Speak No Evil

Book Three Of

The Society Series

By

Ivy Fox

COPYRIGHT

Speak No Evil – The Society
Copyright © 2021 Ivy Fox

All rights reserved. No part of this publication may be reproduced, distributed, or transmitted in any form or by any means, including photocopying, recording, or other electronic or mechanical methods, without the prior written permission of the author, except in the case of brief quotations embodied in critical reviews and certain other noncommercial uses permitted by copyright law.

This is a work of fiction. The names, characters, places, and incidents are a product of the author's imagination or have been used fictitiously. Any resemblance to actual persons, living or dead is entirely coincidental. The author acknowledges the copyrighted or trademarked status and trademark owners of all word marks, products, brands, TV shows, movies, music, bands and celebrities mentioned in this work of fiction.

Cover photo courtesy of Wander Aguiar
Cover model – Lucas Loyola
Cover design, formatting, and editing courtesy of X-Factory Designs

For more information, visit:

https://www.facebook.com/IvyFoxAuthor

https://ivyfoxauthor.wixsite.com/ivyfox

ISBN: 9798701028973

Table of Contents

Prologue	15
Chapter 1	25
Chapter 2	38
Chapter 3	52
Chapter 4	74
Chapter 5	92
Chapter 6	109
Chapter 7	126
Chapter 8	133
Chapter 9	157
Chapter 10	174
Chapter 11	184
Chapter 12	194
Chapter 13	210
Chapter 14	225
Chapter 15	245
Chapter 16	262
Chapter 17	273
Chapter 18	284
Chapter 19	295
Chapter 20	304
Chapter 21	320
Chapter 22	327
Chapter 23	347
Chapter 24	363
Chapter 25	373
Chapter 26	395
Chapter 27	407
Chapter 28	427
Chapter 29	441
Epilogue	464
Ivy Fox Novels	475

Dedication

To all the redeemable Alphaholes out there, my muse thanks you.

AUTHOR NOTE

Thank you for purchasing Speak No Evil. I'm so thrilled that you're on this rollercoaster ride with me.

I would like to reinforce that The Society series has an entwining subplot that will only be resolved in the final book. Although each story centers around one couple at a time with a happily for now ending, only in the very last book will you obtain all the answers you seek. I will say that this book will be filled with new revelations and some more theories on who is behind The Society since we are so close to the finish line.

I would like to ask one small favor of you, if I may.

Reviews are life for an author. I treasure each one since they enable other readers to find my book babies. But I would like to ask that if you decide to write a review to make it as spoiler free as possible. Like I said, this book has bombshell revelations after another, and I'd love it if every reader was surprised when reading it. It will make everyone's reading experience so much more enjoyable and in the end, that's every author's main goal—to offer an escape into the imaginary.

As always, I don't consider my books to be full-on dark, but more in the shades-of-gray category. Therefore, I thought it best to give you the heads-up that some scenarios may be triggering. All I ask is that you put your trust in me and have faith that everything turns out as it should.

If you're okay with all that I've mentioned above, please proceed and get ready for Asheville's favorite alphahole to melt your heart.

He sure as hell sneaked his way into mine.

Much love,

Ivy

Hear No Evil Playlist

The Society

Listen to the full playlist on Spotify (search: Speak No Evil - The Society Book Three)

"All The King's Men" by The Rig

"Feel Something" by Jaymes Young

"Playing With Fire" by Sam Tinnesz feat. Yacht Money

"Do It For Me" by Rosenfeld

"Power" by Isak Danielson

"Flames" by Tedy

"Bones" by Wens

"Silhouette" by Aquilo

"Body" by SYML

"Ghost Town" by Kanye West feat PartyNextDoor

"Walk Through The Fire" by Zayde Wølf feat. Ruelle

"Lost My Mind" by Alice Kristiansen

"Bad Dream" by Ruelle

"Talking In Your Sleep" by AG feat. Daniella Mason

"Hurricane" by Tommy Profitt feat. Brooke

"Serious Love" by Anya Marina

"Can't Help Falling in Love" by Tommy Profitt feat. Brooke

"Lost The Game" by Two Feet

"Glass Heart" by Tommy Profitt feat. Sam Tinnesz

"Animal" by AG feat. MOONZz

"A FOOL'S MOUTH IS HIS RUIN, AND HIS LIPS ARE A SNARE TO HIS SOUL."

-PROVERBS 18:7

PROLOGUE

The cold Richfield heir sat proudly on his wall,

But all it would take was one good push to watch him fall.

Not even all the king's horses or all the king's men,

Would be able to put Colt Richfield Turner back together again.

I've always been fond of nursery rhymes. Growing up, I loved putting my own little spin on them, making the childish poems that much more enjoyable for me. My mother used to do it all the time when she tucked me in at night. While other kids my age loved to hear fabled tales about slaying dragons and conquering monsters, she knew no bedtime story could ever compare to when she sang these little rhymes to me. Especially when she made sure they depicted the people in my life so perfectly.

At this very minute, unbeknownst to him, the altered Humpty Dumpty rhyme suits Colt like a fine leather glove.

Discreetly I lean back against my auditorium chair, watching my prey from my peripheral as he scrolls through his feed on his phone, ignoring the lecture taking place. In his wine-colored Tommy Hilfiger sweater, a color he intentionally picked out, knowing it would accentuate his best feature—his sparkling emerald eyes—he dons his usual cool expression, broadcasting how his mere presence in this classroom should be considered a privilege and not a given. It's no secret Colt is vain to his very core. He enjoys the regal air he puts out into the world, the very one he's showcasing now, intent on reminding us mere mortals that no one in this room could ever measure up. That he's better than everyone he could ever come in contact with, and it would serve us well to remember that.

And in most cases, he's right.

He is better.

Colt was born and bred into a family whose sovereign power can be felt just by walking down any Asheville street that bears their last name. Everyone knows that he, along with his three sisters and cousin, is the last Richfield heir—a dynasty that most would sell their souls to be a part of. Colt has been disciplined to be refined and elevated in his stature, so his pretentious vanity isn't mind-boggling. It's just fucking infuriating to watch.

Cold.

Heartless.

Narcissistic.

That is the very definition of who Colt Turner is.

He only shows a sliver of humanity when he has some woman underneath him, and even then, he discards them as easily as most would day-old trash. Yet despite all his faults, the female population around campus can't seem to get enough of him. It's almost as if they believe one of them might hold the power to change his stone-cold heart into feeling something.

But I know better.

Colt doesn't feel. He's incapable of it.

Most people would constitute his cold apathy as being his biggest flaw, but for me, I actually believe it's his best asset. One I've made sure to take into account in my carefully laid out plans of revenge.

In war, it's not only relevant to have the best weapons in your arsenal, but also aim it where it will do the most damage. And to a man like Colt, who seems impervious to everything around him, your aim needs to be precise and true. In the art of destruction and carnage, I've learned that every great general has a weakness. The chink in Colt's cleverly fabricated armor is secrets—ones that he keeps hidden under such a callous exterior, and others that people close to him have kept concealed from him all his life.

Yes.

Secrets can be a powerful weapon if you have the fortitude to use them correctly, and to Colt's misfortune, I am more than equipped to handle his downfall. I *yearn* for it. Hunger and thirst about the upcoming day where I witness his case-hardened heart break into a thousand small fragments before my very eyes. The ice in his veins will boil over as madness sets in, betrayal living rent-free in his mind. Although I won't be able to boast I had a hand in his suffering, I'll bask in the glory of his demise just the same. It's sure to be one of my biggest triumphs against the Richfields.

That is until I go after Lincoln.

But as the saying goes, the best should always be left for last. Yet, I can't help the smile that tugs at my lips, knowing that Lincoln will suffer just as much as Colt will, soon enough. The warmth that flutters in my chest regarding both cousins' impending ruin has the mimicking effects of an illegal drug—addictive and all-consuming. For so long, I have deprived myself of indulging in it, but when the day finally arrives, it will only make their misfortune taste that much sweeter to me.

However, my focus must remain purely on Colt for now. Not that I'm complaining. When I sink my teeth into his devastation, I'll make a feast out of the pretentious, arrogant heir. I'll gorge in his misery and suffering like it's a banquet prepared solely in my honor. It's time that I am sat at the head of the table and be given the retribution that's so rightfully mine. I've been starved for it long enough.

But then again, all good things come to those who wait.

My mother used to say—beware of the fury of a patient man because there is nothing more lethal than a person who is a master at biding his time to achieve his most nefarious desires. Aside from Teddy, she was probably the only other person who knew all too well what lies dormant in my resentful soul and the lengths to which I would go to get what was owed to me.

And for years, I did just that. I played my part to perfection, knowing all my sacrifices would be rewarded in the end and that I would finally have the life that was always destined for me.

But it only took the events of one spring night for my sacrifices to be laid to waste. I had to stand by and silently watch all my grueling work be undone by the four men I have vowed to destroy. Like his so-called best friends, Colt played his detrimental part that night, ripping my very future away from my grasp, making sure that never again would I be able to get such a golden opportunity. He killed a part of me, and I will make sure to kill a part of him because of that.

The life and reality he so cherishes and flaunts in our faces will cease to exist. I'll reveal the lies and secrets he's lived all his life being oblivious to, and in the end, where he once saw kinship, he'll recognize as a foe. He had a hand in destroying my future, so it's only fair I have a hand in obliterating his sanity.

All I need is a distraction.

A decoy.

I straighten my spine, knowing the answer will reveal itself to me soon enough, and the probabilities that I will get them in my ethics class are zero to none. I try to stay focused on the lecture, but I find the task incredibly difficult since listening to Professor Harper's voice grates on my nerves. It's not her no-nonsense approach to the class that irks me to no end, but it's the way she doesn't raise her voice a decibel higher than needed that really aggravates me. It's a calculative move that ensures everyone in the room is silent enough to pay close attention to her every word. That is if they want to have any chance of getting a passing grade at the end of the semester.

I'm proof that a calculating mind is a dangerous thing; therefore, Emma Harper's manipulative tactic makes the skin on the back of my neck prick. Still, I put on my best-winning smile as her eyes bounce from one student to the next, finally landing on me. I don't miss how she pretends to see right through me, acting as if I'm not worthy of her attention or time as her gaze continues to scour the student-filled rows. I fist my hands to the side as I watch her dismissive gaze continue with her hunt, only to finally fall on the man I've also set my sights on. A sudden satisfied grin threatens to unleash itself as I pay close attention to the hard-nosed professor and what she's about to do.

"Mr. Turner, can I have your input on the matter?"

To her chagrin, Colt continues scrolling through his phone, ignoring her completely.

"Mr. Turner?"

He lets out a huff and places the phone face down on his desk, unintimidated by her disgruntled scowl.

"Did you even hear the scenario I presented just now to you and your colleagues, Mr. Turner?"

Colt keeps the blank expression stitched on his face instead of answering her.

"No, I didn't think so. Very well, then. Although I hate repeating myself, I'll indulge you this once for the sake of your declining grade. The scenario I threw out to the classroom is as follows. You are a member of the city planning department. You are made aware that an old friend of yours, one who runs a planning consulting firm, has submitted a competitive proposal to work as a consultant for your department. She then calls you up on your work phone during office hours, inviting you to be her guest for dinner that same evening. Do you accept the invitation, or do you decline it until the contract has been awarded?"

"That all depends." He shrugs noncommittally.

"On what, Mr. Turner? And please be precise."

"If I'm fucking her or not."

The class breaks out in a fit of giggles, flutters of laughter filling the room, but Emma Harper doesn't seem amused in the least by his reply. She leans against her desk, crossing her legs at the ankle as she glowers at him, her blood-red nails repeatedly tapping on the desk's edge.

"Enlighten me how that bears any weight in this ethical dilemma."

"Well, if this *friend* is as good of a friend as you say, then I must be fucking her. And if I am, there is no way I'll stop just because she wants a job. Besides, I can guarantee you if she's calling me, she's not thinking about her contract either. She just wants a good old-fashioned fuck. Getting a job is the last thing on her mind."

The laughter in the auditorium only increases at Colt's honest response.

Professor Harper crosses her arms over her ample chest and pushes herself off the desk's edge to take two steps closer to Colt's row.

"I'm sure this is a rude awakening for you, Mr. Turner, but there are plenty of people in this world who are motivated by their ambitions and obtain greater satisfaction in achieving their goals than any mere sexual encounter could possibly offer. To some, prestige and power can be highly seductive and more alluring than whatever you believe your sexual prowess can give them."

Another howl of chuckles ensues, making it challenging to hear Colt's retort. But lucky for me, I'm close enough to hear every word that falls from his smug lips.

"I have to be honest with you, professor. You talking about my sexual prowess is aphrodisiacal enough. Isn't there some ethical dilemma in getting a student hard in class just so he can pay attention to your boring ass lecture?"

"The only dilemma I see here is whether I should report you to the dean's office for sexual misconduct or just fail you for your lackluster academic response. I must admit I'm conflicted at which one would truly grab your attention, seeing as very little does."

Colt leans back in his chair, his arms thrown back so his hands can cup the back of his head, as he stares the professor down.

"I prefer our sexual tension to your brand of intimidation any day of the week, to keep my attention. You were almost able to make me care about this class, professor. Don't ruin it with unfounded threats. We both know whose signature signs your teacher's salary."

They stare into each other's eyes with such loathing that my mind begins to wander at all the endless possibilities. I school my delighted features as best as I can, and the minute the rest of the class has quieted down, I chime in on their one on one battle.

"If I may, professor? I think the answer is quite obvious. It would be a blatant conflict of interest in accepting the dinner date, even if the invitation weren't made with the intent of enhancing said friend's chances of getting the job. You didn't say if we had any influence on the decision to award the contract or not. However, it is still good optics that we postpone any contact with our friend for the time being since it would be hard for us to keep the same distance from the actual decision-makers of who gets the contract."

Professor Harper doesn't even look at me as she takes in my answer, her deadlock gaze still set on Colt.

"Correct. I'm glad to see some of my students aren't as ethically challenged as Mr. Turner here."

"So, in other words, just use your hand to get off," I whisper over to Colt, throwing him a goading wink for good measure.

His nose flares, but he doesn't say anything in return, his glower still focused on Professor Harper as she sashays back to her spot at the center of the room and continues with her lesson.

As I take their animosity toward each other, the light bulb in my head only brightens. Emma Harper has been a thorn in my side since senior year began, but it seems she has the same annoying effect on Colt. Not one to ever look a gift horse in the mouth, I decided to include the professor in my scheme. I wasn't planning on messing with her since all her efforts regarding Stone Bennett went nowhere, but making room in my plan for the prestigious professor just feels right to me.

Fated even.

Almost as if the universe agrees that I shouldn't let her off the hook for her meddling. Putting Emma Harper in Colt's path won't be difficult. In fact, it will be all too enjoyable for me to watch them butt heads while the true nature of my game begins to unfold.

Ironic how in a room destined for us to learn about ethics, I'm about to make sure they both lose theirs.

Evil men reap what they sow, Colt.

And your day of reckoning has finally arrived.

CHAPTER 1

COLT

Halloween night – one month ago

I keep my steps silent, my eyes glued to the nape of her neck as Kennedy slowly walks further down the dark corridor. She's so consumed in her task, she completely forgets to check her flank, letting me follow her every step while being none the wiser of my presence.

What are you up to, Ken?

Making sure I always keep a good safe distance between us, I continue to lurk behind one of my dearest friends, wondering what the hell she's up to now. Because in all the years I've known her, Kennedy Ryland is always up to something. My forehead crinkles in curiosity as she continues on with her pursuit in a Kill Bill jumpsuit no less. All that is missing from her costume is a samurai sword, and I wouldn't put it past her if she has one hidden away somewhere. Good thing she's unarmed, because hell has no fury than a pissed off Ken. And by the way I can hear her grind her teeth, she's definitely fuming with rage. Whatever she came back here to find has slipped through her grasp.

No, not something—more like someone.

When Ken finally reaches the servant's quarters at the back of the house, and sees that no one is there, she throws her arms up in the air with a disgruntled huff, kicking the wall for good measure.

"Shit!" she mumbles, aggravated.

Whatever she was up to, it's obvious she failed miserably at it and Ken hates losing. She always has. Seeing as she's about to turn around and head back to the party, I can't pass up the opportunity to confront her here, where she's alone and less likely to be able to dodge my questions. I grab her by the waist and clasp my hand over her mouth, stifling the little shriek she lets out.

"Boo," I whisper teasingly in her ear.

She elbows me hard in the gut, resulting in her release, as I chuckle with her knee jerk reaction of hitting first and asking questions second.

"Damn you, Colt! You almost gave me a heart attack."

I can't help but continue laughing at the deep-rooted scowl she's trying to level me with.

"It looked like you were about to have a coronary long before I came along. Just what are you doing back here all by your lonesome?" I cock a mocking brow.

"What are you talking about? I was just checking if all the rooms had enough beverages. Linc did appoint me as this party's hostess, right? I'm just doing my part, that's all. Geez, paranoid much?" she retorts, crossing her arms over her chest.

"Sure you were." I chuckle, closing the small gap between us, my fixed gaze never leaving her annoyed blue eyes.

But for every step I take in Kennedy's direction, she takes two steps backward, until finally her back is flush up against the wall.

"Where's your fiancé?"

"I don't know. I haven't seen him yet." She shrugs feigning boredom.

"You don't look like you're too bothered that he hasn't shown up to your party."

"It's not *my* party. It's Lincoln's."

"We both know it's *your* party, Ken. Everyone does. That's why people came."

She mauls her lower lip, not happy with my observation. Truth is that ever since Aunt Sierra and Uncle Crawford died so abruptly last spring, no one is in a rush to get chummy with my cousin. Unless of course he's writing them a big fat check, then everyone can't get enough of Asheville's golden boy.

Fucking leeches.

"You didn't answer my question. You don't look like you care if your fiancé comes to this party one way or the other. Why is that, Ken?" I ask, leaning in and pressing my forearm above her head, trapping her completely.

"Of course, I care. Stop being so obtuse," she reprimands with a roll of her eyes, before trying to shove me away.

But I don't move an inch. Ever since Ken accepted Tommyboy's proposal earlier this year, she's tried her best to evade my questions at every turn. Finn would never come right out and tell her that Tommyboy is a douche. Easton respects her decision even if he thinks it's a bad one. And Linc… well, Linc has no say in the matter, and he never will. I, on the other hand, don't give a fuck about letting her or Tommyboy know that I'm opposed to this fucked-up arrangement. And Ken knows that I've never been one to keep my mouth shut.

"Why are you even with that guy?" I ask point-blank.

"Not this again. Seriously, Colt, this conversation is getting stale."

"Well, tough shit, because I'm going to keep asking you until you give me a real answer."

"I have given you one. It's not my fault you refuse to accept it."

"If you're going to feed me that bullshit of how in love you are with Tommyboy, I'm going to hurl. We both know you don't love him."

"You sound pretty sure of yourself. I'm marrying him, aren't I?!" She hikes a defiant brow.

"I stand by what I said. Just because you're willing to put his damn diamond ring on your finger doesn't mean you love the prick."

I know she doesn't. We all do.

She turns her face away to the side, but I grab her chin to make her look at me.

"End it, Ken. Tommyboy is not the one who you should end up with."

"Oh yeah? Then who is?"

My cold heart bleeds, as we both know the answer to that very question but are too cowardly to say it out loud.

"You have other choices," I whisper, instead of giving her the name she yearns to hear.

"Sure I do."

When she lowers her eyes to our feet in defeat, it damn right kills me. Ken is a fucking fighter. She is fearless and without remorse. But when it comes to her heart, she's just a lost girl who wants what she can never have.

"Look at me, Ken. You do have other choices. If you're so gung ho on getting hitched, I'll marry you, if you want?"

Her eyes go wide, her jaw agape as we both stare at each other digesting the absurdity that just left my mouth.

Did I just fucking propose to Kennedy Ryland?

Fuck me!

But the more I think about it, the more it makes sense. I always assumed I'd never get married anyway. Thanks to my parents, I don't believe in the institution. But if it would give Ken an out from the current predicament she somehow has gotten herself into, then why the fuck not? My alternative is ten times better than walking down the aisle to marry Thomas Maxwell Junior. Even though Ken won't tell me the real reason why she said yes to Tommyboy's proposal in the first place, I know in my gut it's not what she wants. And if I listen to my intuition I'd bet good money that the culprit behind her decision is her asshole of a power-hungry father. So if he's the one who is pressuring her to marry into the Maxwell family, I'm sure he'll change his tune if a Richfield heir is willing to take his daughter off his hands. He might have no love for my family at the moment, but we all know that wasn't always the case. I'm sure if I knocked on his door and gave him another opportunity to be a part of the Richfield legacy, he wouldn't think twice, no matter how bitter he is about the past.

"Well, say something!" I exclaim when a few minutes have passed by and Ken still has that shocked expression on her face.

"What do you want me to say? It's obvious you've lost your goddamn mind," she chastises, slapping my chest.

"Why not me? I'm better than Tommyboy," I reply, feigning hurt.

"If you say so," she mumbles under her breath, unconvinced.

"Don't even deny it. I am definitely a better catch and you know it. Besides, if you're willing to marry that douche, who you don't love by the way, then why not marry me?"

"Geez. Now that you put it that way... I'd be a fool not to marry you, huh?"

My smile is only halfway up when I realize she's being fucking sarcastic.

"I'll talk to your father tomorrow and set it all up," I explain assertively.

"Colt Turner, you will do no such thing! Jesus. Are you high?"

"Like I'd ever poison my body." I scoff.

"Okay, then you must be drunk because you are not making any sense right now."

"I'm sober as a judge, Ken."

"Then you hit your head somewhere because you have completely lost it!"

"Ken—"

"No."

"Come on, just think about it."

"I said no!" She deadpans, jabbing a finger into my chest.

"Why the fuck not?"

"Colt… just stop, okay?"

"I could be good for you," I whisper, using all my charm, thinking this might be a better approach to use against her stubbornness. But before I can caress her cheek with the back of my hand, she just slaps it away.

"No, you couldn't."

"I could, Ken. If you just gave me the chance, I could. I loved you once when I was a kid, I'm sure I could do it again if I put my mind to it."

She claps her hands over my lips, shaking her head profusely.

"Don't you dare say another word, Colt Turner. You've said too much as it is. And besides, you never loved me. We both know what you had was an infatuation over the girl who didn't come to your beck and call every time you snapped your fingers. You didn't care about me that way then, and you don't now. So just stop it."

I wish I could tell Ken she's wrong, but deep in my faulty assembled heart I know she's right. The minute I saw what type of misery could come out of truly loving someone, I swore to never put myself in that type of predicament. It only took witnessing my cousin's suffering to realize I had never loved anyone in my life. Not her. Not anyone. Nor will I ever. Not if I have anything to say about it.

"Would you leave Tommyboy if *he* asked?" The question has already left my lips before I can take it back, surprising me just as much as her.

Kennedy's gaze falls to the floor again, as if trying to hide the hurt caused with that one question.

"He won't ask," she mumbles solemnly, her expression reflecting the same pain I've seen on Lincoln's face time and time again.

"But would you?"

She raises her head to look me in the eye, sadness dwelling in them.

"Yes. I would," she admits, her sorrow piercing through my cold heart.

"He'll never ask, Ken. You know that, don't you?"

"Why?" she asks on a somber cry. "Why won't he, Colt?"

I thin my lips, feeling helpless to take her pain away. Even if I told her why, the answer to that question would only hurt her more and it wouldn't change anything. Linc will never be able to love her like she wants him to. Ken needs to move on. I just wish she wasn't trying to do that with fucking Tommyboy, of all people. I'm grasping for the right words to say, unable to deal with the misery hanging densely in the air between us, when a throat clears, alerting Kennedy and I that we're no longer alone in the dark hall.

"Everything okay?" Easton questions with a disapproving tone, as I step away from Ken.

"Of course," Kennedy replies upbeat, trying hard to hide the broken girl that was here just a few seconds ago.

"You sure about that?" he repeats unconvinced, crossing his arms over his chest, staring directly at me.

I throw him an annoyed glower, yet the dark prince isn't one bit intimidated by it.

"Don't be silly. Everything is fine."

If only that were true.

And by the way her voice just jumped up about two octaves, Easton isn't buying it either. As Ken does her best to ease the tension, I look behind Easton's shoulder and see a figure down the hall in an angel costume waiting for his return. It must be Pastor Davis' niece who is shifting uncomfortably from left to right. Seems Easton brought his society homework to tonight's party. I keep my mouth shut while Ken walks over to the girl, linking her arm with hers, heading back to the party.

"Care to explain what the fuck that was all about?" Easton interrogates after he's made sure both girls are out of hearing range.

"I have no idea what you're talking about."

"Don't you fucking dare lie to me, asshole. I'm not having your shit today," he shouts, poking me hard in the chest. "I thought you were done with that shit."

I almost sigh out in relief at the conclusion Easton leapt to so quickly. With the death glare he's leveling me with, it's clear he thinks I still harbor feelings for our best friend. If only I could. Maybe then she'd take my proposal seriously and end it with Tommyboy. But if our little rendezvous taught me anything, it's that only one man could do the job, and unfortunately for Ken, he never will.

"It's none of your business, East," I reply harshly, feeding into his unfounded suspicion.

"Don't do something you'll regret."

"Too late for that. Just worry about what you got going on, and leave Ken to me."

"This cannot happen again, you feel me?" he warns me, getting all up in my face.

"Fuck off."

"Jesus, Colt. I know you're stubborn as fuck, but you've never been stupid. What if Tommyboy had seen you two? Or her brother? You know those assholes are both here tonight, right?"

"Like I give two fucks about either one of them." I scoff, running my fingers through my hair, unbothered by his scenario.

"Oh, yeah? Then what if it had been Lincoln who caught you two instead of me?"

Go for the jugular East, why don't ya?

"If she wanted him, she'd be with him. But she's not, now is she? She's fucking engaged to Maxwell's sperm accident." I play off, hoping he believes the lie.

"You know what? I take it back. You are fucking stupid as shit! Did it ever occur to you that the reason she isn't with Linc is because *he's* the one putting on the brakes?"

I bow my head, knowing how right he is.

"Don't be an asshole, brother. You know she's all he cares about. Sooner or later Linc will get his head out of his ass and tell Ken as much. And when he does, she won't pick anyone but him. She loves him."

"You think I don't know that shit?!" I yell, pushing myself away from the wall, but Easton holds me still by placing his hands on my shoulders, trying to soothe my rage.

"I think sometimes you try to forget it."

If only I could. Jesus, I wish I could.

I wish Linc could just follow his heart instead of being forced to live with the unending torment of his feelings. I wish Ken didn't feel she had no other way to move on with her life than to marry a man who will make her the butt of every crude joke. I wish for a lot of things, but am powerless to make any of them true.

"When did things get so fucked up?"

"Haven't they always been?" He shrugs sadly.

"Fuck it. Go and get back to your girl. I gotta go and find something to take the edge off."

"You do that," he retorts, feeling as if he's done his job here.

Little does he know that things are more fucked up in our lives than he realizes.

I leave Easton and go look for anyone that might take my mind off shit I can't solve. Right now any warm body or mouth will do to just switch off. But as I walk through the halls filled with happy drunk college students, resentment of their carefree happiness begins to settle within me.

We'll never have that again.

Just being in this house of lies and secrets suffocates me.

I need to get out of here for my own sanity.

And with that thought in mind, I get in my Bugatti, putting as many miles as I can between me and the Hamilton's estate—the house that stole our youth from us.

And could quite possibly still rob us of our freedom.

Chapter 2

Emma

Halloween night – one month ago

As I walk closer to the vending machine on the far end of the long corridor, the overhead light keeps blinking on and off, giving the hallway a sinister feel to the narrow space. I guess any empty dark corridor in a library that has been standing for close to a hundred years can look awfully spine-chilling if you let your imagination run wild. With its creaky floorboards and the unnatural wind blowing up against the fragile single-paned windows, making the building's ancient walls vibrate profusely, any active mind might be inclined to conjure up a ghost or two to explain such eerie surroundings—especially on a Halloween night like this one.

I, however, am not prone to such misgivings and foolish supernatural suspicions. My logical mind latches onto real, harsh facts to justify everything in my life, even something as mundane as questioning the reason behind Charlotte Public Library having all the traits and foreboding characteristics of a haunted house.

The boards under my four-inch heels squeak with the weight of my steps, the old wood flooring in desperate need of some TLC. Unfortunately, using public funds to upkeep the old library is the last thing the City Council believes its money should go to. The howling cry heard coming from outside is just the wind promising the arrival of winter to a town's inhabitants, who have been spoiled with warm weather for far too long to remember what wind even sounds like. All perfectly logical explanations as to why this secluded part of the library feels as if an ominous force will attack at any moment.

But this isn't a Stephen King novel, and I'm not a helpless heroine on the verge of tripping into an unknown ghastly fate on All Hallow's Eve. I'm just a woman who got too caught up in her research for her book to even remember to eat dinner until her stomach started to grumble in disapproval. Hence the walk into this secluded part of the library in search of some form of nourishment.

I tilt my head to the side, taking in what is on tonight's menu, tapping my thigh repeatedly with my phone.

This is fucking depressing, Emma, my subconscious castigates as I try to choose between the varied empty calories sealed in small packaging on the other side of the glass.

I push the self-deprecating thought from my mind, slipping a dollar bill into the slot, only for it to be spit back at me. I flatten the bill on the vending machine's surface and try my chances a second time and then a third.

"Even the vending machine thinks your dinner choices for tonight are pathetic," I mumble to myself after my fourth unsuccessful attempt.

Luckily the machine eats up my dollar bill the fifth time around. I take a step back and search yet again for my meal, my gaze landing on a vanilla cupcake with pink frosting. It's probably a week old, but beggars can't be choosers.

"Why the fuck not?" I shrug, pressing the combination on the keypad.

I cross my arms over my chest as I wait for the vending machine to cough up my poor excuse of a celebratory cake. When it begins to stutter, stopping its levers midway and fully trapping my treat in its clutches, I throw my arms in the air in frustration.

"You have got to be shitting me?!" I groan.

I slap the glass repeatedly, and it still doesn't budge. I begin to kick at the damn thing while furiously white-knuckling my phone in my hand, only for the cupcake to mock me further as it remains in the machine's grasp. Defeated, I slam my forehead on the glass, and by some miracle, the grips decide to release the package, dropping it into the bottom drawer. I bend down as much as my gray pencil skirt will allow and pick up my cupcake. I should feel a sense of triumph that I finally have my snack in my hands, but celebrating such a small victory feels goddamn sad.

Not one for dwelling in self-loathing or things I have no control over for too long, I turn around and head back toward the library's entrance, where a long night of work still awaits. I'm halfway to its doors when my mobile phone begins vibrating in my hand, my editor's name popping up on its screen.

"Hey, Jenna. Just give me a second," I say before letting her have a word in, so I can step outside where I can talk freely. "Okay, I'm here."

"Emma!" she greets gleefully, making me let out a sigh of relief.

I can tell how a call with my editor, Jenna Miller, is going to go all by the way she says my name. Today isn't going to be one of those calls where she pesters me for new material or reminds me of deadlines. She sounds too chipper, which means she's read the last email I sent her and is pleased with my findings.

"So I take it you like the recent chapters I sent you."

"I not only liked but FLOVED it!"

I wipe one sweaty palm on my thigh, realizing just how much I was dreading her call.

"It's still rough, but so far, I am loving what you've been able to dig up," she adds, instantly creating a slump to my shoulders where there was only relief a second ago.

Rough.

In other words, there is still so much she wants me to either change, elaborate, or erase completely. 'Rough' is Jenna-talk for you're on the right track, but what else can you give me.

Sigh.

Considering I've been stressing with how she was going to react to my latest chapters, I'm going to take this as a win. I can handle *rough*. It's when she uses words like *unacceptable* or *not up to Ivory Publishing House standards* that I get worried. Jenna has gone up to bat for me more times than I can count with the publishing house. Even going as far as granting me more time to deliver on a book idea I had pitched to her bosses almost four years ago to the day, so I hate it when I feel that I've let her down.

Four years. Has it really been that long?

It feels like it was just yesterday when I decided to finish what he started.

"I think everything is finally coming together nicely. I wouldn't be surprised if this time next year your name is on the New York Times bestseller list," she continues on cheerfully.

"I like your optimism," I mumble, less certain.

"Emma, both you and I know I'm not an optimist. I'm a New Yorker. There isn't room for wishful thinking in this town. If I tell you that you are definitely on the right track with this book, then it's not me stroking your ego—it's my honest opinion."

"Isn't stroking a writer's ego part of every editor's job description?"

"No. That's their agent's. Not mine." She laughs. "My job is to make sure everyone reads the work you have been slaving over for the past four years. And believe me, they will. I might even be able to wrangle a movie deal out of it. I know plenty of studios out west that are hungry for material like this."

"It's not a romance book, Jenna."

"No, but it would make one hell of a documentary. You'll be singing a different tune when this book gets you some Netflix money," she singsongs.

"This has never been about the money for me. You know that," I retort somberly, not one bit excited about the notoriety she's promising.

"Yes, I do," she replies with less glee in her voice. "He'd be very proud of you, Emma. You know that, right?"

I chew my lower lip and look up at the cloudy North Carolina sky that successfully hides the full moon above.

"Anyhooooo," Jenna continues, sensing my need for a subject change. "That's not why I'm calling you tonight. Don't think I forgot what day it is."

I look down at the snack in my hand and sigh.

"Thanks," I reply before she has time to make a big deal out of my birthday.

"So, what are you going to do? Nice dinner with your friends? Hit a few bars and go clubbing? I would just die if my birthday were on Halloween. I'd make all my parties Halloween themed."

"Hmm," I mumble noncommittally to her idea of how my twenty-ninth birthday should be celebrated.

No use in telling my editor that since I moved to North Carolina, she's the closest friend I have. Putting that into words is even more pathetic than the cupcake I'm holding onto.

"Emma…"

"Yes?"

"Where are you right now?"

I could lie. I could. But why bother?

"The library."

"Jesus Christ, Emma! It's your birthday, woman—the last one you'll have before turning thirty. Go out and have some fun. Work will be there in the morning."

Work is *always* there in the morning. It's been my constant companion for longer than I care to admit. Even if I wanted to ditch work and just enjoy myself for one night like Jenna is so keen on me doing, where the hell would I go anyway?

"Even your grandfather would have understood you taking the night off on your birthday."

"Cheap shot, Jenna," I reprimand with little ire behind it. "And trust me, my grandfather would not have understood. He was as much a workaholic as I am."

I mean, where does she think I got it from?

"You know what they say—all work and no play makes for a fucking dull Emma. I mean, when was the last time you just blew off some steam? Or better yet, when was the last time you had a good orgasm?"

"Just this morning," I reply assertively, hoping it's enough to quiet her concern, but from the exaggerated exhale she lets out, it's obvious it didn't work.

"If you got the big O from something that runs on batteries, it doesn't count. Seriously, Emma. You need to have some downtime, too. I know this work is important to you, and as your editor, I praise your work ethic, but as your friend, I think you really need to get out there more. Have some fun. Meet a cute stranger in a bar and just bang his brains out. You'd be surprised at what a good release can do to your stamina. And I bet you that, right now, you're running on fumes."

"Is this why you called? You're worried about my sex life?"

"No, of course not. I just care about you and want to see you happy."

"I'll be happy once I meet my deadline."

"That too." She laughs. "I will say this—the last chapters you sent had me reeling. Any new information you can get on The Society? I mean, you moved to Asheville because you assured us that was where they originated from, but so far, you haven't been able to have one source on record to back up your findings."

"It's not for lack of trying. I can promise you that." I huff out in exasperation. "They're ghosts in that town."

"Hmm. Could it be possible they don't exist then? That this secret society is nothing but an urban legend?" she asks with dismal concern.

I can hear in her tone how that Netflix money she was going on about a minute ago is slowly flying away from her grasp in her mind, and she's not one bit happy about it.

"Oh, they exist, Jenna," I deadpan assuredly. "I know they do. My grandfather spent most of his life trying to prove it. Now it's up to me to pick up where he left off, and I won't quit until I confirm their existence."

"Easy tiger." She giggles, but I don't miss the sigh of relief that came out beforehand. "If there is anyone that can prove The Society exists, it's you. I have no doubts about that. Still, it would be nice to have a living source to back up your findings. What about the town's founding family that you mentioned in your notes, the Richfields? Have you been able to talk to any of them on the record?"

"Unfortunately, no. Colleen Richfield won't take any of my calls. Believe me. I've tried."

"You could just request a meeting with the Richfield Foundation. I'm sure she wouldn't refuse meeting you under the disguise of writing a puff piece on her family's philanthropic foundation."

"I tried that already. I only got an interview with their public relations representative. It was a total bust and a waste of time." I huff, kicking the air at my feet in frustration.

"Hmm. What about one of her children? Didn't you tell me her son was in one of your classes?"

"Colt Turner. Yes, he is, but I doubt he has any ties with The Society. He's too standoffish and egocentric to be involved in such an establishment."

Plus, that boy only has his own interests in the brain.

And when I say 'interests,' I mean bedding every woman within a fifty-mile radius. His insatiability has even made for juicy gossip in the teacher lounge. I doubt very much a self-involved man like Colt is the mastermind behind such a secretive club as The Society.

"I bet he is," Jenna coos as if in sync with my thoughts. "Being the king of the world will do that to a man. Trust me. I've met a few who think they're gods but lack Colt's bank account to back up their claim."

Or deviously handsome looks, but that tidbit I keep to myself.

"What about his cousin?" Jenna continues. "Didn't you say he was the golden boy of the town or something? Wait, just give me a second," she mutters to herself while shuffling some papers around. "Ah, here it is. Lincoln Richfield Hamilton. Have you tried to talk to him about his possible involvement? He seems the type of guy The Society would recruit."

She's right. He does.

Unlike his cousin, Lincoln Hamilton would be a prime candidate for The Society.

He ticks all the boxes.

"I do have him on my list of possible sources. Unfortunately, he's not in any of my classes, so I haven't had an opportunity to meet him face to face yet. And no one in Asheville invites me to any of the Northside soirees that he attends for me to get close to him. I could just bite the bullet and knock on his door and ask Lincoln for an interview, but it would be awkward considering the year he's been having."

"Ah, right. The burglary where his parents got killed. Yes, I would assume you'd have to wear kid gloves with him. But don't worry, Emma. You'll think of something. You always do." Jenna tries to placate, hearing the frustration in my voice. "There is nothing you can do about it tonight, though. My advice to you is to get out of that stuffy library and go have some fun. Go to a bar, grab a drink and find the cutest guy there to take back to your place."

"Sure." I lie, throwing my gaze up at the heavens at her suggestion.

"Good. Next time I call, I hope you've gotten a really good fuck with a smoking hot southern stranger," she goads like the crude New Yorker that she is. "And I won't stop pestering you until you do either."

It's no use reminding Jenna that Charlotte doesn't have the perks she's accustomed to living in the big city. There is no way I can pick up a total stranger for a one night stand under the assurance I'll never have to see him again. This town is too small for that. Sooner or later, our paths will cross, no matter how hard I try to avoid it. And I, for one, don't need that type of hassle in my life. It's chaotic enough as it is.

We say our goodbyes before I hang up the phone and walk back inside to my desk filled to the brim with unfinished work. I came to North Carolina looking for answers, and that's exactly what I need to focus on. This work is too important for me to be sidetracked by a social life—or lack thereof.

Like my grandfather used to say, you either go with the flow or break from the mold. And no one who achieved greatness did it by going clubbing every night. He spent most of his life in pursuit of The Society, and even in his final days, he obsessed compulsively on trying to solve their puzzle before the cancer took him. After all he did for me, the least I can do is to finish his life's work.

I look at the cupcake on top of the desk, tapping the end of my pencil on a notebook.

Twenty-nine.

Where did the time go?

Most women my age are either getting married or are busy making babies, while I'm still trying to swim up creek against the ruthless current, trying to make my mark on the world. Grandfather made sure to instill that type of independence in me from an early age. He was adamant that friendships and lovers are as inconstant as the wind but that your accomplishments are tangible proof of one's perseverance. I've worked myself to the bone to get to where I am today, though most would consider that I haven't even reached my peak.

I will admit to feeling drained. Jenna is right on that account.

All work and no play does lead to a dull life.

But the thing she doesn't understand is the drive behind every decision I make. My grandfather, if he were still here with me, would understand my sacrifices. He knew that to obtain greatness, you had to forfeit some happiness.

Does it get lonely?

Yes. Yes, it does.

I wouldn't mind sharing my life with someone who understood the person that I am. But for that to happen, I'd have to open myself up to the possibility of meeting someone, and I'm too busy to even bother letting anyone new come into my life. This is the last year of my contract teaching at Richfield, and I'm not sure if the school will keep me on after this year. So as I see it, the clock is ticking. I don't want to return home empty-handed. I can't. I just need to uncover the mystery of The Society, and then I can go back and start living my life.

Or at least I hope I can.

I stare at the mocking cupcake and sigh.

Maybe I should do what Jenna suggested and just go to a bar or a club to pick someone up just to clear the cobwebs. I can't use Tinder, though. I tried the app when I first arrived, and I got some messages from my students thinking they could live out their fantasies of screwing one of their professors. Not something I want to be known for around campus. I worked too hard to have my reputation tarnished that way, and no lonely night in need of a warm body beside me will be enough of a motivator to ruin all that I have built.

Everyone has the life they chose, I guess. Whether willingly and knowingly, or just based on the poor decisions we make. I've made peace with mine. Living a life alone is better than having the company of someone undeserving of it—another gold nugget of wisdom given to me by my grandfather. But aside from me, he lived most of his life in solitude too, so I'm not sure if he is really the one I should be taking lessons from. But back then, we had each other, and that was enough.

I miss him terribly. Especially today.

Now all I have are memories and a gravestone to get advice from.

"Happy birthday, Emma," I mumble, splitting the cupcake in two, not even bothered that there isn't a candle to blow out.

I'm about to take a bite when a bunch of incoming text messages on my phone grab my attention.

Jenna: *Get out of that library, Emma!*

Jenna: *One night of fun won't be the end of the world*

Jenna: *Your cha-cha will thank you for it*

Jenna: *Listen to your cha-cha!*

My nose twitches as I stare at the bold letters on my screen, as well as the various eggplant emojis she sent afterward.

Maybe Jenna is right.

Maybe one night out will do me some good. It's Halloween, so I'm sure there will be plenty of guys from out of town. And if there aren't, then dancing for a few hours will definitely put a smile on my face. Work will always be here in the morning.

What harm could one night off do?

Only one way to find out.

Chapter 3

Colt

Halloween night – one month ago

"Hit me," I order, pushing my glass to the center of the bar for a refill.

The starry-eyed bartender sashays her hips toward me, smiling wickedly with the whiskey bottle in hand. She bends her body over the counter just low enough to give me a clear view of her cleavage as she pours my drink.

Double D's.

Not bad. Not bad at all.

Pity they're fake. Not exactly what I'm in the mood for, unfortunately. I've had enough of fake ass bullshit to last me a lifetime, so I'm in desperate need of a fucking break from the norm. Tonight, I want something real—whatever the fuck that means.

Sorry, sweetheart.

No use shoving those gorgeous tits in my face, but I appreciate the effort, though.

Once she's finished filling up my glass, I throw her a flirtatious wink for her troubles. She does that thing that girls do when they want something and bats her pretty eyelashes at me, thinking that will pique my interest. It doesn't. However, when she turns around in her little pirate costume and moves her heart-shaped ass away from me, I take a moment to reconsider and put her down as tonight's plan B.

I turn around in the barstool and lean back onto the counter, my eyes scouring the nightclub, searching for someone worthy of warming my bed tonight. Nothing will get me out of the current bad mood I find myself in better than getting lost inside a woman's thighs.

My eyes land on a Marilyn Monroe lookalike across the room, with plump red lips sucking on her straw, giving me a little preview of what her mouth can do. Her gaze screams 'come here and fuck me already,' and although the offer is tempting, I rather avoid blondes if I can help it.

In fact, if I could do away with all the golden-haired women in my life, it would make me the happiest motherfucker there is. All of them are a pain in my ass in their own particular way—starting from my stubborn best friend to my annoyingly perfect debutante sisters, and ending of course, on the bane of my existence—the ice queen herself—my mother.

Yeah, tonight I need an escape from blondes in general, so Miss Marilyn won't cut it.

My eyes continue on their search amongst the crowded nightclub until they land on a redhead in a sparkling red Jessica Rabbit costume that reminds me of the knockout hostess back at the Brass Guild—a place Easton spends most of his time nowadays to do The Society's bidding. In retrospect, I could have gone there tonight in search of some female companionship since they have quite a stellar collection to choose from. However, since I know that my father has a habit of frequenting the clandestine club, the Brass Guild lost all its appeal to me.

Besides, I've never once paid for pussy. Like hell, I'm going to start now.

Coming to Charlotte to look for someone to fuck is definitely a new low for me, though, but I needed a fucking change of scenery. Asheville only reminds me of the shitstorm my friends and I are in. Sooner or later, East will be done with his task, meaning The Society will next set their sights on either Linc or me. Unfortunately, my intuition tells me those fuckers are coming for yours truly sooner than I want them to, so I might as well enjoy the last remaining days of freedom I still have before I become The Society's bitch boy.

I comb the room hunting for anyone who will catch my eye, but as the minutes' tick by, I come out empty-handed. Even though the dancefloor promises to be packed with gorgeous women, I'm unable to get a good view from where I'm seated. I could just get my ass off my stool to get a closer look, but that sounds like too much work. I rather my hookups come to me than put in the added effort of going to them. It's worked so far for me these past twenty-two years, so why fuck with a winning formula?

Frustrated that I've probably made the two-hour long drive for nothing, I turn around in my seat and take a long swig of my drink. The music in the club is starting to grate on my nerves, perforating my eardrums with its repetitive high-pitched beat.

Worse still. I'm starting to get bored. That happens a lot.

When you've lived your entire life getting everything you ever wanted, it gets awfully tedious coming up with new ways to get excited about anything. And if I'm really hand-to-God honest with myself, The Society coming into my life has been a great reprieve from the endless dull days of being a Richfield heir.

Of course, that doesn't change the fact that I still want those fuckers gone and dealt with properly. It doesn't sit well with me knowing that someone out there knows what happened that night with Aunt Sierra and my fucking prick of an uncle. I'm all about the adrenaline rush of a new thrill, but being blackmailed with the threat of going to prison for the rest of my life doesn't get me hard. In fact, it kills my libido completely. And no one likes a limp dick.

I take a second look at the bartender, who is knowingly swinging her hips left to right to grab my attention as she goes about her business. If nothing better comes along, then she'll have to do. I try to stay clear of fucking bartenders or staff of any kind as a rule. The term 'don't shit where you eat' comes to mind. It makes for bad publicity when I tell them that I'm not looking for anything serious and that a quick fuck is all I have time for. Sure, my definition of quick could be having a woman's pussy in my face for three whole days straight, but it's a far cry from being the beginning of a promising relationship. Nothing's worse than someone bitching to the media that they didn't get their claws in you. Most women appreciate my level of honesty. And those who do, I make sure to reward them for their understanding with as many orgasms as their limber bodies can handle. But then there are always a small few who throw a tantrum. The ones who spend their days dreaming of landing a Richfield Heir to sweep them off their feet and fling them into the lap of luxury like they're some kind of Cinderella or some shit, and I'm fucking Prince Charming.

I am *not* Prince Charming.

Prince Charming is a fucking pussy.

Gold-diggers who think they can fool me into their bed don't deserve even a finger-fuck from me, let alone my dick. A fact they soon realize and villainize me for on every social platform there is, just to get a reaction from me—or worse—my family. Not that I give a rat's ass what anyone thinks about me. I'm perfectly content in being the cold prick that I am. It's helped me survive the burdens that come with having my last name. But if I want to avoid the migraine of my mother bitching that I've stuck my dick in the wrong hole again, then I have to take precautions. Hence, I only go out with women who won't make too much of a fuss when I give them their marching orders. My preventative measures have served me well so far, leaving satisfied women left and right to boast about how a quick fling with me is better than a lifetime fucking anyone else.

Maybe that makes me cold.

Or egocentrically callous.

I prefer the term survival of the fittest.

And my opinion is the only one that counts. So there's that.

I crack my neck to the side, easing the tension in my shoulders. In one fast tip of the glass, I empty its contents, ready for another round. If tonight's excursion to Charlotte proves to be fruitless, then at least the buzz of the alcohol will lessen the disappointment of going back to my hotel room with no one on my arm. I prefer an empty bed to fill it with someone not worth my time anyway. This is the precise thought running through my mind when I hear a low gravelly voice close by, making my cock instantly twitch in recognition, springing hope that tonight's excursion isn't a complete bust after all.

"Water, please."

Well, hello there.

The pretty brunette bartender struts along with a water bottle in tow, and I make sure to follow her every step to see exactly where she's heading. My lingering gaze is no longer enticed by her suggestive sway of the hip, but curious to see if the owner of that deep Yankee voice belongs to the no-nonsense woman who I've imagined under me more times than I can count.

"Thank you," Professor Harper says, giving the girl a ten-dollar bill before opening the bottle cap and taking a long pull of the cool liquid.

I look up at the heavens and thank the big guy upstairs for sending me this treat. Discreetly, I lean away from my seat so that my eyes can fully appreciate the college professor's get-up. Tonight, she decided to ditch her usual naughty librarian look for the sex-on-a-stick dominatrix vibe. My throat tightens as I take in the black leather mini dress that ends in the middle of her thighs and hugs all her curves like a second skin. The two thin straps pretending to hold the dress up are just for show, when in fact, it's her impressive C cups that keep the provocative fabric in place. Her long legs and sculpted ass look fucking amazing in that tight dress, but it's her man-killer spiked heels that really get me going.

Ding! Ding! Ding!

I think we've found tonight's winner.

I get up from my stool and walk the small distance between me and the sexy as hell professor. Her temple is coated with a sheen of sweat, testifying to her previous hardcore dancing, and I can't help wondering if this is how she'll look after she's been ridden long and hard. She's still drinking her water, her sights fixed on the dance floor, completely unaware of my approach. When I get close enough to stand behind her, the sensual scent of jasmine combined with glowing amber and sun-kissed marigolds, swirled with just a touch of sweet vanilla, has my mouth watering. Not only does Emma Harper look good enough to eat, but she smells fucking delicious, too.

"Professor, fancy meeting you here," I whisper in her ear.

Any other woman would have startled at a stranger leaning so close to her. The good professor, though, doesn't seem at all bothered by it. It is probably because half the men in this place have already hit on her at one point or another during the night, and I'm just the new nuisance who is keeping her away from her beloved dance floor.

She takes a step back and cranes her head up just a smidge to put a face to her new bothersome pest. When her impassive bronze glower finally meets my wolfish smirk, she offers a stiff nod in greeting before going back to staring at the dancers on the main floor.

"Mr. Turner," she retorts dismissively.

My cock instantly throbs at her indifference. Any other teacher caught on a night out by one of their students would have awkwardly come up with a million and one excuses as to why they were here in the first place. My ethics professor, however, is another breed of pedagogical academic. She doesn't give a fuck about her students' opinion where she's concerned, and she isn't shy in letting them know it either. She owns her bitchiness, leaving most of her students confused if they want to murder her, fuck her, or aspire to be her. As for me, I've always been undecided in the first two options, since the last one I've already mastered.

"Didn't take you for the Halloween type." I venture on, excited with the prospect of toying with the stiff upper-lipped professor.

"I'm not."

"Is that so? I haven't seen you here before. So either you needed to blow off some steam tonight, or you're celebrating something."

"That's a very astute observation. Such a shame you don't use the same analytical thinking in my classroom."

"That wasn't an answer, professor. So which is it? Did you feel the sudden urge to let your hair down, or is this outing a celebration?"

"It's the latter," she replies sternly, not once looking up at me.

Although I'd love nothing more than to have a closer inspection of her stunning whiskey eyes again, right now, I don't mind that she's doing everything in her power to ignore me. I quite prefer it, actually. This way, I can admire all her luscious curves up close without running the risk of her biting my head off for it.

"And just what are you celebrating?" I lean closer to her ear and ask once I've had my fill.

She slants her eyes, turning them to meet mine head-on, unimpressed with my inquisitiveness.

"Not that it's any of your business, but it so happens that today is my birthday."

"And drinking water is how you decided to celebrate?" I tsk.

She looks at the bottle in her hand and frowns, her manicured brows creased into a sharp v on her forehead.

"Point taken. I guess water doesn't yell celebration, now does it?"

"No, it fucking does not. It screams old maid, and you're anything but."

I grab the bottle away from her hand and place it back on the counter, snapping my fingers at the pretty bartender, who briskly rushes over. "Give me your best Pérignon."

"That isn't necessary," Emma chimes in, shaking her head in refusal.

"I think it is. I mean, you only turn… how old are you?"

"Nice try, but I'm not telling you my age, Mr. Turner," she retorts, crossing her arms under her ample chest, making the swell of her creamy breasts that much more evident.

By the end of the night, I'll have them marked with either my teeth or my cum.

I haven't made up my mind yet.

"Fair enough, but whatever it is, you only turn it once in a lifetime. You might as well enjoy it."

She purses her lips but lets me buy her a bottle of bubbly anyway.

"Should we grab a seat?"

"The place is packed. I don't think we'll be able to find one."

My predatory grin threatens to appear back on my lips because that wasn't the outright 'no' I was expecting from her.

"Follow me," I reply, throwing her my best panty-dropping smile instead.

I watch her hesitate for a split second, but ultimately, she gives in to her curiosity.

"Send the champagne to the VIP room, will you, darling?" I wink at the bartender.

Her stare bounces from me to the hot teacher at my side, the lust-filled stars in her eyes instantly vanishing with the realization she's been replaced as tonight's entertainment.

'Yeah, babe, you're not getting lucky tonight. Rain check, though,' my smile tells her.

I walk up the stairs to the VIP section, the bouncer pulling the red velvet rope in double time when he sees me approach. When we step into the secluded lounge, I verify that it's busier than it was an hour ago when I came in here. Thankfully my corner table is secluded enough to guarantee some privacy as well as having a perfect view to the dance floor downstairs, something I think the good professor will appreciate. I sit down on the white leather cushion while Emma sits across from me, making it clear that we aren't together.

For now, anyway.

All in due time, professor.

"I'll have one glass with you, and then I'm going back down," she explains firmly, making sure that I don't get any funny ideas.

Too late for that.

She's just made this night interesting, so like hell, I'll be satisfied with the five minutes it will take for her to drink her champagne. Still, I don't say anything on the contrary and just lean back, my arms spread wide on each side of the couch so she can get a good eyeful of all of me. Only fair, since I've been checking her out non-stop since the minute I laid eyes on her.

Unfortunately, Emma doesn't take the bait, preferring to keep her sights down on the dance floor rather than taking in my broad physique. She only turns her attention back to the table once the champagne arrives. While the waitress pours some out for us, I take advantage of the distraction and slide my way next to her. I purposely stretch my arm behind her back, pleased when I see goosebumps coat her naked shoulders. She can pretend all she wants that she's unaffected by my proximity, but her body tells me a different story.

"I think a toast is in order," I propose with a mischievous smirk.

"Happy birthday to me," she mumbles under her breath, downing her drink in one go before I've had time to even take a sip of mine. "Thank you for the champagne, Mr. Turner. Enjoy the rest of your evening," she adds, quickly getting up from her seat.

"It's going to be like that, huh? Take advantage of a man's hospitality and not even placate him with a little small talk for his trouble."

She lets out a long exhale, her hands finding purchase on her hips.

"What could we possibly talk about, Mr. Turner?"

"Well, for starters, you could start by calling me Colt and not Mr. Turner. Every time you call me that, I half expect to see my father standing behind me. I really hate the bastard, you know. So for the sake of having a good time tonight, how about we ditch the formalities and just call me by my name. I'm sure one night won't hurt you, will it?"

"Fine. Colt it is."

"See, that wasn't so hard, was it, *Emma*?"

She chews at her inner cheek but doesn't berate me for using her first name. Still dubious of my intentions, she sits back down on the couch beside me but makes sure to keep a significant berth between us.

"So tell me, *Emma*, why are you celebrating your birthday all by your lonesome?"

"Who says I am?" she rebukes, taking the champagne bottle out of the ice bucket to refill her glass.

I arch a brow, calling bullshit on her insinuation she's here with someone. Any man lucky enough to convince this woman to go out dancing with him would be glued to her ass the whole night. And if this were a girls' night, then her friends would have come running the minute they saw her come up to the VIP section. Just like me, Emma came to this club alone, and by the sexy dress she has on, I don't think she planned on leaving it the same way.

"It was a last-minute impulse," she finally explains.

"Really? You've never struck me as being the impulsive type."

"Mr. Tur… I mean, Colt, I hardly believe you know anything about me to make such an assumption."

"True. How about we remedy that and get to know one another a little better so I can make a fact-based judgment. Tell me, what other impulses have you had tonight?"

Her shrewd amber eyes fix on mine, making my cock swell restlessly in my slacks with only one look.

"Do you honestly think that's the type of question you should be asking your ethics professor?"

"Why not? You already gave me an F on my last exam, so I don't see how my grade can get much worse with me speaking my mind."

"I don't see how your mediocre grade is my fault," she quips in annoyance, running the tip of her finger around the rim of her glass.

"You'd be surprised how at fault you are."

This time I don't hide my gaze traveling up and down her long legs. I lick my lips, remembering how I imagined them wrapped around my head when I was trying to do that damn exam. All the studying in the world wouldn't have helped me pass that test with her in the room.

"Foolish boys get distracted by the silliest of things," she exclaims, unbothered with my wandering eye.

"I can guarantee you the hard-on I have this very minute is anything but silly."

"Again, something you shouldn't say to your teacher," she deadpans, completely unruffled with my remark.

"I don't give a fuck about propriety if that's what you're hinting at. And something tells me you couldn't care less about it either."

The small tug to her upper lip tells me I'm right.

"Correct. I've always thought that the rules of propriety were shackles made by weak men to discourage free-thinking women. I, for one, have never liked being gagged. At least when it comes to speaking my mind, that is."

Fuck.

She must have said that shit on purpose because all I can see now is Emma Harper on her bare knees with tears streaming down her apple cheeks, gagging on my cock. I shift in my seat, trying to get my act together, but the gleam in her eye tells me she got exactly what she wanted.

The joke's on me.

I wanted to toy with her and see the rigid professor flustered, yet I'm the one left in pain.

"Are we done here?" she asks defiantly, confirming my suspicion she deliberately planted the image in my head of her sucking me off just to watch me suffer.

Well played, Emma. Well fucking played.

"Tell you what? How about we drink this glass of champagne and then go back downstairs. All I ask in return is one dance. Then you can consider your debt paid."

"Debt?" She laughs mockingly. "Do you honestly believe buying a woman an expensive drink makes her somehow indebted to you in any way?"

"Fuck no." I scoff, insulted by the insinuation. "But if dancing gets me to spend a few more minutes with such interesting company, then what's the harm?"

I don't miss how her eyes sparkle at the idea of dancing. I should have figured that was the way to soften her up. She hasn't been able to move her eyes from the dance floor for most of the time we've been together. I just bought us a two grand bottle of champagne, yet it's the idea of shaking her ass on the dance floor that has her pulse racing.

"One drink. One dance. That's it."

"That's all I ask." I shrug nonchalantly.

She abuses her lower lip with her front teeth, and I swear I feel them drag along the throbbing vein of my cock. I push that thought away for a later activity to explore and pour her a fresh glass. This time she isn't as impatient and waits until I pour myself one.

"Happy birthday, Emma. Here's to being impulsive."

She tries to hide the small smile that crests her lips by drinking her champagne down. She waits for me to do the same, while my stare never leaves hers. Once I've drank every last drop, I stand up, and she enthusiastically follows suit.

"Shall we then?"

She nods, taking the lead out of the VIP room, but when I place my hand on the small of her back, Emma's rushed steps falter. I feel the weight of her disapproving glare on me, but I keep staring straight ahead, pretending to be unaware of the deep scowl ingrained on her face.

I'm not moving my hand, Emma.

Before the night is done, there won't be a part of your body it hasn't touched.

So you might as well get used to it.

Once we hit the middle of the dance floor, her tense shoulders begin to relax, relieved to be back in her element. However, to her dismay, the song the DJ chooses next is something she wasn't prepared for. It's a slow song for the crowd to cool down, and from what I can tell, Emma only likes it when it's hot. I couldn't have planned the song selection better myself. The minute my hands grip her waist, her eyes slant in further disapproval. I school my expression to remain stoic, considering I'm probably the only student who ever dared touch her in such a way. I pretend to be interested in our surroundings instead of the woman in front of me, knowing that's the only way she'll ever be able to relax in my arms. When I hear an exaggerated exhale passing her lips and her arms wrap around my neck, it takes everything in me not to gloat from the small victory.

Once she's fully at ease, I use it to my full advantage and take in the unique shade of her eyes. Back at Richfield, Emma is fond of using her catlike shaped glasses to hide the beauty of their peculiar color, which is a shame since the golden hue contrasts beautifully with her fair skin and dark raven hair. But I guess her hard-as-nails persona isn't enough to keep horny twenty-year-olds from trying to fuck her, so other props need to be used to make her look severe and authoritarian. Too bad for her, I'm not easily discouraged.

We sway slowly to the music while Emma adamantly tries to maintain the small distance between our two bodies. But as soon as we find our rhythm and the song begins to take effect on her senses, she begins to let go, no longer concerned with the intimate proximity. My lips are so close to her earlobe that there is no way she can't feel the heat coming from them.

"All of this was just impulse, huh?"

"Last minute."

"So no plans whatsoever for your birthday? Ah, Emma, some things shouldn't be so discarded."

Rather than having the banter I crave falling past her luscious full lips, she seals them shut and just keeps on dancing, pretending I'm not even here.

Yeah, that won't do.

"Let me guess. You came out tonight to dance, maybe drink a glass or two and pick up some stranger to fuck and call it a day. Am I right?" When an aggravated expression overpowers her beautiful face, I know I hit the nail on the head. "No shame in wanting to celebrate your birthday with a good fuck. I highly recommend it myself."

"Of course, you would." She thins her lips disapprovingly, eyeing everyone around us but me.

"I want what I want, and I won't apologize for it. I think you and I can agree on that front."

Her nose scrunches, but she doesn't deny it.

"So who is he? Who is the lucky man who gets to rock your world tonight?"

She sighs exasperated, and does the first girly thing I've ever seen her do in all the time I've known her—she rolls her eyes at me. Usually, this little gesture is a turn off for me. Ken does this passive-aggressive shit all the time. But it's kind of cute seeing Emma do something so immature since it's completely out of character for her.

"You won't shut up until I surrender to this line of questioning, will you?"

"Not a chance." I smile widely, my hard cock liking the word surrender coming out of her mouth a little too much.

She discreetly tilts her chin over to an asshole dancing with the Marilyn Monroe doppelganger I had been checking out earlier tonight. His greedy hands on the blonde's ass tell me he's traded down.

"He looks like he's taken."

"I guess he couldn't wait the thirty minutes it took for me to grab a drink with you. Some men are fickle that way," she explains, not one bit bothered she's not taking him home with her.

"Anyone else grab your attention?"

Her eyes linger on my broad chest for a fraction of a second before she shakes her head.

"That's just too bad. It would be a shame to let the night not end up as you planned."

"I'm used to disappointment."

"Fuck that! A gorgeous woman like yourself should never say such bullshit."

It's not a pickup line.

I honestly meant that shit.

Emma Harper is fucking stunning, and any idiot in here would be lucky to take her home, even if for just one night. She's been a fantasy of mine since the day she started teaching at Richfield a few years ago. The only reason why I never made a move was because she made it known that she was off-limits to anyone who tried. Tonight, however, she doesn't seem as indomitable.

"That's very sweet of you to say," she mutters at last, albeit suspiciously.

"You and I both know I'm not sweet, Emma. I just call it as I see it. Any motherfucker in here would be lucky to get you under him. Present company included."

"You're my student, so that's not happening." She waves that ludicrous idea away.

Little does she know that the past half hour with her has been the highlight of my fucking month. And that's saying something. If I can put the cherry on top by eating hers—pun intended—then I'm going all in.

Go big or go home has always been the Richfield way.

"If that's your only argument, then you need to come up with a better one. I'll be graduating in a few months, so being your student is a moot point."

"It doesn't change the fact that you're my student *now*."

"It wouldn't be the first time a teacher fucked their student." I cock a mischievous brow.

"But it would be a first for me. Some lines should never be crossed."

"Sorry, I didn't hear the last part you just said. My cock is still at attention with you saying I'd be the first in regards to anything with you," I confess, pressing my steel rod against her stomach to drive the point home.

She gifts me with yet another eye roll, swelling me further.

"Do you always say everything that's on your mind?" she questions, unamused.

"Most of the time, yeah. Why not?"

"Because not everyone is comfortable with such crude honesty," she chastises.

"Weren't you the one who said that propriety was overrated just a few minutes ago? Don't bullshit me, Emma. We both know I didn't offend you by admitting what we're both thinking," I reply knowingly since her hot pussy has been pressing up on my thigh since we started this dance.

I lower my head to the crook of her neck and whisper what I'm sure will seal the deal.

"No one will ever know."

"I will," she whimpers as her tender breasts rub against my chest.

"It's one night. One memory, Emma. Consider it a birthday present. One memory of your hottest student making you cum all over his cock more than once is bound to put your next birthday to shame."

"You sound very confident in your abilities."

"I might have flunked my last exam, but making women cum and see God is my specialty."

"Somehow, I don't doubt it," she mumbles under her breath, her eyes locked on our feet.

I tilt her head toward me, my knuckles under her chin as I stare deep into her eyes.

"What do you have to lose?"

She licks her lips, and I can't help but trace my thumb over her lower lip where her tongue has been. So fucking soft and warm. Just like I picture them to be.

"You ready for some more truth? Here's a dose of it. Every time you talk in class, I imagine these lips around my cock, milking me dry. Every time you wear that one low cut white blouse you have where I can see your black bra beneath, I imagine ruining them with my cum after I've fucked your gorgeous tits with it on. When you bend over your desk, I imagine ramming my nine-inch cock into your pussy in front of the whole classroom, making you wail and scream out my name for all of them to hear. So you see, it's kind of hard to ace an exam when all I think about is fucking you raw until you can't walk anymore. Is that truthful enough for you? Can you take my level of honesty, or is it too crude for your sensitive ears?"

Her breathing turns shallow, her breasts heaving up and down with the images I just planted in her head. It serves her right since she did the same to me up in the VIP room with fantasies of her on her knees.

Emma Harper really has been a wet dream of mine, so if there is any way I can make it happen, it seems tonight is as good an opportunity as I am ever going to get.

"So I'm going to ask you one more time, Emma," I add, once the song we had been dancing to officially ends, leaving us standing in the middle of the dance floor staring into each other's eyes.

"What do you have to lose?"

"Nothing." She breathes out.

Good fucking answer.

Chapter 4

Emma

Halloween night – one month ago

Colt Turner.

Egotistically vain.

Unapologetically arrogant.

Self-centered.

Morally bankrupt.

And to top it off, too damn handsome for his own good.

I could spend the rest of my night listing his many faults and barely scratch the surface of his shortcomings by dawn.

What do you have to lose, he asked.

There are so many variables I could throw at him in response. If someone found out I slept with one of my students, there would be hell to pay. The most prominent fallout would be that I'd end up tarnishing my stellar reputation, one that I've worked long and hard to build for myself. I would jeopardize years of work if anyone got wind I was even considering doing such a thing. Not only would I lose the respect of my esteemed colleagues and peers, but possibly my job for fraternizing in such an intimate way with one of my students. The repercussions of such a decision are endless.

So why am I hesitating?

His deep forest-green eyes never leave mine, intent on raising the pulse in my veins with the heady, smoldering look. I try to remain impervious to his blatant hungry stare, but I doubt I'm fooling him any by the way my body is reacting to him.

I can't believe I'm actually pondering accepting this crazy proposal.

You must be drunk, Emma, to consider having sex with your student.

But I'm not drunk. I had just three measly glasses of champagne, definitely not enough to take me off my game. Therefore, I can't blame intoxication for being the culprit behind my indecision.

And this isn't just any student.

Standing before me with his hands gripping my waist is none other than Colt Turner himself—a Richfield heir with the cocky good looks of an Olympian god. A man who puts most Vogue cover models to shame, with a face that would stop anyone in their tracks just to gawk and admire it. With a well-defined, sharp jaw and angular cheekbones, his emerald eyes take center stage in his glorious face—the complexion of his tanned skin only accentuating their beauty.

But if his inherited handsome features weren't enough to make grown-ass women fawn all over him, the lethal way he uses them to his advantage guarantees his bed is always occupied with a new conquest.

Everything about this man is calculated and premeditated.

From the way he has his sleeves rolled up inches below his elbows, meant to showcase his toned, roped forearms, to the wolfish smirk on his lips that promises the fulfillment of every erotic desire a woman could ever conjure up. Even the fair stubble on his perfect chin is just short enough to entice fantasies of having it deliciously brush against a woman's inner thigh before his plush full lips find her weak spot.

What do you have to lose?

Aside from my reputation, the one thing that is really giving me pause is the damage it will do to my own self-respect. Taking such a shallow man to my bed will undoubtedly leave a foul taste in my mouth. And make no mistake, Colt is as shallow as a pool of rainwater. I have no doubts he can deliver in the bedroom, but the empty vessel that is his soul makes his exquisite packaging lose all its shine in my eyes. There are so many things I can lose if I let Colt have his way with me, but that one is what truly has me wavering.

Unfortunately, my mind and body aren't in agreement.

I hate how my treacherous body hums in delight with his every soft caress. The way his thumbs graze against my stomach, scorching my sensitive skin beneath my dress. Even my core clenches at the idea of him making good on his word to fuck me until I don't know my own name.

But the real killer to my resistance is the sparkle in his jeweled eyes.

It reminds me of why I came into this club, to begin with. Just for one night, I followed Jenna's advice and came here looking for something that would make me feel something.

Something besides loneliness.

I'd settle for anything that would do the trick of taking my mind off of how much of a workaholic recluse I've become in the pursuit of fulfilling my grandfather's lifelong mission of exposing The Society. The burning longing inside me to feel wanted, desired, even if only for a few hours, was the force that drove me to come to this club, and the twinkle in Colt's green eyes, filled with pure eagerness at fulfilling that very desire, is just adding fuel to an already hot flame.

"Nothing," is the word that ends up spilling from my lips, and the predatory grin he gives me instantly has my pussy aching in anticipation.

"Do you want to dance a little more?" he asks, his steel hard-on pushing at my belly, making me roll my eyes to the back of my head with how good it would probably feel to have it inside me.

The little chuckle he lets out when I take a step back from him, just so his cock doesn't tease me further, should infuriate me, but it actually gives him a boyish charm I didn't think could possibly come from him.

"Do you want to go back to your place?"

Yeah, that's not happening, buddy.

Like hell, I'm taking him back to my apartment. Just indulging in this conversation is dangerous enough. Having Colt know where I live is not how I want to end this night.

"I can take you here if you want?" he adds, sensing my silence to mean that my home is off-limits to him.

Hmm, he really is quite astute when the subject matter interests him, isn't he?

I get the feeling that very little else does, though.

Instead of pointing out how I wish he were as perceptive in my classroom as he seems to be with the inner workings on a woman's mind, I hike a challenging brow at his suggestion of a quickie in some nightclub bathroom or broom closet. Of course, I can't fault him for where his mind went. A man like Colt, who gets any woman he desires with just a snap of his fingers, has probably seen his fair share of closets and bathroom stalls.

"How about we go back to my hotel room, then?" he finally says, that stupid twinkle in his eyes making it hard for me to snap out of the current sex-infused fog I'm in.

Thankfully a moment of clarity jerks me awake, and before he's able to move an inch, I place my open palms against his broad chest, successfully stopping his next move. His dark brows crease in puzzlement when I step away from him, unlatching his grip on my waist.

"Thank you for the champagne and dance, Mr. Turner. You made this night… interesting, to say the least. Enjoy the rest of your night."

I don't wait for his reply and turn my back to him, quickly making my way to the front entrance of the club.

Even if I wanted to stay and dance a little longer, I wouldn't have a moment's peace while he's here. But just as I'm reaching the coat check girl to grab my belongings, I feel a soft tug to my elbow, halting my next step. His decadent masculine cologne reaches my senses long before his body gently slides behind me.

"So that's the end of it, huh?"

"It's the end of my night if that's what you are referring to."

Ever so dutifully, he pulls my hair to one shoulder, leaving my neck exposed to him.

As he draws in closer, his warm breath kissing my bare skin, it takes every ounce of my self-control not to lean back into him.

"Pity. That's not at all how I envisioned our night ending, Emma. I had such big plans for us."

I keep my lips sealed in a stern, thin line, not sure I trust myself enough not to throw caution to the wind and just fuck his brains out like every nerve in my body is demanding me to do. As much as I denied it earlier tonight when talking with my editor, an orgasm given by my trusty vibrator really can't compare to the real thing. And I'll admit, Colt bragging about his nine inches did intrigue me. But with my luck, he'd end up being all talk and very little follow-through.

"Can I at least walk you to your car?" he questions politely, running a finger over my bare shoulder.

Left to right.

Slowly and purposeful.

The seductive touch alone tells me his cavalier offer has very little to do with proper southern chivalry. Still, I don't see the harm of having him accompany me to my car. Charlotte, compared to the streets of Boston, isn't the least bit menacing, but it never hurts to have company especially given the late hour.

I throw him a clipped nod, feeling his megawatt smile behind me burn my skin just as much as his finger had managed to do seconds ago. Once we've gathered our coats, Colt surprises me by grabbing my hand when leading me out of the club. My heart pounds erratically in my chest as we both walk out hand in hand, and to my utter embarrassment and shame, I don't pull away from his touch.

Let go, Emma.

No.

Not yet.

I need this.

If I can't have the orgasm Colt promised, at least I won't deny myself a bit of physical connection with another human being, even if it's something as innocent as holding hands.

Maybe Jenna is right. I should just go out with someone. I know dating seems pointless since I'm sure to return to Boston the minute my book is complete, so the idea of getting attached to someone here is bound to be more trouble than it's worth.

But then again, even before I came to North Carolina, I never had more than a few meaningless flings back home. No ex-husband or former fiancé. No mountain loads of ex-boyfriends milling about, just waiting for my return to Beacon Hill. Relationships were always a hard pass for me. Even as a teenager, I was never the type of girl who lost track of time doodling the name of her boyfriend on notebooks. I never got stars in my eyes or swooned over a guy. And as the years passed into adulthood, I found I preferred having the easy, uncomplicated one night stands here and there to a messy, lengthy relationship. Men have always been intimidated by my focused, aggressive nature. And being put last on my list of priorities has never been something men find appealing or attractive. Their egos bruise far too easily when faced with such independence, and I, for one, don't have the patience, time, or tolerance to placate any man's wounded pride.

But it does get lonely.

As much as I value my independence, it still doesn't keep me warm at night. The feminist in me cringes at such a thought, but it is what it is.

"Emma, are you still with me?" Colt asks when we've gone a few minutes without exchanging a word to one another.

I just nod in reply, too scared that I'll hear the dismay in my own voice and end up taking him home against my better judgment. Colt looks down at me hesitantly and gives my hand a tiny, comforting squeeze.

"Good. Now, which one is yours?" he asks, scanning the parked cars on both sides of the street.

"It's just a block away from here. I couldn't find a closer parking space, unfortunately."

I'm sure Colt found one just fine. I bet the club even has a parking spot reserved just for him—one of the many perks of having Richfield as a surname.

"You think you're up for a walk in those killer heels?" he teases, his gaze falling once again to my legs.

I slant my eyes at his unabashed ogling.

"Why don't I just walk myself to the car, and you can turn back around and salvage the rest of your night?" I reply, thinking maybe it wasn't the best decision to accept his offer of walking me to my car.

Lord knows that with each second that passes by, my resolve in not taking Colt up on his offer slowly begins to waver.

"That's not happening."

I huff out, frustrated at his insistence of playing the role of a gentleman when we both know he's anything but, and start walking in the direction of my car. To my utter chagrin, the silence that stretches out between us only increases the already heightened sexual tension. His thumb keeps gently caressing over mine, turning the simple touch into the most sensual displays of affection I've received since God knows when. It doesn't help that the street is eerily quiet and abandoned of all life, making it feel as if we are the only people on Earth.

Relief fills me when I see my car just a few rows down, but before I'm able to point it out to him, Colt turns me around by my waist, slamming our chests together.

"What are you doing?" I stammer, surprised by his sudden assault.

His eyes fall to my lips, his hands now firmly wrapped around my waist, making my chest heave up and down at the proximity of our bodies. I swallow dryly when his front teeth bite the corner of his bottom lip, that damn sparkle in his eyes back with a vengeance. When my skin begins to break out in goosebumps in anticipation of his next move, the last remnants of logic snaps my spine in place, determined to put a stop to this once and for all.

"Take your hands off of me. I won't warn you a second time, Mr. Turner," I threaten with an annoyed tone, trying my damndest to break free from his hold. But the man is granite steel, so my attempts are meaningless.

Instead of releasing me as I ordered, Colt changes tactics by grabbing me by the wrist and pulling me into a nearby alley. He crowds me until my back is flush against the cool brick wall, but I keep my expression blank and unbothered, showing him I'm not one bit intimidated by the move.

"You turned me down."

"You'll live," I reply sternly with a roll of my eyes.

Men and their egos.

It doesn't matter how old they are. If they don't get their hands on the new shiny toy that appeared in front of them, they pout like fucking toddlers.

"Tell that to my blue balls," he jokes, but the humor never meets his emerald eyes.

"Why did you pull me in here?" I ask in an attempt to divert the conversation as far away as I can from his dick. It's bad enough I feel its hard length poke me in the stomach.

"Because I want to hear the words come out of your mouth."

"What words?" My brows crease in confusion.

"*I don't want to fuck you, Colt.* Those words."

I bite my inner cheek because he's decided to play dirty. If I say I'm not the least bit interested in sleeping with him, he'll read the lie stamped on my forehead. If I don't say it, then I'm a coward—the same coward who is too preoccupied with what people will think if they find out, rather than giving in to my urges.

"I won't be the teacher who will play out your schoolboy fantasy," I counter coolly.

"Is that why you backed out, Emma?" He leans closer to the crook of my neck, his hot breath tickling my earlobe, sending shivers down my spine. "I told you before I wouldn't tell a soul. No one will ever know."

"I don't believe you."

"I'm a Richfield. Believe me. Fucking you wouldn't even make it in our family's monthly newsletter of exploits. Whether I fuck you or not is completely inconsequential. So why would I tell anyone?" he rebukes with a tone so arctic that it silences me.

Well, that was a blow to my ego. Ouch.

It's only with the way he runs the back of his knuckles up and down my cheek that I still feel any type of warmth run down my body.

"Still… it's such a shame that you won't get to cum on your birthday. Such a fucking waste."

I laugh at that.

"You think you're the only one who can make a woman cum on demand? Please. I can do that just fine on my own."

"Wouldn't you prefer a man do it for you, though?"

"If there were one here in front of me, then I might consider it. Right now, all I see is a boy who is sulking because he didn't get what he wanted."

"Say that again," he growls menacingly, grabbing the nape of my neck, pulling my face to meet his. "Call me a boy again, Emma. I fucking dare you."

The faint sound of the 'b' barely has time to escape my lips before Colt's mouth latches onto mine. I gasp in both surprise and elation at how good it feels just to be kissed again. Colt takes advantage of my parted lips, breaking through the seams with his tongue, waging war on mine. I'm assaulted by a myriad of overwhelming sensations. He tastes like rich champagne, his warm tongue a complete contrast to the cool air touching my cheeks. He sucks on my bottom lip, nibbling at it so deliciously my core clenches again, reminding me how empty it feels. I hear myself whimper as one of his hands travels up my thigh while the other still cradles the base of my neck. I feel like I'm going to run out of oxygen with his overpowering dominance, and yet, even air doesn't seem as vital as continuing with this kiss.

"Jesus, you taste good," he grunts after breaking free from the maddening kiss to nibble on my lower lip, his hard cock rubbing against my empty core.

I am not fucking Colt Turner in an alley.

I AM NOT fucking my student in a godforsaken alley.

Emma! Don't you fucking do it!

I repeat the mantra like a lifeline to keep my movements in check, but the way I grind on his thigh tells me that my body isn't listening to a word I tell it.

"You don't want to fuck. Then we won't. But let me make you cum, Em. Let me make you fucking cum like you deserve," he pleads, biting into my neck on a groan as he strips me of my coat.

Breathless and powerless to stop this from progressing any further, my head falls back onto the brick wall behind me, my hands pushing down on his shoulders with all my might.

It's my silent agreement to this reckless contract between us.

Colt doesn't even flinch with the request. He goes down on his haunches, eagerly pushing my dress up my thighs. It fucking takes forever for it to rise up enough for his face to be exactly where I need it most.

"Is this a good enough alternative for you, professor?" He winks up at me defiantly, pulling my wet panties to the side. Tired of his arrogant, smug smirk, I grab his throat, Colt's eyes going wide in alarm with the unexpected force.

"I've had enough of your mouth, Mr. Turner. This is a once in a lifetime opportunity for you. I wouldn't ruin your chances by saying the wrong fucking thing that will ensure I change my mind."

His eyes go half-mast before he sinks his teeth into my inner thigh.

"Argh," I cry before I'm able to silence my wail with my palm.

"My name is Colt. Remember that, Em, because you'll be screaming it out in about a minute."

"Always so cocky," I whisper hoarsely, pulling at the ends of his hair. "Why don't you put your money where your mouth is—or in this case, your tongue. Prove to me that you can put it to better use than just bore me with your never-ending wit."

"Yes, ma'am," he says before licking his lips and doing what he's told.

The minute his strong tongue taps my sensitive nub, I see stars.

God help me, but it's been too long.

Colt drags his tongue over my slit, my clit swelling with each deliberate stroke. He pulls my left leg over his shoulder, followed by my right, my fingers entwined in his hair. The brick wall behind me is the only thing keeping me from falling. Colt never falters, though. His large hands squeeze my ass cheeks, pushing my wet pussy closer to his mouth so he can continue to devour me with a hunger that matches my own. The sound of him eating me out is just as stimulating as his masterful touch. I gasp out loud with each talented stroke, weaving my fingers through his silky brown hair until my nails bite into his scalp when he scrapes my clit with his teeth. Either due to the fact that I haven't had a man go down on me in ages, or because Colt is a pro at using his tongue, my orgasm begins to build up, threatening to end this sooner than I'd expected. I close my eyes to keep myself centered, just so I can ride this wave a little longer. But it's no use. Without my consent, my body begins to contract, a telltale sign that I'm right on the verge of coming undone.

"Fuck," he growls, pissed when I let out an earthshattering wail, the orgasm ripping through me. "That one didn't count, Em. Not by a fucking long shot. Consider it a warm-up."

With each sharp intake of breath, I command my heart to slow down, but it's an impossible feat with such a man on his knees intent on tearing me apart.

Colt slows down his ministrations, giving my body just enough time to recover before he rekindles the flame still burning inside me. This time his stabbing tongue dives deep into my core, making me crave the feel of his hard cock. The way he lavishes me with slow, torturous thrusts of the tongue has me gasping for air, but that doesn't satisfy him. Colt's thumb eagerly seeks out my swollen clit, ruthlessly teasing it until I'm a panting mess and writhing again within seconds. Broken moans fall from my lips, encouraging him to accelerate his intense tempo. My chest heaves with each ragged breath, my tender breasts aching for his attention.

I'm so punch drunk on the moment it takes me a while to hear the lively chatter coming from across the street. Two couples dressed from head to toe in Halloween costumes talk and laugh animatedly with each other, completely unaware that just a few feet away from them, I have my student on his knees, intent on making me cum for a second time tonight.

My eyes fall to Colt in warning, my heels digging into his back to grab his attention. Sensing my gaze on him, his green eyes latch onto mine. I tilt my head to the side, alerting him of our unexpected audience. With an arrogant smirk, he breaches my wet pussy with two of his fingers, his mouth never leaving my dripping wet entrance. As punishment, I dig my heels harder into his back, biting my knuckles to prevent giving our location away with my moans. His fierce grip on my ass only aids him in fucking me blind with his fingers. It's when he inserts another digit inside me all of me begins to quiver. My legs stiffen around his shoulders, my core threatening to spasm around his digits and well-versed tongue at any second. Just as Colt intended, the last thing on my mind is who could possibly be watching us right now. All I want is to fall a second time over the precipice, and damn who sees it. My head falls back onto the brick wall, my teeth biting into my lip as the heat of white light overtakes all my senses.

He was right.

The first orgasm was just a warm-up because this one just blew it out of the water.

All of my body is on fire, the two orgasms just a taste of what promises to be some of the best sex of my life. Gently, Colt puts me down and rises to his full height, my arousal coating his chin. He leans in and kisses me, my taste still wet on his lips. Just like his first kiss, this one is intoxicating and dominant. My fingers weave into his hair, loving how his chest rubs against my sensitive nipples.

"Fuck," he groans, breaking our kiss. "I want to be inside you right now, Em. Are you sure there isn't anything I can say to change your mind?"

With one hand, I trail a finger down his chest until I find his stiff cock ready and eager to do just that. He bites into my shoulder as I cup his steel cock. "Jesus, you're going to make me cum if you keep that shit up."

"It doesn't bode well for your reputation if you can cum with just a gentle stroke," I tease before adding more pressure to his suffering member.

"God, you're infuriating. Sexy as hell, but still infuriating."

"The same can be said about you, Mr. Turner."

"I'd bet you'd be singing a different tune with your pussy clenched around my cock."

"All I see is a boy who talks a good game but probably doesn't have the skills to deal with a real woman." I bait him, my voice dripping with want.

The dark look returns to his face, flipping my body around in one fell swoop.

"Fuck this," he growls, gently pressing my face against the wall. "That's the second time you called me a boy, Em. Put your hands up against the wall. Now!" he orders, before biting my lobe, so exquisitely that my toes curl in my heels.

"What are you doing?" I ask with bated breath.

"If I can't fuck you, then at least I'm going to use this fine ass to jerk me off into oblivion. Don't worry. I'll have you cumming before you know it."

With my dress still hiked up to my waist and my bare ass at his mercy, I spread my hands on the cool brick wall just as he ordered. With one hand, he plays with my pussy while his other holds the back of my neck to keep me in place, his cock at the crook of my ass.

The next few minutes are filthy and dirty.

And God help me, it's exactly what I needed.

Just as he forewarned, Colt has me wailing out his name as hot greedy spurts of cum are sprayed on my ass cheeks. We're both gasping for air by the time he's done with me. He holds me close from behind since I can barely keep myself upright from the impact of this last orgasm.

"Happy birthday, Em," he whispers huskily before placing a tender kiss on my bare shoulder.

And even though he just made me cum three times, it's this little, gentle kiss that I'll remember most from this night.

Chapter 5

Colt

My seething gaze bores into Sheriff Travis's furrowed brow, demonstrating how the unconvinced expression he's got stitched onto the center of his forehead doesn't impress me in the least.

Does he really believe he can unnerve Lincoln or me with that stupid ass scowl he's got going on?

He should know better than to think he can intimidate a Richfield. We were brought up with scrutinizing and disapproving glowers all our lives, and an outsider thinking he can unnerve us in any way is just plain laughable, if not borderline pathetic.

"What I can't understand is why you didn't report the gun missing," he continues with his rant of how Lincoln not reporting his father's gun missing on the night that he and Aunt Sierra were murdered has raised a number of red flags in his investigation.

"As I told you before, sheriff, my father had a vast collection of guns. Even relics going as far back as the Civil War. It was a hobby of his, and one I didn't partake in as I have no tolerance for such things. I respect our second amendment rights, but keeping such a large armory goes against my very nature. Until you made me aware of it, I couldn't possibly tell you if a gun was missing from our home or not," Lincoln repeats calmly.

My cousin comfortably leans back into the living room couch, looking right as rain, while Sheriff Travis looks like he's sitting on a throne of rusty nails by the way he keeps shifting about. I keep rooted to my spot, preferring to stand against the grand piano, leering down at the man before us. While Lincoln acts as if we are just having a casual conversation with the sheriff, I know better.

This is an interrogation.

"Hmm. You must agree that it's odd that you didn't report it after the fact, though."

"I'm sorry you feel that way, sheriff, but unfortunately, there was no way for me to know that it had been stolen from our property since nothing else was taken."

"Hmm," Sheriff Travis mumbles again, and I make a note of having his pretty little wife Betty Lee hum out the same tune while I'm nine inches deep in her throat, just so the fucker knows how aggravating the sound is. "Yes, that's another discrepancy that I'm still trying to wrap my head around. If your mother and father were killed in a robbery gone wrong, then why didn't the thieves use their deaths to their advantage and take something?"

"Isn't your job to find out?" I butt in, giving Sheriff Travis my best fuck-you smile.

"Whoever came into our home that night and took said gun must also have been the same perpetrator who killed my parents. Whether they were successful or not in robbing us blind is insignificant. Whatever their original thieving intentions were that night, they ended up committing the worst crime of all. The gun that killed my parents being in your possession is still a lead to their killer, is it not?" Lincoln interjects assertively before Sheriff Travis has time to respond to my provocation.

"Yes, yes. You're right. It is a lead. The only one we've had so far, I'm afraid. As I told you earlier, ballistics proved that it was your father's gun the assailants used on your parents that awful night. Somehow it made its way into Tucker Dixon's possession. Now, as he was in prison when your parents were murdered, we've ruled him out as our shooter. Unfortunately, since Dixon also passed away unexpectedly, we can't determine where he got the gun in the first place. But we are talking to members we know belong to his Southside gang. We believe with enough pressure, one of them will end up giving us something we can work with. Some inkling of how your father's gun got into Tucker Dixon's hands."

"That's good," Lincoln retorts, sounding somberly optimistic, playing the part of a grieving son needing closure for his parents' untimely death to a fault. If I could applaud my cousin for his earnest performance right now, I would. Years of acting like our shit doesn't stink are finally paying off.

"However, I do have just one more question to ask you."

"If it helps with your investigation in solving my parents' murder, then please go ahead and ask."

"Does the name John Bennett mean anything to you?"

My spine stiffens ramrod straight at the mention of the name.

Fuck.

I knew Lincoln's bleeding heart would bite us in the ass someday, and here is the good ole fucking sheriff proving me right.

"Yes, he's the father of a close friend of mine," Lincoln replies without breaking a sweat.

"Stone Bennett's father, you mean?"

"Sheriff, just get on with what you really want to ask because this shit is getting tiresome."

"Colt—" Linc begins to warn under his breath at my outburst, but I've had enough of this unsolicited tête-à-tête.

"Nah, cuz. It's Friday night, and both you and I have got shit to do. We don't have time to watch Sheriff Travis here drag his feet. Just ask what you want and be done with it."

He glares at me with disdain, but I got the fucker beat. No one can turn down the temperature in the room better than I can with just one look. When a shiver runs down his spine, causing him to shudder, it takes everything in me not to laugh in his face.

"As I was saying," he begins to stammer, "I have been informed that the Richfield Foundation has taken on the responsibility of getting John Bennett out of prison. From what the District Attorney has told me, it seems you are actually going to be successful in your mission as the governor is also pressuring the DA's office into reassessing the case."

"Governor Peterson is a close family friend, yes, but if he's pressuring the DA's office in any way, then it's only because he wants the judicial system in Asheville to work instead of throwing innocent men behind bars just to close a case. John Bennett is the perfect example of the faulty system, and my family's foundation has always supported causes that better our community."

"How are you so sure he's innocent?" He arches one bushy eyebrow in contempt.

I watch Lincoln's jaw tic, the only indication Sheriff Travis has officially pissed him off.

Oh, you've gone and done it now, motherfucker.

You really shouldn't push Linc's buttons, chief.

You never know if you'll end up with a bullet carved into your skull because of it.

"Because, sheriff," he starts with a menacing gaze so threatening that even I get chills. "Your department didn't have any concrete evidence against John Bennett to even bring him in for questioning. The whole case against him was built on biased social profiling and hearsay, with no shred of proof. The circumstantial evidence to back your claim up was minimal, and as far as I'm aware, you weren't able to prove he was even at the scene of the crime when it took place. Yet your department and the DA's office worked tirelessly to put him away and pressured his assigned attorney into a plea deal when he maintained his innocence throughout."

The sheriff's scowl twitches in place as he rubs his sweaty hands on his khaki-clad knees.

"He was the only suspect we had at the time."

"That doesn't mean my friend's father is guilty of any crime aside from having the misfortune of being born on the Southside."

"Again, he was our only suspect."

"Then you should have done a better job," I chime in.

He snaps his head in my direction, fury in his eyes.

"Believe me. I intend to do my job much better in the future with *all* my cases."

Did this fucker just threaten us?

"May I ask why you are asking me about Stone's father, anyway?" Lincoln interjects, more composed in an effort to break the sheriff's and my staring match.

"As you must already know, he belonged to the same Southside gang as Tucker Dixon. I found it odd that the Richfield Foundation would go to such lengths to free a man who is a known member of the same gang that could have had a hand in killing your parents."

"Again with this 'I find it odd' bullshit," I sneer. "Is there anything you don't find peculiar, sheriff? Because from where I'm standing, it looks like it's extremely easy to cause your head to spin in all directions from the most insignificant drivel."

"Colt, that's enough," Linc interjects, throwing me his less-than-subtle 'shut the fuck up' glare. "The sheriff's question is a fair one, and I can assure you that the Richfield Foundation only wants to set right a wrong. I see no relevance between my family's philanthropic endeavors, my parents' case, or Tucker Dixon and his known associates."

"But there lies the problem, Lincoln. We do," Sheriff Travis deadpans. "Seeing such an esteemed foundation use their extensive funds to set free a man who is known to have ties with a Southside criminal organization needs to be addressed."

"Hmm," I hum, using the sheriff's own verbal crutch against him. "Maybe you think our family's money should be used for better projects. Say, to be your benefactor in the next election coming up in a few months? I have to say, sheriff, your visit today kind of feels like it's either coercion or extortion. Lucky for you, our family is immune to both."

"That… that was never my intention," he stutters aghast, his whole face going deathly pale. "I'm merely trying to alert your cousin to the optics of the situation."

"Sure you were. But you know what they say about people with good intentions. Hell is filled with them."

My wolfish grin only slants wider as Sheriff Travis takes out his handkerchief from his blazer pocket to pad away the cold sweat that suddenly made its way to his bald forehead.

I feel the weight of my cousin's disapproving glower, but I couldn't pass up the chance to watch the sheriff squirm.

"We understand your concern, but I can assure you it's completely unfounded. Again, anything I can do to help, I'm more than happy to oblige," Lincoln says as he begins to stand up from the couch, indicating this little chit-chat has reached its end.

The sheriff gets the hint and all too eagerly gets up from his own seat.

"I appreciate that," he mumbles.

"You should. Most people don't like having house calls from Asheville's finest, especially when they make victims feel like perps. In my opinion, my cousin has been very patient in talking to you. Maybe next time, our family's lawyer should also be in attendance, seeing as the sheriff's department doesn't have the best track record when it comes to putting innocent men behind bars. We would hate to see history repeat itself, now wouldn't we?"

The sheriff's face turns from sickly green to hateful beet red, but I couldn't give a fuck.

"Thank you for your time, Lincoln."

"Of course," my cousin replies politely, his arm already stretched out to show the good sheriff his way to the front door. Sheriff Travis offers him a clipped nod and gifts me a black look.

Like that shit scares me.

"See you around, sheriff. And please give my love to that gorgeous wife of yours." I wink at the bastard just to ruffle his feathers a little further.

He doesn't have time to say anything in return since Lincoln has already shut the door on him, but just the quick glimpse I caught of his livid face was enough to make me feel all warm inside.

"Did you really have to go there?" Linc mumbles in irritation, pulling me away from the foyer in the direction of the kitchen.

"What?" I chuckle in amusement, with a little spring to my step.

Linc, however, doesn't find my ass funny today. He stops mid-step just so he can look me dead in the eye. Even if he didn't have that damn grimace on his face, I could still feel his irritation roll off him in threatening waves. My cousin has the purest heart I know, but push him beyond his breaking point, and well, we all saw what could happen when he loses his temper.

"You should be done with the sheriff's wife by now," he reprimands on a deep exhale, turning to head to the kitchen once more, trying hard not to blow up in my face.

"What can I tell you? She's a clinger. I can't exactly ghost her just like that, now can I?"

Never missing a beat, Lincoln's eyes travel throughout the kitchen, making sure no one will hear our conversation. Ever since Finn moved in with his girl, we never know what we'll find by turning a corner. Just the other day, I caught the two of them going at it in the pool house. Finn and Stone getting caught fucking like rabbits against the kitchen counter is bound to happen eventually. Lucky for us, it doesn't seem like today's the day, which means Linc and I can talk freely.

Linc opens the refrigerator door, his blank stare telling me he doesn't see a damn thing inside, too wrapped up with the muddled thoughts running through his head. He's still brooding, and it's starting to touch a nerve.

"Why are you so fucking upset with me right now? You were the one who told me to fuck her in the first place."

He snaps his arctic blue eyes at me, and I feel myself freezing in place.

"I said for you to use your charm and get close to Betty Lee so you could find out what the sheriff knows. Not make her your sidepiece."

"First of all, my charm is my dick. And secondly, not my fault you weren't more specific."

"This is not a joke, Colt." He growls, slamming the refrigerator door.

"You think I don't know that? If we played by your rules, one of us would be in jail already."

"Not one of us. Me!" He points his index finger at his chest.

"As if I'd ever let that happen." I scoff.

Like hell, I'd let Linc turn himself in. If he hadn't killed Uncle Crawford that night, I would have done it for him. The way I see it, my cousin did the world a fucking favor in putting a bullet in that fucker's head. No use in crying a river over the asshole now. He got exactly what was coming to him.

"Look, don't worry about Betty Lee, okay? I told you, I haven't slept with her in ages, and I don't intend to either. She got good enough taste to keep her loyal. She gave us the heads up about the gun and her husband paying us a visit, didn't she? So cool your jets and just breathe, Linc. We got this." I try to assure him.

His upper lip twitches unconvinced, but we've got other shit to focus on.

"Did East deal with the kid? He's not going to run his mouth, is he?" I ask him, worried that the Southside punk may be more troublesome than Easton speculated.

"I wrote him a check, but he hasn't cashed it yet."

"Then maybe East needs to pay Chase Dixon another visit. Make him understand that, whether he takes our money or not, he needs to keep his mouth shut."

"Perhaps," Linc mumbles under his breath, deep in thought.

"What are you thinking about, cuz?"

"I'm thinking that there are too many loose ends we didn't account for."

"We'll deal with them as they come. We always do," I counter comfortingly.

"Will we, Colt? I'm not so sure anymore."

I walk up to him and squeeze his shoulder, hoping to squash the doubt and guilt he has been afflicted with for the better part of a year now.

"The sheriff has squat on us, cuz. He's an incompetent buffoon that isn't equipped to tie his own shoelaces, let alone figure out what went down that night."

"He's not the one I'm worried about."

"Ah, right. I almost forgot about the boogeyman." I huff out, taking a step back to lean on the counter.

I cross my arms over my chest, tilting my head to the side to see where my cousin's head is at. I should have figured the sheriff was the least of his worries when it's The Society who is the real threat to our freedom.

"You think they're done with East?"

"I do. Which means you're next," he counters wisely.

"Yeah, I was thinking the same thing. They'll leave you for last, considering they probably think that you're the one who has *offended* them the most," I reply with extra sarcasm on the word offended. "How is the digging going? Were you able to confirm your prick of a father was a member?"

He shakes his head in defeat.

"I tore this place apart from top to bottom and couldn't find one thing tying him to The Society. Checked every inch of his computer and came up empty-handed, too. Either he covered his tracks, or The Society did it for him. But he must have been involved with them somehow. It's the only logical explanation for this backlash."

A stretch of silence ensues as we take that thought in.

Neither one of us has discussed our suspicion that the late governor must have been a member of the ominous boys club with East or Finn. For the past few months, they've had their hands full with The Society intent on pulling their strings. Adding this worry onto their shoulders would be overkill. And besides, being a Richfield, Linc and I are used to keeping secrets—even from our best friends.

But it's the only logical explanation. Not only was Uncle Crawford an only child from an esteemed Asheville family, but as governor, he had his fingers in many pots and in even more pockets. With his sadistic personality and hunger for power, he must have been the perfect member of The Society. Hence why they are so pissed that my cousin killed the fucker.

"What about you?" Lincoln turns to me and asks. "Has the Charlotte Library reached out to you yet, or have you made any leeway with Professor Harper? We need that book, Colt."

"Not yet," I mumble, less self-assured.

Now, this is the part that gets tricky for me.

Not only has the library not reached out to me yet, but after what went down between Emma and me over Halloween, I can't just walk up to her all charming and shit and try to sweet-talk her into giving me the damn thing.

First off, because Emma is not like the other bored out of their minds housewives from the Northside looking to jump on my dick for the thrill of it like Betty Lee was. The woman has class and little tolerance for my bullshit, even if her pretty cunt did drip all over my hand and tongue that night. I knew the deal was a one and done sort of thing, even if my cock still hates me for not insisting on taking things further.

And second, if I breathe a word of that night to Linc, he will have my balls—literally and figuratively. He'd be pissed I threw our best chance of finding more info about The Society out the window just because I decided it would be fun to hook up with my ethics professor. Telling him that when I saw her at the club wearing that little leather dress and fuck-me high heels, all thoughts of The Society and that stupid ass book flew from my mind, won't win me any brownie points. And it sure as fuck won't help my case if I admit I have thought of little else but that night in the alley with her either.

"Maybe I should be the one to deal with Harper," he muses more to himself than to me.

"No!" I slam my palm on the kitchen counter. My quick stern reply added with the impulsive reaction surprises us both, but I quickly rectify the mistake with my usual aloof grin. "Leave her to me. I can handle her." But just by the way his hand rubs over his chin, I can tell he's not convinced. "I said, I got it, Linc. You just stick to looking for anything that ties your prick of a father to The Society. That's what you should be focusing on. I'll deal with the professor."

He lets out an exaggerated exhale, but before he has time to argue with me, his phone starts blowing up from his back pocket. I catch a glimpse of a familiar blonde's smiling face on his screen, the same one who holds the power to relax his stiff demeanor instantly.

Kennedy Ryland—the only girl who can offer my cousin some semblance of peace as well as ensure his hellish torment continues, all in the same breath.

While Lincoln's body relaxes as he takes the call, mine begins to tense.

Why does he do this?

Why keep her close when it hurts him so much? When it fucks with his head? Does he really think his feelings will change throughout the years if he carries on with this charade of just being friends? Because from what I've seen, it fucking won't. Linc is as much in love with her now as he was when his whole world blew up in his face and his heart broke at sixteen.

I don't get it.

Is it the masochist in him that needs to be a part of her life somehow?

Is it the martyr in him?

What?

For the life of me, I can't wrap my head around why my cousin prefers a life filled with pain, guilt, and anguish when he could be perfectly content having someone else in his arms. He could pick anyone else to make him forget the one girl who is completely off-limits to him, and yet he does nothing. I know he's tried plenty of times before, hooking up here and there, just to get Ken out of his head, but he always ends up making fucking excuses why those girls aren't for him. Lies he feeds himself as well as me. He should just push her away and be done with it. That's what I would have done if the roles were reversed. Ken might be family to me, but if her presence caused me a sliver of the same pain my cousin lives with on a day to day basis, I wouldn't think twice at cutting ties with her. I value my fucking sanity, and Linc has been dancing over that trapeze wire for longer than any sane person could bear.

One day he'll fall.

And he won't be able to live with the degradation of it all when he does.

When he hangs up the phone, I level him with a knowing glower, showing him exactly what thoughts are on my mind.

"Don't start, Colt," he whispers, shame already robbing the smile Kennedy's call put on his face.

"You have to stop this shit, Linc."

His ocean eyes sear me with such despair it hurts to breathe.

"I can't. God forgive me, but I can't."

Love—the ultimate bullet to the heart—is the real reason why he'll never let her go.

Out of stupid fucking love.

It's that wasteful feeling that makes him endure the cruelest of torments.

I don't get it.

Love has always been a foreign concept for me. Sex, I understand fine.

Love, not so much.

I can count on one hand the people I can honestly say I love. Linc, Ken, Easton, and Finn are the only ones that come close to coaxing the feeling out of me. Sometimes my sisters too, but that all depends on the day I'm having. My friends are the only ones worthy of the sentiment, and that's just because of another feeling behind it—loyalty.

My unconditional trust in them trumps love in my book any day of the week.

They would never betray me.

They would rather die than be disloyal.

That, to me, is stronger than any love I could ever aspire to have or even want.

I just wish I could have the same certainty with every other person in my life as I have with them.

The thing about being a Richfield is that you always have a target on your back, and you never know who will come out of the woodwork to stab you next. Experience has shown me that if you love something, then you make yourself vulnerable for the jagged edge blade of betrayal to do its number on you.

I may not know the first thing about love, but I know a thing or two about betrayal.

And nothing cuts deeper than the wound inflicted by a person you love.

Chapter 6

Colt

Once Lincoln tells me his plan for the night is to go to the Brass Guild to watch Scarlett perform with the rest of the guys, I tell him that I'd rather skip it and do my own thing. Between Finn and Stone never taking their hands off one another, Easton making googly eyes at his new girlfriend on stage, and the mindfuck that is watching Ken and Lincoln together, going to the same elitist club where my father is sure to make an appearance isn't exactly my idea of a good time, and definitely not how I want to spend my Friday night.

Instead, I find myself going to the one place I usually try to avoid spending any time at, and that, of course, is my house—the original Richfield Estate. Considered to be Asheville's crown jewel, it boasts sixty thousand square feet and eighty-acre surroundings, making it one of the country's largest and oldest family homes. The over the top mansion where I lay my head at night is every historian's wet dream.

I almost gag whenever I hear such compliments.

This place is not a home.

It's a fucking prison, and the Richfield name is the iron shackle that binds me to it.

Luckily I can roam around most of this place without running into one of my parents—a small joy in exchange for living in a cold museum of a house.

Feeling restless since I've conceded to spending my night here, I decide to put on my trunks and go for a midnight swim in our indoor Olympic pool to clear my head. Lately, my mind has been overwhelmed with problem after problem, and I would rather enjoy the tranquility of swimming through chlorine-infested waters than spend another minute being drowned by my murky thoughts. Between The Society's impending letter, the sheriff's visit, and Ken still determined to see her engagement through, I've thought of little else.

Well, that's not entirely true.

Golden whiskey eyes and pouty, red lips have also kept me up at night, but entirely for different reasons—more pleasurable ones at that.

If I had half a brain, I would have made the two-hour drive to Charlotte to see if the good professor was in the mood for a repeat of our alley encounter. Unfortunately for the past month, whenever I did make the drive out, Emma Harper evaded me by not showing her pretty little face at the club. The only time I do see her is when I go to class, and I can't exactly have my way with her there when she's trying to do her damn job as well as pretend to ignore my presence in the room.

As I pass my father's study on the way to the pool, the memory of Emma's supple lips on mine is interrupted by the loud growl coming from inside.

"I'm warning you, Turner. Stay the fuck away from my son!"

Well, well, well. What do we have here?

I lean in closer to the door, the small gap in between giving me a perfect view of Richard Price slamming his fist against my father's precious eighteenth-century oak desk.

That will definitely leave a mark and devalue the damn thing.

Too bad Price decided to break a piece of the expensive furniture and not my father's face.

"You're being irrational," my father retorts, sounding almost bored.

"Don't fucking patronize me! I'm not stupid, you arrogant prick."

My father rises to his challenge by taking a sip of his bourbon and leaning comfortably back in his chair. All of him screams that he doesn't give two shits about Price's threat. I have to give it to my old man since Easton's stepfather looks like he's about to go on a murderous rampage.

"I'm fucking serious, Turner. Don't mess with my family. You know I'm not one to let bygones be bygones."

"Oh, believe me, I know that." My father smirks. "And if I recall correctly, so do the men who harmed your wife once upon a time. I'd love to ask them but I can't, now can I? And why is that, Richard? Why can't I ask them to what lengths you would go to teach your enemies a lesson?"

The eerie silence that transcends the room can be felt from way over here in the corridor.

What the fuck are they talking about?

"Are you threatening me?" Price spits out.

"We're friends. Why would I threaten a friend?"

"We are not friends."

"Yes, we are," my father deadpans, never once raising his voice. "You're a good man, Richard. And because I know that about you, I'm going to forgive such an accusation."

"You are one condescending piece of shit. You know that?" Price growls through bared teeth.

"Tsk, tsk." My father wags a patronizing finger at him. "Now, is that any way to talk to me?"

Jesus, my father's an asshole.

Well, it takes one to know one, I guess.

Whatever he's gone and done now, I wish Price would just lose it already and slap the smug grin off his face.

Come on, Price. Grow a pair.

"Just keep the hell away from my family!" he barks out instead, disappointing me.

"That won't be possible, and you know it. Not now anyway," my father mutters the last part more to himself than to Easton's dad before taking a sip of his drink.

"Ah. You mean Scarlett? I can protect the girl. She doesn't need you anymore."

The sound of a loud fist slamming onto the top of his desk has me frozen in place. My father rises up from his seat, no longer capable of keeping up with his aloof demeanor.

"Listen here, Price. I have been more than patient with you. But no one, and I mean *no one*, can protect her better than me. And neither you nor your son will keep me from her. Do you understand that?!"

Price throws him a disdainful sneer, while my father tries to recompose himself back to his stoic form.

But it's no use.

My father has just shown all his cards.

Little does he know Price isn't the only one who had a peek at them.

"You really are something, aren't you? Your wife is probably upstairs blissfully sleeping in your bed, completely unaware that you're here threatening me about my son's girlfriend. Who by the way will be *my* family soon enough, therefore my responsibility—not yours."

"She's in love and free to choose who she wants. That doesn't mean she is no longer my concern."

"Always with the riddles." Price scoffs. "You might be able to play these little games with everyone else, but not with me, Turner. You forget I grew up in this town, too. I know all your dirty little secrets."

"And I know yours. Just because you've stepped away from the fray doesn't mean a damn thing. Don't forget who you really belong to."

"I belong to no one!" Price hollers, his face fuming with rage.

"Yes, you do. The minute you came to me with those names fifteen years ago, you signed your fate. You knew what it meant, so don't delude yourself."

"Fuck you, Turner."

"Noted. Now, is there anything else you want to say?" my father counters calmly, sitting back in his chair completely unbothered by the unhinged man in front of him.

"If any harm comes to mine, you best believe I'm coming for yours." Price throws an accusing finger in my father's direction.

"I gave Scarlett my word that no harm would come to the boy. I have never broken a promise to her, nor do I ever intend to. So don't trouble yourself with idle threats when I've already guaranteed that not a hair on Easton's head will be harmed."

Another bout of silence ensues, Price's shoulders visibly relaxing before my very eyes, while I stand baffled and confused with their heated argument.

"Then why?" he asks, sounding just as perplexed as I am at this point. "What's the point of all this?"

I try to lean in closer to hear my father's whispered reply, but to my aggravation, all I catch is Easton's dad's huff in contempt at whatever explanation my father just gave.

"You fucking Richfields. You always end up poisoning everything around you. Just keep this little game of yours the fuck away from my family."

"You're becoming repetitive in your old age, Richard. You said that already." My father arches a smug brow, drinking the rest of his liquor.

In true Easton fashion, Price flips the bird in my father's unrepentant face.

So that's where he gets it from.

"Don't make me come back here, Owen. You think you know the lengths to which I would go to protect my family, but you have no clue. I'm not afraid of getting my hands dirty."

"And you don't know what I've done to protect mine. So let's stop with the threats, shall we? It's beneath us. Real men don't warn. We act."

Price throws him another disdainful glare and rushes in my direction. When he opens the door and sees me rooted to my spot, there is so much hate in his deep chestnut eyes that I take a step back just in case he wants to unleash hell on the wrong Turner.

"Come in, Colt," my father calls out as Price clips my shoulder to get the hell out of our house.

"What was that about?" I ask point-blank as I walk into the study.

"It's nothing that you should concern yourself with."

"Didn't look like nothing to me."

"Believe me, it was. Richard and I have known each other since we were kids, so I don't take offense when he jumps to unfounded conclusions. I can't hold it against him since he's always been headstrong."

"Easton is like that, too."

"Yes, I know," he retorts ambiguously, his smile thin on his lips.

"Why were you talking about his girlfriend?"

"Who?" my father questions absentmindedly as he refills his glass with bourbon.

"I heard you both talking about Scarlett."

"Did you? I don't recall her name coming up. She's Pastor Davis' niece, correct?" he asks before drinking his chalice in one fell swoop.

His brazen lie makes me want to wring my hands around his neck and make him choke on his favorite bourbon.

He's fucking lying right to my goddamn face and doesn't look one bit remorseful while doing it.

"One and the same."

I cross my arms over my chest, unimpressed that my own father is playing me.

"Hmm," he mumbles dismissively, placing his empty glass on the coaster in favor of grabbing the coat behind his brown leather chair.

"Going somewhere?"

"Yes. I have some matters to attend to."

I bite my inner cheek at the gall of him.

"Must be pretty important stuff if it means you have to deal with it after midnight."

"Quite," is his non-committal reply.

Knowing my father, he's probably going to get his dick wet with whichever bimbo he has for a mistress these days and try to forget that his so-called childhood friend just threatened him and his entire family.

Fucking two-timing asshole.

He's about to pass me by, only stopping next to me to squeeze my shoulder.

"Have a nice swim, son. It's a lovely night for it."

With that farewell passing his lips, I'm left in his study to fume alone.

And this is why I hate spending any time here.

It only reminds me how my whole fucking family is a lie.

The next morning I'm sprawled in my bed, staring at the ceiling recounting what I heard last night in my father's study.

Why the fuck was Dick Price all up in my dad's face?

For all I know, dear old dad probably made a pass at Easton's mom. I wouldn't put it past him since all of Northside knows what type of player he is.

And let's face it.

Naomi Price is hot as fuck.

When I was growing up, I wouldn't have minded playing the whole Mrs. Robinson scenario with her. Of course, the only thing that stopped me from trying my shot with her was the certainty that if East ever found out, he'd cut my dick off and have his stepfather feed it to me. They might not see eye to eye on a lot of things, but when it comes to Naomi, they are always on the same page.

It must be nice to have something in common with your old man. Linc and I got shafted in the father department, so I can't say I understand what that feels like.

But as I try to recall their cryptic conversation, Naomi's name wasn't the one mentioned.

Scarlett's name, however, was.

But why?

I run my hand over my morning scruff, trying to make sense of their conversation, but all I get is a headache for my troubles.

Fuck this.

I'm not going to spend a perfectly good Saturday morning thinking about my shitty, adulterous father and whatever beef Price has with him. As my go-to move, I grab my cock and close my eyes, thinking of anything that will get my mind off my father's wandering dick and focus on my own. It should be the only one that matters to me anyway.

I don't have to think too hard on the person I want to sink inside of. She's been the only woman on my mind since Halloween night.

I must be slipping.

My phone blows up with hot hookups left and right, and none of them whet my appetite as much as the idea of Emma Harper cumming on my mouth again.

Who knew I was into the whole hot for teacher kink?

I grab the base of my cock, imagining her sweet pussy squeezing around me and milking it dry. In my mind, she's here in my bedroom on top of me, running those deep red nails all over my chest, getting me off while giving me just a sliver of pain to go with it. Even my fantasies of Emma are better than whatever thirst trap is DMing me nudes late at night, asking if I want to meet up. I keep to a gentle rhythm as I picture Emma in nothing but her catlike glasses, her hair up in a bun looking all respectable, while her filthy mouth orders me around.

Words like harder, faster, deeper, and more sung in her sweet voice have me close to coming undone. When she wraps her hands around my throat, suffocating me while riding me into oblivion, I cum like a prepubescent teenager who just found Pornhub on his phone.

Fuck.

It was hard enough being in her class and not fantasizing about being inside her, but now that I got a little taste, every time I leave her classroom, I suffer a severe case of blue balls. Not that she flirts with me or anything. As far as she's concerned, that night never happened. I wish I could dismiss it so easily, but then again, I've always been a sucker for a good challenge. Before the year is done, I'll have Emma on all fours with my cum dripping down her thighs, my name on her lips.

Now that's the type of morning wake-up call I'm talking about.

But until then, I guess my hand will have to do.

I get out of bed and wash up before putting on my sweats for my ritual morning run. People have no idea the amount of work that goes into keeping this body in shape. They like to gawk and stare, but no one is really interested in the daily sacrifices I make to look this good. Then again, no one is interested in taking a peek behind the curtain at anything that has to do with me. All they want is the superficial image I portray, the untouchable Richfield heir who has the world at his feet.

What a fucking joke.

If only they knew the true cost of being a part of this family.

Goddamn it.

There I go again.

Bringing shit up that I should be accustomed to by now is not how I want to start my day. It was that fucking conversation that I walked in on last night that has me overthinking this morning. I just need to clear my head with a good run and then go over to Linc's place to tell him what I witnessed last night. Unlike me, I'm sure he'll be able to put two and two together easily enough. He's always been the brains in our little group.

As I walk down the large spiral staircase, animated laughter coming from the dining room can be heard throughout the large foyer. Instead of heading out, I walk toward the sound, and just as I expected it, the giggling stops the minute I pop my head in the room.

"Here comes the alphahole," my sister Irene singsongs before picking up her orange juice, her long blonde hair combed back into a no-nonsense ponytail.

"Not just any alphahole, but Asheville's favorite alphahole. Good morning, dear brother." Abigail winks at me playfully.

"Just Asheville, Abby?" Meredith counters evenly, shaking her head. "Why be modest about our brother's amazing accomplishments when he's worked so hard for them?"

Always busting my balls these three.

I swear they came out of the womb knowing exactly what to say to push my buttons.

"Meredith," my mother reprimands without any heat behind it.

God forbid she give Mer—her favorite—any grief.

I have no idea why my mother insisted on having any more children when it's so painfully obvious she got it right with her firstborn. In her eyes, my eldest sister Meredith can do no wrong—Irene coming in a close second. Little Abby and I got the short end of the stick where my mother's approval is concerned. Colleen Richfield doesn't suffer fools well, and unfortunately for my baby sister Abby, she's a lot like me on that front.

She talks before she thinks.

Impulsively acts before considering the consequences.

And is too damn cocky for her own good.

If the stories are true, that means we got the wrong end of the gene pool and are both a lot like our father when he was our age. In other words, we fail to meet my mother's well-versed sense of decorum. While our father had a reputation of being wild and carefree in his youth, our mother has had an ice stick rammed up her butt since birth.

Duty, honor, and family have always been her mantra.

It's ironic she values such things since she has failed miserably at the last one.

My sisters and I don't have a mother—we have a general intent on preserving the Richfield family name at all costs.

Her very air reeks of privileged entitlement and matriarchal authoritarianism—a far cry from what one would expect of a southern bell. While other women of her stature and age go out to brunch with their friends for the sole purpose of gossiping and throwing jabs at each other as they sip on sweet ice tea, my mother puts up no pretenses. She makes you feel like a minuscule ant that she can squash easily enough with her heel, not giving you a second thought after the deed is done.

Cold.

Uncaring.

And unsympathetic to failure of any kind.

The world could be collapsing in on itself, and my mother would coolly slap it across the face and demand its composure.

But my baby sister Abby still has time to redeem herself in our mother's eyes. She's still in high school with plenty of time to become the little Stepford cold robot our mother wishes her to be. I, however, have been dubbed as a lost cause, hence the lack of even a good morning greeting to her only son.

"Morning, ladies," I greet animatedly, brushing away my mother's disapproving stare while taking a grape off my baby sister's plate and popping it into my mouth.

Abby just slaps my hand away, but the mirth in her deep green eyes tells me she doesn't mind me messing with her one bit.

That's the other difference between Abby and me and our other sisters. We got our father's emerald eyes while Meredith and Irene got the traditional arctic blue of my mother's side of the family.

I place my chin on my baby sister's head and steal another grape.

"What the hell is an alphahole, anyway?" I whisper in her ear.

Abby opens her mouth to explain, but Irene beats her to the punch.

"Google it, big brother. I'm sure you'll see a picture of yourself when you do," she explains mockingly while buttering her toast.

"Funny," I retort inattentively since my father's empty chair has my full attention. "Dad not up yet?"

"He had a long night and is sleeping in this morning."

I bet the fucker did.

My gaze trails over to my mother, who doesn't seem one bit upset that my father's nocturnal activities have prevented him from having breakfast with his family. Not that I'm surprised. A woman like her is too busy with more pressing Richfield matters to attend to than waste a single second of her time paying her husband's extramarital affairs any mind. I bet if he brought his sidepiece home and fucked her right on their shared bed, my mother wouldn't even flinch or bat an eye.

Colleen Richfield has an ice sculpture for a heart and frozen hailstones running through her veins.

No one can squeeze blood from a stone.

So how can I expect any emotion to bleed from her?

"Are you having breakfast with us this morning like a normal person?" she quips flatly, eyeing me up and down, showing her discontentment with the clothes I've got on for breakfast.

"As much as that backhanded invitation sounds appealing, I'm off for a run."

"Of course you are. God forbid you to take part in anything this family does."

"Aw shucks, Mom. I didn't know you cared." I place my hands to my chest, taking mock offense.

"Your attitude is getting rather dull, Colt. How about you switch it up from time to time?" Meredith interjects, using the same words and tone my mother taught her to perfection.

I flip her off, causing her to slant her eyes in disgust, as Irene almost chokes on her juice at the gesture. My baby sister, however, giggles in amusement into her napkin. Unlike the other three women present, Abby loves my ass even if she does give me a hard time. I ruffle her hair and stroll away from the room, not even bothering to tell my mother goodbye. It's not as if she expects me to, anyway.

With my earbuds in place, I go outside to stretch before I get my morning jog in. I'm mid-lunge when a familiar black envelope on the windshield of my car breaks my concentration and makes certain to shoot all my morning plans to hell.

Chapter 7

Colt

Shit.

Guess it's my turn now.

Motherfuckers!

Ever so cautiously, I casually tread to my car, all the while discreetly searching my surroundings in case anyone is watching me. If they are, they sure are keeping their presence well hidden. I pull the damn thing from my windshield, the weight of the black envelope in my hands feeling heavier than the ones sent out before. When my thumb traces over a lump, a sudden knot in the pit of my stomach surges, reminding me of the last time The Society sent more than just a simple letter with their demands.

Hiding the envelope in the waistband of my sweats, I run back to the house, bypassing Abby on her phone in the foyer.

"That was fast."

"I changed my mind."

"Hey, you okay?" she asks with concern, holding onto my forearm to keep me in place. "You know we were just messing with you at breakfast, right?"

She might have been, but no one else at that table was. But instead of adding to my baby sister's worry, I throw her a devil-may-care grin.

"I know, shortstop. It's all good. I just remembered I've got somewhere to be, that's all."

I ruffle her hair endearingly before heading back upstairs to the confinement and safety of my room. Once I've made sure to lock myself in, I take the envelope out of my waistband and throw it on my unmade bed. The red wax with The Society symbol mocks me as I pace back and forth, running my hand through my hair while my eyes never leave the wretched thing.

I should just get changed and take it over to Linc's.

That's what I should do.

But then why did they send it to me directly? Why not send it over to the Hamilton Estate like they did Finn's and Easton's letters?

Fuck it.

I grab the envelope and rip it apart to find the dreaded letter inside, and low and behold, another flash drive just as I suspected. The ominous small device even came with its own note, ordering me to open whatever is inside first. Now last time we got one of these, it was fucking brutal. East almost lost his mind having to watch his mom and stepdad fuck. Mind you, I found it kind of hot, but then again, it wasn't my parents' sex tape on show. Just the idea of it makes me nauseous.

Shit!

Is this another sex-tape scandal in the works?

Nah, it can't be. Colleen is too uptight to be filmed fucking. With my luck, it's a tape of my dad screwing some Brass Guild whore, and who the fuck wants to see that shit? If that's all The Society has on me, then they can go fuck themselves. Every Tom, Dick, and Harry in both Carolinas knows my old man steps out on my mother and that she doesn't give two shits about it either. For all her poise and sophistication, and her endless rants on Richfield pride and proper behavior, the outing of an affair doesn't seem to rattle her cage any.

My attention goes back to the drive on my bed, and as hard as I try to rack my brain on what could possibly be on the damn thing, the answer evades me.

Only one way to find out, and like hell, I'll be doing it with everyone else around me glued to the screen like East had to endure.

Fuck that.

I would rather watch it on my own first and prepare myself than take my chances of losing my shit in front of everyone. I'm not as hot-blooded as East, but every man has his breaking point, and it seems The Society are masters at uncovering what those are.

Unlike last time, I don't have my cousin's patience to buy a new computer in case the flash drive has any virus attached to it. It's not like they're going to get anything from my laptop's hard drive anyway. While Lincoln has been doing his part in the Richfield Foundation since Aunt Sierra passed away, my mother doesn't feel I'm mature enough yet to take the responsibility on, leaving Meredith to take the full burden on her shoulders. No skin off my back. I'm in no hurry to be another cog in the Richfield wheel. Right now, my mother's reluctance in getting me involved with anything pertaining to this family means that there is nothing on my computer that can be of any worth to The Society.

After I've inserted the flash drive into my laptop, I sit on the edge of the bed, taking a deep breath before opening the dreadful yellow folder with my name on it. When I see another video in there, the hairs at the back of my neck begin to rise. I press play, and just like with Easton's video, the same black screen appears with The Society's golden symbol at its very center.

And then nothing.

Just black.

The fuck?

My brows crease, wondering what the hell is going on when suddenly an image appears, one I'm all too fucking familiar with since that night is seared into my brain, branded with a hot iron. The video of the library is grainy, almost as if someone filmed us through a dirty glass. It's enough to confirm our suspicions that whoever was there that night was able to hide away in the secret passageways of the house without us knowing.

Before I can make sense of what point of the night I'm looking at, a white flash blurs the image, making whoever was holding onto the phone recording the whole shitshow lose their focus for a split second. The image trembles for a bit, but when it zooms back on us, it's unmistakable what just happened.

Finn and East have my Uncle Crawford bound tight on the floor, wailing in pain from the gunshot to his leg. My hand is still clutching his gun, staring my uncle down with such loathing that it's a wonder I didn't finish him then and there.

My heart beats rapidly in my chest, remembering perfectly all the words said that night even though the video doesn't have any sound to it. I'm sure the real one does, though, since it's obvious this has been cut and edited only to focus on my part of the despicable night. I fist my hand on the duvet, thankful that Lincoln and Aunt Sierra aren't in the shot as my uncle continues to spew his filth. But hell must have heard me because, all too soon, my cousin walks into view, slowly heading in our direction. I swallow dryly as I remember the tempest in his blue eyes as he unclenches my hand off the gun and takes it into his own. With a steady hand, Linc holds the gun under Crawford's jaw, whispering the last words the fucker will ever hear.

My breath catches in my throat as I watch for a second time Lincoln pulling the trigger, making sure that my uncle's brain matter spills in all directions, his hot blood on our skin sealing the four of us to this unknown fate.

I didn't feel remorse then, and I don't feel it now. Even when watching the replay, I feel nothing. The only thing that troubles me is that The Society has ironclad proof of what went down that night, which means we are officially fucked. They've got us by the shorthairs, and they know it.

And now so do I.

One wrong move, and we're all done for.

With the faint smell of blood and gore resurfacing all around me, the video ends. In its place, the same black screen comes up with The Society symbol, only this time, it's paired with a sinister robotic voice coming through the speakers.

"Colt Turner—Richfield heir and Asheville's most notorious son. We've been watching you, as you can tell by our little home movie. What a murderous web you and your friends have weaved for yourselves. We're sure by now you've realized this is only a small recorded sample of your misgivings. We're keeping the full show close to the vest, but don't worry. We're not going to use this against you. Not yet anyway. Not if you play by our rules. Unlike your friends, we've decided that you are different, and therefore, worthy of special consideration."

"I'll show you different, motherfucker." I grind my teeth.

"Just like your friends, in the letter attached, you will be given a task. However, bear in mind it is not the assignment we are really interested in you performing. Think of it as a decoy in order not to raise suspicion from your *so-called* brothers. Lying should come as second nature to you now, so we're sure you're not uncomfortable with keeping up pretenses even with them. We are going to give you a once in a lifetime opportunity to redeem yourself. Finn and Easton have failed their missions and therefore have been punished for it. You, on the other hand, can set the wrongs they have done right. If you do as you are told, then we will destroy this piece of evidence."

"Liar." I scoff.

Just how fucking stupid do these shitheads think I am?

"Remember what is a stake here—your freedom. Our patience is running thin with your friends' disobedience, yet here we are, offering you a golden opportunity to redeem yourselves. Mercy is not something we shell out often, but we believe your task will be one you want answers to as well. Are you ready?"

"Yeah, asshole, I'm ready," I spit out like the fucker can hear me.

"You have been lied to."

My brows crease.

"And this lie is one that we want to be uncovered and told to the world. In exchange for exposing this secret, we will make sure to keep yours buried. No one will know that you were the one who drew first blood that night. No one will know the depravity of your actions. All you have to do is dig deep and unbury the secret that the people closest to you have been trying to keep hidden. Consider it one dirty secret for another. That is our proposal. Succeed in your mission, and we will expunge the wrongs you and your friends have afflicted on us. But for this to occur, you must not divulge a single word about this deal to anyone. If you do, we will find out, and this 'get out of jail free card' will be null and void. Your friends' fate, as well as your own, is now solely in your hands. Do with it what you will. Oh, and Colt, one more word of advice. *Trust no one.*"

And with that ill-omened warning hanging in the air, the video ends, and my torment begins.

Chapter 8

Colt

The minute I step foot inside the Hamilton mansion, I know something is amiss. Linc and East are frozen still at the center of the large entrance hall, listening in on the heated argument taking place inside Finn's room upstairs.

"Trouble in paradise, I see."

"Shh. Linc and I have a bet going that Stone is going to throw something any minute now."

"We should give them their privacy instead of eavesdropping like this," Linc suggests, concerned, but doesn't move an inch from his post.

"And miss the show? Not a chance."

While Easton looks like he's enjoying the lover's spat, Linc doesn't seem to find the two lovebirds arguing with each other very funny. And why would he? Walker spilled his guts out to the Southie on what happened in this very house last spring, the first chance he got. If Stone gives him the boot, then not only will she break his oversized heart, but she'll leave with all our secrets, too. And no one wants someone else holding our crimes against us. We already have The

Society on our tail. We sure as fuck don't need a scorned ex-girlfriend to add to the mix.

At this point, the cynic in me would be pissed that Walker doesn't have a hold on his woman by the way I hear her chew him out upstairs, but unlike my cousin, I'm not the least bit concerned. I've seen enough in the past few months to know that those two are meant for each other. If Stone didn't run for the hills when Finn fessed up that he was an accomplice to murder, then whatever little squabble they are fighting over now won't scare her off either. The tattooed Southie is a ride-or-die kind of girl, so Linc has nothing to worry about.

"Don't fret, cuz. This shit is their version of kinky foreplay. Instead of them shouting at each other, soon all we'll hear is loud moaning and grunting."

"I'm not so sure. They've been at it for a while now."

"Only means the hate fuck afterward will be ten times better." I wink, but my amused chuckle is interrupted when Stone rushes out of Finn's room upstairs, slamming the door in his face like a possessed woman.

"Argh!" She belts out in aggravation at the same time Finn scrambles out of his room.

"Don't walk away from me, brat. We need to sort this out."

"I'm done talking. You're not going to change my mind."

"I said no, Stone! No fucking way am I letting you do this!" Finn yells, stampeding down the stairs right behind her.

"It's already done. And you telling me what I can and cannot do is pissing me off!"

We watch Finn pull his hair out of his skull, trying hard not to lose his cool but failing miserably at it, while an enraged Stone keeps tapping her heel on the floor, waiting for what he'll say next. The two are so wrapped up in whatever drama they've got going on they don't even acknowledge that they have an attentive audience in their midst.

"Stone, you are not doing this."

"I am."

"No, you're not. The man is as slimy as they come. How can you even consider working for him?"

"*That* man is in the running to be one of next year's presidential candidates. This is the job of a lifetime, Finn, and not you or anybody else is going to change my mind about taking it."

"What the hell are you talking about?" Easton interrupts, no longer amused with their heated banter but curious about the subject at hand.

"East, can you please tell my girlfriend that working for Senator Maxwell is a fucking bad idea?"

"You're going to work for Tommyboy's dad?!" Easton exclaims, aghast.

"I am. Finn's mom got me the job on his electoral campaign, and I'm taking it," she explains with her hands on her hips while eyeballing her boyfriend.

"Hold up. Just wait a second. Maxwell is going to run for president?"

"God, East. You're usually quicker than this. It's what I said, isn't it? The whole thing is still very hush-hush, but Senator Maxwell is slowly putting a team together."

"And my mother decided it would be a good idea to pull some strings and get Stone involved in his presidential campaign," Finn chimes in, disheartened.

"I thought your mom liked your girl, Walker?" I ask him in confusion.

"She does! Hence the job!" Stone throws her arms in the air in exasperation. "Most of the senator's aides are volunteers, yet Charlene got me a paying job as an assistant to his number two. She knows I'll need to sustain myself through law school next year and that this job is a godsend for me. Why can't anyone see that?"

"I told you, I can take care of you," Finn retorts.

"And who said I need to be taken care of? I was taking care of myself before you came along, quarterback. I don't need a knight in shining armor. I never have."

"No, what you need is a good fucking spanking," he mumbles under his breath.

"I'm with Walker on that one," I add my two cents, not ecstatic with the idea either.

Her resentful stare bores into me.

"Please don't do this, brat," Finn pleads, pulling her into his arms in an effort to convince her.

Her eyes soften at his new tender approach to deal with this shitshow, but everyone can tell she's made up her stubborn mind.

"It's only a job, and it pays good money, Finn."

"I can get you a job. Linc, get my girl a job before she has to work for that sleaze bag."

Linc begins to open his mouth but seals it shut when Stone shakes her head at him.

"I already accepted it. I won't go back on my word."

Finn looks absolutely defeated, but when Stone wraps her hands around him, placing her head on his chest, his resolve begins to waver. The rest of us, however, aren't as easily swayed.

"It's just a job, quarterback. Nothing more. Why are you so against it?"

"Ah, well, maybe because Senator Maxwell might be behind The Society," Easton points out, arms crossed on his chest.

"You don't know that," she counters, pulling away from Finn to look Easton in the eye. "You said so yourself that Scarlett saw Linc's mom get into Tommyboy's car. You have no proof it was the senator behind the wheel that day. It could just as easily have been his son. More probable, even."

"True. But do you really want to get involved with that family? Knowing full well one of those motherfuckers is blackmailing us?" Easton retorts bitterly, but his tone doesn't seem to have any effect on the Southie.

"If I remember correctly, Kennedy is about to marry into that family. And not one of you has lifted a finger in trying to stop her. A job versus being forever linked to them doesn't seem so bad to me."

I tried to stop her.

On Halloween night, I tried, yet again, to talk Ken out of making the worst mistake of her life. But I'm not the one who can change her mind. Only one man in this room can, and unfortunately for everyone involved, he'll never be able to. I don't need to look at my cousin beside me to know what self-deprecating thoughts are ruling his mind at this very moment.

Having had enough of the stilted silence around us, I decide now is as good a time as any to do what I came here for.

"If Walker's girl wants to work for the next Clarence Thomas, that's her prerogative. We've got bigger fish to fry."

And before Finn or Stone can ream me with whatever harsh reply is on the tip of their tongues, I take out the sinister black letter from my back pocket and wave it around. Astounding how the mere sight of the eerie envelope is capable of silencing any room and filling it with dread.

"Good. I have your attention." I smirk.

"Shit. You've been summoned already, huh?" Easton mutters, trying to be his usual witty self, but there's no mistaking the apprehension coating his gray eyes. "So who do they want you to go after?"

"I don't know. I haven't read it yet." I shrug, handing the evil thing over to Linc.

He holds it carefully in his hands and walks over to the living room. We all follow and surround him as he places the letter flat on top of the grand piano. When I see a familiar name embossed in perfect gold lettering, I kick myself for not having read the damn thing back at my place before I came over.

IVY FOX

AND THEN THERE WERE TWO.

TWO RICHFIELD HEIRS, WHO UNLIKE THEIR PREDECESSORS,
ARE MORE DESERVING OF OUR WRATH
FOR THE SINS THEY HAVE COMMITTED.

YET FOR NOW, ONE OF YOU WILL GET THE CHANCE TO SHOW US
IF HE MERITS OUR BENEVOLENCE, OR OUR RETALIATION.

THE TIME HAS ARRIVED TO USE THE SELF-SERVING
TURNER CHARM TO OUR ADVANTAGE,
AND RID US OF PESTERING NUISANCES.

EMMA HARPER HAS OVERSTAYED
HER WELCOME IN OUR FAIR TOWN,
HER ONLY TIE TO IT — HER EMPLOYMENT
PROVIDED BY THE RICHFIELDS THEMSELVES.

FREE HER OF THIS BURDEN BEFORE THE FIRST SNOWFALL
LANDS ON ASHEVILLE SOIL, AND GAIN OUR MERCY.

WE WILL BE WATCHING.

THE SOCIETY

Fuck my life. These fuckers sure do know how to pick them, don't they?

They want Emma.

No, wait. They don't.

She's only a decoy.

But is she really?

Fuck.

How can I be sure?

I keep my expression as blank as possible while everyone takes turns reading The Society's demands word for word.

"I guess I lucked out," I gloat, leaning against the piano, knowing everyone in this room will expect such a comment from me. "One call to the dean, and the pretty professor goes back to where she came from. I'll talk to him Monday. There, done. Next."

What a fucking shame, though.

I had so many plans for the young professor, and these assholes just blew all of them completely out of the water. But while my mind is on the loss of the dirty things I had in store for Emma, everyone else in the room looks troubled by something else.

"What?"

"We can't get her fired. Not yet anyway," Lincoln explains pensively.

"Why the fuck not? This is the easiest gig they have given us so far. We should be celebrating, but you all look like we're at a funeral or something."

"Will you please explain it to your cousin? The damn vain idiot can't see past his own fucking reflection in a mirror, much less see what the real problem here is," Easton interjects, disappointed, while Linc lets out an exaggerated exhale.

I throw East a seething look cause he's being a prick, but that doesn't change the fact that I really don't understand why everyone has their panties in a twist.

"Am I missing something?"

"Yes!" they all rebuke simultaneously.

"What?!"

"They want professor Harper gone because she must have found out something about them in that book of hers back at the Charlotte Library. Maybe she even stumbled on who they are," Lincoln explains patiently. "We can't fire her. She's too important. What we urgently need to do is find out what she knows and be quick about it. Because this time, The Society gave us a time frame, and by my count, we have until Christmas before the first snowfalls. If we're lucky, maybe early January at the latest, which means you're on a deadline."

"A short one at that," Finn chimes in.

I muse over what Linc is trying to warn me about and pair it with the instructions given on the flash drive. Emma was supposed to be just a front for my true task, but that doesn't mean there isn't some truth to what Linc is saying. The Society knows that it would be child's play for me to terminate her contract with the school. Our family is the one who holds the purse strings for the Richfield School Board, so one word from us about our dissatisfaction with any teacher and they'd be kicked to the curb. It really is that easy. So why this precise decoy?

Trust no one.

That was their parting advice, and I should have taken it to heart earlier.

Especially when it concerns them.

Linc's right.

Emma must have been getting too close for comfort for them to bear, and what better tool to get rid of her than use one of the two Richfield heirs they are currently blackmailing. When they said not to pay their written task any mind, like a fool, I took their word. That was my first mistake, and it took my friends reading their demands to make me realize it.

It's obvious to me now that they purposely tried to divert my attention off Emma and made sure all I centered on was trying to decipher the riddle they posed to me—uncover whatever lie they want unburied.

Like I have a clue what that's about.

That video had me so consumed with trying to understand what they were alluding to and how I would have to conceal its existence from the rest of the guys—more importantly, from Lincoln—that I didn't even read the letter until I got here, for crying out loud.

They played me like a fiddle, but now it's my turn to return the favor.

They think we have no clue Emma has been digging into them, and that's the leverage we can use to our benefit. While I pretend to be their little puppet, I'll get whatever discovery Emma obtained and use it against them. With any luck, she knows who these fuckers are by name. And if that's the case, we can finally put an end to all this once and for all. Of course, before I can do that, I'll still need to get my hands on that fucking video. So many loose threads to deal with, but I guess I should start with the main one.

I look around to face all the forlorn expressions on my friends' faces and throw them my best wolfish grin.

"Leave the professor to me. I know exactly how to play this."

I smack my lips, feeling confident in how to go about this, but it doesn't seem like anyone else in the room shares in my conviction.

"We're so fucking screwed," East mumbles under his breath, anxiously searching his pockets for his nicotine fix.

"What?"

"Don't play dumb, Colt. If you think Professor Harper is going to swoon and give you all her secrets just because you shine those fake veneers at her, then you have another thing coming," Stone chastises.

So that's what they're thinking I'm going to do—lure Emma into my bed, hoping for some pillow talk about The Society.

Instead of explaining how I'm really going to go about solving our boogeyman problems, I let them believe what they will and add fire to the flame with a cocky comeback.

"This is all real, sweetheart. If your boyfriend doesn't mind, go ahead and check for yourself."

I wink.

"Oh, please. You're anything but *real*."

My jaw ticks at her smart mouth.

"Control your woman, Walker. She's getting on my nerves now. If you're not man enough to give her that spanking you were promising a few minutes ago, then trust me—I am."

The Southie rushes toward me, all claws and teeth, but Finn quickly grabs her by the waist and pulls her away. Stone's legs continue to wiggle in the air in an attempt to kick me as Finn begins to retreat to their room.

"Let's go, brat, before we have another murder to clean up afterward."

I can hear her mumbling all the way upstairs what a conceited prick I am, but thankfully her irksome voice is silenced the minute Finn has her locked away inside his bedroom.

"She's right, you know," Easton adds, puffing on his cancer stick. "You might think your dick works miracles, but it won't do the trick with a woman like Emma Harper."

"Enough. Colt isn't going to try to sleep with her. He just needs to get his hands on whatever she found in that book." Lincoln walks over to me, his expression hard as steel. "Tell me you got this?"

"I told you I did. Have I ever not kept my word to you? Ever?"

He gives me a tight nod and then turns to face the dark prince of our little group.

"If my cousin says he can handle it, then I believe him. Everyone else should too."

"Whatever you say, Linc. It's not like our lives are on the line," Easton remarks sarcastically, blowing rings of smoke into the air. "What are we going to do about Stone, though?"

"What about her?"

"Are we really going to let her work for the senator? It's a fucking bad idea sending her into shark-infested waters, if you ask me. Especially if we think Tommyboy and his sleazy father are members of The Society and the ones who are after us."

"She's a big girl and can hold her own," I defend, bored, pretending to flick an imaginary piece of lint off my shoulder. "She's also stubborn as fuck, so if Walker can't talk some sense into her, then neither can any one of us."

I look over at Lincoln to back me up in my assessment, but he's oddly silent throughout the whole exchange.

"What's wrong?"

"Nothing," he states evenly. "I'm going for a walk."

He leaves us without another word or explanation. I stand silent, watching him walk over to Oakley Woods through the living room window.

"It's not you that he's pissed at. It was Stone saying that we haven't done anything to get Ken out of her engagement that has him all wound up."

"Speak for yourself," I bite back, watching Lincoln's shadow get further away from the house. "I've been trying to get her to call the whole thing off since the day she announced she was going to get married to the dipshit."

"You can't change her mind. Only he can."

"Hell has a better chance of freezing over," I reply sadly, the knots in my stomach twisting profusely.

"You have got to let that shit go, Colt."

Easton forcefully stubs the rest of his cigarette in the ashtray, thinking the reason behind my disapproval of Ken getting hitched is because I'm still harboring feelings for her.

If only that were possible.

"Yeah, I heard you the first time."

"Just focus on the shit that you have on your plate and leave Ken alone."

It's his authoritarian tone that hits a nerve.

"It's funny how deluded some people are to be under the impression they can order me around. I'm my own man, you know? I do what I want, when I want. Don't ever forget that."

"You're an asshole. A man is a stretch."

I throw him the finger, beating him to the punch, and walk toward the front door.

"Where are you going?"

"Where does it look like? He needs me."

I don't need to explain anything further and begin my search to find my pensive, somber cousin through the vast woods. When I finally catch up to him, I don't say a word. Lincoln knowing I'm here is enough. I'd follow him to hell and back if he'd asked me to. Because while everyone is so quick to point out all my flaws or try to change me in every way, my cousin has always accepted me for who I am. Acceptance in a world intent on wanting to mold you into a version of themselves is only one of the reasons why Lincoln is better than most of us.

As the fall leaves crunch under our feet, my mind wanders onto another dismal day that we walked through these very woods trying to escape the ugliness of our lives and deal with the reality of who we are.

I'm texting Ken a funny meme when my bedroom door flies open, my mother standing stiffly under its threshold.

"Come with me," she orders, snapping her fingers.

"Why? Where are we going?" I stammer, stunned, placing my phone down beside me.

My mother hardly ever talks to me, much less comes into my room out of her own free will.

"Your cousin needs you," is all the explanation she gives before turning her back on me.

On any other occasion, I would be reluctant to go anywhere with that woman, but the very mention of my cousin is enough to persuade me to follow her willingly. I get off the bed, making sure to grab my shoes and coat, and rush to keep up with her long strides, struggling to put my clothes on. Once we get into our car, she orders the driver to take us to Aunt Sierra's house across town. I try not to fidget in my seat, wondering what could possibly have happened to my cousin to warrant a visit from my mother. Even though I have a million and one questions to ask her, we spend most of the ride to his house in silence. Whatever is wrong must be serious, though.

My mother's shoulders look tense and rigid even if her stoic expression says differently.

Colleen Richfield doesn't show emotion.

Ever.

"Feelings are for the weak," she says. "And Richfields are never weak."

My older sister Meredith is just like her, cold and unfeeling. She just turned fifteen last month, two years older than me, but by the way she mimics our mother so perfectly, you'd swear she had celebrated her fortieth birthday.

I know Mom wants me to be more like my sister, but it's harder for me.

If I find something funny, I laugh.

If I find something sad, I cry.

If something gets me upset, I shout and break stuff.

And if I love something, I show that, too.

This is unacceptable behavior for my mother. She says I have too much of my father in me like that's a bad thing or something. I don't mind that I'm like Dad. At least he still kisses me goodnight, even though I keep telling him I'm too old for it. He still plays catch with me when I ask him to and surprises me with trips to the movies and promises of eating junk food afterward. He isn't ashamed of showing his feelings and showers me with attention and love at every opportunity he gets.

But that all changes when Mom is around, though.

Then he switches off all emotion to everyone around him, just as easily as one does a faucet.

I've been trying to see how he does it, so I can do it, too. I almost have the hang of it, but I have to keep practicing to be really good at it. That way, when Mom is around, she won't be upset with me once I show her that I can be made of stone, too.

She'll finally be proud, and for her, pride is as close as she will ever get to loving me.

Unfortunately for me, I'm unable to conceal what I'm feeling right now. Proof of that is how my heart is beating a mile a minute. Wiping my clammy hands over and over on my knees, I wonder what could have happened to my cousin for my mother's well-mannered poise to show some cracks.

"What's wrong with Linc?" I ask, unable to keep it in any longer, but my mother refuses to even look at me.

Another pearl of wisdom from dear old mom is that a person should only speak once they have been spoken to. She is adamant that you can learn a lot more from a person through observation instead of filling the time with empty chit-chat. "Talk is cheap and can easily distort the truth." She's fond of saying. "Observing one's actions, however, is worth its weight in gold."

"Mom. Why are we going to see Linc?" I repeat, tired of her silent treatment.

"All you need to know is that he needs you. That's all."

"But why?"

"Colt! Enough with the questions. Should he feel the need to tell you himself, he will. Right now, all I want from you is your presence, not your endless babbling," she snaps, turning her gaze to the passing scenery out her window. "And remember—duty, honor, and family is all that's important in this world."

I hope that's not true since I mostly hate mine.

When the driver pulls up to the Hamilton Estate, I run up to the house only to stop mid-step when my mother doesn't follow me. Instead of going inside, she turns around in the opposite direction and heads over to the Oakley Woods. Confused, I trail behind her when suddenly I hear a pained wail coming from somewhere deep inside the woods.

Lincoln.

I race in the direction of his cry, completely bypassing my mother at maddening speed. When I finally find him, he's on his knees, crying hysterically and shouting at the wind. I'm taken aback by the sight of it, frozen in place.

Lincoln is more than just my cousin.

He's always been like a brother to me—one that protects and stands up for me when no one else does. While everyone else in our family is fake and cold, he's the only one that refuses to submit to our heartless legacy. His kindness and gentle soul outshines us all, so seeing him like this hurts my heart.

"Linc? What's wrong? What's wrong, Linc?" I stammer while slowly inching closer to him.

I shake his shoulders, trying to coax an explanation out of him, but he doesn't answer me. He just keeps crying, rocking back and forth in the dirt, mumbling incoherently under his breath.

"Help him!" I yell over to my mother, but she stands back, watching my cousin fall apart.

"Mom, I said help him!" I shout again, but still, she keeps to her immovable state.

How can she just stand there and do nothing?

I've never hated her more.

I hug him to me, feeling completely powerless to help him. My tears begin to freefall from my cheeks and dampen the earth beneath, mingling with his. It takes forever for Linc to calm himself down, but once he stops his manic rocking, I sigh out in relief. After all his tears have dried up, his bloodshot eyes look up at my mother.

"Did you know?" His voice is so hoarse from all the yelling that it takes me a minute to grasp what he asked her.

"Yes," she answers him stiffly.

"Who else?"

"All you need to know is that no one outside this family will ever divulge what you learned today."

"Right." He scoffs, sounding older than his twelve years. He swipes the dirt off his knees but refuses to stand up. "I always knew he hated me. Now I know why."

My mother takes three quick strides to us, pushing me away to grasp his chin so forcefully, Lincoln has no choice but to look up at her from his kneeling position.

"Look at me, Lincoln. You are a Richfield. That is all that matters. Do you understand me?"

His eyes begin to water again, but he refuses to lower his fixed gaze from hers.

"Say it, child! I am a Richfield!"

"You're hurting him!" I cry out, trying to pull my mother away, but her nails just end up sinking further into his skin, creating maroon indents on his chin.

"I said say it, Lincoln! I am a Richfield!"

His ocean eyes turn a violent color as he begins to stand up.

"I am a Richfield."

"Louder."

"I am a Richfield."

"I said louder!" she yells.

"I am a Richfield!"

"That's right! You are. Everything else doesn't matter. Only that. Am I making myself clear?"

He nods, drying the errant tears that managed to break free during her brutal assault.

"Good. Now tell me. Where is that wretched sister of mine?"

"Inside," *he croaks, squaring his shoulders and tilting his bruised chin to the main house.*

"I'll have a talk with your mother. She should have been the one to remind you of who your true family is."

"She's not doing so well."

In other words, Aunt Sierra must be wasted and crawled off into a corner somewhere.

"My sister never is," *my mother says with a disgusted snarl and then turns to me.*

"Stay here with your cousin. I don't want either of you in the house for the next hour or so. I have to set a few things straight and remind the dear governor who really runs this town."

I nod, too afraid to utter a single word. I've never seen my mother like this. The woman standing in front of me might as well be a stranger since I don't recognize her one bit. For someone who has tried to drill into me that showing emotion, no matter what it may be, is a sign of failure at its worst degree, she sure let it all out a second ago.

This wasn't being disgruntled or upset.

This was a show of unrestrained rage.

When she leaves, I look over to Lincoln for answers. "What the hell just happened? Why were you crying?"

"It doesn't matter anymore. Aunt Colleen is right." *He shrugs.*

"About what?"

"About who I am."

My brows furrow in confusion with the vague explanation, as well as the faint smile that is on his lips.

"You came for me," he says, changing the subject.

"Of course, I did. If you need me, I'll always be here for you."

His blue eyes are back to shining their bright light, making me feel like I'm the most important person to him. He wraps his arm over my shoulder, the sides of our heads touching.

"I love you, Colt. You're the brother I should have had."

"Ahh, don't get all mushy on me." I tease, jabbing my elbow playfully into his gut.

It would be pointless for me to tell him I feel the same way. He knows I do.

"So, what do you want to do for the next hour?"

"We walk." He smiles, wiping the tears from his cheek, smearing dirty streaks onto his face. "And maybe if I'm lucky, I'll get lost in these woods and forget there is a life outside of them," he adds softly, looking deep into the woods as if it holds the escape he longs for. The pain that is back in his voice has my chest tightening in fear.

"If you ever get lost, I'll find you," I vow, not wanting to let the woods keep him.

He's all I've got.

He tilts his head toward me, his genuine smile back on his lips.

"I know you would, Colt. You always do."

CHAPTER 9

EMMA

The Charlotte Library is filled with its usual hushed silence. The blissful quiet only interrupted every so often by a faraway cough or a clearing of a throat by the handful of souls here. While the devout are known to spend their Sunday mornings on their knees in prayer, and the sinful in bed, sleeping off the debaucheries they committed the night before, I find myself in the only place that reminds me of home. There is nowhere I would rather be than right here surrounded by the written word of great philosophers, poets, and historians—their accomplishments giving me the fortitude that I need to achieve mine.

Unfortunately, my happy place is perturbed by the sound of an unwelcome intruder's footsteps drawing closer to me. I keep my head bowed, pretending to focus on my scribbled notes when the chair opposite me slides back, scraping against the old flooring with the sole intent of grabbing my attention.

"Mr. Turner."

"Professor Harper."

How bad is it that I knew it was him all along, even before he uttered a single word?

To my displeasure, I've become much attuned to the man sitting in front of me. It's been a secret burden I've been carrying for the better part of a month now. I've tried every trick in the book to push the images of my infuriating sexy-as-hell student from my mind, but he's determined not to make it easy for me.

In class, if I so much as have the misfortune of glancing in his direction, his plastered on cocky grin tells me every illicit thing that he's reminiscing about. Each time I catch him chewing the corner of his lower lip, eyeing my legs so unabashedly, I know he's picturing them spread apart, his tongue lapping at my center. For that very reason, I avoid making any eye contact with him, but it's of little use. I don't have to look at Colt to feel his eyes peeling every garment of clothing off my body. It only takes one of his heady stares to place me right back in that abandoned alley, the memory of his lust-filled words a never-ending torture.

Every time you talk in class, I imagine your lips around my cock.

When you bend over your desk, I want to ram my nine-inch cock into your pussy in front of the whole damn class.

And when I see your black bra beneath the low cut white shirt that you like to wear so much, I imagine ruining them with my cum.

Safe to say, I threw that shirt in the trash the first chance I got.

It has taken all my willpower, and then some, to pretend I don't feel his lingering gaze on me at all times or disguise the way my skin heats up whenever he's near. How my core clenches in anticipation, that he follows through on all his wicked promises, and that I once again fall to the mercy of my desires as I did on that fateful Halloween night. And now, if tormenting me in my own classroom wasn't enough, Colt has decided to come to my holy church to antagonize me further.

Argh.

Instead of having to bear looking at his godlike features for another second, I return my attention to my notes, pretending that they are far more interesting than my present company.

"I have to admit I'm surprised to see you here, Mr. Turner. On a Sunday morning, no less. Lost, are you?" I state, my tone reserved as I flick a page of my notebook.

"Not at all. Since you've been a no-show at the club, I thought my best chance to see you again would be to come here. Happy to see I was right," he explains, his voice thick and luscious.

I stiffen my back and flip yet another page, a tad too brusquely.

"You see me all the time back in school. You shouldn't have bothered making the long drive to Charlotte for that."

Flip.

"Some things are worth the effort."

"Not in this case. You know what my office hours are. For the sake of your environmental footprint, just walk there the next time you want to annoy me."

Flip.

"And miss seeing you this flustered? I'd fly my family's Learjet not to miss this."

"Of course you would."

Flip.

Flip.

Flip.

When his hand comfortingly covers mine to stop my incessant flicking, it throws me completely off-kilter. He surprises me yet again with his uncharacteristic demure smile. Still, the way the soft green shimmer of his eyes successfully slows my heartbeat to its normal smooth rhythm is what really confuses me. Once he's made sure I'm more composed, he removes his hand from mine and sits back into his seat as if this vulnerable moment between us never happened.

"So this is how you spend your free time, huh? Reading old books?"

He picks up one of the various books I have lying around on the desk and begins to examine it.

"I don't see how that is any of your business, Mr. Turner," I retort, standing up from my seat just enough to snatch the book away from his hands.

"Colt."

"What?" I question distractedly, still trying to find my bearings.

"You know my name, Emma," he replies teasingly, apparently back to his old cocky self. "Or are you fishing for me to remind you like I did last time?"

He arches a mischievous brow, making sure to put the image in my head of how he had me screaming out his name last time we were alone like this.

"Colt, it is," I quip back sternly, praying that my tone will keep him from elaborating further.

"Good. No need for the whole Mr. Turner bullshit. Like I told you before, it sounds like you're talking to my father, and I would rather not think of him while I'm talking to you if you don't mind."

"That's the second time you said something along those lines. I gather you don't like your father much?"

"There isn't much to like," he replies aloofly, his gaze falling to the open notebook in front of me.

I stretch out my arms on top of it and clasp my hands together, making sure to block his view.

"From what I hear, Owen Turner is quite the likable guy."

"If by likable you mean he's a cheating scumbag who likes to fuck anything in a skirt, then yeah, my dad is a peach."

The apple didn't fall far from the tree, from what I hear either.

But instead of saying what instantly came to mind, I force myself not to divulge my inner thoughts, too keen for him to elaborate further. I school my features as best I can so that Colt doesn't realize how truly interested I am in learning more about his family. Not that I care much about his father's extramarital affairs, but you never know what small detail Colt might let slip that can help me in my quest for some answers.

"So the rumors are true." I probe further.

"Where there is smoke, there is always fire, Professor," he replies, leaning back in the chair, cupping his hands behind his head, the shine in his eyes back to their usual predatory shade.

It's just another one of his signature moves, primarily used to show off his taut forearms and broad physique. I wonder how much time he's spent perfecting each vain gesture, each alluring move. Is there anything genuine about him at all? I let out an aggravated sigh, unimpressed by the gun show.

"I'll bear that in mind," I mutter disappointedly, focusing back on my notes rather than wasting my time.

Colt is like a forgery of a beautiful painting. Yes, it might hold the same elaborate colors, skillful strokes, and defined textures that are meant to please the senses, but it will always lack what only the original can offer—soul. The true beauty of art is that it appeals to and connects with our basic human emotions. That it stimulates and coaxes out feelings that overwhelm and leave us forever changed. And although Colt ticks all of the boxes of being a living, breathing work of art, all I see is a lackluster canvas with pretty colors but little depth.

Dull.

Unimaginative.

Uninspiring and worse of all—completely soulless.

Aside from a fleeting moment of pleasure, there's nothing real in this man for anyone to truly experience or appreciate—nothing life-altering at least. It is a shame how someone could be gifted with such breathtaking features and yet be so painfully empty on the inside.

"So what are you up to?" he ventures, his tone sounding less confident, almost as if he can read the thoughts running through my mind.

But that can't be. Colt is too vain to care about anyone but himself, let alone be affected by my inner condemnation.

"You're not going to give me a little clue?"

"Just because you have no qualms in divulging personal information about yourself doesn't mean I am as likely to do the same."

"Ah, come on, professor. Whatever happened to *quid pro quo?*"

I let out an exaggerated exhale because he's relentless and won't leave me alone until I answer him. Right now, all I want is for Colt to return to where he came from and let me get back to work. He might be a beautiful distraction to admire, but he's a distraction all the same.

"If I tell you what I'm doing, will you leave?"

"If that's what you want."

I don't miss how his jaw clenches, obviously not used to having someone less than eager to bask in the glory of his presence.

"It is," I state evenly.

"Fine, then. I'll leave, but only after you tell me what you're doing."

"Research."

"Research for what?"

"A book."

"A book?" he repeats, confusion etched on his face.

"Yes, Colt. A book."

"I didn't know you were a writer."

"I'm not." I shake my head. "Or not yet, at least. I am, however, an enthusiast of American history, most importantly on the side of history that you can't find merely by searching Wikipedia."

"I thought you could find anything online these days."

"Not everything can be learned with a simple push of a button. Sometimes you need to dig deeper. Work harder to get to the nitty-gritty of things."

"How long have you been working on this?"

"Four years now," I admit, hoping he doesn't hear the feeling of failure in my voice.

"That's a long time, Em. This must be very important to you if you've dedicated so much time to it."

"It is." I bow my head, not liking the sound of empathy in his tone.

"What's it about?"

"I think I've answered enough of your questions for one day, Colt," I interject, not comfortable with the way his eyes are assessing me much in the way mine had been scrutinizing him a few minutes ago.

"A promise is a promise." He smiles, getting up from his seat, but to my chagrin, he doesn't leave quite yet, preferring to walk over to my side of the table first. "I hope you find what you're looking for, Em," he whispers and then leans down to place a gentle, subdued kiss on my cheek.

True to his word, he doesn't say anything else and leaves so that I may continue with my work in peace. But as I watch his figure slowly vanish from my sight, reinstating the familiar silence within the library, his parting words summon an unnerving feeling settling within me.

I hope you find what you're looking for, Em.

Hope is of no use to me, Colt.

I need a miracle.

I'm still thinking about the unexpected visit I got yesterday in the library when a light knock on my office door brings me out of my reverie.

"Come in," I say without lifting my head from my lesson plan.

The smell of sandalwood cologne seeps into the room, making me stifle my groan when I realize who I just invited into my domain.

"Dean Ryland. What a pleasant surprise."

"Emma. Are you busy?" he asks with his usual well-mannered tone, closing my office door behind him.

"If I tell you that I am, would you leave?" I think to myself while pasting on the fake smile he expects to receive from me. "I always have time for you, dean."

"Now, now, Emma. I'm sure we know each other well enough to discard such formalities. Please. Call me Montgomery."

My false smile hurts every inch of my face as I widen it for him.

"How does the first semester look?" he questions, grabbing the seat in front of my desk.

"So far, so good. I have a few students that are struggling but none that I didn't expect."

"Both Jefferson and Kennedy are doing well, I hope?"

"They are."

"That's what I like to hear."

"Is that why you came to see me today? To check up on your children's progress in my class?"

"Actually, no. I popped in because I was wondering if you gave my proposal some more thought. You know, the one about having dinner with me?"

Shit.

I totally forgot he had asked me out a few weeks ago. Usually, I wouldn't have forgotten such a thing, but my mind has been split into too many directions to keep it all straight in my head. Between my book's deadline, trying to get a verified source on record about The Society, and the fantasies of riding Colt Turner like a mechanical bull keeping me up at night, the dean's dinner invitation completely slipped my mind. Now, instead of a simple text turning him down, I'll have to do it face to face.

Shit.

"Dean—"

"Montgomery."

What is it with these Asheville men and their first names?!

"I'm not sure us going out is wise. I have a lot on my plate at the moment."

"Too much that you can't spare an hour or two to have a meal with a colleague?"

We're not exactly on the same paygrade, Montgomery. You're my boss, not my colleague.

Montgomery never passes up the opportunity to touch me in some fashion or another whenever I walk into a room. Be it a light squeeze on the shoulder or a graze on the small of my back, I can always count on his hands finding their way onto my body to some extent. The only reason why I put up with it is because he's not sleazy in his unsolicited affection. However, if I accept his offer of us going out to dinner, I'm not sure if he won't misread my intentions and blur the lines of professional decorum.

"Emma, it's just dinner. Not a marriage proposal," he adds playfully.

"Doesn't the university frown upon such things?"

"I *am* the university. Do you see me frowning?" he jokes, but I can read the expression on his face that he believes every word of what he just said.

No, you're not, Montgomery.

You're not a Richfield.

You only wish you were.

Aside from his self-inflated sense of importance, Dean Ryland is actually quite appealing to the eye. Although his sense of fashion consists mostly of sporting the traditional tweed jacket with suede elbow patches, his dirty blonde hair and light blue eyes make him look younger than his forty-something years. Always clean-shaven and well put together, he's a dead ringer for Harvey Specter in Suits, sans sarcastic repertoire that is. If our roles were different, I probably wouldn't hesitate to go out with him, even if only to eat a meal with someone who at least could carry an intelligent conversation.

"We could go to Alphonso's if you like?"

"That's quite a fancy restaurant."

"It is," he retorts confidently, thinking the overpriced restaurant will be the thing that convinces me to go out with him. But it's not the extravagant French menu that has me considering his invitation. It's my editor's words that give me the extra push to concede.

You moved to Asheville because you assured us that was where The Society originated from, but so far, you haven't been able to have one source on record to back up your findings.

Montgomery Ryland might not be a Richfield, but it's a well-known fact his past is entangled with the elitist family to some extent. Born and bred in Asheville, he's climbed the social ladder with enough ease to have gained the favor of the most prominent Northside families. So much so that, if it wasn't for his humble origins, he too could have been a candidate worthy of The Society's notice, which means he may have some knowledge regarding the organization that might be of use to me.

"Alright. Dinner sounds lovely. But as friends."

I add the last part just so he knows that his notion of dessert is off the table. If my snub offended him in any way, he doesn't show it. Instead, he stands from his seat, all smiles like he's just won the state lottery. He's about to say something else when another knock on my door stops him in his tracks.

In his majestic six-foot-two frame, Colt Turner waltzes into the room like he owns the place. And unlike Dean Ryland, he can honestly boast about this being *his* university.

"Am I interrupting?"

When Montgomery's wide, cheerful smile disappears, his face morphing into a stern authoritarian expression, I can't help but assess the two men's odd interaction with one another in odd fascination.

"Colt."

"Montgomery."

Seeing as Colt's family is the one who holds rank over the dean, I never assumed they were at odds with each other. I would have bet good money that Montgomery treated all the Richfield heirs like royalty, yet here he is poking holes in my theory by gifting Colt this less-than-lukewarm greeting. As the temperature in the room continues to plummet down into sub-zero conditions, my curiosity only increases.

Interesting.

"If you're busy, Professor, I can come back at another time."

"I was just leaving. Emma, I'll call you later to set things up."

"I look forward to it."

Montgomery throws Colt another curt nod before passing him by. Colt immediately closes the door behind the dean, mumbling something under his breath too low for me to hear.

"Mr. Turner, two unexpected visits in as many days. What can I do for you this time?"

"You once said that if I needed your assistance that I should see you during office hours."

"I did, didn't I?" I take a good look at him, his serious expression giving me pause.

"You gave me an F on the last exam. I'll need at least a C to graduate."

"Then I suggest you study. You still have time to improve your grade."

"I do. But I'm not my best when taking your tests. I get distracted. I think I've told you this before."

It's a miracle my skin doesn't turn beet red, but thankfully I'm able to look unaffected by his remark.

"Yes, I remember. So what do you suggest as an alternative?"

Images of him on his knees, widening my legs so his tongue can lap at my clit surge in my brain.

Jesus, Emma. Get a hold of yourself, woman.

"I was thinking about the book that you're writing and all the work that you've been putting into it on your own. I was hoping that maybe you would consider taking me on as a research aide and that it could qualify as extra credit for my grade."

"You want to help me research my book?" I ask, dumbfounded.

"I do. I figured you might need a hand with that side of the project so you can focus on writing."

"That's very thoughtful of you." I bite the end of my pencil, taking stock of this Asheville god before me. "I didn't think you were capable of being so noble."

"Is it noble to want to spend more time with a beautiful woman *and* get my grade up? All my intentions are purely selfish. I can guarantee you that much."

"That does sound more like you." I relax, remembering who I'm talking to.

"So is that a yes?"

"Just a minute. If I accept, then I have to tell you there will be long hours. I won't take any excuses about you not having time for your hectic social life or other courses you might be failing that need your attention too."

"The only class I'm failing is yours. And you don't have to worry about my social life being affected by me helping you. I'm not what you would call a people person."

"I've heard the contrary."

"Don't believe everything you hear." He throws me a wolfish grin.

"I'll keep that in mind."

"Good. So is that yes?"

I tap my fingers on my armchair, taking in every inch of the man before me.

"It is," I finally relent.

"When can we start then?"

"This afternoon. Meet me at the Charlotte Library once your classes have finished."

I half-expected him to protest about the long ride over to Charlotte, but he surprises me yet again by not complaining.

"I'll see you there."

When Colt leaves my office, I rush out of my seat and lock the door behind him, knowing that the call I need to make shouldn't be disrupted or overheard.

"Emmaaaaaaa!" Jenna singsongs on the other line. "What's up?" The weight of anxiety that I had been carrying for the past four years begins to disintegrate, and miraculously enough, a new feeling takes its place—hope.

"Tell me you have good news for me?"

"I do." I smile. "You wanted a source, Jenna? How does two sound?"

Chapter 10

Emma

I'm typing away on my laptop when a familiar shadow blocks the little afternoon sun remaining from my view. I tilt my head up and see Colt boasting his trademark panty-dropping grin, ready to wreak havoc on my work schedule.

"Mr. Turner, you're late," I greet, less than impressed with his tardiness, returning my focus to the open word document on my screen.

"Couldn't be avoided, Professor. The drive here was a bitch. You sure we can't do this back at school?"

"No, Mr. Turner, we cannot. Here," I state before he has time to say anything else. "I need you to fact check everything written on that list."

"Putting me to work already, huh?" He smirks.

"That's what you're here for, isn't it?"

The roguish gleam in his eyes makes the pulse between my thighs throb. While my head insists on telling me that Colt has nothing worth offering me aside from information on his family, my traitorous body doesn't seem to share the same mindset.

"Whatever you say. You're the boss."

My lips turn to a fine line as I drag my focus back to my chapter, forcing myself not to pay any mind to my body's natural reaction to him. When Colt grabs the chair next to me, my spine goes ramrod straight with his unwanted proximity.

"You haven't told me what your book is about yet."

"Yes, I have. American history, remember?"

"American history, huh? I didn't know the Illuminati had a hand in molding our country." He jokes, pointing to one of the quotes I need him to double check.

Seeing as I'm not going to get anything done until his curiosity is fed, I stop what I'm doing and look him dead in the eye.

"Precisely why I'm writing about them. To educate the clueless as you seem to be."

"Is that what you want to do?" He smacks his lips.

"Very much so, yes."

"And writing a book on what… secret societies is how you're going to enlighten the world?"

The way his forehead wrinkles when he says 'secret societies,' as if the topic is completely ludicrous and idiotic to him, hits a sensitive nerve. My grandfather had to endure the same ridicule when he told people about his obsession. They laughed in his face and made fun of him at every turn. So much so that he pulled me out of middle school and decided to homeschool me. He took every precaution that in no shape or form would I be bullied or ostracized for his eccentric beliefs. But while he went to great lengths to shelter me from such ugly behavior, he braved going to work every day as a college professor, knowing full well he'd lost the respect of his peers and was the butt of every joke on campus, as well as the staff room.

"I never figured you'd be into this type of thing," he adds with a hint of disillusionment, only increasing my defensiveness.

"Have I ever given you the impression that I'm naive or gullible in any way?"

"No, but—"

"Do you consider me intellectually challenged?"

"I didn't say that."

"No, you merely implied it."

"Em," he coos gently, squeezing my knee to stop me from continuing on with my rant, "I would never dream of insulting you. I respect you too much to ever do that. It just took me a bit off-guard that this is what you spent the last four years of your life working on. That's all. I didn't mean anything by it."

The sincerity in his eyes is the only reason why I don't bite his head off.

"Fair enough," I retort coldly, squaring my shoulders and snapping my head back to my screen. "Now can you do what I asked so that I can go back to work, please?"

I wait for his usual witty reply, but to my amazement, he doesn't utter another word. Instead, he stands up, list in hand, ready to tackle his assignment. I watch in my peripheral as he tries to locate the books on my list to fact check, looking completely out of his element. I stifle my snickering laugh when I witness his face light up after having correctly discovered the first book on his list without any help.

Focus, Emma.

You're not here to gawk or fawn over your student.

This work is too important to be distracted by the likes of him.

I shake the reprimand away and get back to work.

For the next couple of hours, we both work side by side in total silence, my focus only interrupted by the odd question here or there about his task. When my foot starts to cramp up, I decide this is as good a time as any to stretch my legs and retrieve another book I need that I forgot to add to his list. It's only when I'm on my way back to our shared table that I realize most of the women in this library can't take their eyes off my new assistant. Some men, too.

Even on a dreary Monday afternoon like today, Colt looks like he's about to step onto a photoshoot set to get his picture taken. I've taught enough boys his age to know that their sense of fashion consists solely of jeans and hoodies, but nothing could be further from the truth when it comes to Colt. In designer black slacks that hug his thighs and sculpted ass to perfection, and a navy sweater that screams out it's in heaven just to touch his muscular biceps and abs, he looks as dignified as any Forbes entrepreneur ever could. It's not only his clothes that reek of wealth and privilege, but the way he carries himself, too.

I've tried my best not to notice him back at Richfield, yet little things still manage to wiggle themselves to my subconscious. How I rarely see him talk to anyone, save for the few friends in his close unit. The way I sometimes catch a glimpse of him through my classroom window, lying on the grass on the campus green, his eyes shut while he lets the sun kiss his cheeks, completely oblivious of the world around him.

And in the few times our paths have crossed through the school's halls, he's either in deep discussion with his cousin or solely on his own. For a man who's reputed as Asheville's notorious 'lady killer', he sure seems to treasure his solitude immensely, which raises the question of how he's able to romance so many women to his bed when he doesn't seem to make any elaborate effort. Aside from Kennedy Ryland, I've never caught him saying two words to a woman in broad daylight.

Discreetly I hide behind the bookshelf, just so I can inspect him further without his knowledge.

He really is spectacular to look at.

He might consider himself not to be a people person, but with his high cheekbones and sharp jawline—not to mention the rest of his well-defined body—he'll never be fully capable of preventing people from naturally seeking him out. With short dark brown hair in the back, but longer on top so that silky soft strands fall to his temple, even I find myself taking a beat to marvel at the stunning color of piercing eyes on his prominent face. Colt could have the most obnoxious and unpleasant personality, and still, the world would be captivated by him. So unfair that men like Montgomery Ryland are all I have to aspire to when such fine specimens walk the earth.

But then again, Colt gives a whole other meaning to the word eye-candy.

You might want to take a big bite of it, but in the end, it's nothing but empty calories.

Still, can I really blame these women here for looking?

You mean like you're doing now, Emma?

I roll my eyes and get back to our table, pretending not to have heard my censuring reprimand. But as I try to focus on work and ignore my new assistant completely, his faint chuckle breaks through my concentration.

"What's so funny?"

"This bullshit right here." He points to the open book in front of him, squeezing my knee.

While I'm on my best behavior to keep our relationship purely professional, Colt isn't as careful.

I really wish he would stop doing that.

No, you don't. Otherwise, you'd have said something by now.

"It says here that secret societies were the very incubators of today's current democracy."

"I take it you disagree with that assessment?" I arch a brow, genuinely interested in what he has to say, especially considering the family he was born into.

"You don't?" he asks instead of answering my question.

"I can name you twenty U.S. presidents from the top of my head that belonged to one secret society or another. You have to understand that these same secret boys' clubs elected their own leaders and drew up constitutions to govern their secret operations. So it's not by accident that men such as George Washington and Ben Franklin—who had important roles in these secret organizations—also carried influential positions in the real world. It would be foolish of us to believe that their way of thinking didn't mold our current democracy in some way."

When he doesn't look convinced, I continue on.

"Okay, consider this then. The power of these societies stemmed from having the ability to stay anonymous and keep their communications secret, correct? Doesn't our own government use the same models in their own institution? The CIA? The FBI? Secret Service?"

"So what you're saying is that all the conspiracy theories out there are true?"

"No. What I'm saying is that every urban legend has a sliver of truth to it, no matter how minuscule. What is extraordinary to me is how people prefer to label these legends as delusional fiction, rather than face the possibility that these secret organizations not only exist but also have unchecked power to do as they please."

"Huh," he muses to himself, his forehead creasing. "So how would you be able to tell fact from fiction?"

"Research," I tease, knocking my knee playfully with his. "And a lot of it, I'm afraid."

"What if the answer to your question wasn't in some book or newspaper clipping? What would you do then?"

I don't need to think too hard on the matter since, by default, that's the reason why he's here.

"I'd go to the first plausible suspect and do my due diligence. Try to find any shred of proof to support my suspicions."

When his emerald eyes shimmer with something I can't quite name, my heartbeat accelerates, and my mouth begins to dry. I clear my throat and immediately turn my attention back to my laptop, kicking myself for letting out such a passionate rant.

"My book will be completely impartial, though. My aim is to find out the truth about such organizations. Nothing more."

He opens his mouth on the verge of asking something else when my phone begins to vibrate on top of the desk. I quickly pick it up when I see it's Montgomery and decline the call. Unfortunately for me, Colt recognizes the number.

"Why is the dean calling you? School hours are over, aren't they?"

"I don't see how that is any of your concern," is my curt reply.

"Right." He unclenches his jaw, making it pop.

I don't miss how his tone has gone from being enthralled and intrigued with our previous conversation to downright cold. The sudden chill between us gnaws at my throat. I dart my attention back to the screen, trying not to squirm under his scrutiny, yet I can't help the cold shudder that ripples through me as I try my best to remain impervious to his insidious stare. Colt is wound up so tight that he might snap at the littlest provocation.

"It's getting late. You can leave if you want," I say dismissively, praying he takes the hint and leaves.

His chair scrapes against the floor, and without even as much as a goodbye, he stomps off. I let out the breath that I was holding, my shoulders slumping from his abrasive exit.

What the hell was that?

Snap out of it, Emma.

He's just a means to an end.

You shouldn't be wasting your time thinking of why his mood changed so suddenly.

Minutes later, I'm still trying to push away the guilty feeling of how abrupt I was with him when someone places two brown paper bags on the table. I look up to find Colt has returned, thankfully less taciturn.

"I thought you left."

"Why did you think that? You told me that this job meant long hours, and I promised you that I'd be down for the long haul. I just went to get us some dinner. You'll work better on a full stomach."

"I don't know what to say," I mumble, honestly surprised by the kind gesture.

"Just eat, Em," he orders, placing a bowl of shrimp garlic pasta in front of me.

It's only when the rich aroma hits my senses that my stomach begins to growl. Too hungry to feign embarrassment, I pick up my plate and do just that. As we eat our meal in silence, I'm reminded of what I needed to ask him. Since Colt seems to be in better spirits, this is as good a time as any to bring the topic up.

"I heard your family has quite the extensive library of their own. Is that true?"

He nods.

"Is there any way I could visit?"

He places his plate back on the desk, using his napkin to clean up before answering.

"You want to come over to my place?" He wiggles his brows.

"I wouldn't phrase it exactly like that, but yes."

He runs the pad of his thumb over his lower lip, the crippling fear that he can somehow read my inner thoughts, making it hard to keep my breathing in check.

"I could do you one better. Let me just get the okay from the parentals, and instead of working here, we can work there for a few days. How does that sound?"

Like exactly what I needed to hear.

CHAPTER 11

EMMA

Although the recently arrived December chill can be felt in the air, Montgomery insists we eat out on the terrace. Not that I mind the cold so much. It's the company I'm still debating over. While the decision of having Colt as my aide seems to be bearing fruit, I'm still on the fence in regards to Montgomery.

"I thought a lunch date would be less intimidating for you. Was I right?"

I offer him a thin smile, not really comfortable with him labeling this simple lunch as a date, but in retrospect, I didn't have to accept his invitation if I didn't want to. The only reason I did was because I have my own agenda behind it.

"I gather you don't date much?" I ask, taking a bite of my Caesar salad.

"If I'm totally honest, the school and my kids keep me too busy to think about socializing. But sometimes it feels good just to have a meal with a beautiful woman and indulge in delicious food to remind me that I'm still a man."

I know he's expecting me to gush over such flattery, but I do no such thing and move onto a safer topic.

"Your children are full-grown adults. I would assume they don't need much of your attention."

"Spoken like a woman who doesn't have kids of her own."

I bite my fork to keep myself from giving him the reply he deserves.

"I'm sorry. I don't mean to offend," he quickly backpedals, seeing that his offhand comment dampened the romantic mood he was aiming for.

I gift him another one of my fabricated smiles instead of telling him where he can shove his condescending remark. Thank God I have class in an hour. Otherwise, I'd end up with lockjaw from forcing myself to smile so much.

"It's just that, no matter how old my children get, I will always worry about them and their future. It's my job as their father to guide them in the right direction. The day you become a mother, I'm sure you'll be the same way, too."

Just because I'm a woman doesn't mean my maternal clock is ticking, Montgomery.

"Mmm," I mumble noncommittally before taking a sip of my white wine. I had no intention of drinking during lunch since I still have classes, but Montgomery isn't making it easy on me with his douchebag remarks. "Both Kennedy and Jefferson seem to have good heads on their shoulders, so you must be doing something right."

When his grin splits his face in two, I see that although I may be immune to his flattery, Montgomery takes my compliment at face value. I don't, however, add that both his kids give me hives. Jefferson is an overachiever who doesn't take failure lightly, while his sister Kennedy seems to be oddly manipulative, only saying what she thinks a person wants to hear and never her true thoughts.

"I try my best. It hasn't always been easy without a woman in their lives. I can be quite strict with them. I know that. But it's only in their best interest."

Tired of talking about his kids, I try to divert the conversation to something that has more of my interest.

"If you don't mind me asking, how long has it been since your wife passed?"

"Close to ten years now, God bless her soul."

His eyes take on a purposely saddened hue. I know what words he expects to spill out of my lips next since it's obvious this isn't his first rodeo. Something along the lines of how lonely it must have been to raise two children all by himself, or how remarkable he is to have managed to balance a prestigious career and a family so flawlessly. But inflating a man's ego has never been my style.

Does he want a fucking parade or something?

Why is it that single mothers are never half as praised for raising their children and bringing a steady income home as men are for doing the bare minimum? Sure he did it all by himself, but so did my grandfather, who never expected a pat on the back.

"I've heard lovely things about her," I say instead of blurting out my true inner thoughts.

"Oh, have you?"

"Yes. I spend most of my free time at the Charlotte Library, so I couldn't help but admire the section there called Dorethea's books. I was told the children's book section was specifically dedicated in your wife's honor."

"Ah. Of course." He seals his lips in a fine line, his attention now on his risotto.

"I didn't mean to embarrass you. I thought it was a lovely gesture to keep her memory alive."

"As much as I would like to take full credit for that, I had no hand in doing it."

I know.

Why do you think I brought it up?

If we can speed this along and get to the good stuff, that would be great, Montgomery.

I keep my interested look branded on my face, even though I'm becoming impatient with the way he's chewing his food, intentionally trying to avoid the subject.

"I just assumed it had been you. Another family member, perhaps?"

"In a manner of speaking." He takes a drink of his wine.

Oh, come on!

Give me more than that!

I take another forkful of my salad, waiting for him to just fess up and lead our conversation to where I need it to go, but it feels like I'm pulling teeth with this one.

"Your late wife's parents, then?"

He lets out a resentful exhale.

"No. By the time my wife passed away, they were no longer with us."

"I don't mean to intrude. Please forget I even brought it up if it brings you such discomfort."

I pat his hand and bat my eyelashes at him. I'm not particularly proud of the lengths to which I'm willing to go, but I can't turn back now. When his azure eyes begin to glimmer, I almost gag at what I can see so vividly in them. Montgomery has me naked and under him already, and all I had to do was flutter my lashes at him.

Yeah, that's not going to happen.

"It's quite alright," he relents, taking my hand in his and caressing it. "I really shouldn't be bitter about the gesture. It was made out of love, after all, and considering the person who did it, I should be honored that she was even capable of summoning such a sentiment. But my wife had that ability in her—to make even the most cold-blooded people fall for her enchantment." Although he's using his usual soft-spoken manner, I detect an undertone of resentment to his words.

"Oh. So it was a previous lover?"

"God, no." He laughs, enabling me to release my hand from his hold. "It was her best friend, Colleen Richfield. She's the one who did it."

The way he says Colleen's name seems to leave a foul taste on the tip of his tongue. The hate is so tangible that if I lunged myself over our table, I could grab it. Although I fully intend to commit every word to memory, I make a note to be smarter next time and record our conversation on my phone.

"I didn't realize your family was so close to Richfields," I lie.

"Not my family, but my wife sure was. She and Colleen grew up together and were joined at the hip, you might say. Colleen cared more for my wife than she did for her own younger sister, Sierra. But that was inevitable since Sierra was a different breed—alive and hungry to experience the world. Colleen and Dorethea were more tempered in their dispositions, down to earth."

I don't miss how the mention of the youngest Richfield sister brought a more heated sparkle to his eye that his own wife failed to inspire.

"How did you all meet?"

"Funnily enough, I was a student at Richfield when I met all three. To make ends meet, like so many scholarship students, I did some catering work to get by at the Richfield Country Club. I was introduced to them at one of their Northside galas. But here I am going on and on about myself when we haven't talked about you yet."

"There isn't much to tell," I reply pleasantly, hoping he takes the hint and brings us back to the conversation at hand.

"Why so modest, Emma? A woman like you with all her accomplishments shouldn't be so humble in her achievements."

"I'm not. I just don't really enjoy talking about myself."

"Hmm. I can relate."

Shit.

But I want you to talk.

I need you to.

If I want him to be forthcoming about his past, I have to bite the bullet and be somewhat transparent with my own. To a small degree, that is.

"But ask away. What do you want to know?"

"The only thing I know about you aside from your academic career is that you're from Boston. Any family there?"

"No. The only family I had left died five years ago."

"I'm so sorry to hear that." He gives me a forlorn look, brushing his hand over mine once again.

"It's quite alright."

"So nothing ties you to Boston? No friends or ex-boyfriends?" he asks inquisitively.

I shake my head, slipping my hand away from his with the excuse of fixing my napkin.

"Good to know."

No matter how charming he's trying to be, it's completely wasted on me.

Yes, Montgomery Ryland is quite charismatic if I let myself go there. With his dirty blond hair and big blue eyes, he is definitely appealing to the eye. Even if sometimes what he says rubs me the wrong way, I have to admit he is quite handsome. Still, my body doesn't respond to him as he might wish. Maybe I'm broken, but when I look at him, all I see is a job, nothing else.

"Tell me a bit about Boston. I've been there a few times for some conventions, but I never really ventured into the city."

For the remainder of our lunch, we talk about my birthplace, but not once do I give him any real personal details about my childhood or how I lived before coming to work for him.

"You sound like you miss it," he says, as he orders us two cappuccinos.

"I do. It's the city I was brought up in, and it holds my most cherished memories."

"And Asheville hasn't given you any yet?"

Smoldering green eyes in an empty alleyway suddenly flash before me.

"I don't live in Asheville, now do I?" I reply, praying that Montgomery mistakes the blush that crept up my cheeks as a reaction to his company.

"Yes. Why is that?"

"Now, dean, you know my salary. If I wanted to live in the Northside, I'd have to ask for a raise, and living in the Southside doesn't seem like a clever thing to do for a single woman like me. Charlotte is quiet and calm, and it doesn't have such a division between the rich and the poor."

"Yes, of course."

We drink our coffee, filling the time with talk about school and other mundane things. What I really want is for him to fess up more about the Richfields, but I guess I need to have a few more of these 'so-called dates' to get him to relax and be more forthcoming.

When I tell him that I should be getting back to school or risk being tardy for my class, he pays for lunch and then accompanies me back to my car. When I feel his hand on my back, my knee jerk reaction is to flinch away. But since I need a second date with this man, I let it slide.

"I had a lovely time," he coos once we've reached my car.

"Me, too."

When I see him lean in for a kiss, I turn my face so his lips land on my cheek.

"Thank you for a lovely lunch. I look forward to doing it again," I state quickly, hoping it's enough to take the sting away.

"I'll call you and set that up." He smiles broadly. "Maybe next time we can do dinner instead?"

"That sounds great. I'd like that very much."

Although I'm not looking forward to having dinner with my boss, to get the information I need sacrifices have to be made. I need to be patient. And if Montgomery doesn't pan out, I still have Colt.

I don't know why I genuinely smile at the thought of my mercurial student or why he came to mind when the dean asked me if I had made any memories here.

But one thing I am certain of—when all of this is done and over with, Colt Turner will definitely be hard to forget.

Chapter 12

Colt

For the first time in what seems like forever, I wake up with a purpose.

Today, I need to dazzle Emma with a tour of this cold-ass mausoleum of a home. I'm hoping that she'll be enchanted enough with it to slip some tiny detail about the book she's writing or—more importantly—whatever intel she was able to get about The Society.

It's been two days since I convinced her to take me on as an assistant, and so far, I haven't gotten the answers I need from the evasive professor, but only a small insight into her work, which happens to be a tell-all novel about secret societies. The irony isn't lost on me how Emma has been slaving away for the past four years to prove such organizations are real and that the first assistant she takes on to help her in her mission winds up being living proof one of them truly exists.

Not that I'll ever tell her.

True to her word, she's put me to work and let me fact check her findings on the Freemasons, the Illuminati, and the Invisible College. And although her detailed research has me blown away with ironclad proof of their existence, the true thorn in my backside hasn't been mentioned once. It also doesn't help that the one library book that holds something regarding our blackmailers, she's made sure to keep hidden away from my greedy hands.

To say that I'm frustrated is an understatement. With any other woman, I'd have the information by now. All I would have to do was give out a few earth-shattering orgasms, and that would have been the end of it. She'd be fessing up every last secret she'd ever had and even some she had forgotten about.

Emma Harper, however, is in a class of her own.

She won't be easily fooled or persuaded just because I flash my toothpaste-commercial smile at her.

No.

She's different from all the others.

Most of the Northside women I've screwed senseless needed a spark in their dull lives and were eager enough to have me satisfy their cravings for excitement.

Emma, on the other hand, doesn't need me to bring meaning to her life.

She already has it.

Her work gives her all the passion that she needs, which is new for me since I've never been passionate about anything in my life.

Even though the sexual tension between us is undeniable, Emma never seems to acknowledge it for more than a quick, vulnerable minute, too consumed with the work at hand to be sidetracked by a little thing like desire or lust. If I didn't have such a high opinion of myself, my ego would have definitely taken a hit with the way she focuses so obsessively over her work that, at times, she forgets I'm sitting right beside her.

So if sex isn't the key to unlock all her secrets, I'm banking that knowledge is. The Richfield family library has been visited enough times over the years by great historians for me to know that it's in high demand as *the* library to visit.

Hopefully, Emma's guarded nature will change after today, but for that to happen, I have to ask the ice queen herself if she doesn't mind me bringing a playdate home. Since breakfast is the only meal this family has together, it's as good an opportunity as any to bring the subject up.

I walk downstairs to the dining room with that one purpose in mind, unsurprised to see everyone there already. I greet my pain in the ass sisters and parents with a curt nod and grab the chair next to my baby sister, Abby, who throws me one of her brilliant smiles. I might as well enjoy them while they last since it's only a matter of time before my mother snuffs the sweet rebellion out of her. Right now, she still loves my ass, but once my mother is through with her, she'll see me as nothing but a disappointment to our family, just like Mer and Irene do.

"Morning, dear brother."

"Morning, shortstop."

I smile widely at her, playfully pulling on the end of her ponytail. Once I've settled into my seat, I pour some coffee into my mug, eyeing my mother at the head of the table to establish what mood the ice queen is in today—Antarctica-glacial or just your run-of-the-mill walk-in freezer cold.

"You sure came in late last night. Hot date?" Irene instigates, always ready to stir the pot in front of our mother while pretending to look innocent spreading jam on her toast.

"And how would you know that? Aren't good girls supposed to go to bed early on school nights?" I wink roguishly, not taking the bait she threw at me.

"If their irritating brothers let them sleep, then yes. You're the one who woke me up. I heard your obnoxious car pull in around midnight."

"First off, my Bugatti isn't obnoxious. It's a monster. And secondly, I suggested picking another bedroom in this house that isn't so close to our driveway, otherwise your beauty sleep is going to get interrupted a lot in the upcoming weeks."

"What's going to be happening a lot?" Meredith asks from across the table, obviously eavesdropping on our conversation.

"You butting in on other people's discussions. Oh, wait. No. You already do that, don't you?"

"Funny," she groans.

"I thought so." I smile widely, always happy to get on Meredith's shitlist so early in the day.

When my mother doesn't once acknowledge my little spat with her favorite offspring, I think this is my shot to do what I came for.

"I'm bringing someone to the house today, FYI."

Like fuck, I'm going to *ask* my mother for permission to bring anyone over here. But if I don't want her to be a total bitch to Emma when she meets her, I at least need to make the effort of pretending to ask for permission for appearance's sake.

"Can't you take your hoochie mommas somewhere else? Do we really need to deal with your hookups in our own home?" Irene declares with a disgusted sneer, trying to sound older than her seventeen years of age, in an attempt to win some brownie points with mommy dearest.

"Your brother didn't say he was bringing a girl home, Irene. In fact, to my knowledge, he never has. So I'd be more careful with your accusations, sweetheart," my father interjects with a serious tone.

"Sorry, Daddy," Irene stammers, bowing her head to her plate to hide her red cheeks.

Although both Meredith and Irene love nothing more than to suck up to our mother, when it comes to our father, all my sisters are big-time daddy's girls. One strong word from our mother might cause them discomfort, but if it comes from our father, then they don't know what to do with themselves. I guess it has to do with the fact that my mother's stern discipline is to be expected. Not so much when it comes from the one parent that actually pretends to have a beating heart.

Like them, I used to think my father hung the moon and stars in the sky. For most of my childhood, he had been my hero, and there was nothing anyone could say that would make me think differently. But that all changed when I saw with my very eyes who my father really was.

He wasn't a hero.

He was just another piece of trash husband who couldn't keep it in his pants.

"Is it Lincoln who is coming over?" my mother's voice rings out for the first time since I came into the room.

"No."

"I see. I haven't seen much of him lately."

And by lately, what she really means is that she hasn't put eyes on my cousin since her sister's funeral. Save for sending a few business-like emails and texts concerning the Richfield Foundation, my mother has avoided Lincoln like the plague. Her only nephew suffered like crazy over his mother's death for months, and yet my mother kept a wide berth between the two of them, not once reaching out to console him in his moment of grief.

And these two assholes, ladies and gentlemen, are my parents.

Is it any wonder that I have the asshole gene with them as my progenitors?

"So, who are you bringing over? Is it a girlfriend?" Abby asks jovially, her bright green eyes glimmering with romantic notions only a fifteen-year-old girl could have.

"Sorry to burst whatever teenage dream you've got going in that head of yours, shortstop, but it's not a girlfriend. In fact, it's my ethics professor."

By the sound of silverware hitting her plate, my remark has definitely grabbed my mother's attention.

"Do you mean Emma Harper?"

"One and the same."

"I've heard she's very pretty. Young, too," my mother adds, taking a sip of her orange juice as her scrutinizing gaze tries to read me.

"Is she? I hadn't noticed."

"No? Then you seem to be the only one. I've heard Montgomery Ryland is quite enamored with her... *intellect.*"

Motherfucker.

I knew there had to be a reason for that prick to be calling Emma the other night. I try to relax my clenched jaw, so my mother doesn't see how her comment hit its target. She wants a reaction out of me to see what my true intentions are in regards to the good professor, and like hell will I roll out the red carpet to my inner thoughts for her.

"Seems awfully unprofessional to have her over, don't you think? When I attended Richfield, not once did I ever bring a college professor home with me. But then again, I'm not you." The less-than-subtle accusation proffered by Meredith has me fisting my hands under the table.

Do I want to fuck Emma?

Yes. Yes, I do.

Do I want my whole family to think that the only reason any professor could be interested in visiting our home is because I'm fucking her every which way till Sunday?

No. No, I fucking do not.

My older sister thinking that Emma could be easily corrupted by my charm would be laughable if it weren't intended as an insult to humiliate me. In their eyes, I have no worth—nothing that will bring honor to the Richfield name. Fucking half of Asheville is proof enough that I only know how to do one thing, and knowing how to fuck isn't exactly on their list of honorable accomplishments.

"If you must know, Professor Harper has taken me on as her assistant. She's writing a book on American history and heard that our home library has books on the subject. Being that we Richfields are known to be hospitable as fuck, I insisted on her visit."

The whole table grows so quiet I can almost hear the sound of their jaws dropping onto their plates while looking at me as if I've grown two heads all of a sudden. "What are you all staring at?" I ask defensively, still tense from my sister's remark.

"Don't mind us, son. It's that your news just surprised us. That's all," my father explains, a sly smirk planted on his lips. "You have to admit academia has never interested you before."

"Or anything else for that matter," my mother interrupts critically.

"But," my father continues on, "if your professor has found a way to excite you on any topic, then I'm all for it."

I brush his prideful remark to the side and snap my attention to the actual person who calls the shots in this house.

"So is that a yes or what? Can I give her the tour and use the library for a few days?"

My father looks over to my oddly pensive mother, the proud gleam in his eyes unnerving me so much that my knee keeps repeatedly bouncing up and down like I've got restless leg syndrome or something.

"I don't see the harm. What do you think, dear?"

"If your father doesn't see an issue with it, then neither do I."

"Good. That's all I needed to hear," I retort abrasively, immediately getting up from my seat to leave before I give them any reason to withdraw their approval or have to endure my father's prideful stares a minute longer.

But before I'm able to make my quick exit, the cheating bastard halts my steps with his next remark.

"I look forward to meeting this professor of yours, son. Anyone who can spark such enthusiasm from you is definitely worth meeting."

Not if I can help it, asshole.

When I arrive back at Richfield, my previous foul disposition improves immensely with the knowledge that I'm about to turn the imperturbable professor into putty in my hands. Again I have to remind myself that this woman is unique, and therefore, my usual approach won't work on her.

Emma has made it clear that she wants nothing to do with me. Too bad for her. I've always been a sucker for a good challenge.

When I see Easton and Stone walking up the steep flight of stairs to the ethics' hall, I call out their names and rush to catch up with them. It's safe to say that the pep in my step doesn't go unnoticed by the exceedingly perceptive duo.

"Did hell freeze over, or is that an actual smile I see on your face?"

"I hope your good mood means what I think it means," Easton adds on to Stone's snarky comment.

"If you're asking if I'm closer to finding out who the fuckers are that are trying to ruin our lives, then yes. Yes, I am."

"Thank Christ," he belts out, relieved, patting my back as I've just solved all his problems.

Maybe I'm overselling this, but failure has never been in my vocabulary. If you show no weakness, then there isn't any to exploit. Mommy dearest taught me that trick when I was still in diapers. But I don't need to fake my confidence. My plan is solid. I might not be able to sweep Emma off her feet with my charm, but I will gain her trust. I just need enough of it for her to tell me everything she knows about The Society. And once that's done, I'll get rid of her just as they ordered me to. One call to the dean should do it.

Montgomery Ryland is quite enamored with her.

Hmm.

That fucker might be a problem.

Not that I'm too thrilled with the idea of firing Emma either, but if that's what The Society wants, then my hands are tied. Her lack of fawning all over my dick might have me intrigued, but not enough that I would trade my freedom for her to keep her job. And if Ryland gets in my way, then I'll just have to remind him of his place. He loves the prestige that comes with being the dean of an Ivy League University like Richfield too much to have it threatened.

Then there is the other issue at hand.

The one that I have been keeping a secret from all of my friends—the task The Society really wants me to accomplish. Guilt comes easily enough for most people, but thankfully I've never been afflicted with such a futile sentiment. I will admit, though, keeping something of this magnitude from Lincoln has been challenging. He's never once kept a secret from me. Not even the one that damns him. Once I figure out what the fuck The Society wants, then I'll tell both him and the rest of the guys what I've been up to. Not a second before.

When we step into Emma's class, I head over to my usual front-row seat next to Ken and her brother, while Easton and Stone sit a few rows back. The whole room goes quiet the minute Emma walks in. She really does know how to command a room to do her bidding without so much as opening her mouth.

And what a pretty mouth it is.

Before our little rendezvous Halloween night, I had to keep my mind elsewhere when she delivered her lectures. I was either on my phone or laptop, scrolling through every social media platform I had access to, instead of showing her how captivated I was with each word that slipped from her lips. But after I got a little taste of how sweet they are, I no longer feel the need to pretend what is really running through my mind when she teaches a class.

Even now, as she goes on and on about the philosophical study of morality, mine is completely shattered with fantasies about all the ways I could use those lips to my benefit. When an idea pops into my head on how I can savor them again, I begin to count down the minutes until class finishes. When the bell rings, ending my agony, I stay in my seat while everyone else exits the room. I don't miss how Ken looks back at me curiously as she leaves the room. I'll have to come up with something to satiate her inquisitiveness.

"Mr. Turner, is there something you need?" Emma asks firmly, her back turned to me as she wipes down the whiteboard in front of her. Like a lion approaching an unsuspecting gazelle, I get up from my seat and slide right behind her.

"There are so many things I need, Em," I whisper in her ear, running a finger up and down the slope of her neck.

She instantly turns around, arms crossed, to show she's not one bit amused with my unsolicited caress. Little does she know that's about to change.

"But today, I'm the one bearing gifts."

"Oh. How so?" She raises an eyebrow, intrigued.

"Consider the Richfield Library at your disposal."

When her whiskey eyes turn into liquid gold, my breath catches. Everyone with a pair of eyes knows that Emma is a fucking knockout, but when she's excited about something, she's fucking breathtaking. I had tiny glimpses of it when she went on a rant about her work back at Charlotte the other night, but seeing her light up like this, does something to me.

And I'm not sure how I feel about it all.

"I've made you happy."

"Tremendously!" She beams, her genuine bright smile having a direct line to my cock. "I've heard so many great things about your family's library."

"Well, I hope it can live up to the hype."

"It will. Of that, I have no doubt."

"So, I did good?" I ask, eating up the small distance between us until her back is against the board behind her.

"Very good." She swallows dryly.

"Good enough to merit a reward?"

"What kind of reward would you want?"

When my eyes fix on her pouty lips, her breasts begin to heave.

"My next class should be arriving any minute now."

I can't help but chuckle at where her mind went.

"Don't worry, professor. I'm not going to fuck you here. When you finally come to your senses and realize that it's going to happen, I want to take my time, and a handful of minutes won't cut it."

"Then what do you want?"

My broad smile only widens when she doesn't correct me. Both she and I know that sooner or later I'll have her under me. It's all a question of time now.

"All I want is a kiss."

"A kiss?" She rasps, her own amber eyes falling to my mouth.

I run my finger over her lush, full bottom lip.

"Shouldn't be too hard for you. We've done it before."

"That was different."

"Was it?"

"Yes, it was. If someone sees us together, I might lose my job."

Aw, Em, you're going to lose it anyway.

"Then I guess I should quit stalling."

She opens her mouth to protest, but I silence her with my lips. The instant they press on hers, all thoughts of limited time evaporate. She's just as sweet as I remember—pliant to my touch and hungry for my possession.

Gently my tongue breaks the seam of her lips, entangling with its counterpart. Unable to hold back, I pull her closer to me by the nape of her neck with one hand while gripping her hip with the other. Her body molds with mine so perfectly it's almost as if she were made just for me. I push the idiotic notion away and savor each second of our kiss. My hard cock rubs against her hot core, making her whimper into my mouth. This woman's fire is scorching enough to thaw my ice-filled veins, and right now I'm beginning to resent my previous remark that I won't take this any further than just a kiss. I want to hear her scream out my name again when she's cumming. I want to feel her pussy swallowing me whole. There is so much I want at this moment that I can't help but be irritated with the fact that I can't have it. I brutalize her mouth, sucking out all her sweetness as punishment for having me feel this way after one kiss. When I gain enough fortitude to pull away, the crimson flush of her cheeks, her swollen lips, and her shallow breathing only aggravate me further.

"That's enough," I snap harshly, trying to get my bearings.

When her fingers lightly touch her lips, I'm unable to stifle my unsatiated groan.

"For someone so young, you sure know how to deliver a kiss," she whispers under her breath.

"I've had loads of practice," I reply coldly.

"I'm sure you have."

Unable to control it, I replace her fingers on her bottom lip with my thumb, her half-mast eyes gaining another simmering golden hue to them.

"You're not too bad yourself."

My aloof remark is meant to belittle the moment, but it's all for show since all I can think about is having her lips on mine again.

"Coming from someone who has kissed his fair share of women, I'll take that as a compliment," she states just as dispassionately, snapping out of her lust-filled haze.

I lean in until her breathing stops when she feels my mouth once again inches away from hers.

"Not all kisses are memorable, Em," I state evenly. "The same can be said for women."

She squares her shoulders, my backhanded comment successfully bringing her back to her senses.

"Good to know, Mr. Turner."

She stiffly turns around to continue wiping the board down, so she doesn't have to spend another second looking at me. This is when I should leave. This is the moment I should turn the fuck around and just put as much distance between us as I possibly can.

But that's not what I do.

Instead, I lean in just enough so she can feel my breath touch her skin.

"I really wish yours didn't leave a mark."

I press a chaste kiss behind her ear then rush out the door, leaving her just as confused as I am.

Chapter 13

Colt

I slump on the leather couch, trying to pretend I'm not one bit infatuated with the gorgeous creature strolling absentmindedly through my family's library. Emma slowly walks around every inch of the eight hundred square foot room, lightly touching every book in her reach as she goes about it as if each one is some precious gift that needs to be treasured and esteemed.

Never in my wildest dreams did I ever think that one day I'd be jealous of the attention a woman gave a hardback.

Fuck me.

Yesterday afternoon when I brought her here for the first time and gave her the full two-hour tour of my home, this was the only room that left her completely speechless.

Not our indoor Olympic pool or the home cinema.

Not the pretentious conservatory or the elaborate hedge maze outside.

None of those ostentatious displays of wealth impressed her in the slightest, much less left her tongue-tied. But the minute she set eyes on our library, it was love at first sight.

So it came as no surprise that when I offered to ditch going to the Charlotte Library and make this our primary working place for a couple of weeks, she jumped at the chance. It's been two days since we started working here, and already she has her little rituals. The minute Emma passes through this room's oval-shaped threshold, she can't help but take a few minutes to appreciate her surroundings, leaving me to twiddle my thumbs and act like I'm not fixated on her every move.

The way her amber eyes light up when she has a first edition book in her hands, carefully flipping each page with the delicateness one would treat a newborn with has me just as spellbound. Most women would take one look at the Richfield Estate and begin scheming ways of how to seduce me so that they could get a piece of this life. Emma is so enamored with her new happy place that she hardly even registers I'm right at her side. She'd be over the moon with just one book from my family's collection, yet she's content enough to appreciate it for the limited time given to her. I have to admit, sitting still and reading a four hundred page book has me yawning, but watching her fawn over a book? Well, I could do this shit for hours on end and never get bored.

But I'm on a deadline, and as much as I enjoy the view, I won't get any answers this way.

"Hate to spoil your fun, Professor, but we've got work to do," I tease, jumping to my feet and walking over to the workstation we set up in the center of the room.

"What? Oh yes, of course," she stutters in embarrassment, the soft crimson blush on her cheeks making her look sweet and inviting.

I let out a chuckle while getting settled for another afternoon of grueling research.

"You're laughing at me, aren't you?" she says, pulling out the chair beside me.

"Just a bit, Em. But don't worry, I'm not making fun of you. I think it's cute how you go all gaga for books."

"You call me that a lot," she mutters under her breath while opening her laptop.

"Huh?" I question, utterly clueless at what she's referring to.

"Em. You've called me that a few times now."

Have I? I hadn't noticed.

"Sorry. It won't happen again."

I straighten my spine, but my sudden tense demeanor softens when she covers my hand on the table with hers.

"No, it's okay, Colt. My grandfather used to call me Em, too. I hadn't realized how much I missed hearing it until you started calling me that."

"You sure it's not too personal for you? You're usually a stickler for keeping things professional between us."

"I think that ship sailed a long time ago. Don't you?"

Images of our kiss from yesterday immediately assault me, and just the faint memory of it has my cock rising to attention. She goes back to her notes and dismisses me once more. Instead of using this slip up of hers to pull her closer and get a repeat of that quick make-out session, I concentrate on what I have to do and try not to obsess over one simple kiss.

That shit sounds like something Finn would do.

And even though I love Walker as if he were my own flesh and blood, I'm not going to be pussy-whipped over a little thing as insignificant as a kiss. I'm here to do a job, and as much as the thought pleases me, ripping Emma's panties off with my teeth at this precise moment isn't it. Yes, it'll be a great perk once I'm finished with her, but I've got bigger concerns to tackle presently.

"Can I ask you a question?"

"All depends on the question," she replies, back to her stiff upper lip manner.

I guess the sliver of vulnerability she let out when she was talking about her grandfather was more insight into her personal life than she's comfortable showing. She's back to being all about the work, and luckily for me, her work is precisely what I want to talk about.

"Don't worry, professor. It's purely professional."

"Okay, then. Go ahead. I'm all ears."

She turns in her seat, just enough to look me in the eye, adamant in keeping a good gap of space between us. If fucking Emma were my goal right now, I'd have pulled her onto my lap to teach her a lesson—she can't keep me away from her if I set my mind to it.

But that's not my end goal.

Not yet, anyway.

"It's about your book. I couldn't help but see that in your synopsis, you wrote that this historical novel of yours would be about four of the most influential secret organizations to exist in this country, yet so far, I've only worked on three."

"I don't hear a question." She pushes her catlike glasses up to the bridge of her nose.

"Is there any reason why you haven't let me work on the fourth yet?"

"Yes."

"Are you going to tell me?"

"No," she quips.

"I can't do my job if I'm left in the dark, Em."

It's probably a shitty thing that I just used her grandfather's pet name for her on purpose. I might have had no clue that word came out of my mouth before, but now that I know it holds meaning, I might as well use it to my advantage.

She mauls her lower lip and looks deep into my eyes. For the first time since I've met her, I'm the one who becomes flustered with the way she's scrutinizing me with a single look. The seriousness in her stare takes me aback, and I wonder just what she's trying to find.

"You're right," she states finally, closing her laptop. "Have you ever heard about The Society?"

This is it.

This is fucking it.

I try to keep my features as stoic as possible, so she doesn't realize how much I need her to spill her guts. If I tell her that I don't know who they are, she might smell something shady going on. The Society is a joke told over kegs at fraternities, so telling her I've never heard the name before will set off alarm bells in her head. And we can't fucking have that, now can we?

"It's a Richfield University urban legend," I reply with a blank expression.

"What did I tell you about those?" She cocks an accusing brow at me.

"That no matter how small, there is always a sliver of truth to them."

"Correct. Glad to see you've been paying attention."

"I always pay attention to everything you say."

"Now tell me what you've heard about them?"

She brushes my cocky remark out of the way as one would swat a pestering fly so that we can focus on the subject at hand. I tell her all I know, leaving out the part that they have been blackmailing my friends and me since school began.

"I don't know much aside from what every other so-called secret college society seems to promise. It's supposed to be this super cagey boys' club that says they can ensure the rich and privileged gain all their hearts' desires as long as they are okay in selling their souls to become members." I laugh as if the mere thought of such a club is ludicrous.

When Emma begins to scowl, my hackles rise. She's starting to lose interest in continuing this conversation with me since it's apparent I'm not taking this seriously. I quickly change gears and rectify my mistake.

"If I remember correctly," I begin with a more pondering tone this time, "myth says that every firstborn son is promised to the establishment to keep the bloodlines pure. That they make sure, their members stay within the same families, only opening up a few exceptions from time to time to those they deem worthy. It feels like a bunch of misogynistic assholes on a power trip, but then again, inspired thought isn't their forte. I mean, just their name is disappointing to me. Look at Yale, for example. They named their society The Skulls and Bones. Just naming their cult The Society doesn't necessarily induce fear. More like laziness, if you ask me." I scoff, leaning against my chair, linking my hands at the back of my head.

"There lies the difference between those other societies and this one," she chimes in enthusiastically. "They don't need a name to hold power. That's what's so ingenious about them. Only in the last century did people start referring to them as The Society. The century before that, they went nameless, yet everyone still feared them."

"Is that why you picked them? Why not go after the Bilderbergs and their influence on the economy, or something more religious, like The Knights Templar. Hell, if you wanted to go after assholes, why not write a piece about the KKK?"

She shakes her head.

"They've all been written about before, while The Society has dumbfounded most historians. We know of their existence, but we still don't have any tangible proof to back it up. It's all hearsay. And that's why I'm focused on them more. This book is very important to me, Colt. I got the book deal because I promised that I'd be the first one to get tangible proof and unmask them to the world."

Fuck me.

That can't happen.

"If they are as dangerous as you say they are, doesn't it seem foolish to go after them? Aren't you afraid they might retaliate?"

"No. They won't hurt me."

"How can you be so sure?" I ask, not liking the exceeding self-assurance in her tone.

"I just am."

Unlike Emma, I know The Society and the lengths to which they will go to get what they want. Emma's impudence comes with the fact that she believes she's working under the radar, and they have no clue she's onto them. But I know better. Not only are they already on her tail, but I'm positive

The Society will also hurt her if she tries to push them into a corner.

Fuck.

I no longer have until the first snowfall. My timeframe to finish my task has just shortened immensely. I need to get Em out of Asheville as fast as possible. If I don't, those antsy bastards might come after her themselves, and who knows what they'll do to her to keep her quiet.

She gets up from her seat and starts walking through the library, turning her back to me and giving me a view of her ass. As much as I like what she's throwing in my direction, it's not enough to settle my nerves.

"Now it's my turn to ask you something."

"I'm an open book."

To this, she laughs, but even the sweet timbre of it can't ease the tightness in my chest.

"If only that were true," she mumbles but then shakes it off and walks over to a clear bookcase.

"What are these?" She taps the glass with the tip of her nails.

I get up from my seat and walk over to her, needing to be near her for some inexplicable reason.

"What do they look like?"

"Diaries of some sort. Very old diaries."

"Correct. These are my family's ledgers, passed down from generation to generation. It goes back to the first Richfields who settled in this house–Lionel and Laura Richfield. Since then, every head of the family writes down their experiences and then locks it here for the next head of the family."

"Does that mean you'll get to add to this collection?"

"That privilege goes to someone else," I retort coldly.

"Have you read them?"

"No. My older sister Meredith has, though. She's the first in line. Not me. I'm what you can call a spare."

"Is that how you see yourself?"

"No. That would be too kind of an adjective to describe me."

A deep v settles on the bridge of her nose where her glasses sit. She surprises me by holding onto my hand a second time today and taking one step closer to me.

"I guess being a part of this family isn't as easy as one would assume."

"Prison never is."

The pregnant pause that ensues has me paralyzed to the spot. The energy between us crackles as if a magnetic current has wrapped itself around us with the sole purpose of pulling us closer to one another. I lift her chin gently with my knuckles so that I can get a better view of her face. No alcohol in the world can intoxicate me more than staring into Emma's whiskey-colored eyes. Her long lashes bat a mile a minute under her catlike glasses, and when her tongue peeks out to moisten her lips, my cock aches to feel her touch. The moment, however, is ruined when we hear footsteps approach. She drops my hand like a hot potato and takes two steps away from me, looking everywhere but at me.

"Am I interrupting something?" my father's velvety voice rings out through the room.

"Yes. Go away," I tell him in annoyance but the fucker only broadens his smile, walking directly over to where Emma is standing.

"We haven't been officially introduced. You must be the teacher that has surprised us all by getting Colt interested in something less self-serving than what we are accustomed to from him. Now I can see why."

"Emma Harper," she states evenly, reaching out her hand for my father to shake. I watch her back go ramrod straight when my father takes her hand and places a kiss on it instead.

Motherfucker.

"Owen," he replies, all smiles and sparkling emerald eyes.

Emma pulls her hand away, squaring her shoulders and planting the stern expression on her face that she loves to use in class.

"I think you don't give your son enough credit. He's been quite helpful to me."

"I bet he has."

His less-than-subtle insinuation is as loud as the rage rattling in my chest. I want to slap his fucking smug smile off his face, but Emma beats me to the punch.

"Ah, now I see where Colt gets it from," Emma interjects.

"What might that be?"

"The ability to speak his mind without forethought."

Instead of being insulted, my father actually laughs.

"Yes. Quite true." His continued chuckle aggravates my nerves. "Colt takes after me more than he'd like to admit. Don't you, son?"

"If that's true, I might as well kill myself now." I gift him my best wolfish grin.

"See? He's exactly how I used to be at his age, but time will ease his rough edges soon enough. Either that or a good woman who is perseverant and patient enough to tame him."

I don't like the way he's staring at Emma as he goes about spewing his warped wisdom.

"Is there a point to this little visit of yours, or can we get back to work?"

"Colt's right. We really should continue," Emma adds, her smile as fake as a cubic zirconia simulated diamond.

"Of course. God forbid I interrupt my son's scholarly devotion."

He begins to walk out of the room but then halts halfway.

What now?

"Professor Harper, my family hosts a New Year's Eve party every year. I've been told you don't have any family nearby, so maybe you'd consider being my family's guest."

"That would be lovely. Thank you," Emma responds politely.

"Glad to hear it. I hope it's not too forward of me to ask, but is it true that you live in Charlotte?"

"It is," she replies, puzzled at his left-field question.

What are you up to, old man?

"I thought I heard as much. I've seen that your sessions with my son have run quite late into the night, and it concerned me that you still had such a long ride ahead of you to return back home. If you ever need to prolong your work here, one of the guest rooms will always be at your disposal. I'd feel much better knowing your safety is taken care of."

"Thank you. That's very considerate of you."

"Well, I guess I best leave you two to it then. Nice to meet you, Emma."

"Likewise."

When my father finally leaves, I snap my attention to Emma, taking three long strides to reach her. I grip her chin forcefully, her eyes widening in alarm.

"What are you doing?!"

"You are not sleeping one night under this roof. Do you understand me?" I bark out like a possessed man.

"Let go of me!" she seethes, her nails sinking into my wrist.

"Not until you tell me you understand! Spit it out, Em, before I run out of patience."

"Yes! Okay! I won't sleep here."

Before I can stop myself, I lean in and bruise her lips with mine.

This isn't the same inquisitive slow tempo kiss she let me steal from her yesterday in class. It's hard and brutal, intent on making my point. This kiss tells her not to fuck with me. The only Turner that gets to taste her is me, and it will serve her well to remember that shit. When I feel her hands unlatch from my wrist so they can rest on my chest, I pull away.

"Now that's settled, let's get back to work. I want you gone before dinner."

Instead of giving me an attitude, Emma sits back in her chair, mute as a Buddhist monk, and does exactly what I ordered. Her unexpected obedience should make me happy, but it doesn't.

It's forced and entirely against her nature.

But Emma isn't stupid.

Far from it.

She knows that when an animal is close to breaking out of its cage, poking at it will only guarantee to infuriate the beast further.

And right now, she's the only thing I want to sink my teeth in.

Chapter 14

Colt

Secrets are my family's most treasured heirlooms, and our various homes are the very mortuaries that keep our lies hidden. Keeping secrets has been in my veins for as long as I can remember, and now The Society wants me to uncover one of the many and shine a light on it. Their only hint is that this dark, mysterious secret has been withheld from me by the people I'm closest to.

Like that's supposed to narrow it down.

Out of the many Richfield skeletons that my family keeps under lock and key, how am I to know which one they want, let alone be able to find out the ones no one talks about?

What if the secret they want is Linc's?

I can't let my thoughts go there. Sure these assholes know a lot, but I doubt they know that clusterfuck. And if they did, wouldn't they leave it for Linc to disclose in his own task?

I pinch the bridge of my nose to ease the headache that's fast approaching. Between The Society and my family, I don't know which is more fucked up or causes more migraines. But while I've been dealing with my family's baggage for all of my life, The Society is the only one who has the means to ruin me.

Ruin us.

And since Emma let the cat out of the bag yesterday, revealing she is determined to out them in her book, putting herself in harm's way, they are the ones who I need to focus on.

What did she tell me the other day regarding uncovering hidden truths?

Go to the first plausible suspect and do your due diligence.

So in my case, there are only two people who immediately come to mind, and those, of course, would be my parents. In their very particular cunning way, they are both experts at covering up the truth with well-fabricated lies and making everyone believe that they are what every southern-born elitist family should aspire to be. It sickens me to my very core how well they both play their part in the charade of the perfect couple.

I look at my watch and confirm that it's close to midday. No one will be home at this hour, so if I want to do some serious snooping, this is my best chance.

As I expected, when I arrive home early from school, the cold mausoleum is empty save for a few servants running about the place to keep everything spick and span like the lady of the house demands. My father should be golfing or whatever he does at this hour, while my mother and Meredith should be busy with their usual Richfield Foundation tasks. Abby and Irene will be home from high school around four, which leaves me with enough time to search around and see if I can find something that will give me an idea of what The Society expects from me.

I don't even have to think about where to go first.

Intuitively I head directly to my father's favorite hiding place in the whole house. If there is anything worth discovering, it will be in his study. I step inside his sanctuary and take a good look around the place filled with books and family memorabilia, the scent of bourbon and his cologne still hanging in the air. There are endless pictures of us kids on the mantle above his fireplace, making him look like the family man he's not.

I walk over to his desk and see two framed pictures—one of me, my sisters, and Lincoln at some party taken at the Hamilton Estate and another of my mother on their wedding day.

What a fucking joke.

I sit in his chair and pick my mother's frame up, feeling disgusted with the pretense. If he felt anything for her, he wouldn't be sticking his dick in everything around town. And he sure as hell wouldn't be inviting women he just met to spend the night in the same house his wife and kids sleep in.

Every time I remember his offer to Emma, my blood boils.

The fucker had the audacity to offer her one of our guest rooms right under my nose and use her supposed safety as an excuse. It's a good thing Emma got the hint that her spending one night here would be one night too many.

I know my father.

He'd seduce and find his way into her bed eventually.

And that betrayal would kill any lasting speck of love I could still have for him.

And as to Emma?

The Society could do whatever the fuck they wanted to her.

I wouldn't care.

She'd be as dead to me as he is.

The tumultuous thoughts continue to run wild in my head as I keep looking at my mother's uncharacteristically smiling face. But then something else grabs my attention, pulling me out of my animus mood. My mother's wedding picture is slanted somewhat, its angle inclining down just a bit. I can tell there is something else beneath the picture. I turn it over, unclasping the back end of the frame, and sure enough, two pictures fall onto the desk.

One of my mother.

And the other…

Of Scarlett.

Heat rushes through me, and it takes everything in me not to rip it into tiny pieces. There is only one reason a man would hide a picture of another woman amongst his prized possessions—he's fucking her.

I guess it didn't take me much time to discover what The Society wanted after all. They want me to humiliate my mother by exposing what looks to be my father's new mistress. Hate bleeds through me, not only for the betrayal done against the woman who gave me life but for the girl who looks so innocent in her drab clothes and large glasses.

Easton loves her, and she does this to him?!

Fucking cold-hearted bitch!

Easy, Colt.

Think.

If I go to Easton with this, he'll never believe me. Or worse, he will, and it'll end him.

I can't have that.

The dark prince and I have always had this unspoken bond in our little band of brothers. While Finn is all heart and Lincoln is slowly on his way to sainthood, East and I have always been the odd men out when it comes to genuine goodness. We don't have that gene in us. However, I have seen a change in him since Scarlett came into his life. The gloomy, dark cloud that always seemed to hover above him is nowhere in sight, and in its place, love shines through him. He managed to find peace when there was only a raging battlefield inside of him before.

No. I can't tell Easton.

Scarlett is the one I have to pay a visit to. I want to hear her deny it to my face, and when she can't, I'll tell her to get the fuck out of Asheville before Easton ever finds out what a two-timing snake she is. Easton might suffer from her sudden disappearance, but it's better than the alternative. Knowing that the person he put his trust and love in could betray him so coldly is something Easton could never recover from.

I know that feeling, and if I can spare him that ugly, gut-wrenching pain, I will.

Luckily for me, tomorrow is Friday night.

Which means it's about time I pay the Brass Guild another visit.

I watch from the sidelines as Scarlett belts out her song, leaving everyone awestruck by her vocal range. As expected, Easton is at his usual table with his eyes fixed on the woman on stage. I need to get Scarlett alone, but it's going to be difficult with him being here. I scour the room until I find the red-haired vixen I'm looking for. When Ruby finishes charming one of the Brass Guild's members and begins to walk over to her next client, I make my move.

"Mr. Turner. What a surprise," she greets, plopping two kisses on my cheeks, sure to leave a mark with her blood-red lipstick. "I do believe this is the first time I've seen you here without your entourage."

"Sometimes we just have to do our thing solo, don't you agree?"

"Quite so. How can I help you this evening? Maybe some company while you watch Angel's show?"

"Actually, I was wondering if I could get a private audience with your star singer."

I watch her gaze travel over to her protégée, and instantly her expression morphs from flirtatious to protective.

"I don't think that can be arranged," she replies, less hospitable than she was a minute ago.

"Now Ruby, I thought the Brass Guild was all about indulging its guests."

"If talking to Angel is so important, shouldn't you ask her boyfriend first? Maybe he'll be more indulging. He's sitting right there. Shall I ask him?" she coos, placing her head on my shoulder, pointing at East.

"I don't see why he should be bothered." My jaw ticks when I see that just like Emma, Ruby is also immune to my charms, making me have to think quickly on my feet. "Especially since that's exactly why I'd like to talk to her alone. It has to do with Easton, and I would rather not have him know I talked to her."

She instantly pulls away from me, her brows pinched in worry.

"Don't worry. He's not stepping out on her or anything."

Your precious Angel is.

"I'm not sure if you know this, but East and his family have been going through a lot recently. I thought maybe if I talked to Scarlett in private, she might know how we, his friends, can help them recover better without hurting his pride."

"Yes, I heard what happened to Easton's mother. Scarlett has nothing but praise for Naomi Price. A true shame."

"So, will you help me, Ruby? For Easton? I know it would mean a lot to Scarlett."

When Ruby's eyes soften, I know I've got her.

"Fine. I can get you five minutes."

"Make it ten, and I'll make it worth your while." I wink.

"That would mean that I would have to keep Easton busy."

"I'm sure you can come up with something." I scan up and down at her voluptuous figure.

"That boy only has eyes for Angel, so if you are insinuating that I seduce him, then I'm sorry to disappoint you, but he won't buy that."

Jesus. Am I the only guy in Asheville that isn't pussy-whipped?

"Christmas is coming. How about you just talk about something he can buy Scarlett as a present. I'm sure he'd be grateful for your help."

"I guess that can work. But Colt, if I find out that you are lying to me and harass Scarlett in any way, consider this your last visit to The Brass Guild. Do we understand each other?"

"Perfectly."

"Come with me then." She huffs and begins to take me backstage. I follow her lead, and within minutes we enter a room filled with elaborate costumes and dresses all over the place.

"This is Angel's dressing room. She'll come here to freshen up and change before she leaves. I can give you ten minutes at best since Easton usually comes in after she's done with her shows."

"Ten minutes is more than I need."

There is hesitance in her gaze, which I try to reassure with my best southern aristocrat smile. The minute she leaves me alone in the dressing room, I do my due diligence and check if there is anything in this room that can be tied back to my father. As I come up empty-handed, I hear faint applause coming from the lounge. I might not have found any physical proof to link the two fucked-up lovebirds together, but when Scarlett waltzes through her door, her verbal confession will do just fine.

I lean against her vanity, arms crossed at my chest, ready for her. When she swings the door open and sees me in here, her smile turns uneasy.

"Colt? I didn't know you were coming to tonight's show," she stammers nervously, rooted in place. "If you came here for Easton, he's just outside."

"I'm not here for him. I'm here for you."

"For me?" she asks, baffled.

I tap my lips with my index finger as I eat away the distance between us.

"I can't figure you out, Scarlett, and that unsettles me."

"I don't know what you mean," she retorts, trying not to shift from one foot to the other.

"Outside of the Brass Guild walls, you act like a scared little girl, but on stage, you transform into a siren luring dollar bills out of men's pockets."

Her brown eyes turn cold.

"You make me sound like a prostitute."

"If the stiletto fits." I shrug, feigning boredom.

"Are you drunk?!" she chastises, bypassing me to walk over to her vanity.

"Far from it. I'm as sober as a judge. Huh. Funny I just said that, considering I'm still debating what the best punishment is for the crime you've committed."

She throws her wig onto the floor, staring daggers at me over her shoulder.

"Colt, you're not making any sense, and if I'm being honest, you being here is making me feel uncomfortable. I'm going to have to ask you to leave."

A sinister chuckle leaves me as I walk over to her.

"I'm not leaving, Scarlett. Not until you tell me what your connection to my father is."

Her big brown eyes go wide as saucers before she's able to school her features to look impassive.

"I have no idea what you're talking about," she quips, turning away from me and facing her mirror.

I grab the edge of her chair, leaning down to her ear, while never breaking my gaze that's fixed on our reflection.

"Are you fucking him?"

She throws her wipe on the vanity, pure venom in her glower.

"I'm getting real sick of that question."

"Are you, now?" I laugh, standing back up to my full height. "And who exactly asked you that question before me? Easton perhaps?"

"It's none of your business either way."

"So there is something going on between the two of you." My nostrils flare in disgust.

Her lips morph into a fine line, her resolve to keep her secret affair iron-strong.

"Now, Scarlett, don't go all mute on me. Just tell me what the deal with you and my dad is. And don't insult my intelligence by telling me it's nothing."

"The only thing I'm telling you is to leave, Colt."

"I'm not budging an inch."

"Leave, Colt, before I get your ass thrown out of not only my dressing room but out of this club!"

"You sound like you have a lot of influence. Why is that Scarlett?"

She opens her mouth to reply but then shuts it.

"Just who else are you fucking for you to feel you have all this clout?"

"Please leave. I won't ask you again," she replies, wounded, pretending to be hurt by my remark.

But I know better.

This is all an act.

She's a performer, after all. She duped Easton into falling in love with her, seduced a man old enough to be her father, and if I let her, she'll fool me too into believing I'm being unjust with her. Having had enough of her games, I grab her shoulders and turn her around in her chair to face me head-on, her loud gasp bouncing off the walls.

"I told you I'm not leaving here without you answering me. Just out with it already!" I demand impatiently, but before I have time to shake her into giving me an answer, someone pulls me back and punches me so hard in the jaw that my entire body falls onto a nearby couch.

"What the fuck do you think you're doing?!" Easton shouts at me.

I get up to my feet and point to the woman he's shielding with his body.

"What I have to. Now get out of my way. You don't want to be here for this. Trust me."

"The fuck are you talking about?!"

"Your girlfriend has some explaining to do, and I'm not leaving this room until she does."

I rush toward her, but East pushes me off.

"Colt, I swear to God you're not leaving this room without a busted lip if you try to get near Scar again!"

I huff.

"You think I'm bluffing, asshole? Try and put a finger on her, and I'll knock your teeth in. Don't test me, Colt. Not on this."

This motherfucker is going to make me break his heart.

Goddamn him!

"Then you ask her. Ask her what her relationship with my father is," I deadpan, waiting for the ground to swallow him whole.

But to my surprise, Easton doesn't as much as flinch.

"Ask him yourself. Scar doesn't have to tell you a goddamn thing."

The fuck?!

"You know, don't you?" I stammer, taking two steps away from him.

But instead of answering me, East just purses his lips, fists still clenched at his side.

Something isn't adding up. If Easton is still standing strong, unaffected by my father's relationship with his girl, that can only mean the two aren't screwing around his back.

Then what the fuck is the connection?

"You're supposed to be my best friend. No secrets, remember?" I accuse him.

"Brother, I'm trying really hard to remember why I'm even friends with you in the first place. You want answers? Then ask your fucking father, man to man. Stop intimidating Scar. Believe me, Colt. You won't win here."

With that threat hanging in the air between us, I do the first decent thing all night.

I turn around and leave.

The following Sunday morning, I find myself in the last place I'd ever think to be—parked outside Asheville's First Baptist Church just on the outskirts of the Northside. I'm in my car, eyes closed, trying to get some shut-eye since the past few nights all I've done was toss and turn, when a knock at my window startles me awake.

Scarlett pulls her long chocolate brown hair in a bun while I open the side door to let her in.

"Does your boyfriend know you texted me to come see you this morning?"

"No. He's still upset with you. I thought it best that I come and talk to you alone."

"Right," I mumble, slamming my head back.

It's not the first time Easton's been pissed at me. Come to think of it, I usually end up getting on his nerves, and him on mine, a couple of times a week. But I love the fucker, and that's not something I feel about most people in my life. I've got to find a way to make this right, but I know while East is seething in his corner, it's best I keep my distance from him.

Scarlett fidgets in her seat, awkwardly cleaning her wet palms over the ugliest pale gray skirt I've ever seen on a woman. She looks more like she's someone's sister-wife instead of the knockout who sings her heart out in a clandestine nightclub over the weekend.

"Did you ask Owen?" she finally questions, breaking the silence between us.

Owen.

"You're on a first-name basis with my father, huh? Pretty intimate thing if you ask me."

She lets out a long exhale before turning to the side to face me.

"Colt, I want to have this conversation with you, but if you're going to act like an ass, then there's no point. Are you going to act like a grown-ass man like I know you are capable of, or am I wasting my time?"

"Fine. You win. I'll shut up."

"I shouldn't be the one telling you this. It should have been him. But I don't think he ever will." She starts off pensively, and the taint of affection in her tone for my father doesn't go unnoticed by me.

"My father loves his secrets, Scarlett."

"Yes, I know that, too," she says more sternly.

"Ahh." I chuckle, happy to see I'm not the only one he's disappointed. "He's kept some from you as well, hasn't he?"

"He has," she retorts angrily.

"And you're pissed. That's why you texted me to come. You want to get back at him?"

She shakes her head, a frown now on her cupid bow mouth.

"I'm upset with him, yes, but I know I'll forgive him eventually. I hope you do, too."

"Why would I forgive my cheating-ass father for anything?"

"Because you love him. And that's what you do for the people you love. You forgive their shortcomings even if they hurt you."

"I'm no doormat." I scoff.

"I didn't say you were. But you're his son. And whether you like to admit it or not, there is a piece of you that wants to understand your father's actions. Believe me when I tell you I'm trying to wrap my head around them, too. But I just have to trust him, because he's always been there for me.

Through the good and bad times, he's been the one person I could always count on. I'm not going to turn my back on him just because his actions don't sit well with me."

"How has my father been there for you?" I ask, utterly confused.

"Does the name Angela Davis mean anything to you?"

I shake my head.

"She was my mother, Colt. You see, they grew up together, my mom and your dad, and became best friends when they were kids. She told him everything, and in turn, he confided everything in her, too. My mom left Asheville when she was eighteen in search of her big break in Vegas, but she always kept in touch with your father. A few years later, when she got pregnant with me, he became my godfather and the only male parental figure I had. I never met my dad, but that never mattered to me because I had yours. He never stayed away from Vegas for long, always trying to visit us every couple of months. Both Mom and I lived for those visits because Owen was such a force of nature. You remind me a lot of him in a way. When my mother died, he was the first to know about it and told my uncle. He made sure I had everything I needed when I arrived in Asheville. And I'm not sure I could have made it without him. He's always been like a father to me, Colt. Not a lover like you assumed, but a guardian that I could lean on."

My throat is dry with the loving way Scarlett talks about him. I knew that adoration once upon a time. But not anymore. Scarlett might still have shutters for eyes, but I see him well enough. The *real* Owen Turner.

"Why didn't he ever tell my sisters or me about you? Why keep you a secret?"

She bites her lower lip, thinking about the right response to give me.

"I think his friendship with my mother might have been seen differently by yours. Maybe he didn't want your mom to think he was having an affair with mine. I can tell you I never saw anything intimate with her more than a few hugs and kisses on her forehead. My mother was no homewrecker." She reasons defensively, trying to preserve the image of a woman I never met.

"Still sounds like cheating to me. You don't have to have sex to emotionally cheat on your family."

She twiddles her thumbs and bows her head.

"I admit I think so, too. And I think Owen is of the same mindset. Maybe that's why he kept us a secret to spare your mom's feelings as well as yours and your sisters."

"It wouldn't matter anyway. Like you, my sisters might have rose-colored glasses on when it comes to my father, but both my mom and I know differently. Once a cheater, always a cheater."

The look of pity on her angelic face makes me want to punch something. I turn my face away from her, pretending to look out my window so that I don't have to feel the guilt her sympathy evokes in me.

"I just wanted you to know, but I would prefer if you kept this to yourself. Maybe one day he'll tell you about me. But until then, if you could keep what I told you between us, I would appreciate it."

"Does East know?"

"He went to see your father once since he also jumped to the same conclusion you did."

"Great," I sneer as my jaw ticks, knowing that even my supposed best friend didn't tell me about this.

"Don't be cross with East. Your father asked him not to say anything to either of us."

East doesn't owe any loyalty toward my dad, but he sure as shit should have had some for me. Sensing that there isn't much more she can do, Scarlett opens the car door and starts getting out.

"Scarlett."

"Yes?"

"I'm sorry I was such an ass to you the other night. You got the brunt of my rage and didn't deserve it. I know when I've fucked up."

"Apology accepted." She smiles timidly.

"Scarlett, can I ask you something?"

She nods.

"Why are you angry at him? With my dad, I mean?"

"Because I'm tired of living a life filled with unspoken lies. Their only purpose is to cause pain."

"Ahh, but that's the catch, isn't it? My father loves his secrets too much to give them up."

"So I'm learning."

Chapter 15

Colt

Linc: *We need to talk. Come to the Grind before school.*

That was the only text I got from my cousin this whole weekend since I blew up at The Brass Guild. He didn't have to write anything else for me to know—that just like East—he's pissed at me.

No, fuck that.

Worse.

Disappointed.

My head leans back into my car seat's headrest, thinking of how far I've fucked up that even Linc is upset with me. It wasn't always like this. There was a time that Lincoln believed I could never be in the wrong. He'd place his hands over a hot stove, confident in his belief that whatever fucked-up thing I got messed up in, it was never my fault.

A specific memory of a lazy summer afternoon from our past comes to the forefront of my mind, and as hard as I try to push it away, I'm helpless to resist it.

I slice through the water like a shark, my expert strokes bringing me closer to the floating board where she's sunbathing in her yellow polka dot bikini. I know I'm showing off, but if I want Kennedy to look at me the same way she does my cousin, I have to give her a reason to. Maybe swimming like a gold-medal champion won't do the trick, but I have to try something. And forcing a kiss out of her won't work since the last time I tried to pull that shit, she pushed me out of our treehouse and broke my damn arm in the process. This time she has to come to me if she wants to get her first kiss. We all know Lincoln has been dragging his feet and won't do it himself.

Guilt consumes me as I think of the reason why he still hasn't made his move.

He knows I like her.

And because he loves me, he won't stand in my way where Ken is concerned.

He's always been selfless like that.

I, on the other hand, don't know the meaning of the word.

With those distracting thoughts in my head, I lose my rhythm and end up swallowing lake water as a result. As I pull myself up onto the wooden float, I don't know if I should feel grateful or pissed no one noticed me completely fucking up my less than perfect butterfly attempts. Grabbing a towel to dry off, I sit next to the girl I was trying to impress. Her legs dance in the water as her gaze remains fixed on Lincoln, who is rowing her canoe.

If Kennedy is anywhere near a body of water, then it is a safe bet that her trusty canoe is always nearby. She can't swim for shit, but like hell would she ever let that stop her from joining us on lake days. Her pride won't let her wear floaties on her arms or a life jacket, preferring to use them only when she's paddling her canoe. And even then, she always reminds us that even the best swimmers have to use one when they grow.

"You know, I could always teach you how to swim," I tell her when I catch her enviously looking over at my sisters having a grand old time swimming closer to the shore.

"Doubtful. You looked like you were about to drown a minute ago."

"Ahh, so you were watching," I gloat, nudging her shoulder with mine.

"Hard not to when you act like a pompous ass all the time."

"That hurt," I joke, placing my palm over my chest.

"Sure it did." She laughs.

"I can teach you if you want," Teddy chimes in behind us, his voice making my skin crawl.

Kennedy throws her head over her shoulder and gifts him her weak-ass, fake smile.

"No need, Teddy. If I ever want to learn, I'll ask Lincoln. But thanks for the offer, though," she replies sweetly.

"Suit yourself," he counters in a bored tone, lying back on his beach towel.

Ken turns around and rolls her eyes. She hates the sicko just as much as I do, but since he's Linc's older brother, she puts up with him for his sake. Ken would do anything for Lincoln, even if that means acting like she likes his creepy-ass older brother. I see how she tries not to cringe when the asshole undresses her with his eyes. The fucker is already a freshman in high school, but apparently, only thirteen-year-old girls do it for him.

It's fucking disgusting.

But I wouldn't expect anything else from him. I know the asshole had something to do with what happened with my younger sisters' cat, Whiskers, last month. The cat was fine one minute, and the next, Irene found him in our hedge maze with his neck broken. She had nightmares for weeks while little Abby cried for days on end. Even Meredith shed a tear when Dad buried Whiskers next to our conservatory, and she's made of stone. The only ones at the house that day were Teddy and Linc for our usual Sunday family brunch, and I know my cousin wouldn't hurt a damn fly, much less kill my kid sisters' pet.

It was that fucker, I'm sure of it. I just can't prove it.

I get up to grab a bottle of water from the cooler, my mind still elsewhere, when suddenly I hear a loud splash coming from behind me. My neck turns left to right, fear gripping my heart when there's no sign of Kennedy anywhere on the float.

"Where's Ken?" I yell over to her brother, who is glued to his phone.

"What?" he asks absentmindedly, scrolling away.

"Teddy, where's Ken?!"

"I have no idea what you're talking about," he mumbles, eyes shut, taking in the sun.

These two fuckers!

I look all over the lake only to find Finn and East on their jet skis far away while Lincoln is slowly paddling his way to us. My chest tightens as I run around looking for her in the water. It's only when I see blond hair and a stretched-out hand trying to break through the surface a couple of feet away that I scream.

"KENNEDY!!!"

I watch my cousin splash into the water, Lincoln's face filled with pure determination to reach her. I dive in right after him, dread making each of my strokes uneven and awkward. Near the bank, I can hear a loud commotion coming from our parents. Easton's stepdad and my dad run to the water in an attempt to reach her in time. I'm out of breath, panting away when Lincoln finally pulls her out of the water and onto his back. He swims to shore while I do my best to follow suit. When my feet find sand, I run like hell to the bank, Linc already blowing oxygen into her lungs, while my father pumps her small chest. Tears threaten to run down my cheeks as I stand by helplessly watching Linc call out to her.

"Stay with me, Ken. Stay with me," he repeats desperately every time he breaks free from her lips.

When Kennedy coughs up lake water, my dad pushes her to her side to let all of it out. I'm still in shock when I feel nails sink into my shoulder, jerking me around in one fast swoosh.

"This was your doing, wasn't it?" my mother yells at me.

I'm so out of it that I don't even understand what she's saying.

"Did you think your practical joke would be funny? Kennedy could have gotten seriously hurt, you insolent child!" she shouts right before I feel her hard slap on my cheek.

My whole body shakes with anger, but I'm unable to say a word in my defense. I'm not taken aback by the fact she hit me since my mother has always been a big believer that if you spare the rod, you end up spoiling the child. No. It's the way my mother's eyes bore into my skull as if she hates the very sight of me that has me tongue-tied.

"Answer me!" she shouts again, and when she raises her hand to give me another blow, I just stand there waiting for it to happen.

But then nothing comes.

I open my eyes and watch Lincoln hold my mother's wrist, preventing her palm from striking me twice.

"Enough," he orders menacingly, placing himself in the line of fire.

My mother's ice blue eyes slant, but I see her calm composure reestablish itself.

"Is that so?"

"It is," he deadpans. "You will never lay a finger on Colt again."

I swallow dryly as I watch the two stare each other down. My stomach falls when I see there is pride in her eyes with how he just talked back to her. I've never once dared to confront my mother the way Linc is doing now, too afraid of the retaliation that would follow. Yet, he doesn't look one bit fearful. He looks ready to chew her up and spit her out. And to my utter astonishment, my mother seems pleased by his defiance.

"And why is that?" my mother counters with a chilling smirk.

"You know why. Colt is a Richfield. And neither you nor anyone else will make him feel less than."

"You learn quickly," she muses, unlatching Linc's grip from her wrist.

"When I need to. Can you say the same?"

There is a deathly stilled silence in the air. Even the adults standing around us hold their breaths, waiting to see how my mother will react to my cousin's impudence. I'm still trying to get my bearings when I feel a quivering wet body slide next to me. Ken looks up at my face with unshed tears in her eyes. She rises to the balls of her bare feet and places a chaste kiss where my mother's fingers are probably imprinted. She then snaps her neck to my mother, her nostrils flaring in anger and disgust.

"Ken, don't," *I whisper, but it's no use. She's already standing shoulder to shoulder with Lincoln, ready to take my mother down.*

"Colt did nothing wrong, Aunt Colleen. You are always so quick to pass judgment on him without having all the facts. Shame, Auntie. Shame on you!"

"Kennedy! What has gotten into you, girl?!" *her father yells, appalled, from somewhere behind us, but Ken doesn't so much as flinch.*

"No, Daddy. Auntie is wrong. She should apologize to Colt. He did nothing wrong."

I watch my mother's scrutinizing gaze bounce from Linc to Ken in deep thought.

"Fair enough. I'll apologize to my son if you tell me who pushed you into the water."

Yeah, I want to know too, since there is no way in hell Ken fell on her own. Whoever pushed her in, I'm going to make sure to break every bone in their body.

Kennedy glances to the wooden float at the lake's center, Finn and Easton now there along with Teddy and Jefferson. She then turns back to my mother, resolve in her stare.

"I slipped."

"Did you, now?"

"Yes."

My mother's lips thin into two fine lines, not buying the lie that Ken just gave. I then freeze in place when my mother looks past the two blonde heads in my way, to focus her sole attention on me.

"My apologies, Colt. It seems as if you're not the one at fault—this time."

That's all she says before turning her back to me and heading back to the house. Her apology is as contrived as Kennedy's account of what happened. As my mother's silhouette gets farther and farther away, I don't know who I'm angrier at most. I wrap my hand around Ken's and pull her to me.

"You didn't slip. You're lying."

"No, I'm not."

"Yes you are, Ken." Linc backs me up, crossing his arms over his chest, just as adamant.

"I'm not. I swear I'm not. So just drop it, okay?" she insists, pulling her hand away from me.

"Whatever," I bite back, pissed. "Have it your way. But next time, I don't want either one of you to bother with my mother. She's not worth it."

I kick the sand at my feet, fuming at my mother's knee jerk reaction of always blaming me for everything that goes wrong in this family. And if I'm honest, I'm angry at Linc and Ken too for trying to come to my rescue when I know nothing that anyone says or does will ever change how my mother sees me.

"She might not be worth it, but you are," Ken states, wholeheartedly. "I'll never let anyone hurt my friends. No matter who they are."

"Big words for a girl who just swallowed a gallon of lake water because she's too afraid to learn how to swim," I tease, her sass beginning to thaw away my rage.

"Colt's right, Ken. You can't take everyone down who might have it in for us."

"Oh, no?" She cocks a defiant blonde brow, her little fists placed on her hips. "You boys just watch me."

I slam my car door, hands in pockets, and cross the street over to Richfield University's preferred hangout. As per the norm, the place is packed with the sound of baristas filling the pretentious coffee orders of kids that live off ramen noodles in their dorm rooms. It doesn't take me long to spot Linc sitting in a booth by himself. I slide in opposite him, crossing my arms over my chest to protect me from his tongue lashing.

"Go on. Get it over with," I tell him.

He taps the table with his knuckles, his assessing gaze making me feel even more uncomfortable than I already am. His scrutiny has my throat swelling up and my palms sweaty.

Here's the thing.

I don't give a fuck if I'm a living, breathing disappointment to my entire family. I don't give two shits what anyone thinks of me, for that matter. I only value one person's opinion, and that's the man sitting in front of me. If Lincoln can still see some good in me, then I know I'm not as lost as the world perceives me to be.

"Jesus, Linc. Just come out and say it already. I fucked up. I get it, okay?"

He leans back, his lips in a firm straight line.

"Easton is pissed."

"Yeah, I know," I mumble under my breath.

"You need to make things right."

"I know that, too."

He leans forward, his arms spread on the table.

"He thinks you blew up for no reason. But I know you, Colt. You've spent most of your life holding your feelings in, so whatever pushed you over the edge must have been provoked. You want to tell me about it?"

My jaw ticks, thinking that this is all The Society's fault. They're the ones who caused the rift between East and me. They had me snooping around, trying to find things best left unfound. But I can't tell Linc that. I've come this far not to let anyone know what The Society's true intentions are. I can't reveal them now. I feel like I'm deceiving the one person who always has my back, but it's for his own good. One more failed mission and I know my bleeding-heart cousin will turn himself in and make it so the rest of us aren't to blame. Like a samurai who has failed his duty, he'll throw himself on his sword, sacrificing himself for the people he loves.

I can't have that.

Who's there for him, if not me?

"What happened, Colt?" he finally demands.

Since I can't tell him what's really going on, half-truths are all I have for him.

"I found a picture of Scarlett in my father's study. He hid it behind a picture of my mother no less," I explain, purposely leaving out why I was nosing around my father's stuff in the first place.

"I see." He leans back in his seat once more, taking all of this in. "That doesn't mean what you think it does, though."

"Doesn't it?" I scoff.

He lets out a long, exaggerated exhale.

"You should have come to me, Colt, instead of going to the Brass Guild and confronting her like that. I'm serious when I say that Easton is pissed. He loves the ground she walks on and will char it to ash if someone hurts her in any way."

"Yeah, I got the memo," I reply, rubbing my sore jaw. "The fucker laid it on me good."

"That's the second time in as many months that you two have butted heads. Do you know why that is?"

"Because I can't keep my mouth shut?" I goad with little steam.

"No, because you two are too much alike and not in a good way. Whereas he's fire and you're ice, you both have the potential to burn everything you touch."

"Got it, cuz. Stay away from Easton when he's in a mood."

"No, Colt. Apologize to Scarlett. That will be enough for him to cool down. But he won't forgive and forget easily."

"I did that already."

"Good."

I chew the corner of my lip. "So you're not going to ask me why my bastard of a father had a picture of Easton's girl?"

"No, I'm not, because you don't know either. To get the truth, you'd have to actually talk to your father, and we both know you're not going to do that. Besides, Uncle Owen has never been that forthcoming anyway."

"That's the understatement of the year."

"It's just the way he is. We all have our secrets," Linc defends, deflated.

I'm not the least bit surprised Linc is defending my old man. While my mother may have kept a wide berth between herself and my cousin this past year, my father maintained a presence in Linc's life in any way he could—always calling Linc each day to check up on him and taking him out to lunch once a week. Even before my prick of an uncle and Aunt Sierra died, my father always had a soft spot for Linc. He was always his favorite nephew, but then again, compared to Teddy, there wasn't much of a contest. I was never jealous of their friendship, mostly because Governor Crawford was a dick of massive proportions to Linc, and if my father could make my cousin's life easier, I was all for it. Owen Turner might be a disloyal two-timing bastard, but he has never been cruel. Not like Crawford could be.

I hope the fucker is burning in hell.

"So, how is the other thing going? Your time with the Professor, I mean."

"It's been interesting." I grin mischievously, which only ends up gaining another long exhale from him. "What now?" I complain.

"Please tell me you haven't slept with her?"

"Don't get your panties in a twist, cuz. I haven't."

Technically it isn't a lie. I haven't slept with Emma.

"But you want to, don't you?" he accuses, knowing me inside out.

"I'll take the fifth. Answering that question honestly will only get me in trouble." I laugh.

"I thought you lived for getting into trouble," Kennedy interjects, making her presence known and sliding in next to me, all bright smiles. "What did you do now?"

Jefferson takes the seat next to Linc.

"Oh, you know the usual. Pissing people off left, right and center."

"Just another day of being you, then," she teases.

"I heard Easton wants to rearrange your face. Is that what we're talking about?" Jeff asks, taking a sip of his coffee.

Ken snaps her head at me.

"Please don't tell me you tried something with Scarlett?" she questions, horrified.

"Hell no! Scarlett's his girl. I wouldn't touch her with a ten-foot pole. You know that."

"Thank God." She breathes out in relief.

"Why so worried about Scarlett? She doesn't seem to like you very much," I counter inquisitively.

"Yeah, I've been getting that vibe from her, too," she mumbles, concerned, running the tip of her finger over the rim of her macchiato.

"You have to be less intimidating, sis. Otherwise, you'll lose all your friends," Jeff jokes lightheartedly, picking on his twin.

"I don't mean to be with her. I have to put more effort into welcoming her into the fold. Scarlett just needs time. I'm sure once she realizes we're on the same team, she'll warm up to me."

"You mean like you did with Finn's girl? Don't think I haven't noticed you all up in Stone's business," I taunt in amusement.

Their sudden friendship might be mind-boggling to some, but not to me. The Southie is hard as nails, and well, Ken can be downright scary when she wants to be. Both of them have grit and an iron will to go after what they want. Scarlett, on the other hand, is more closed off. Like Easton, that girl keeps everyone at arm's length until she's sure of their intentions.

"I like Stone. She's feisty." Ken laughs.

"She's a pain in the butt but whatever. Walker seems to be happy."

"Now all we have to do is find someone who makes *you* happy." She wiggles her brows at me.

The sudden image of Emma, biting at the end of her pen as she researches some passage in a book, comes to the forefront of my mind. I shrug that shit away before a perceptive Ken reads my inner thoughts.

"I think you have a better chance at setting Lincoln up with someone. Colt doesn't do commitment, do you?" Jeff interjects smugly.

I try to relax my smile and not tell Jeff where he can shove his advice. Unlike everyone else sitting at this table, I've never jumped on the Jefferson bandwagon. I get why he's important to Linc, but he's too much like his old man for me to like. Montgomery Ryland is a power-hungry animal with no scruples, and Jeff is happy to follow his pop's lead.

"Well, well, well. What do we have here?" Tommyboy coos, alerting us to his presence by planting both palms on the edge of our table.

Shit! Doesn't anyone go to class anymore?

I can handle having coffee with one asshole, but two at a time is beyond my tolerance threshold.

"Are my eyes deceiving me, or is this a Dead Presidents' reunion?" He chuckles, amused at himself. "Oh no, wait. It can't be. Last time I checked, Teddy was in the club, not Colt. Little late in trying to step into his shoes, aren't you?"

"Tom," Kennedy begins to chastise, uncomfortable that her fucking fiancé just brought up Teddy's name.

"Don't be like that, babe. I'm just messing with Turner here. He can take a joke, can't you?"

"If by taking a joke, you mean having to look at your face, then yeah, I'm all about having a good laugh."

His smug smile instantly disappears, and as he's about to throw whatever lame-ass witty comeback my way, Linc beats him to the punch.

"I think you should have coffee with your boyfriend somewhere else, Ken."

Kennedy's cheeks flush red as if Linc just slapped her. She doesn't say a word while getting up from the booth and hauling ass out of The Grind.

"I always thought Colt was the heartless one in your group. Guess I was wrong," Jeff says before getting up and following his sister out the door.

Tommyboy just smiles like he won something and strolls away.

"The fuck was that about, Linc?" I ask, astonished.

My cousin has always taken in stride all of Tommyboy's past provocations, so what gives?

Lincoln doesn't open his mouth to explain and instead reaches into his jacket pocket and hands over a pale pink envelope to me. I open it up and immediately understand why he's not acting like himself.

It's a save the date card for Kennedy's wedding.

"It arrived in the mail this morning. It's real now."

Shit.

"I'm sorry, cuz."

The suffering in his ocean eyes physically hurts my insides.

"I knew it was coming. I guess I just wanted to live in denial a little longer."

"You've been living in denial since you were sixteen. It's time, Linc. You gotta move on. Let her go and save yourself the grief."

"I don't know how," he confesses, hanging his head down low, his hands keeping it from falling on the table.

"Yes, you do. Hurt her. Like you did just now."

The self-deprecating laugh that leaves him hurts me just as much as the pain swimming in his eyes.

"I can't. When you finally fall in love with someone, you'll understand why."

For the second time today, Em's whiskey eyes flash into my mind, and I don't know what to make of that unbidden thought.

Chapter 16

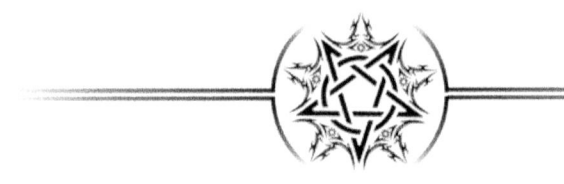

Emma

I sneak small glances at the exquisitely gorgeous man sitting at my side, so engrossed in what he's reading that he is utterly unaware of the captive audience he's gained in me. We've been working together nonstop going on two weeks now, and I have to say his work ethic has surprised me. Although I had my motives in accepting his offer to be my assistant, I was sure that Colt's intentions also had a hidden reason behind them—a more self-serving one. That somehow he would use the time we were spending together to his advantage and worm his way into my bed. I'm not sure if I should be elated he hasn't made one move in that regard or bitterly disappointed.

Not only did I not think he'd ever take this job seriously, but never in my wildest expectations would I have anticipated him being such an enthusiastic and proficient aide. I hate how sexier that makes him to me. It's difficult enough to concentrate on the job at hand with him in the same room, but add his focused determination to my cause, and I'm done for.

"Do you need something?" he asks, breaking up my thoughts while keeping his bowed head on the book in front of him.

"Huh?"

"I can feel your eyes on me, Professor." He smiles, a grin so genuine it takes my breath away.

"I'm sorry," I croak, embarrassed he caught my blatant ogling.

"Don't be. I like it when you look." He smirks, but it fails to have the same swagger and cockiness to it that I've become accustomed to seeing planted on his face.

It's playful and without malice.

And God help me, highly seductive.

"I was just thinking," I begin to say in an effort to do some serious damage control on my libido, "how amazing it must have been for you to have grown up in a house like this."

When his glowing smile falls from his face, I almost kick myself for opening my mouth.

"Nothing amazing about it."

"How can you say that?" I ask in astonishment, my gaze scouring his beautiful home library that puts many of the ones I have visited in my lifetime to shame. "There are literally millions of people who would disagree with you and love nothing more than to live in such splendor as you have."

"Whoever envies my life is an idiot. Didn't anyone ever tell you that money can't buy happiness?"

"Are you saying that you're not happy?"

He thinks about it for a moment, which leaves me even more perplexed.

"No. I don't think I ever have been."

"Privilege has spoiled you," I snap, displeased with his reply.

"I've made you angry, even though I told you the truth."

I raise my face his way, stern and unrelenting.

"How can you say that you're unhappy? Look around you. This home is fit for royalty, and yet you spit on it. Not to mention the fact that you have two living breathing parents and three siblings, yet you continue to be ungrateful."

His smile returns to his lips, only making my brows crease in confusion.

"What?!" I snarl.

"How do you do it?"

"Do what?!"

"Live with so much passion inside of you?"

I chew my inner cheek, his statement taking the wind out of my sails.

"I've never met someone like you. Someone who puts all of herself into everything she does. Your work, your classes, even your opinions."

"A life without passion isn't much of one."

"I agree. You asked me if I was happy, and I told you the truth—my truth. I'm not like you, Em. I don't have that lust for life or drive burning within me. How could I? My whole life I've been given everything I ever wanted, even when constantly reminded that I was unworthy of it. I never had to work for anything you see around you. But I would trade all of it like that," he snaps his fingers to drive the point home, "if I could have just a sliver of your passion."

"It couldn't have been that bad."

"Believe me, it was. Where you see grandeur, I see bars meant to imprison me into being someone I'm not. Where you see privilege, I see the expectation of living up to a name I have grown up to hate. Everyone orders me to be a certain way, and I refuse to be anything but myself. I would rather trade places with someone from the Southside and live a life of squalor than have to endure another minute of trying to live up to impossible expectations."

"Was it always that way growing up?"

"In this house, yes. But I had my friends and my cousin. They were the ones who kept me from drowning in misery. They're my real family."

"You never gave me the impression that you were miserable."

"Looks can be deceiving."

I let his admission sink in as I stare into his jeweled eyes.

"Again, you surprise me. You're not just a pretty face, are you?"

"You think I'm pretty?" He smirks, trying to lighten the tense mood. "Say handsome, at least. I may be a miserable prick, but I've still got an ego the size of the Eiffel Tower."

I laugh.

"Yes. You're very handsome."

Stunning, actually, but I keep that to myself.

"Happy you approve," he replies softly, his eyes falling to my lips.

We go silent for a moment, the taut air around us shifting to something far more alluring. I clear my throat and return my attention to the notes on my screen, praying it's enough to cool both of us down.

The little chuckle he lets out tells me I'm not fooling anyone.

"What about you? I hardly know a thing about you."

"There's nothing much to tell," I reply firmly, straightening my spine.

"I highly doubt that. Just give me one little tidbit of your life. Only fair after what I confessed, don't you think?"

He's right.

He gave me much food for thought. While Colt was unloading all his baggage on me, I was able to confirm my preconceived notions of him. Not only does Colt have no ties to The Society, but he's completely clueless as to who they are.

"Come on, professor. Don't leave me hanging."

He squeezes my knee, sending an electric current to my bloodstream. I pull his hand off me and place it back on his thigh.

"Fine. If you must know, I was raised by my grandfather. My parents died when I was six in a car accident," I tell him, surprising even myself that I chose that bit of personal information to give him.

"I'm sorry."

"Don't be. It's not like I remember much about them anymore."

"Hmm. That's the fucking saddest thing I've ever heard, Em."

"Even sadder than an heir to a billion-dollar dynasty wanting to trade places with a Southie?"

"Touché."

I can't help how my chest swells in response to the heartfelt smile he gives me.

"You've spoken about your grandfather before. He must be very special to you."

I nod, not trusting myself to use my own words when faced with the uncharacteristically compassionate smile he brandishes.

"Does he live back in Boston, where you're from?"

I shake my head. "No. He passed away five years ago. Cancer."

"I'm sorry," he repeats, pulling a stray lock of hair from my bun and placing it delicately back behind my ear.

There is another silent moment between us as we both recognize the suffering in each other's eyes, powerless against letting the other see the stifling despair we've tried so hard to hide.

"I… hmm… we should really get back to work." I clear my throat again before I do something stupid like kiss my student.

Again.

"Of course," he concedes, and this time goes back to his notes and lets me return to mine.

After an hour or so, Colt tells me he's going to fix a snack for us to eat. For someone as narcissistic as he portrays himself to be, he is oddly considerate at times.

While he's gone, I get up from my seat and stretch my legs, walking through the library filled to the brim with first edition books. But as always, my feet lead me to the one place in this library that is still a mystery to me—the closed vitrine bookcase. The leather bound diaries under the pale glass mock me, whispering to me how inside their pages I will finally unlock the secrets I've spent most of my adult life chasing after.

I know Colt will be at least ten to twenty minutes before he returns.

Do I dare?

Yes. Yes, I do.

I take a bobby pin out of my hair and begin to unlock the case. It takes me a few tries, but I jump for joy when I finally hear it click open. I pull out the first ledger on the upper shelf, thinking the beginning is always a good place to start. I flip page after page, ever so carefully, in order not to rip the ancient book. I wish I could take it home with me, but I'm not sure if its disappearance would go unnoticed. Just as I'm thinking of taking the gamble and taking it with me anyway, a particular entry grabs my attention.

Ivy Fox

Ah, my sweetest love, what has become of our humanity?
Everywhere I turn, I see brother fighting against brother, and for what?
Where some seek liberty, the other sees struggle and strife. Yet my eyes only see evil men with blood on their hands in their individualistic pursuits of supremacy.
Who is left to put balance in an otherwise imperfect world, my dearest love?
Who will stand up for those who don't have a voice?
Who cannot defend themselves against the powerful, the ruthless, and cruel.
Something needs to be done, my love.
Wicked men cannot win the war between good and evil.
Only the brave and selfless can give their lives to the cause and guarantee that justice always prevails.
Am I such a creature, or should I stay silently by, while good men fall under the tyranny of others?
I believe I've stumbled across the answer, but I am struggling with what that will entail.
Have me in your prayers, my dearest heart, as your name is always in mine.
Ask that a merciful god bestow such inclination down upon me.
For I fear all mercy has disappeared from my very soul only to be replaced by retribution for the guilty.

Forever lovingly yours,

L. Richfield

"This is it," I whisper, my heart pounding so loudly I miss the clicking sound of high heels approaching me. I close the ledger in my hands and pray the smile on my lips is enough to fool the woman who is currently staring daggers at me.

"You must be the spirited young professor I've heard so much about," Colleen Richfield says in greeting.

Even without introducing herself, no one could mistake the immaculately dressed blonde for anyone other than the lady of the house. If her designer clothes and expensive jewelry didn't out her, the regal air around her does.

"I'm sure anything Colt has said about me is highly exaggerated."

"My son hasn't breathed a word for or against you, Miss Harper," she adds, eyeing me up and down.

"Oh? Then who?"

I straighten my spine as her scrutinizing glower persists in skating over my body, head to toe, instead of answering me.

"It's a pleasure to finally meet you, Mrs. Richfield," I add, finally remembering my manners, even if she has not.

"Hmm," she hums, slowly sauntering toward me. Each click of her heel is in sync with my racing heartbeat.

"Thank you for letting me into your home. Your library has helped immensely with my research."

"So I see," she retorts, only a few inches away from me now.

In her red sole stiletto heels and cream fitted dress, the blonde woman before me doesn't look old enough to have children, let alone four almost full-grown ones. But it's not her ageless beauty that has me frozen to my spot. It's the arctic coldness in her gaze that chills me to the bone.

"Mother." Colt's voice rings out from behind us, and the audible sigh of relief that leaves my lungs echoes through the room.

Colleen doesn't acknowledge her son as she takes the ledger from my hands and places it back into the bookcase. Once she's ascertained the bookshelf is once again locked, she heads toward the door, only stopping for a brief second when she's about to bypass her son.

"Next time, don't leave your friends unattended, dear. You never know what trouble they'll find themselves in."

Chapter 17

Emma

"I must say I was surprised to receive your call."

"You were?"

"Yes. Although I thought our lunch date last time was lovely, I figured it was a one-time sort of situation," Montgomery explains, composed, sipping on his wine. "You didn't seem very invested in us socializing off-campus. Or am I completely off base?"

'Not by a long shot,' I think to myself.

I offer him a meek smile because that's how Montgomery Ryland likes his women—subdued and polite. I've done enough homework on the dean enough to know that about him.

"I'm sorry I made you feel that way. I guess I'm rustier than I thought I was with this whole dating thing. But I do enjoy your company."

"I'm so happy to hear that."

The waiter comes with our order and places the plates in front of us. Unlike last time, I couldn't wait by the phone for him to arrange a meal together. I knew if I called him with a dinner invitation, he would jump at the chance, even if it meant him driving all the way to Charlotte to join me. I made sure to pick a restaurant that had an inviting southern feel to it to placate his expectations of tonight, but avoiding anything along the lines of a candlelit dinner.

I bide my time and talk shop until I can insert what I really want to know.

"I heard a little tidbit about you recently."

"Have you? Doing your background check on me?" he muses, cutting into his steak.

"Nothing of the sort. It just came up in idle conversation with one of the faculty members."

"My name came up in conversation that wasn't regarding work?"

"Is that so hard to believe? You're a highly respected member of the Asheville community. I would assume you were accustomed to having people talk about you all the time." I try and stroke his ego.

"It's been my experience that when your name is in the mouths of some people, not all of them will have kind words to say. But I do admit I'm now intrigued by what you might have heard about me."

"I was told you were born on the Southside. Is that true?"

A smirk plays on his lips as he keeps slicing through his sirloin.

"Does that surprise you?"

"If I'm honest, yes it does. It's rare that someone from that part of town can rise and make a name for himself in Asheville."

He plays with his wine glass as he gazes upon me.

"You're quite right. It was difficult. However, as you can see, not unheard of."

I take a sip of my wine, wondering if every piece of information will be this difficult to obtain. Just like last time, Montgomery measures his words.

"You must have worked very hard to get where you are today," I say at last.

"I won't lie to you. There were plenty of sacrifices I needed to make, and not everyone in this town made it easy for me."

"How so?"

"Let's just say that most of Asheville prefer their poor not to cross the invisible line between Southside and Northside. I guess I was lucky I made it through the crack. Once I got a scholarship to Richfield, they couldn't deny my potential, no matter how many were skeptical of it to begin with."

That's it, Montgomery. We're almost there.

"It was fortunate that you attended such a school then. Both professionally and personally. If I recall, last time you told me you ended up meeting your wife at a Northside soiree."

"You have quite the memory." He frowns.

Uh, oh. Not this shit again.

Come on, dean. You're so close.

Don't go mute on me now.

"I try to memorize important details regarding the people I care about." Just as I intended, this little comment is enough to break through his skyscraper-high walls and get us back to where we need to be. "So tell me, was it love at first sight?" I bat my eyes at him, acting as if I'm desperate to hear a love story rather than the real information I hunger for.

"You really aren't from Asheville, are you?" He chuckles, amused with himself.

No, I'm not Montgomery.

Good thing I'm hiding my Beantown temper since normally I'd have slapped that stupid high and mighty look off your condescending brow by now.

"Does that mean you don't fall in love in Asheville as you do everywhere else in the world?" I counter teasingly, clenching my fist under the table.

"Let's just say the Northside has its particular way of doing things and love hardly ever comes into the equation."

"Hmm, sounds oddly cold to me."

"It can be for some." His eyes darken in displeasure.

"Looks to me as if you might have some experience in the matter."

"Nothing gets past you, does it, sweetheart?"

"I guess you can say that."

Call me sweetheart again and see how well that works out for you.

Breathe, Em.

He's only a means to an end.

If my intel doesn't pan out, I can show him how I truly feel about him.

Until then, suck it up and get the job done.

I can't believe I ever thought this man handsome or appealing in any way. His pompous attitude irks me to no end. At first, I thought him charming intellectually, but the more time I spend time with him, the more I realize his intellect isn't to impart wisdom but to make others feel minuscule for not having the same high IQ. I've witnessed firsthand him ridicule his colleagues with backhanded comments in staff meetings and belittle them in his office. At first I thought him to be a perfectionist like me, only satisfied when the job is done right. But now I see him for what he really is—a narcissistic bully in a suede jacket.

"Are you going to share your experience, or do I have to pry it out of you?"

"As you wish." He laughs before taking another sip of his wine. "As I told you before, I was one of the lucky ones to get accepted into Richfield. My whole life changed the minute I started school. The classes were so demanding and stimulating that I found myself on cloud nine. The world was finally opening its doors to me, where once they had been closed shut in my face. And then my world toppled over once more when one fateful night I catered a party and met a girl."

"Your future wife, you mean," I add.

"Yes, I did meet Dorethea that night, but she wasn't the one I became enamored with. It was Sierra Richfield that left me completely in awe."

"Oh, the plot thickens. I didn't expect that."

Yes, I did. Keep talking, Montgomery.

"Not many people do, but there are a few who still recall that night and like to gossip about it whenever they are short of current rumors to entertain themselves with."

"I take it your crush was one-sided then."

"Quite the contrary. After that night, Sierra and I became inseparable and fell deeply in love. So much so we schemed to leave Asheville and elope. I was ready to lay waste to all my well-laid plans for the future because of one woman's love. But her family had other expectations for her. When a person is born into such a dynasty, your will is not your own. Neither is your heart. I learned the hard way that some families will accept you at their dinner table but not into their family."

"I'm so sorry to hear that. It must have been heartbreaking."

"It was. Her older sister found out about Sierra's plans to run away with me and told their mother. If Colleen Richfield is a cold shrew, then their mother was a heartless wench. They used the fact that I took a summer job down in Atlanta to save enough for our marriage, to conspire and hold a wedding they found more favorable. When I learned that Sierra married Crawford Hamilton, a man ten years her senior, I felt an excruciating pain I wouldn't wish on my worst enemy. I thought my world ended there and then. Even the rumors that Colleen hated Crawford more than she disliked me couldn't mend my broken heart. But luckily, Dorethea came into my life and healed those wounds. And to Colleen's bitter disappointment, I ended up being a permanent fixture in their lives anyway, since my wife was her best friend. It's true, I didn't marry the woman I was in love with, but I had a suitable replacement—a friend and a God-fearing woman who was an excellent mother to my children."

"I can't believe the Richfields would arrange a marriage in this day and age."

"Oh, I can tell you that they still do. I hate to confess to it, but I've also had a hand in doing something similar to my daughter. Crawford must have been at odds with either his wife or sister-in-law for one reason or another when he barged into my home one night wanting to arrange a union between his eldest son and my Kennedy. Out of spite, I conceded to the courtship, knowing Colleen would be furious at the match."

"Do you mean Theodore Richfield Hamilton??" I ask, completely surprised at what he's confessing.

This I did not see coming.

"One and the same, I'm afraid. I hate to talk ill of the dead, but I was relieved my daughter no longer had to continue the romance after he overdosed. I know her heart was never in it, and it pained me to put her in such a position. But my Kennedy has always been a good girl and knows how to live up to my demands. Thankfully this one she didn't have to keep. However, if you ask the Richfields, that will not be how they recall the events. They thought I was trying to get my hands on their fortune yet again. Since I had failed to wed Sierra, Colleen accused me of using my daughter to do it for me by marrying Teddy, as if I would stoop so low."

"That's quite an accusation."

"Yes. But that family always sees outsiders as enemies, unfortunately. Even Kennedy, who was Colleen's godchild, I might add. Cold, unfeeling creatures, the lot of them. Ah, my poor sweet girl. Kennedy hasn't had it easy. My pride has taken plenty away from her. When Teddy died, the poor thing came to me, begging that I talk to her godmother and arrange another Richfield match, thinking that was what I wanted, but I declined. It damn well broke her heart knowing she failed me, even though Teddy's death was no fault of her own. But I made sure she understood that I was done with that family once and for all. I have had my fill of them."

"Kennedy wanted you to arrange a marriage between her and Colt?" I stammer, feeling like someone just punched me in the gut.

"Lord, no!" He laughs. "My daughter might have been enamored with a particular Richfield heir when she was younger, but Colt Turner was definitely not it. Kennedy has more sense than to fall for that pompous jackass. I meant Lincoln Hamilton, his cousin. I told her it was out of the question and began conversations with Senator Maxwell and his son as an alternative for my daughter."

I shake my head, not believing what I'm hearing.

"So your daughter doesn't want to marry Thomas Junior, either."

"As I said, Emma, the Northside does things differently. Every marriage you see here is a business transaction. There is rarely ever love at the foundation of matrimony. Even the high and mighty Colleen Richfield married under those same conditions. I'm sure she never wanted to marry a man like Owen Turner, who is known to have shared the bed with half the women in both the Carolinas, but when the time came, she did her duty and married him anyway, because of his own prestigious family. I heard Colt is even more promiscuous, but as they say, like father like son."

"This is a lot to take in," I choke, flattening the linen napkin over my lap.

"Welcome to Asheville, sweetheart. It's a world all its own. Not many make it here, and those who do end up scarred because of it."

"I see that. So does this mean you no longer have any ties to the Richfields?"

"I'm the dean of their university, a position granted to me while my dear Dorethea still was amongst us. But that is as far as our relationship goes."

"Oh."

"Besides, Colleen never forgave my shortcomings when her best friend was concerned. I must confess, I could have been a better husband to Dorethea. She didn't deserve half the things I put her through early on in our marriage. But when the heart talks, the mind has no say."

"Sierra's recent unexpected death must have been painful for you."

His face turns somber.

"As if my heart had been ripped from my chest."

"Is that the real reason why you never remarried?"

"Again, very perceptive of you. I guess I always thought one day Sierra would gain the courage to leave her husband and find her way back to me, especially after Dorethea died. Unfortunately, I'll never know if one day we could have had our happily ever after. Someone made sure to extinguish her beautiful light before she got the chance. I hope whoever did it gets the death penalty. I'll be sure to be seated in the first row when that happens."

I swallow dryly, not expecting the hatred spewing from him.

"May I offer you some advice, Emma, on how to survive Asheville?"

I nod, trying my hardest not to look too shaken by his vengeful gaze.

"It's all about perception in this town. Everyone has their way of perceiving things here. Don't believe everything you see, don't trust everything you hear, and don't take what's spoken to you as fact. Rarely are the things seen, heard, or spoken the truth."

Speak No Evil

"Understood. See no evil, hear no evil, speak no evil, right?"

"Exactly."

Chapter 18

Colt

I take stock of Emma's stiff demeanor. Her back is ramrod straight, and her neck is so taut she keeps constantly rubbing at its nape to relieve the pressure.

"Any plans for Christmas? It's just right around the corner, you know?" I ask, wondering if idle chit-chat will do the trick of getting her mind off of whatever she's obsessing about.

"I'll probably do what I always do. Read Wuthering Heights and order Chinese," she responds mechanically.

"Nothing says Christmas more than a story of revenge and take-out."

"Hmm."

"Okay, that's enough," I say, closing my laptop and pulling her chair to face me.

"What are you doing?" She gasps in shock.

"Something is eating at you. I can see the wheels in that brain of yours turning nonstop. What's wrong?"

She chews on her bottom lip.

"It's time we continue our research back in Charlotte. I think I've overstayed my welcome with your mother here."

"Why would you say that?"

"Just a hunch."

I follow her gaze to the now empty bookcase where my family's ledgers used to be. Either Meredith or my mother took them for some light reading, it seems. I swear I'll never understand either of them.

"Who's L. Richfield?" Emma questions out of left field, bringing my attention back to her.

"Huh?"

She plants her palms on my knees, leaning in closer to me as if she's about to tell me a secret.

"Who was L. Richfield, Colt? It's important. Please."

My brows furrow more at the desperation in her voice than the question itself.

"I wasn't expecting a pop quiz on my family tree, professor, but I'll humor you. He was the pretentious genius who actually ordered this house to be built as a wedding gift to his wife. My family lived on the Hamilton Estate before then, but I guess my great-great—how many greats it is—grandpa was compensating for either a small dick or a wandering one if he needed all this to make his woman happy. Not that the poor bastard even saw it finished, though. He died in battle during the Civil War. However, legend has it that he didn't die on the battlefield like the history books say but was assassinated down at Fort Macon by his superior officer when he found out dear old Lionel had been slipping confederate secrets to the Yankees."

Emma bows her head in deep contemplation.

"What is this all about?" I ask, covering her hands with mine and giving them a light squeeze.

"Nothing." She slumps back in her seat, pulling her hands away from me.

Okay, enough of this shit.

"You need to relax, Em. You've been working nonstop, and it's getting to you."

"You have no idea what I need," she retorts, rubbing at the tension in her neck.

"Don't I?" I muse, running my hand up and down her thigh.

"Colt, what are you doing?" She snaps her head back at me, her amber eyes piercing into my emerald ones.

"I told you. You need a break. You've been working yourself to the bone. When was the last time you did something just for yourself?" I ask, my hand continuing to creep up her skirt.

She licks her lips, her eyes going half-mast as they follow inch by inch where my hand is leading.

"I don't remember," she whispers.

"Then when was the last time you let someone do something for you?"

"I don't remember that either."

She lets out a soft laugh, but it quickly dies on her lips when my fingers brush against her panties.

"Halloween, perhaps?"

The soft pink that colors her cheeks gives her away.

"You need a release, Em. Just a few minutes where your brain goes blank, and all you feel is the nerve endings of your skin spark alive."

"Sounds tempting." She licks her lips again, my cock instantly hardening, thinking about all the ways I'd love to use that gorgeous mouth of hers.

"Close your eyes," I order, stifling my grin when the good professor does what she's told.

Her breathing stills when I start playing with her clit over her underwear.

"All work and no play is no way to live, Em."

"What makes you such an expert on how I should live?"

"I think after you cum on my fingers, you'll see just how knowledgeable I can be."

Her chest begins to heave as I draw in closer. I only stop when my mouth is right in her ear. Her sun-kissed marigold scent filling my senses and tantalizing me further.

"Open your legs."

She does as she's told, her skirt rising up her thighs. I pull her underwear to the side, happy when my fingers find her pussy already wet for me. My lips never leave her ear as I continue to toy with her wet slit.

"Does that feel good?"

She nods, her lips opening just enough to intake air.

"Tell me how much you need to cum right now."

"So much," she whispers hoarsely, her temple finding purchase on my shoulder for balance.

"Imagine it's my tongue on you. I'm eating you out, and at any moment, someone could come in here and catch us."

It's not a lie. Someone could pop in at any time. But then again, that's half the fun.

"Hmm," she whimpers.

"I'm on my knees while you're holding onto my hair, depriving me of oxygen. But I don't care because your pussy is all the nourishment I need."

She sinks her teeth into her lower lip, and I wish she were biting into mine. Her legs begin to quiver as I add pressure to her clit, while breaching her wet core with my fingers. My free hand grabs the back of her neck, my thumb brushing lightly over her skin. Her nipples harden with each caress, making my mind wonder how they'd taste on my tongue.

"Would you like that? My mouth on you?"

"Yes," she moans again, her arms wrapping around my neck, her fingers tugging at my shorthairs.

"What about my cock, Em? Do you want that, too? Would you like to know how it feels to be properly fucked?"

The way she shifts closer to my fingers tells me she does.

"Tell me you want my cock inside you, and I'll let you cum," I tell her, adding pressure to her swollen clit.

When she doesn't say the words I want to hear, I pull away. She raises her head in astonishment, her eyes burning in both frustration and desire. I lean back, cupping my head with both hands, as I stare her down.

"This could all be much simpler if you just do as you're told."

The fire in her gold eyes takes my very breath away, and when I think she's about to cave and give me what I want, she surprises me by doing the exact opposite. Instead of begging me to touch her, she raises her skirt a little more and widens her legs until I can see her dripping wet pussy in front of me.

Fuck!

She then starts fucking herself with her fingers, her head leaning backwards in ecstasy, as she strums her clit to perfection. I've never been so fucking turned on and pissed off all at the same time.

"Do you think you can do that better than me?" I ask, to which the little temptress nods, keeping to her tempo. I slap her hand away, earning a hostile snarl from her.

My Em is a fierce wild animal when she's horny.

Before she has time to say anything, I insert two fingers inside her core, her eyes going wide at the intrusion.

"You're going to cum by my hand, not yours!" I growl, my lips so close to her mouth I can almost breathe the air out of her lungs. I add another digit, making sure my thumb is always rubbing her clit. I fuck her so hard that all her walls begin to seize around me. She's so fucking tight I think I'm about to pass out with want.

"Now you can cum, Em! And you better fucking cum hard if you know what's good for you!" I order, the sounds of her wet core being viciously abused by my hand, making pre-cum coat the crown of my cock. As Emma's lips part and her body begins to convulse around me, I breach the small gap between us, joining our mouths together. I eat up her cry of ecstasy as she plummets into one of the sexiest orgasms I have ever seen. I pull my lips off hers, her body now sated and limp, and I lick her cum off my fingers.

"Both your pussy and your mouth taste sweet, Em."

"We shouldn't have done that," she murmurs, leaning against her chair while still gasping for air.

"Who says I'm done?"

Her long lashes flutter, her eyes falling to the unmistakable bulge in my pants.

"Sit on my lap."

When she doesn't move, I pick her up by the waist and place her on my lap, cowgirl style.

"That wasn't a question. It was an order."

"I'm not having sex with you," she proclaims steadfastly, her heart beating as loud as my own.

"Are you really going to keep fighting this?"

She refuses to give me an answer, preferring to look away from my relentless gaze. I grip her chin and pull her whiskey eyes back on me, where they never should have left in the first place.

"Fine, have it your way. You want to fight this? Go for it. As long as you know that this," I point between her chest and mine, "is a done deal. It's happening, Em. So make your peace with it because sooner or later, you will be riding my cock to oblivion, and you know it."

"No, I won't," she states flatly, but the little she-devil begins to rub her pussy on my junk.

"Yes, you will," I choke out, loving the feel of her on top of me.

"Keep telling yourself that," she taunts as her hand goes to my zipper and pulls it down.

My breath catches in my throat as I watch her deft fingers release my swollen cock from its confinement. The touch of her warm hand alone sends shockwaves throughout my system, but it's when she places my cock just at the edge of her slit that I lose it.

"You think you can play with me?" I slur, gripping her ass cheeks to speed up her tempo.

"I think you're all about the game, Colt. You love the chase. Isn't that what this is all about?"

"That all depends on who I'm chasing," I groan when my cock slides perfectly against her folds.

"What are you chasing now?" She breathes onto me, her teeth pulling on my bottom lip.

"Right now? Fucking restraint not to fuck you raw," I confess, fisting her skirt.

She lets out a soft moan, her lids falling of their own accord before capturing my mouth in the sexiest kiss a woman has ever given me. Emma keeps stroking my cock with her bare pussy, the intoxicating smell of sex in the air just adding fuel to the fire she lit inside me.

"Em," I groan when I feel I'm seconds away from cumming.

"How badly do you want to cum right now?" she taunts, turning the table on me. "How much do you want to fuck me right here and now?"

"Shit! So fucking much."

Her shallow breathing reaches my ear before she bites my lobe, making my eyes roll to the back of my head.

"This," she whispers huskily while her pressured strokes pick up speed, "is all you'll ever get."

I pull her hair back with such force she has no other option but to look me in the eye.

"If I wanted, I'd be nine inches deep inside you right now," I growl, pissed.

"Are you saying you don't want me?"

"You know I do."

"But you won't take what's not given to you, will you?"

"No," I seethe, so fucking hot for this woman I can't even think straight.

"Hmm. Whoever thought there would be a gentleman under that cocky bravado after all?"

"I've had enough of your mouth, Em."

"Shame. I haven't had enough of yours."

She goes back to kissing me stupid, and God help me, but it's her velvet tongue entwined with mine that pushes me over the edge. My cum spills all over her bare pussy, while Emma continues to use and abuse my cock until she reaches her release. I hold her close, our temples kissing as the vibrant colors of our orgasms begin to fade away, reality trickling back in and returning us to the dull world that awaits.

Emma gets off my lap, straightens her skirt, and begins to pack her stuff up off the table.

"What are you doing?"

"What does it look like? You're right. I do need a break. We'll start fresh tomorrow afternoon at the Charlotte Library."

"You're leaving?"

Her eyes fall onto my still half-mast cock, the very one that bobs to life when it feels her eyes on it.

"Yes. I think we've done enough for today. Don't you?"

She arches a knowing brow at me, and to my utter frustration, leaves me to tend to my stiff dick on my own, all the while wondering who is playing who here.

Chapter 19

Colt

"Mr. Turner, I'd like to see you in my office after class," Emma states the next morning as I'm about to leave her classroom.

"Is that so?"

"I think we need to make some things clear," she adds, keeping her explanation vague solely for the benefit of the other students who are still milling around her classroom.

"Sure. I have class until two."

"That's fine. I will see you after." She dismisses me with a curt nod.

Suffice it to say that the rest of my day goes to shit. I already know what Emma wants to talk to me about. It'll be something along the lines of what happened yesterday afternoon at my house being wrong and that she won't let it happen again.

Fuck that.

I told her this only ends one way. It's not my fault she's as immovable as a brick wall. Once my last class is finished, I rush over to her office, intent on reminding her of that fact.

"Come in," she answers after I've knocked on her door.

Even her voice just uttering the word 'come' in any manner has me hard already.

I close the door behind me, making sure to lock it without her knowing.

"Mr. Turner, please have a seat. I'll be right with you," she adds coolly, shuffling some papers furiously around her desk. It's obvious she's buying time to get her lecture down pat.

"We're back to Mr. Turner, I see?" I can't help but tease.

"I think it best. It will help immensely with setting some clear boundaries between us."

And here it is—the talk.

Usually, I'd be bored with the predictability of it all, but one thing I've learned is that Emma Harper is anything but dull. She wants this as much as I do. She either needs more time to process it all or hates that someone like me got under her skin. I've got to say I know the feeling.

Instead of grabbing a seat as she requested, I walk over toward her desk.

"And what boundaries are those, professor?"

"Colt, please sit down," she says, frustrated, taking her catlike reading glasses off and slamming them onto a pile of papers.

"I think I'm good right here," I tell her, leaning on the edge of the desk in front of her. When she crosses those long damn legs of hers, my cock twitches in anticipation of seeing my plan through. Emma shakes her head, trying to rein the thin ribbons of her sophisticated composure back in.

"I'm your teacher, Colt. And because I am, I should have dealt with things very differently yesterday. I apologize for letting my urges get the better of me. It won't happen again, and if you feel you need to report the incident to the school, I completely understand. I'll be more than happy to write a letter to the dean myself and explain my wrongdoings."

"What we did wasn't on college grounds, professor. I don't think Dean Ryland or any other asshole has a say in the matter. You were tense and needed to cum. I was happy to oblige." I wink mischievously, throwing in my wolfish grin.

"You make it sound like it was a business transaction."

"Not a transaction, but more like one friend looking after another. Although, I do feel like you got the better end of the deal. You got to cum twice, while I've been suffering ever since."

I cup my hard cock in my hands to drive the point across, her eyes falling straight to my erection.

"I think you should make it up to me."

"Is this your subtle attempt at blackmail?"

"I'm not here to strong-arm you into anything. I'm just telling you that the taste of your pussy is still on my lips, and my cock is envious."

"I can't have a serious conversation with you when you are acting like this," she counters, turning her head away from me.

"Good because I didn't come here to talk," I admit before unlatching my belt buckle.

"Colt, don't you dare," she protests when she hears me pulling down my zipper.

"Nah, professor. The time for talking is over. I told you before, I don't want to talk. But I do want that mouth of yours," I tell her as my cock springs free.

Her beautiful golden eyes turn into liquid fire the minute they land on my impressive hard length.

"You can keep your pretty ass right there if you want, Em. But I'm cumming while staring at that mouth of yours and imagining your lips around my cock. I haven't been able to think of anything else since you first started teaching here anyway, and that's the truth."

She clenches her thighs together while I wrap my hand around my shaft and begin to pump it up and down. I caress her cheek as she vigilantly keeps her attention on me, desperate hunger in her eyes.

"Do you want a taste?"

She doesn't say anything, but the way her nipples go hard as diamonds through her thin blouse tells me she does.

"Are you afraid someone might come in?"

She lifts her head to look into my eyes instead of giving me an answer.

"Let them. I'm sure half of your students have beat their cock into submission numerous times while thinking of you. They just never had the pleasure of having your eyes on them as they go about it."

"Is that what you like? Me watching you?"

"With you, Em, I've learned to be happy with whatever I can get. It's a fucking humbling feeling, that's for goddamn sure. So if I can't have your mouth, then this is enough."

My dick doesn't necessarily agree with the words spilling from my lips, but the rest of me knows I'm telling her the truth. She licks her lips, and I watch with bated breath as her hand reaches out to mine. When her fingers lightly caress the crown of my cock, I hiss.

Fuck.

"See what you do to me?"

"I'm not doing anything. You're the one making yourself hurt," she taunts, her hand completely covering mine, following the slow tempo of my strokes.

"Emma," I growl.

"What?"

"If you don't get on your knees and wrap those pretty lips around my cock in five seconds, I'm fucking you in this office. I don't care who hears or sees it!"

She bats her eyelashes at me and leans her head down, her tongue teasing my swollen crown. Another hiss leaves me, my hand letting go of my cock so that my fingers can weave themselves into her silky raven hair. I grasp her scalp as she takes me into her hot mouth, so deep inside I almost cum.

Fuck.

"I gave you an order, professor. Don't half-ass this shit, and get on your knees."

The way she squirms in her seat tells me the naughty professor loves it when I'm the one calling the shots—or at least when she's so inclined. When her bare knees fall to the floor, never once taking her mouth off me, I can't help but praise her.

"You're so fucking beautiful, Em. You take my damn breath away sometimes just by looking at you. But like this? On your knees, sucking me off, you are a fucking vision."

I've never been one to say shit like this when I'm with a woman, but fuck if Emma doesn't bring out the closeted romantic in me.

She sighs around my cock, taking all of me in until I feel myself hitting the back of her throat. I know I'm bigger than your average guy, and that most women shy away from sucking me off since they can only handle so much.

But not my Em.

She swallows me whole, sinking her nails into my ass cheeks to push me further inside her.

"Jesus fuck, Em," I rasp, my fingers digging into her scalp to keep me centered.

She's barely even started, and already she has me weak in the knees, bursting to cum.

"You like my cock in your mouth, don't you, professor?" I tease, hoping to gain some power back since it's blatant that she's the one in charge even in her submission.

Her thighs rub up against each other as dark mascara tears run down her gorgeous cheeks. I have never wanted to fuck a woman more than Emma Harper at this very moment. But my determination to finally screw her brains out is taken away when she begins to hum around my cock, making it impossible not to cum down her throat. I pull at her hair, forcing her to take every last inch of me, and in three pumps she has me cumming.

Jesus.

She pulls back, licking her lips, her amber eyes half-mast as they meet mine. I don't have to touch her to know her body is on fire, needy for me. I pick her up from the floor and sit her ass down on the desk, going right to my haunches. Like the ravenous animals we've become, she raises her skirt while I open her legs wide, placing her stiletto heels on the edge of her desk—her pink pussy ready to greet me.

"No underwear today, professor?"

"No," she whimpers.

"How come?"

"I'd end up ruining them. It's been a nasty reoccurrence lately."

I smirk and begin to caress her pussy lips with the back of my knuckles.

"Are you saying I'm at fault?"

"Can't you tell?"

Taking the challenge on, two digits break the seam of her core, finding her utterly drenched. I stand up to grab the nape of her neck and pull her to me so she can look me in the eye.

"Did you like me fucking your mouth, Em? Is that what got you so wet?"

"Yes," she sighs.

"Did you like swallowing my cum?"

"Yes."

Fuck this woman.

I kiss her madly as one hand fondles her pussy while the other keeps her still by moving to the base of her throat. I release her from our brutal kiss and kneel before her like she deserves and begin to lick her till my heart's content. Her sweet nectar drives me insane, making blood swell my cock yet again and readying it for an encore performance. But the blowjob was too much for Emma, and before I can devour her like I want to, Emma cums on my lips. I rise to my full height and capture her mouth in mine until we're both out of breath with just one kiss.

"So what was that you were saying, professor? Something about boundaries?"

She arches her brow accusingly, but it hardly has any effect since I'm still taking in how breathtaking she looks in her afterglow.

"This can't happen, Colt." She tries again. "We have to stop this before we get to the point of no return."

"Stop? Oh, professor, I haven't even started with you yet."

Chapter 20

Emma

I try to concentrate on my notes as Colt reads over his. He's been nothing but professional since the minute he walked into the library. I should be grateful that at least one of us has their head screwed on straight. While his mind is focused on the work at hand, honestly invested in my research, all I can think about is his mouth on mine—the taste of him dancing on my tongue.

This is wrong, and I know it.

I could lose my job over this.

Or something far more precious like my stupid heart.

It's not as if I haven't had students come onto me before. Since I came to teach at Richfield, hardly a week has passed by that some overly confident student doesn't try their luck in asking me out. They are easy enough to dismiss. Colt Richfield-Turner on the other hand, not so much.

I pull at my necklace, my skin instantly heating up with memories of him ordering me to my knees. I clear my throat at the seductive thought, his head immediately snapping in my direction.

"Everything okay there, Em?" he asks in his deep southern drawl.

Dear Lord Almighty, but why does he insist on calling me that?

Doesn't he know what it does to me?

Knowing Colt, he's doing it on purpose.

"I... um... I'm just going to check these three books out. Be back in a minute."

He nods, throwing me one of those panty-melting smiles, resulting in me getting up out of my seat in quick haste. I don't need any of these books at this precise moment, but I definitely need a breather from Colt's close proximity.

When I agreed to let him be my research aide, it was with the sole intention of using him for his knowledge—not his body. I wanted to coax out as much information as I could about his family from the arrogant heir, thinking he'd be more than willing to boast about his origins. I never imagined he felt so miserable being born into such a legacy. My initial assessment of him has been slowly disintegrating with each passing day we've spent together. And where once I thought him to be a shallow, empty hole of a man, I now find him complex, with too many layers for me to decipher what is real and what is pretense he uses to protect himself.

If all of this didn't spell trouble for my unequipped heart, his fearless dedication to my book has left me both impressed and enthralled that somehow my life's work—and my grandfather's—has resonated so deeply with him. Colt has always given me the impression that everything either bored or annoyed him somehow. I assumed he was perfectly content in sleepwalking through his entire life without actually feeling passionate about anything besides his looks and whichever new conquest he could get into his bed. To see him now so diligently helping me in my cause, working long hours side by side with me, and forgoing all other social commitments is highly seductive to my workaholic nature.

Before we started these sessions, I'd bet the only way Colt would have ever been convinced to see the inside of a library would be with the understanding he would be hooking up with some college girl in the dead languages section.

Who am I kidding?

Knowing Colt, he'd probably demand a whole orgy of women to get him to pass through those doors. Not that I'd be surprised if anyone ever told me that had indeed happened once upon a time.

It's just who he is.

He oozes sexual magnetism. It bleeds from his pores even when he puts up the facade of being cold and apathetic. Brave is the woman who can resist such charms because clearly, I'm not as resilient.

When the lights begin to blink repeatedly in the library, I look at my watch and confirm it's closing time. Disappointment hits me like a slap in the face because Colt didn't instigate any intimacy tonight.

Emma, get a grip. He's a child.

My eyes rake over his body as I make my way to our table.

Colt may be in his early twenties, but he's no child.

He's all man—broody, charismatic, Adonis-like perfection of a man.

I start packing up my stuff, as does the man I've been obsessing over. Once we have gathered everything, we walk to the parking lot, my compact car parked next to his.

"Well, goodnight," I stammer, opening my car door.

"Goodnight, Em."

He leans in and places a chaste kiss on my cheek, my shoulders instantly slumping that this is as far as he'll go tonight. I turn around to unlock my car when a twisted epiphany hits me.

Why am I resisting this?

I already started this insanity the minute I let him touch me on Halloween night. Sure, I probably deserve to be put into a straightjacket for what is clearly lust-filled madness over one of my students—a Richfield heir no less—but who says I can't enjoy a little bit of crazy in my stagnant life?

Colt's broad back is turned to me as he searches for his car keys in his pockets. I grab his forearm, making him turn around. I wrap my arms around his neck and go to the balls of my feet and kiss him. His surprise only lasts a few seconds before he deepens our kiss. His hands grab my ass, pulling me to rub against his engorged cock. He picks me up in the air, my legs instantly wrapping themselves around his waist, as he continues to devour my mouth.

"I've wanted to do this all night," he mumbles. "It fucking took you long enough."

I pull at his hair so I can kiss him again, my core desperately emptied without him.

The small glow coming from the streetlight illuminates us both, the expression on his face just as feral as my own. He places my feet on the ground and turns me swiftly around, hiking up my skirt.

"Put your hands on the hood."

"Colt," I whisper, doing exactly as he demands while looking around the parking lot to see if anyone can see us.

But if I expected a response or any vocalized concern about us being watched, he doesn't give me one. Instead, the next sound I hear is him unzipping his pants, followed by a foil packet being ripped open.

"Do you want me?"

God yes.

I nod.

He sinks his teeth into my neck from behind, sucking on my flesh as he rubs his cock on the crack of my ass.

"How much do you want me, Em?"

I bite into my lower lip, unable to stifle the desperate whimper that comes out. His hands go to my wet pussy, the evidence of my want right at his fingertips.

"Answer me. How much do you want me right now?"

"So much."

"Do you want all of me? This is it, Em—your last chance to tell me to stop. Tell me. Tell me you want me."

"Yes," I beg, not able to fight it anymore.

"Then you have me," he groans before thrusting his huge cock inside me.

"Oh, my God!" I yell, my core stretching invitingly to accommodate huge length.

"Almost there, baby," he grunts, trying to go slowly, aware that his size is too much to take in all at once.

"Don't call me that," I wail softly, loving how full I feel right now.

He chuckles in my ear as he enters in further, my eyes squinting at the delicious pain of it all.

"No baby. Got it."

When his cock finally sinks to the hilt, we both moan out. Colt grows serious as he starts to thrust inside me, his lips latching onto the crook of my neck.

"Jesus, this pussy, Em. If I knew this is what it felt like to fuck you, I'd have done it sooner."

"Don't stop," is all the self-control I have to say.

Colt grips onto my hips as my nails scratch his car's paint job to keep me steady. He fucks me hard and ruthlessly, taking weeks, months, years of frustration out on my body. All I can do is take his punishment, my teeth slicing into my bottom lip to keep me from screaming out in utter rapture. My temple meets to the hood as well, bending my body halfway so he can drive deeper inside me. When he uses this position to his advantage, the head of his cock hitting that one spot inside me that has eluded all other men before him, all my futile attempts to keep quiet disappear.

"Colt!" I scream out, my entire body shaking, threatening to explode at any moment.

"Em," he rasps raggedly, wrapping my hair around his wrist, pulling it back so he can eat my wails with his mouth.

The symphony of our bodies brutishly slapping against each other only heightens my need to come undone. Unable to contain it any longer, I wail out my release, Colt's punishing onslaught increasing my orgasm tenfold.

"Em!" he growls just before following me over the cliff, his tongue seeking refuge with mine. He promptly turns me to face him, slamming me back against the car and kissing me with such need, I almost combust again. When he ends the kiss, I'm left in a pool of desire.

"Is your place close by?" he asks, rearranging my skirt before taking care of his condom.

I nod.

"Good. Get in the car, Em."

A gorgeous smile plants itself on his lips, making my whole body quiver. He takes me by the hand and walks me over to the other side of his Bugatti. He opens the door for me, fastening my seat belt and brushing his lips against mine before he rushes around to his side. We take the five-minute drive to my place in silence. The only sound I can focus on is my erratic heartbeat as Colt keeps squeezing my thigh with his hand. Once he's parked the car on my street, he leans in to unbuckle me.

"You really are an extraordinary woman. I'll make sure to remind you of that tonight."

My heart jumps up to my throat. I grab his wrist on reflex before he opens the car door.

"If we do this, we need ground rules," I tell him, trying to minimize the repercussions of this situation somehow.

The smile he throws me is just as addictive as the man himself, a silent warning that I don't hold a shot in hell in denying him anything anymore.

"Whatever you need, Em."

The gentle way he says my name obliterates whatever defenses I have left. He gets out of the car, opening the door for me and when he pulls me gently by the hand out of my seat, hesitation digs its ugly claws back into me.

"We're being reckless. *I'm* being reckless. Maybe you should just leave, Colt."

"I could do that. But I won't," he whispers ever so tenderly, leaving just a tiny sliver of space between us. "You fought against this long enough. Just let go, Em. I'll catch you. I promise."

"I wish I didn't believe you."

"You're scared," he hushes, caressing my cheek with his knuckles.

"Aren't you?"

"No."

"You're young. *Too young*. You have youth to use as an excuse for your rash choices."

"Em, look at me."

My eyes soften as I stare at him.

"Age has nothing to do with what's happening here. I want you. I can't make it any clearer than that. Now, do you still want me? Or are you going to let a little thing like fear get in the way of this? Of us?"

"There isn't an us. This is just sex," I lie, wanting to kick that amorous notion as far away from me as possible.

Colt lets out a chuckle, entwining his hand in mine and placing a gentle kiss on my wrist.

"You're laughing at me again."

"No, babe. I'm not. I'm laughing at how similar we both are. The whole ride over, I kept telling myself this is just sex, too. Guess we're both liars."

My brows crease in the middle of my forehead.

"Don't call me babe, either."

The broad smile that splits his face in two has butterflies taking flight in my stomach, turning me into a hot irrational mess of a woman.

"Got it. No babe and no baby. Any other requests?"

I shake my head.

"Good. Now, are you going to invite me in, or will I be driving back to Asheville tonight?"

I tighten my hand around his and start walking toward my apartment building. I don't even have to look at him to feel his triumphant smile kiss my skin. The five-story ride up in the elevator crackles with nervous electricity, promising that after tonight nothing will ever be the same again. Once we've reached my floor, I walk over to my apartment, my hand trembling so hard I can't even get the key in the lock.

Get it together, Em.

It's just sex.

It's just meaningless, hot sex.

Seeing the difficulty I'm having in getting into my goddamn apartment, Colt gently takes my house key away from me and opens my door on his first try. My back is flush against the wall while Colt takes center stage in my living room. Compared to his home, my apartment isn't lavish or exquisite, yet somehow he looks more in his element here, amongst my humble things, than he did in the place he grew up in. My heart drums madly inside my chest as he strolls over to my bedroom, not even waiting for me to lead him there. Like a lamb to the slaughter, I follow the sinful wolf all too willingly, counting down the seconds until his sharp teeth sink into my skin and eat me whole.

Colt is already seated at the edge of my bed when I reach my room's doorway, palms face down on either side of him, legs sprawled wide.

"So fucking beautiful," he praises as his eyes skate down my body.

My breasts feel heavy from his lingering gaze, my core clenching in anticipation of a repeat of our parking lot rendezvous.

"That outfit suits you, Professor. But I want it off you now," he commands, chewing the corner of his mouth.

I keep the small distance between us as I begin to unbutton my blouse. My eyes never leave his as I pull the satin material off my shoulders, dropping it to the floor, my gray pencil skirt following right behind it. I slip out of my heels, his emerald eyes sparkling as I unlatch the hook of my bra.

"Is this better?" I ask defiantly, letting him take in every inch of my naked form.

"Come here." He slaps his knee.

I walk over to him, his greedy hands immediately reaching out and pulling me hurriedly against him. His gaze continues to rake over my body, considering all his options, making me ache for him even more. Although I'm impatient to feel the weight of his body on top of mine, Colt seems to have other plans in mind.

In the parking lot, the way we fucked was fast and intense. Now it's clear he wants to savor each second, make each caress and kiss count for something, prolonging this magnetic tug and pull between us a little longer before diving in and succumbing to its power.

And I'll let him torture me since I'm no longer able to resist him anymore.

I gasp out when one of his hands grips my breast, pinching its nipple with his fingers. He pulls me to settle on his knee, his mouth sucking on my tender nub. His teeth scrap over my sensitive bud in a way that has me seeing stars. I run my fingers through his lush, dark hair, loving the feel of it against my skin. His mouth switches to my other breast, lavishing it with the same care and devotion as its twin. I'm gasping for air by the time his hand brushes my wet folds.

"So fucking beautiful," he mumbles to himself as he kisses his way from my neck up to my cheek and then my lips. I let the kiss wash away any scrap of lingering logic I may still have that tells me what we are doing is wrong. It can't be. Because in this very minute, all of this feels too right to be condemned. I kiss him fervidly, mimicking his hungry tongue stroke for stroke, my core drenched with desire. He plays with my clit, adding pressure until he has me whimpering and gasping for air.

Playing my body like his own personal ragdoll, his two brawny hands lift me off his lap to settle my legs around his waist. Colt stands up only to lay me down with care on my mattress, never once breaking our heated kiss. I place my hands on his chest to push him away, and he obeys my command not to come any further.

"Take off your shirt," I command.

His predatory grin comes out again as he pulls himself off me and back to his feet. He unbuttons his shirt, dropping it lazily to the floor, revealing mouthwatering six-pack abs that I fully intend to lick all over before the night is done.

"Now your pants."

The devious tug to his upper lip has me biting my inner cheek. I grope my breasts with each hand, captivated by the show he's giving me. Colt pulls his pants down, black briefs with a noticeable bulge underneath them.

"Do you want me to go on?" he teases.

"Yes."

He pulls down his boxers, kicking them off to the other side of the room, his cock bobbing freely and hitting his navel.

He really does have it all.

Looks, wealth, and a cock that would make most men weep with envy.

He strokes his steel shaft with his hand, his eyes searing through me.

"Open your legs, Em. Let me see how wet you are for me."

I lay on the bed, my elbows pulling me up as I widen my legs so he can have a good, hard look at what he's done to me. He groans when I begin to play with my lower lips.

"Taste yourself. Tell me how sweet you are."

I do as he says, humming in delight as I suck each finger.

"I don't believe you," he grumbles. "I need to see and taste for myself."

Going to his knees on the bed, he pulls me closer to him, a loud wail ripping out of my throat when his mouth meets my pussy. In long, hard strokes, he laps me up, my heated skin singing in utter bliss. I hold onto his hair for dear life and keep his head exactly where it always ought to be, right between my thighs.

"Fuck," I growl, which elicits an amused snicker from him.

But he doesn't quit. Only when I cum on his tongue does he slow his brutal assault.

"Lay back, Em," he orders.

I crawl up the mattress on my elbows, waiting impatiently for him. He looms over me, nibbling his way up my body until his mushroom head reaches my core.

"Condom," I yell at him, slapping his shoulder, so he can give me enough room to open my bedside table drawer.

He laughs, picking up a condom from my stash and dropping it next to the pillow beside my head.

"In due time," he taunts, sliding his impressive length against my slick folds. The crown of his cock rubs against my clit so deliciously that by the time he gets the condom, I'm all nerves and live wires.

"Put it on me," he orders, placing the edge of the sealed square in my mouth.

I rip through the wrapper with my teeth and then sheath him with it. I want to taste him again, but the need to have him stretch me is all I can think about. When his cock breaches inside me in one fast thrust, we both cry out in elation.

"Fuck."

"Jesus, Em. How can you still be this fucking tight?" he grunts, thrusting deeper inside me.

My nails dig into his shoulder blades as he starts to slowly fuck me senseless, his measured tempo making me lose my goddamned mind. His leisured thrusts, combined with the way he keeps kissing me with such fervor, decimate all my walls. I've never felt this full before—this wanted and desired.

This is not just sex.

This is adoration.

"Harder," I beg, wanting to be back on familiar ground, one that I can control.

"Fuck," he grunts, driving in deeper.

All my senses are consumed with this man as he pounds into me with more than just his hard cock.

"Harder."

Frustrated tears fall to my pillow, unable to keep my heart from becoming entangled in our reckless lovemaking.

"Colt, please."

"I know, baby. I know," he whispers, licking my tears with his tongue.

In my tormented lust-filled haze, I don't even have the will to reprimand him for the nickname. Grasping that this has become too much for me to take, Colt pulls my legs upward, wrapping them around his shoulders. He begins ramming into me with such force I forget my own name, let alone the unnamed feelings bubbling up inside me.

"That's it. Let go, Em. I got you. I got you."

Just as he calculated, in this position, composed thought becomes an impossible feat. All I can do with my ankles locked behind his neck is surrender to the myriad of sensations coaxed out by being wholly dominated.

What finally pushes me to the point of no return is Colt's ragged breathing against my calf and kissing it with the same passion as my lips. The loud wail that erupts from my chest vibrates throughout the room, my core clenching around him in a vice grip, ensuring that we both cum simultaneously. I hear Colt call out my name as he pounds into my pussy once more before shattering on top of me. The blinding light that washes over my body and soul is so devastatingly profound that in my head, I reach out to grab hold of it before it vanishes into thin air.

And in my euphoria, all the stunning colors that took over seconds ago fade into a never-ending black.

Chapter 21

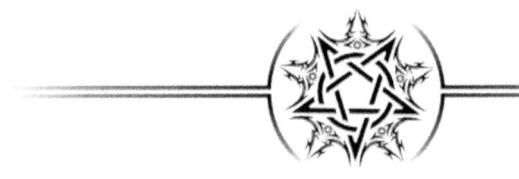

Emma

I'm not sure how long I've slept for, but when my eyes finally slide open, a sense of inner peace flutters through me. No longer conflicted over what transpired in my bedroom with my student of all people, I inch in closer to the crook of Colt's neck, who is lightly running his fingers up and down my back.

"There you are," he coos once he realizes I'm awake. "You fell asleep on me, Em."

"Don't sugarcoat it, Colt. I blacked out. You can say it."

"Nah. It would sound too much like bragging." He chuckles, brushing his nose against mine before kissing the tip.

"What about you? Did you sleep at all last night?" I ask, rubbing the remaining vestiges of sleep away from my eyes.

"Not really, no."

"Why not?"

"Nothing you have to worry about." He offers me a soft smile.

I stroke his chest while Colt moves his feather-light touch from my back to run his fingers through my hair. Needing to have a clear view of his face, I move on top of him. I purchase my chin on his chest as he plays around with a lock of my hair.

"Are you going to tell me to go home now, Em?" he asks, his jade-colored eyes as clear and tranquil as a green meadow on a spring day.

I shake my head.

"Why not?"

"You know why."

"I do." He smirks. "Doesn't mean I don't want to hear you say it."

"Because you were right. I'm done fighting this."

His jeweled eyes take on a whole new shine, mirroring the complex feelings I refuse to give name to.

"Hmm," he hums, his thumb now trailing over the outside of my cheek.

"What?"

"I like when you're the first face I wake up to in the morning."

"Is that supposed to mean something?"

"Does it have to mean anything for it to be true?"

"No," I reply softly, understanding him perfectly, all the while wishing I didn't.

He lets out another heartfelt chuckle, warming my insides with the sound alone.

"How about a shower?"

I nod, thinking that preferable to continuing this line of conversation.

He pulls the sheet off us, picking me up into his arms and walking us over to my ensuite. He places me on my feet to turn on the showerhead, and once he's happy with the temperature, we both slip inside. He pours some liquid soap into his palms and begins to wash my aching limbs as the water cleans last night's sweat off our bodies.

"That feels good," I confess, closing my lids to enjoy his tender ministrations.

Once he's finished washing my body, he turns me around to face the shower tiles and moves onto my hair next, kneading my scalp until I'm so relaxed I run the risk of falling asleep standing up. The only thing that keeps me alert is his bobbing hard-on pressed against the crack of my ass.

You can't beat the stamina of a twenty-two-year-old, I guess.

Once he's finished rinsing all the shampoo from my hair, I turn around to face him.

"My turn," I order, switching places, so he's the one under the falling stream of water.

His Adam's apple bobs furiously as I wash every speck of his body, from his luscious, dark brown hair down to his taut, hard abs to his impressive muscular forearms. Once his torso is fully clean, I go to my knees.

"Em," he supplicates as I massage from his calves up to his thick, strapping thighs. It's when I get to his cock, and wrap my hand around the base of it, that he hisses out.

"Jesus Christ, woman, you're fucking killing me."

I continue pumping away at his sturdy length, his cock swelling in my grip. The water drips down his body, rinsing the last of the soapsuds away and leaving every inch of him smelling like a field of marigolds, and yet retains that masculine scent that is his and his alone. Unable to resist any longer, my tongue teases the crown of his cock before my mouth fully wraps around it. He mumbles incoherently, his fingers latching onto my wet hair, pushing my throat down his long, stiff shaft. I suck him with all my might, my eyes prickling with tears as the tip of his mushroom head hits the back of my throat.

"Look at me," he orders.

My eyelids flutter under the pounding water above, doing everything in my power to keep my eyes fixed on his while my tongue licks the angry vein on the underside of his cock, before circling my mouth around it once more. My eyes are still on him when he reaches under my arms, lifting me up and turning me over, kicking my feet to spread apart.

"Hold on to the wall."

"Colt," I begin to protest, since we didn't bring a condom with us.

"Fuck that, Em," he growls, as if reading my thoughts, grabs my throat from behind so my back is slammed up against his chest. "Do you want me?"

"Yes." I squirm.

"Then I'm fucking you raw. I'm clean. I swear on my life that I am. I won't cum inside you if you don't want me to, but this is happening."

"I'm on the pill," is my automatic reply because right now, all I want is to have him inside me.

No, not want.

Need.

Like a burning flame that needs oxygen to survive, I need Colt to spark life back into my body in the only way he knows how.

We hold our breath as his raw length thrusts inside of me.

"Oh, my God!"

"Holy fuck!"

Like this, I won't be able to keep from cumming much longer.

"Colt!"

"I don't know what turns me on more. Fucking you like this, skin to skin, or that you're about to cum just because you're wet and needy after sucking me off."

"Oh, God," is all I say as he pounds into me like he wants to split me open.

I slam my open palms against the tiled wall, unsuccessfully trying to contain the explosion that inches closer to detonation. Colt peppers my shoulder and neck with butterfly kisses, a complete contrast to the way his cock is turning me inside out.

"Em," he whispers in agony, so close to falling off the precipice himself.

With my name sung from his lips, I hand over the reins of my resistance and let him push me off the edge, knowing he'll be here to catch me.

"So fucking beautiful. I never get tired of seeing this look on your face," he cajoles before shutting my mouth with one hard kiss. "Now on your knees, Em," he growls afterward, the feral beast back in his eyes.

I do as he says, licking my lips as he strokes his cock in front of me. It doesn't take long for jets of cum to find their way onto my chest. With his fingers, he spreads his release over the swell of my breasts and then shoves his thumb through the seal of my mouth so I can lick it clean. Once he can't handle the sight of me sucking his finger any longer, he pulls me back up, only to deliver a fiery kiss that leaves me weak in the knees. He pulls me in close, hugging me to him while kissing every inch of my face. I close my eyes and try not to focus on these tender gestures from him.

It'll do neither of us any good if I do.

After he's done washing me for the second time today, Colt turns off the water and wraps a towel around me to dry off. He then picks me up in his arms, walking us to my bedroom, and plants me on my bed. I lie on my side, intent on watching him dry his glorious body off, but my eyes feel heavy after our excursion. I'm almost half asleep when I feel him slide up against me, caressing my face and taking the wet locks of hair off my cheek. I nestle into his warmth, my breathing becoming shallower as I succumb to my slumber.

"No turning back now," he whispers into my hair, pressing a soft kiss to my temple.

I don't say a word in reply, too afraid of what his prediction will mean for us both.

Chapter 22

Colt

It's been two days since I've been shacking up with Emma in her cozy little apartment. I have to admit, living so domestically has a certain appeal to it.

We wake up and fuck.

Eat breakfast, then fuck again.

Work on her book for a while, then fuck some more.

All day long, we are either deep in research mode or wrapped around each other.

A man could get used to living like this. Whenever the urge is there, one of us reaches out for the other, which's enough to get us going. Sometimes all it takes is a searing look, a tentative smile, or a seductive word, and we're both on the floor fucking each other's brains out. I've never felt so relaxed and content as I have this past weekend, and it all falls to my naughty professor, who can't keep her hands—or her mouth— off of me.

Guess it goes both ways.

Emma brings out a ravenous side in me, too. I look at her, and the need to own and mark every inch of her body consumes me. For someone who is used to having everything handed to him on a silver platter, Emma making me work for every touch and caress is just as wondrous and spellbinding as the woman herself.

I pull on the side of my lower lip with my teeth, watching her typing away on her laptop, so focused on the words she's writing down that she doesn't even realize I'm already itching to persuade her to take another study break.

"Don't you even think it, Colt. I'm sore as it is, and I've got five chapters to hand in this week."

She's sit sideways on the couch, a blanket and computer on top of her, with a teasingly amused grin on her lips. I'm sitting just opposite her in the same position with my own work on my lap, but that doesn't stop me from playing with her toes.

"I'm sure there are plenty of other places on your body that aren't sore."

Her cheeks immediately turn pink, but the fiery light twinkling in her amber eyes tells me she is up for my proposal.

"There most certainly are, but if you don't let me finish this chapter today, you won't be able to enjoy any of them."

"You playing dirty with me, Em?" I growl, thinking of taking a big bite out of her ass.

"I've learned that dirty is the only way you like it." She winks flirtatiously.

"I'll settle for your mouth, then. One kiss and I promise to be on my best behavior."

"Liar." She giggles.

Fucking giggles.

I swear I never get tired of the sound. It does something to my frigid insides, while also sending all my blood down south to my eager cock.

Shit, even I'm smiling, and I rarely do that.

"Cross my heart and hope to die." I smack my lips not so innocently.

"Just one?" She lifts up a finger indicating one kiss is all I'll get. For now, anyway.

"Just one."

"Fine. Do what you will with me then." She laughs.

"Oh. I intend to."

I place my laptop on the side table, grabbing hers next and placing it on the floor. I crawl up her body, Emma instantly melting to the couch beneath me, waiting impatiently for my kiss, her big beautiful golden eyes liquefying in feverish anticipation. Her breathing is already shallow by the time she feels my hardness press up against her sensitive core, my breath fanning across her face.

"Colt," she breathes out.

"Just one kiss, Em. Then we can go back to work."

I lean in and tease her bottom lip with my tongue before she greedily opens up to let me into her mouth.

All of Emma is sweet rapture.

Her smell.

Her voice.

Her decadent kiss.

It's enough to make men foam at the mouth just to get the little slice of heaven that only she can provide. In her kiss, I find both peace and the blinding urgency in pinning her to the ground and fuck her hard until all she sees and thinks about is me—and no one else.

I've always been a selfish prick, never one to share my toys with anyone else. But when it comes to the woman who is currently lying beneath me, offering herself so pliantly, so fucking breathlessly, I fear selfish is the kindest word anyone could say about me. Other words suit me far better.

Possessive.

Maddened.

Obsessed.

Take your pick.

I'll fully concede to them all.

When I moan into her mouth, needing to possess more of her, Emma places her open palms on my chest to push me away. Even though she's putting a pin in our make-out session, the way her eyes are half-mast with the same flame of desire that burns inside me ensures that I won't have to wait long to get what I want.

"Only one kiss. You promised," she gasps for breath.

"I remember."

I let out a frustrated sigh and plant my head on her chest. She lovingly runs her fingers through my hair as I hug her. When she lets out another sweet laugh, I pick my head up to look at her.

"What's so funny, Professor?"

She tilts her chin to my duffle bag sitting on the floor.

"I can't believe you actually had clothes packed in your car. You knew that sooner or later I'd be taking you home with me, didn't you? I swear I don't know if I should despise how cocky you are or be in awe of your self-confidence."

I shake my head.

"I didn't know. I might have hoped, but I didn't know."

"Is that so?" she questions disbelievingly. "Then why the change of clothes?"

"Let's just say it's something I picked up from Walker. Always have a spare change of clothes in your trunk. You never know when you'll get yourself dirty and need a quick wardrobe change."

Her brows tighten in confusion, but some things are best left unexplained. Suddenly feeling the weight of The Society's shadow on my shoulders, along with the memory of the night I learned that little trick, I push myself off her. After

I've fixed Emma's blanket and given her back her computer, I sit on the floor, my back leaning against the couch so that I can be close to her a little while longer.

"When do you think you'll have this all done, Em?"

"Why? Are you counting down the days until you're rid of me already?"

I know the comment is made in jest, but what she doesn't know is that our days truly are numbered.

Before the first snowfall touches Asheville soil.

Once that happens, I'll have no choice but to send Emma as far away from here as possible. Just the idea that days like these will soon be a thing of the past spurs a painful pang in my chest, making it hard for me to breathe.

"Colt? I was only kidding. You don't have to look so serious," she explains softly, turning my face by the chin to meet her eyes.

"I know you were. My mind was just elsewhere."

"Oh. And where did it lead you?"

"To The Society," I confess.

The worried lines on her forehead intensify as she stares deeply into my eyes.

"You really do believe The Society is real, don't you?"

She worries her lower lip with her teeth before closing her laptop.

"I wouldn't be writing about them if I didn't."

"You never told me why, though? As far as we know, they really could be just something some college kid made up at a kegger to scare freshmen. You haven't gotten any real proof to prove the contrary."

"What makes you think I haven't?"

My throat closes up, but I school my face to look impassive.

"You don't have anything, Em. If you did, I would have come across it in your research already."

"Maybe I kept whatever proof I have purposely out of your hands."

"And why would you do that? Don't you trust me?" My tone is accusing, but deep down, I know Emma would be smart in not believing a word I say.

I'll just end up hurting her anyway.

"Can I trust you?" she asks, pure hope in her question.

"No," I reply before I have the sense to lie to her.

The soft smile that crests her lips splits my glass heart in two.

"I once told you I was an orphan. Do you remember?" she asks, throwing me a somber smile while running the pad of her thumb over my scruffy chin.

"I remember."

I fucking remember everything you say, Em.

"I was so young when my parents died that I can't remember what they looked like, or even the sound of their voice or the way they smelled. I have no recollection of my parents whatsoever, save for the few things my grandfather told me throughout the years. He was the one who raised me." There is pained nostalgia to her tone as she continues to caress my cheek. "My grandfather was what you would call eccentric. Like me, he was a college professor. He loved his job—lived for it. But when my parents died, he became obsessed with something else."

My throat constricts at what she's insinuating.

"Let me guess? The Society," I chime in.

"Correct. If you recall, I told you my parents died in a car crash, but they weren't the only ones who lost their lives that day. Judge O'Keefe—a renowned magistrate in Boston—rammed into my parents' car on the Longfellow Bridge one night, making both cars drop eight feet into the Charles River. In the dead of winter, neither my parents nor the judge had any chance of survival. Either the fall or the hyperthermia would have killed them."

"I'm so sorry, Em," I whisper, holding on to her wrist to kiss it.

"It's okay. It doesn't hurt me to talk about it as much as it used to. But that's not why I'm telling you all this."

"Why are you then?"

"So you can understand why this book isn't just a book for me. It's the chance to solve the mystery that has haunted my grandfather and me since I was six years old. You see, when my parents died, the police ruled it a freak accident caused by some faulty wiring to the brakes in the judge's car. They chucked it up as some malfunction caused by the subzero temperatures Boston had been experiencing that winter. My grandfather, however, never believed in accidents or macabre coincidences. He was a very logical, factual individual, and didn't particularly appreciate the Boston police's swept-under-the-rug conclusion. So he checked forensic reports and everything else the police would humor him with, but he never got any closer to an explanation that would make sense in his head."

"Sounds like he was as stubborn as you," I tease halfheartedly.

"Moreso, if you can fathom it." She smiles fondly in recollection of the man who raised her. "Since the police weren't much help, my grandfather decided to do some digging into Judge O'Keefe's old court cases, thinking that maybe the culprit behind his faulty brakes had to do with someone the judge had put behind bars."

"Was it?"

She shakes her head, a grave expression tainting her stunning beauty.

"When my grandfather began looking into the judge's old cases, he did some investigating on the judge himself. He found out that Judge O'Keefe had a disturbing fetish for young girls."

"How young?"

"As young as eight."

"Fuck."

"Sick, I know, but that's not all. He learned that the judge had been actively distributing child pornography and that his step-daughter had killed herself the year before his death when some of her photographs were leaked from the dark web to various porn sites. Apparently, some of her classmates had gotten hold of them and shared them around the school. She was only fourteen at the time. But even with all the incriminating evidence that my grandfather found against him, somehow the judge went on unscathed. It's almost as if he had carte blanche around Boston to do whatever he pleased, like he was deemed untouchable."

"Do you think whoever messed with his brakes was seeking vengeance against the sick fuck?"

"I don't think it, Colt. I know it."

"What do you mean?"

There is a spark of excitement in her eyes, one that has me worried.

"A year after the accident, the judge's widow put their family brownstone up for sale. My grandfather used her open house to his advantage and went to the judge's home pretending to be a potential buyer. With so many people there, it was easy enough for him to maneuver around the place without anyone being the wiser of his true intentions."

My hackles continue to rise when Emma gets off the couch to walk over to her bookshelf across the room. Between her Brontë sisters and Jane Austen collections, she picks up an out of place hardcopy of Alexandre Dumas' *The Count of Monte Cristo*. She retrieves a familiar envelope from between its pages that sends dread to the very heart of me. She slowly walks back to where I'm still seated on the floor and sits next to me with that wretched thing in her hands. Ever so carefully, she opens it and takes out the sinister black stationery that has tormented my friends and me for the past months.

"My grandfather found this amongst the judge's things in his study," she explains, handing it over to me.

I swallow dryly, as if a boulder was pressed up against my ribcage, as I begin reading the letter's contents out loud.

CONFESS YOUR SINS.

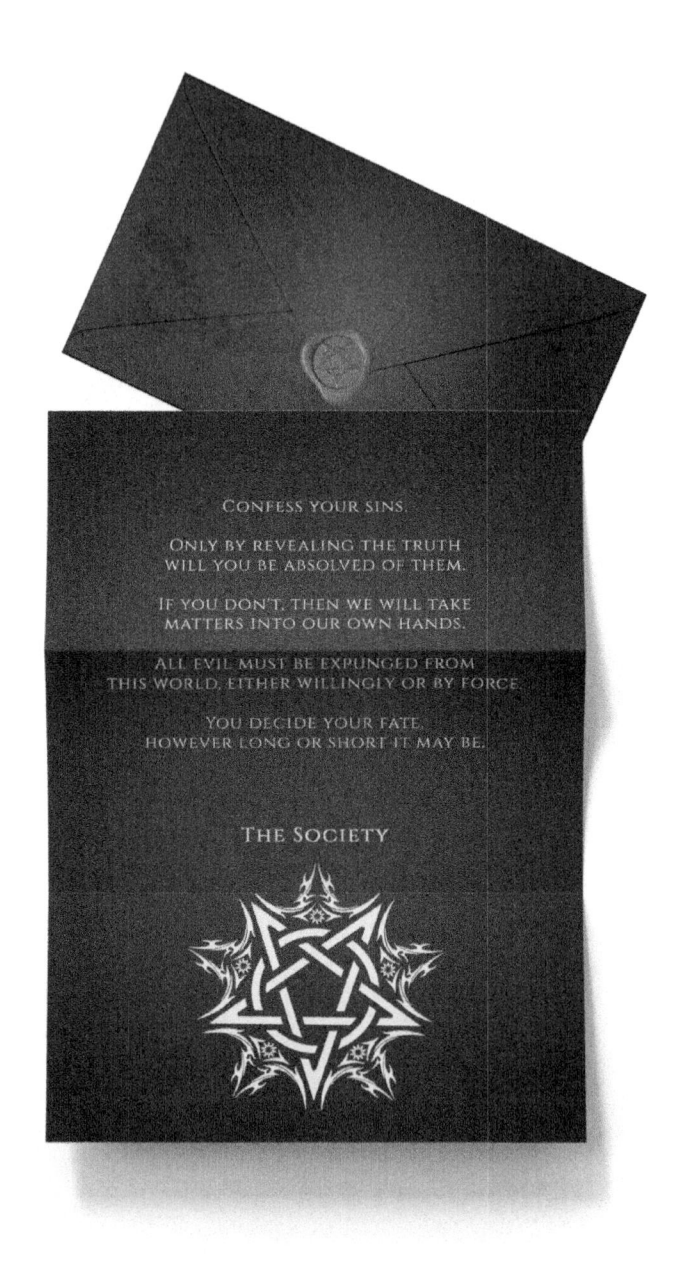

ONLY BY REVEALING THE TRUTH
WILL YOU BE ABSOLVED OF THEM.

IF YOU DON'T, THEN WE WILL TAKE
MATTERS INTO OUR OWN HANDS.

ALL EVIL MUST BE EXPUNGED FROM
THIS WORLD, EITHER WILLINGLY OR BY FORCE.

YOU DECIDE YOUR FATE,
HOWEVER LONG OR SHORT IT MAY BE.

THE SOCIETY

Emma's expression remains serious as she takes the letter out of my hands and places the envelope back inside the book. Genuine fear like I've never felt before prickles my flesh, knowing that something so dangerously vile has managed to get its way into her hands. All I want to do is grab the damn thing and burn it so Emma can be rid of it once and for all.

But the damage is done.

Unbeknownst to me, The Society had touched her life way before I came into the picture.

"That letter could mean anything," I choke out, unable to keep the panic away from my voice.

"My grandfather didn't think so. He believed that The Society found out about the Judge's pastimes and gave him a choice. Either admit to his crimes or deal with the consequences of his inaction. Since he didn't turn himself in, it's safe to assume they dealt with him themselves. It was just bad luck that my parents got caught in the crosshairs and became their collateral damage."

"If someone can take the lives of innocent people just to make sure evil men get punished, doesn't that make them just as immoral? Just as vulnerable to the same kind of retribution," I spit out, my body trembling from equal parts rage and terror.

"I agree with you to some extent, but you have to understand that type of statement only makes sense in a world where the line between good and evil is clearly defined. Not everything is that linear or black and white, Colt. It's just not the kind of world we live in."

"I'm guessing when your grandfather found this letter, he didn't stop there, did he?" I ask, instead of continuing on this discussion path.

"No. Like you, he believed The Society also needed to be brought to justice."

"Sounds like I would have liked him."

"I think he'd have liked you, too," she replies with a deep melancholy tone.

I entwine my hand in hers, giving it a light, comforting squeeze.

"It's okay. I've made my peace with it."

"Have you? Because it doesn't seem like you have, Em. You're writing a tell-all book on these fuckers—continuing where your grandfather left off. All of this sounds dangerous to me. Especially considering that if what you told me is true, then The Society doesn't care if innocent lives are collateral damage," I plead to her common sense, but my shoulders instantly slump when she starts to shake her head in denial.

"I don't think their intention was ever to kill my parents. In that regard, I do believe it was an accident they didn't account for."

"That doesn't justify what they've done! You grew up without a mom and a dad because of them, Em. Who knows what they'll do if they find out what you've been up to all these years. This is dangerous! Too fucking dangerous!"

"I'm not in danger, Colt. I promise you that I'm not," she tries to assure me, cupping my face in her palms.

I know you are.

"Em, listen to me. Please." I hold onto her wrists. "Do you think these fuckers are going to let you publish this book outing all their dirty laundry? You're smarter than that. They will come after you. You know they will."

"You sound afraid. I didn't think anything could make you afraid."

"I'm afraid of you getting hurt."

Fuck that. I'm terrified that she will.

"I'm a big girl, Colt. I can take care of myself."

Not against The Society, you can't.

Her phone starts to vibrate on the table, taking her attention away from me, but as she begins to reach out to grab it, I hold onto her elbow, pulling her to face me.

"Stop this, Em. Please. For me."

Her eyes soften, emotion swimming in her golden pools, terrifying me even more than the ominous society.

"I'll be fine. You have to trust me. I just need to finish what my grandfather started. I owe him that much."

"I don't believe that. I don't believe for a second he'd risk you to go after them."

She pulls away from me, standing up to put some distance between us.

"It doesn't matter what you believe. It's what I want. I will see this through, Colt. And neither you nor The Society themselves will stop me."

I stand up, aggravation and helplessness leaving me unsure on how to change her mind. I stare her down as she picks up her phone, a sudden annoyed expression marring her features.

"I... um... I forgot I have an errand to run this afternoon," she stammers, doing everything in her power not to look me in the eye.

"Whatever. Do you, Em. It seems like that's your MO anyway. I'm going for a walk."

I pick up my winter coat and slam the door on my way out of her apartment.

In my haste to leave Emma's place, I walk past my car and decide that a walk through Charlotte's streets is a good enough solution to temper my foul mood. After all, Emma confided in me, how can she still be so determined to go after The Society? They killed her parents, murdered a judge—even if the fucker did deserve it—and got away with it scot-free for crying out loud. Why isn't she running for the hills? Why did she sacrifice four years of her life into a book that will only ensure their wrath? I don't fucking get it. There has to be more to this—something I'm not seeing.

I grab my phone out of my pocket with the sole purpose of calling Linc. If anyone can figure this mess out, it will be him. He's been on my case about me not having any leads on The Society as it is, always reminding me that I'm on the clock. I'm sure I'm already on his shitlist for evading his calls. My cousin doesn't understand that every time I talk to him, I feel like shit for lying to his face. Not that I've made any headway with figuring out just what the fuck The Society wants from me either. I'm fucking up in every direction, and right now, I feel like I'm drowning.

But before I'm able to bring Linc's name up on my screen, an unanswered text grabs my attention. Between the various messages sent by my asshole of a father wondering where I've been holed up all weekend, to my baby sister, Abby, ordering me to text her proof of life, Easton's text is the one that gives me actual pause.

Easton: *Call me when you see this, asshole* 🖕

Without giving it a second thought, I press call.

"Took you long enough," he greets in an irate tone after the second ring.

"Aw, what? Did you miss me? I was wondering when you'd call for us to kiss and make up."

"Can it, asshole. I'm still fucking pissed at you, so let me say what I have to say and be done with it."

"Right." I grit my teeth. I hate that the motherfucker is still angry with me about what went down at The Brass Guild with Scarlett. Easton has never been the type to forgive and forget easily, but he never held a grudge with me for so long. I hate to admit it, but I fucking miss the melancholic prick. "Go on then."

"Christmas is in two days, and my folks invited the guys over to spend it with us."

"And you wanted to personally invite me over? I'm touched," I reply sarcastically.

The line goes silent, and I don't have to see him to know he's clenching his fists.

"Scarlett's the one who wants me to invite you."

"But not you," I rebuke, already knowing his answer.

"I'm not there yet, Colt," he huffs into the phone.

"Got it. Tell Scarlett that I have plans with the family and I can't make it. She'll buy that." My jaw goes stiff at the pregnant pause that ensues. "Anything else?" I ask, wanting to hurry up and hang up the phone.

"Just one more thing. We're all still going to your parents' place for New Year's."

I let out an frosty chuckle.

"If you want me to be a no-show for that as well, then you're in for a world of disappointment. I can't miss it. My mother will have my balls if I do."

"I figured as much. I just wanted to let you know that I'll be there. With Scarlett."

"I have nothing against your girl, East," I admit in earnest, wanting to make it clear in his mind that my issue was never with his girlfriend. It was always with my asshole of a father.

"Did you really apologize to her?"

"Yeah," I mumble back.

"Good." He sighs. "Just fucking be on your best behavior with her on New Year's. I don't want to have to rearrange your face with your momma and sisters all there. You feel me?"

Like my mother would even care.

"I'll be a perfect gentleman."

"Sure you will." He scoffs, but there is a tinge of humor behind it.

"I am sorry, East. I overstepped and fucked up. I know I did."

"Well, holy shit. Another apology from Colt Turner. Either hell has frozen over, or it's a fucking Christmas miracle."

We both nervously snicker on the phone, and I kick the air with my shoe.

"So, are we good?"

"No." He exhales loudly. "But we'll get there. That's what family does, right? Forgives us when we act like total jackasses."

"Not every family."

"Yeah, well, ours does. We've survived worse trials."

I'm not so sure that we have.

But instead of uttering that depressing thought out loud, I go with a less complicated one.

"Have a Merry Christmas, East."

"Yeah. You too, asshole."

When I hang up the phone, I'm both burdened with the hope that Easton will forgive me eventually and saddened that I was the one who made him hate the sight of me in the first place.

But all those feelings disappear when I lock eyes on a couple across the street, sitting inside a café, deep in intimate conversation.

Rage.

Fury.

Betrayal.

Jealousy.

Those are the burning feelings running through my body when I catch Emma on a date with none other than Montgomery-fucking-Ryland.

Chapter 23

Emma

My heart becomes trapped in my throat as Colt's enraged jade eyes stare daggers into my soul from across the street.

Shit.

Shit.

Shit!!!

"Emma, is there something wrong? You've turned awfully pale all of a sudden. Is everything alright?"

I grab the glass of water in front of me and take a huge gulp.

No, Montgomery. Everything is far from being alright.

"Will you give me a minute? I need to use the powder room." I throw him a conciliatory smile, hoping my excuse will prevent him from asking any other questions.

"Yes, of course."

Like the perfect southern gentleman he pretends to be, Montgomery stands up from his seat as I lift myself onto unsteady legs. I rush out of the room and head to the coffee house's entrance, where Colt's already standing at the door waiting for me.

"What the fuck, Emma?!" he growls through clenched teeth.

"Not here," I chastise and pull him away from the café into a nearby alley where he can't make a scene.

"What?" He pulls away from my grasp. "Are you afraid your boyfriend will see that you've been dipping your professor pen into the student pool?"

"That's not fair. And he's not my boyfriend."

"Are you sure? Because the way he was staring at your boobs when you were talking kind of gave the impression that he is."

"If I dated every man that looked at my breasts, then I wouldn't have any spare time to spend it listening to you spout all this nonsense."

"Ah, look who's full of herself now," he sneers, raking me from top to bottom with such disdain, it clouds my reasoning.

"Will you just shut up? Let me think!"

"Do you honestly believe you can come up with a valid excuse as to why you fucked me not two hours ago in your apartment and are now on a fucking date? With your fucking boss no less, Emma?!"

He grabs me by the chin with such force that I have no choice but to follow his lead and take a step back. Once he has me pinned to the wall, his grip moves from my chin onto my throat.

"Colt, you're hurting me."

He's not, but I sigh out an exhale of relief when his unyielding grip loosens.

"Explain, Em! Cause I'm fucking at my wits' end!"

"It's not what it looks like. I'll explain everything back home. I promise."

He shakes his head profusely and pins my wrists together above my head, his sweet minty breath kissing my face.

"Explain now, Em. Are you fucking him?!"

"No."

"I don't believe you." He shuts his eyes, letting out a pained sigh.

"Colt, look at me. I swear on my parents that Montgomery hasn't laid a finger on me."

His nose flairs in disgust at my remark.

"You just saying his name has me losing my goddamn mind. Why, Em? Why string me along if he was the one you wanted? Did you take some kind of perverse pleasure in fucking your student while trying to entice the dean into your bed as well? Was that your endgame? Or was I just a challenge to you, and now you're off to the next conquest?

"Fucking explain it to me, Em, because the reasons I'm coming up with on my own don't paint a pretty fucking picture, Professor," he spits out, all teeth and rage.

I don't know what has me more conflicted—that Colt so easily jumped to the conclusion that I'm sleeping with Montgomery or that he looks as if his whole world just ended because of it.

"You're upset. Too upset to hear reason or think straight. Go home, Colt. Before you say something we'll both regret."

He pushes away from me, leveling me with such a cold stare, a chill runs down my spine.

"Too late. I already fucking regret ever setting my eyes on you."

"Colt—"

"Goodbye, Professor. Have a fucking spectacular life."

He turns around and leaves me standing there, mouth agape and heart hammering. It takes all the strength I have to walk back to the café and face Montgomery again.

"Feeling better?" he asks, feigning concern the minute I sit at our table.

"Much. Thank you."

"Are you sure? You still look flushed."

"I'm fine," I sneer and then quickly backpedal and offer him a fake smile.

"Alright then, if you're sure. How about we order some food?" he adds, snapping his fingers to the waiter behind the counter.

"No. I think it's best we call it a day and head home."

"Oh?" His eyes light up at the insinuation behind my statement.

"I meant that I should be going home, alone."

"I see. I confess I thought the opposite. I thought we were reaching a stage in our relationship where maybe you'd finally invite me over to your place and we'd get to know each other on a different level."

"There is no relationship," I seethe at him in my head but seal my lips shut. In his self-entitled mind, he thinks since this is our third date, sex must be on the table for him. *Never going to happen.*

"I only came today so that I can tell you in person that I think we should stop having these small get-togethers entirely."

"Did I do something to offend you?"

"No, nothing of the sort. I just think we work better in a professional setting—as colleagues. Nothing more."

"How disappointing. I thought we had a real connection."

The only connection we had was you wanting to jump my bones and me wanting to know if you were in The Society or not. Once you told me you were persona non grata by the Richfields, I knew that could never be the case.

"But I will respect your wishes." He smiles tightly. *As if you had a choice in the matter.* "I hope that at least we can be friends and not just mere work colleagues from here on out."

"Of course." I give him yet another thin smile. "Now, if you will excuse me, I should be getting back. With school out for Christmas break, I have plenty of assignments to grade that I'd like to catch up on."

"Far be it from me to keep you from your scholarly duties. Please, let me walk you to your car."

We both stand up simultaneously and head outside. Thankfully I was able to grab a parking space just a few feet away from the café, so our walk to it is relatively short.

"I will miss these small dates we shared, Emma. If you ever change your mind, call me." He leans in and places a wet kiss on my cheek, too close to the side of my lips for it to be an innocent mistake.

Since I'm in the home stretch now, I decide not to scold him for his unwanted kiss. But as I sit behind the wheel of my car, I catch the sight of piercing light emerald eyes in my rearview mirror, utter misery tarnishing their celestial beauty, causing my heart to break into tiny shards of glass.

Once I arrive home, I try to occupy my mind with anything and everything but thoughts of how I left things with Colt. Not able to focus on work, I succeed in putting up a small pathetic Christmas tree in the corner of my living room, high-fiving myself that I was able to get it up before Christmas Eve this year. I bake gingerbread men to add to the Christmassy feel I've decided to go with as my distraction and end up eating the whole batch for my dinner with a pint of Ben and Jerry's vanilla ice cream to accompany them. I buy a dress online for New Year's, a mistake of monumental proportions since I end up obsessing over whether it's a good idea to go to the Richfield party knowing Colt will be there.

Safe to say that when I finally crawl into my cold bed, I'm miserable. As I stare at the empty pillow beside me where Colt had laid his head for the past two nights, my heart cracks further. How he got under my skin so quickly is beyond my comprehension, but even if I can't grasp how he effortlessly sneaked his way inside my heart, it doesn't change the fact that he's in there now. The time we shared this month has been the highlight of my entire stay in Asheville.

No. That's a lie.

Since Colt came waltzing into my life with his wolfish smirk and light eyes, it's like a spark was lit inside me—a flame that I would do anything to keep from extinguishing. He's the breath of fresh air that brought unpredictability back to my otherwise foreseeable life. Everything in it before he came along, I had planned and carefully thought out. From where I went to school, where I took my first teaching job, and finally, the steps I followed to bring me closer to The Society. All my life, nothing came as a shock to me because I controlled each choice, each outcome.

I never expected Colt.

I never even saw him coming.

Not until it was too late.

I toss and turn in my bed, wondering if it isn't best to call it quits and just pick up a book until sleep finally overtakes me when a faint knock on my door sends my heart racing. I look at my watch and see it's two in the morning. Unable to prevent myself from getting my hopes up, I run in a mad dash for the door. Through the peephole, I see the man who has rattled the cage to my heart until its locked clutch was no match to keep him away. I take two large gulps of air and open the door.

His hair is disheveled, and there are rings under his eyes, so unlike the well put together persona he likes to flaunt.

"I'm sorry," he says.

I lean against the doorframe and cross my arms over my chest.

"For what?"

"Take your pick. Being an asshole, mostly."

I maul my lower lip.

"Have you ever apologized for anything in your life?"

"It's becoming a reoccurrence lately. I don't like it."

"No. I don't expect you do."

"Can I come in?" he asks anxiously.

I move back, allowing him to come inside. I close the door behind me, hoping he doesn't hear how my bruised heart wants nothing more than to fall into his embrace.

"It's pretty late for a house call, Colt."

"I couldn't sleep," he replies with a crestfallen smile.

"I couldn't either," I admit, sitting on the armrest of my couch.

"Why couldn't you sleep?"

"Probably for the same reason you couldn't. I didn't like the way we left things this afternoon."

"Neither did I," he mumbles, sitting on my coffee table.

"Colt—," I begin to explain, but he raises his hand to stop me.

"Em, I need to do this first, okay? I might lose it if I don't."

I nod, allowing him to start this awkward conversation off first.

"I don't know what your deal with Montgomery is. Maybe you were meeting to talk about school or something. I don't know. Maybe I totally fucked this up by thinking it was a date."

"It was," I admit.

"Shit!" he counters, running his fingers nervously through his hair. "Okay. I can deal with that. I gotta say I've never been in this position before. Usually when I'm with a woman, I don't care what they do when I'm not around. I couldn't care less if I'm honest. But I fucking care now. I know we never said we were exclusive, and maybe this thing between us is just a fling for you. I want you to know that it's not for me. I don't know what we are, but I know it's important. Real. And if you don't feel the same, then the least I can do is tell you that Montgomery Ryland is the last person who should take my place."

"Colt—"

"Nah, Em. Just let me have my say, okay? This is fucking eating me alive, and if I don't say it, I'll never fucking forgive myself."

I push myself onto the couch while he leans in and grabs my hands in his.

All of me screams to end his suffering, but I seal my lips shut so he can say his piece, wanting to respect that zealous determination in his eyes.

"I'm not here to condemn your choices, Em. I get it. From the outside, Montgomery has it all. He's older than me, more sophisticated, and has a higher IQ. I even get that some women might find the piece of shit attractive, but Em, don't be fooled. He's as rotten as they come."

"Why do you say that?" I ask, this time my curiosity surpassing the guilt I feel.

He runs his tongue over his teeth, hate lingering in his stare.

"My family doesn't talk about this shit, preferring to act like we let bygones be bygones, but it's not true. Before Montgomery ever became one of Northside's esteemed inhabitants, he was just another pissant Southie that happened to have enough brains to get himself a scholarship at Richfield. I have no issues with people trying to better their circumstances through hard work and sheer determination. Shit, one of my closest friends has a girlfriend from the

Southside, and just by the way she hustles, I have no doubt she'll rule the world one day." He snickers proudly.

"You're talking about Stone Bennett, aren't you?"

He nods.

"She's my student. I always found her to be a very bright and extremely hardworking young woman. I have to say the only thing she disappointed me with was turning down a job offer in New York with Watkins & Ellis. At the time, my editor was dating a senior partner in the firm, and since Stone seemed to need a job to accept her scholarship at Columbia, I offered to help. I had a lot of apologizing to do afterward when Stone withdrew her acceptance."

"That wasn't her fault, Em," Colt explains with a severe expression on his face. "Don't be too hard on her. Sometimes shit just gets too tangled up for one person to sort through."

"Hmm."

"Shit. I don't want to talk about Walker's girl anymore. I need to tell you who you're getting in bed with in regards to Montgomery. Fuck, I can't even say that shit without my blood boiling."

"Colt, you can stop. You've got this all wrong."

"Em, I fucking adore the shit out of you, but can you just keep quiet while I say what I need to."

"Fine." I huff out in frustration, but Colt leans down and places a chaste kiss on my knuckles, successfully improving my disposition.

"Okay, so where was I? Ah, right. Buttmunch Montgomery. As hard as it is to get into Richfield, he won a scholarship, and because of that, he started to mingle with many influential people. He knew to make it in Asheville, he needed to network and create a narrative where the Northside would embrace him as one of their own. If not, then he'd always be perceived as just another Southside loser. That meant death to Montgomery, so he came up with a foolproof plan. What better way to gain the respect he so coveted than to marry one of Asheville's favorite daughters?"

"You mean Dorethea?"

"No, I mean my Aunt Sierra, Lincoln's mom. When Montgomery was a sophomore in college, he did some odd jobs to pay his way, one was catering at fancy parties. The prick met my aunt at her debutante ball when she was sixteen and brainwashed her into running away with him the minute she was of legal age so they could get married."

"Brainwashed? Isn't that extreme for two kids who fell in love and didn't know any better?"

"He never loved Aunt Sierra. The Richfield fortune, however, was another matter. That I'm sure the fucker fell head over heels for. My aunt was just a stupid kid with stars in her eyes, while he had dollar signs in his. He would have gotten away with it, too, if my mother didn't find out about their plans.

"At first, Mom hesitated to tell my grandmother about the affair—too afraid of what the old shrew would do to my aunt. But when my mother found out Montgomery was fucking every short skirt at Richfield while proclaiming his undying love to her baby sister, she didn't think twice and stepped in.

"My grandmother's solution to the shitshow was to arrange a marriage on the down-low between Aunt Sierra and Crawford Hamilton. My mother was against that union, too. She knew that, between Crawford and Montgomery, even the devil would have been strapped to choose which was the worser evil. She pleaded with Easton's dad, Richard Price, to marry my aunt instead, but at the time, Dick was all about Dick. He didn't want a wife, let alone a barely legal one.

"Uncle Crawford wasn't as hesitant. He knew he was getting tarnished goods and that time was of the essence, so he demanded to be well compensated for the trouble of marrying my aunt. My grandmother bent to his will and even gave our previous family home the Hamilton name. This was all done while Montgomery was none the wiser, working in another state for the summer. Of course when he returned, he was fucking livid. So much so that he pulled the wool over my mother's eyes and began courting her best friend in secret."

"Dorethea," I blurt out, entirely captivated by the web of lies and deceit his family history contains.

"Yeah," he mumbles, saddened. "Aunt Dory fell for his charms hook, line, and sinker. The memories I have of her are that she mostly kept to herself, but she always had a cheeky smile planted on her face like she knew some secret that no one else did. Her family wasn't abundantly wealthy, but they did okay for themselves and had good standing within the Northside community. When my grandmother died, I know my mom gave Montgomery the dean position alongside a generous wage package just so her best friend would be taken care of. Still, there were rumors that marrying Mom's best friend right from under her nose wasn't enough to appease Montgomery's need for revenge. Some people say that even after they were both married, he continued an ongoing affair with my Aunt Sierra." His brows crease, upset with his last revelation, while I'm still reeling from all that he's shared with me. "So I guess what I meant by this little history lesson is that the dean is not the man for you. He's a snake—a wolf in sheep's clothing. You deserve better, Em. So much better."

"Someone like you, perhaps?"

"Fuck, no," he laments with sorrow in his timbre. "You deserve better than me. You deserve the fucking world, Em."

"Colt," I whisper, inching closer to him until I'm able to cup his cheeks in my hands. "Can I talk now?"

He nods, his eyes falling to the floor.

"Will you look at me at least?"

"I can't. Not if you're about to break my fucking heart, Em. Let me at least pretend that I took your rejection like a man and not like some fucking pussy."

"Colt, look at me. *Please.*"

His shoulders broaden as he intakes a breath of bravery into his lungs before fixing his eyes on mine.

"I don't want Montgomery. I never did. He was just a means to an end. That's all."

"So who do you want?" he asks expectantly.

"I'm looking at him."

"Thank bloody Christ," he shouts before picking me up in the air. His lips lock with mine while he sits on the couch and places me on his lap. "I was going crazy, Em," he confesses between desperate kisses. "You don't know what you do to me."

"Just kiss me, Colt. Just kiss me," I beg just as desperately, my fingers already at the hem of his T-shirt, pulling it forcefully over his head.

Our kiss isn't pretty.

It's all knocking teeth and warring tongues, but it mimics our desperation for one another perfectly. Because that's precisely what we are. Desperate to love and be loved. And no one can love me better than Colt.

I pull at his zipper, his hands already pulling off my satin nightgown and dropping it to the floor, the urgency for our bodies to be united suffocating the very life out of us.

"Colt!" I scream when he thrusts so deep inside of me that my whole body becomes burning light.

"I thought I lost you," he grunts, jackhammering inside my pussy until all I am is heated flesh, limber limbs, and shallow breath. "But that will never happen, will it? Because you're mine, now. Say it, Em. Say it!"

"I'm yours. Please, Colt. I'm yours," I plead for mercy as he keeps hitting my G-spot with his cock.

But he never relents, his mouth sucking on my sensitive nipples one at a time, as his hard length inside me threatens to become my favorite addiction. His tongue trails up my neck until his lips are yet again dominating my mouth, his fingers digging into my hips to keep his ruthless tempo going.

"I can't. I can't," I yell out breathlessly, not making any sense anymore.

"Yes, you can, Em. Cum, baby. Cum on my cock. It belongs to you. Just as I do."

And with his words stroking my hungry heart, I do as he says and fall off the cliff into blissful rapture, knowing full well that from here on out, wherever I go, Colt will always follow.

Chapter 24

Emma

I feel warm.

I open my eyes to find my body all wrapped around Colt's naked form on my bed, clinging to it as if it's the missing piece to make mine whole.

"Hmm," I hum, the vibration making his cock swell in greeting. "Was I out for long?"

"Just an hour or so. How do you feel?" he asks, running the back of his knuckles against my cheek. "I forgot you were still sore. Was I too rough with you?"

"No. It was perfect." I purr in satisfaction, running a finger up and down his chest. "Come to think of it, I might need a reminder of how perfect it was."

"Is that so?" He licks his lips.

"Hmm." I nod, sliding up his body until I'm seated on his lap.

"You sure you're up for round two?"

"Let me show you how up for it I am."

When my hand grasps the base of his cock, he hisses out, his lids shutting of their own accord for a split second. I lower myself down his body just enough to tease the crown of his cock with the tip of my tongue while my pussy begins to rub against his thigh. He leans back into my pillow, his arms behind his head, watching me, ever so observantly, intent on not missing a single second of this. I trail my tongue up and down his shaft, taking special care of the angry vein alongside it. When I feel my wet core pool with desire, my lips wrap themselves around his cock. My mouth leisurely goes up and down on him to toy with Colt a little longer. He tilts his head to the side just enough so he can have a better view of me. I lift my eyes to his, sucking his cock deep into my mouth until it hits the back of my throat.

"Fuck," he growls, bringing a satisfied grin to my lips. "Em, as much as I want to cum in your mouth, I'd rather have a taste of your pussy first. Come here and sit on my face."

I bite the inside of my cheek, and instead of crawling up his body, I turn around until my drenched pussy is within his reach, while keeping his hard cock in my mouth.

He bites my ass cheek before taking one long swipe of my folds to taste me.

"Argh," I yelp, unable to keep still as he laps at me.

"You started this, Em. Now I'm going to finish it."

And does he ever.

I wrap my hand at the base of his cock to keep me steady, sucking on his steel shaft as best I can while being assaulted by his sweet, torturous tongue. Before I know it, I'm cumming, the taste of his pre-cum only heightening the detonation of fireworks running through my entire body. The sting of a slap to my ass cheeks brings me out of my euphoria and back to our exquisite lovemaking.

"Turn around," he orders.

Still shaking from my orgasm, I do as he says and sit around his midriff.

"Put me inside you."

I grab his cock and slowly insert it into my wet core. But unlike yesterday, all Colt does is hold onto my hips and wait for me to move.

"This is your show, Em," he taunts with a sly smirk.

I plant my open palms over his chest and begin to move slowly at first, just to enjoy him hardening inside me, but when that isn't enough to quench my hunger for him, I increase my speed, his fingers digging deliciously into my flesh in reply. My head falls back, my hair flowing every which way as my nails sink into his torso, leaving my mark on him.

"Em, put your hair up," he grunts.

"Huh?"

"Just do it, baby. Please, for me."

I twist my hair up on my head in a lazy bun, but the messy hairdo seems to please him if his lust-filled grunts are any indication.

"Now put these on," he commands, reaching out for my glasses on the bedside table.

"My reading glasses? Now, Colt? Really?" I gasp, staring down at our joined bodies, my pussy swallowing him whole. I'm so close to cumming, ready for my second orgasm to be triggered, and this man wants a fashion show.

"Baby, please."

"God, you're a kinky asshole," I rebuke playfully, snatching my glasses away from him so I can put them on.

"Enough of that pretty mouth, and keep riding my cock."

"Don't think I'm letting that baby talk slide, Mr. Turner. I'll have words with you after."

"Fuck!" he groans. "Shit, Em. Just like that. Call me Mr. Turner like you do in class."

I want to laugh at his kinky fuckery, but I have to admit it's turning me on.

"Since the first day you started teaching at Richfield, I imagined you just like this—fucking me raw, bouncing on my dick, scratching my chest until it bled out for you."

"Keep going. I'm so close, Colt. So fucking close," I whimper, a coat of sweat dripping down my back.

He begins strumming my clit, his eyes never leaving my face.

"That's it, Professor. Ride my cock. Milk me dry."

"Oh, my God!" I wail, reaching the gates of nirvana.

The sound of Colt grinding his back molars is so loud it reaches my ears. He pounds into me three more times before stepping off the ledge himself. Once we have both reached our peak, I fall to his chest, his strong arms instantly wrapping themselves around me. I concentrate on his drumming heartbeat, a reminder that I'm not alone in this unexpected feeling that has slithered its way into our hearts. The rapid sound returns to a smooth beat, so tranquil it almost lulls me to sleep.

"Em?" Colt whispers while loosening the knot in my hair. "Can I ask you a question?"

"You sure are chatty tonight." I smile, but when he doesn't reply with a witty remark, I lift my head to look at him. "What's wrong?" I ask, handing him my glasses to stash away.

"What did you mean when you said that Montgomery was only a means to an end?"

Like the flip of a switch, my whole body grows rigidly cold.

"Em?"

I maul my bottom lip, wondering if this is when I should come clean with him or not.

"Just say it, Em. Stop choosing which words to say and just tell me already."

"I thought he might be in The Society."

"Montgomery? That prick?" he yelps, straightening himself up on the bed and pulling me along with him. The look in his eye is the same one I had when I entertained the idea that the dean could be the key to unlocking The Society's mystery. But like Colt, I was wrong in my assumptions. It only took me two dates with the man to figure that out.

"It was my mistake. I know now that a man like him could never be part of such a club."

"How can you be so sure? The fucker ticks all the boxes of a sociopath primed to do The Society's dirty work."

I shake my head.

"No, he doesn't. And you're wrong about him being a good candidate for The Society. He told me himself they want nothing to do with him."

"Wait?! Hold the fuck up, Em. The fucker admitted he knows them?"

"No, not in those words." I bite my inner cheek.

"Em, look at me," Colt orders, grabbing me by the shoulders. "If you know who they are, then you have to tell me."

"You wouldn't believe me if I did."

"I will. I promise. Now please, Em. Just tell me."

It's the urgency in his voice that does me in.

"The reason why I think Montgomery could never be a member comes down to the other two men I believe are."

"Okay... who?"

This is it.

Oh God.

"I believe that your father is a member and... your cousin, Lincoln."

His eyes go wide as he stares at me like I've grown an extra head.

"Emma, you can't be serious," he blurts out.

Knowing that he won't believe me until he sees actual proof, I jump off the bed and go into my closet. Behind the hanging winter coats, dresses, and other various skirts and blouses, I pull the book I stole from the Charlotte Library. I run back to the bed, Colt's confused expression still intact. I flip page after page until I find the entry he needs to see.

"Just read this."

He takes the book out of my hands and begins to read the sentence aloud word for word.

Born from the ashes of civil strife, a new dawn arises and with it a symbol of an unmerciful future, where all evil men must be judged and punished for their offenses. Only the selfless and earnest can sacrifice their lives to the betterment of humanity and ensure evil will never have its day.

In the very heart of Asheville, one family heard the call of righteousness and vowed to assemble like-minded individuals to fight the arduous battle for mankind's soul.

'Their name is as rich as the fields that stretch out beyond both of the Carolinas, and their hearts, just as pure as the cotton grown there.'

"It goes on and on about all the good deeds The Society did after that, but see this," I ask, pointing excitedly to the last passage. "I think this is code. *'Their name is as rich as the fields'*—Richfields. Your family, Colt. And this pentagram drawn under it, I saw a similar one sketched inside one of your family's ledgers in the library. You have to agree with me that the coincidence is suspicious."

"That doesn't prove anything," he says, slamming the book shut and throwing it to the floor.

"You don't believe me?"

"Em, you're making it very difficult for me to be able to. My dad and Linc, members of some goody-two-shoes society? Impossible. My father is a philandering womanizer that wouldn't know a good deed if it slapped him across the face."

"And your cousin? Lincoln?"

"Trust me, Em. He's not a part of any of this. And I can tell you this right now, this stuff about The Society being selfless and righteous is complete bullshit!"

"I don't think so. I've spent years researching them, and all my findings tell me that throughout history, The Society has always been on the right side of it. They are not the bad ones here. They are just out to set wrongs right."

"They are vigilantes! Tell me who has the right to be judge, jury, and executioner? Because that's what they are, Em. They're a corrupt militia with their own agenda, wanting to impose on others their beliefs of what is right and wrong.

What if they decide you writing this book is *evil*? That by exposing them to the world, you are putting all their efforts in jeopardy? Tell me, Em, who is going to protect you if they come after you?!"

I press my palm to his face, the deep-rooted fear inside him gnawing at my insides.

"No one is coming after me, Colt. I've never seen you this riled up."

"Well excuse me if hearing that a secret society with blood on their hands could be linked to my family bothers me. Shit! That's not even the worst part. Just thinking that somehow my girlfriend might be on their radar and piss them off is enough to have me lose my mind."

"Girlfriend?" I choke out.

"I said it, didn't I?" His nose crinkles.

"Sometimes I forget how young you are."

"Not this shit again," he belts out, starting to turn away from me, but before he's able to get very far, I pull him closer to me.

"That's not what I meant, Colt. It's sweet. That's all."

"You and I both know I'm not sweet."

"No, I know that. But that doesn't mean you can't be sweet too when you feel like it."

"Only with you, Em," he confesses truthfully, his green eyes softening.

"I like that about you," I whisper, hugging his waist and resting my head on his chest.

He hugs me tighter, placing a chaste kiss on the top of my head.

"Well, don't tell the world about it. I don't want to ruin my rep."

"My lips are sealed," I tease, kissing the special place where his heart beats.

"This conversation isn't over, Em. You know that, right?"

"For tonight it is. Just hold me, Colt. The Society can wait."

And as I'm about to shut my eyes, his whispered reply unsettles me, causing the first sliver of fear to burrow into my bones.

"The Society waits for no one, Em. Not even for us."

Chapter 25

Colt

After being away from it for the past ten days, returning home gives me a strange new perspective on the cold mausoleum. There was a time I thought these walls cold and heartless, but now as I stand here taking in what used to be familiar surroundings, I see something far more sinister at play.

I step into the large foyer of my home with Emma clinging to my arm, and all I want to do is grab her and return back to where we came from. I'm very aware of the influence her research has had on me and how it's affected how I view my childhood home in an entirely different light—a much darker one at that.

Even this elaborate display of power under the disguise of a New Year Eve's bash reeks of control and dominance over its guests. It's a reminder that our family is not to be trifled with. Most of Northside spends twelve months out of the year bending their knee to us Richfields, lusting after the possibility that their names might be written onto the guest list. They all know that being in my family's good graces is crucial to their survival in this town. No one casts a colder shadow than a Richfield when someone doesn't fall in line with our wishes.

Before Emma came into my life with her conspiracy theories, I wouldn't have batted an eye at anyone here. I'd be bored out of my mind, counting down the minutes until I could leave, while looking for a warm mouth to entertain myself with. Now, as my eyes scrutinize my crowded home, filled to the brim with Asheville's high society, I can't help the sinking sensation in my gut warning me to be cautious. I don't see women dressed in their finest jewelry, laughing away at some boring anecdote shared by their monkey-suit companions. I don't hear the celebratory clinking of champagne flutes or the live orchestra playing their violins and cellos. I don't register the loud gasps of appreciation for the over-the-top décor or the bustling of waiters offering hors d'oeuvres.

Everywhere I turn, all I see is the sway of one cruel and unyielding entity—The Society.

Could Emma be right?

Did my family birth the nemesis that has blackmailed my friends and me since school began?

And if so, then why come after us? Why punish would-be heirs to their cause?

After the night Emma revealed who she thought was behind The Society, I persuaded her to hand me her manuscript so I could read for myself what her findings were. As incredulous as I was going in, once I read her extensive research and established for myself how all the pieces seemed to fit so perfectly, her written facts were hard to ignore. Surprisingly enough, the thing that had the small hairs on the back of my neck prickling in fear wasn't how she concluded that my family was the one behind the nefarious boy's club, but how she portrayed the bastards. Emma painted them as selfless soldiers fighting the good fight against all the evils in the world.

But if they are the good guys in this story, then what does that make me?

Make us?

"Colt, are you okay?" Emma questions, beside me, her golden eyes filled with concern.

"I'm good, Em," I reply warmly, kissing her temple to soothe her worry.

Her rigid stance immediately relaxes at my lie, and when she throws me one of her glowing smiles, it sends a punch to my gut.

"How about we do the rounds in this place and then bail early?" I whisper in her ear, wanting to get the two of us out of this house as fast as possible.

"Didn't you say this party was important to your family? Won't your parents be cross with you if we leave so soon?"

Fuck my parents.

If they are the ones making my life and that of the people I care about a living hell, then they can take a long walk off a short pier.

I'm about to open my mouth and give her any excuse that would persuade her to leave early when I hear a girly shriek nearby.

"Colt!" Abby yells as she flings herself into my arms.

She wraps her willowy arms around my waist, her head pressing into my chest, and immediately a sense of guilt washes over me. I never did reply to her countless texts. I ghosted the only sister who gives a crap about me, and now I feel like shit.

Fuck.

I didn't even get her a Christmas present.

Jesus.

Merideth and Irene are right. I am an alphahole—or whatever the fuck that means.

"You scared the bejesus out of me. Where the hell have you been?" she accuses, slapping my chest after she's made sure I'm in one piece.

"With my girlfriend. Abby, meet Emma. Emma, this is my kid sister," I state, tilting my head to the woman beside me.

"Girlfriend?" she yelps excitedly, taking in Emma from top to bottom. "You're the professor, aren't you?"

"I am." Emma blushes. "It's very nice to meet you, Abby. I've heard a lot about you."

"Whatever you heard couldn't have come from my brother since he didn't so much as call me on Christmas." Abby pretends to pout.

"I'm sorry, shortstop. But I'll make it up to you. Whatever you want is yours. Just name it."

"Even your Bugatti?"

Why you little extortionist.

"You said I could ask for anything, big brother." She points an accusatory finger in my face. "And don't say I'm too young either. I already have my driver's permit to learn how to drive, which by the way don't forget, you offered to teach me."

Jesus fucking Christ.

My family must be The Society. Blackmail is in our blood if my baby sister is any proof of it.

"Fine. If you want the Bugatti, then it's yours."

"OH, MY GOD! For real?!" She shrieks again, piercing my eardrums.

"Yeah, yeah, yeah. But I'll only give you the keys after you've passed your exam. Not a day before."

She jumps yet again into my arms, happier than I've seen her in months. The warmth that trickles down to my cold heart, coaxed by my little sister's happiness, feels oddly magical.

I love my Bugatti.

I fucking love that car, but somehow it pales in comparison to the wide smile I was able to put on Abby's face.

"Thank you! Thank you! Thank you!" She continues to jump for joy but then remembers her manners when the mingling guests milling about begin to look sideways at her. "Nice to meet you, Emma. Sorry I didn't say that before."

"It's quite alright." Emma smiles brightly.

"You must be quite the good influence on my brother for him to have become so generous," she goads, her eyebrows jumping up and down on her forehead.

"You can stop gawking at her now, Abby."

"Sorry." The little heathen smirks.

"And who is this?" Just the sound of my sister Meredith coming from behind me has my spine going ramrod straight.

"This is Emma. Colt's girlfriend," Abby explains excitedly, as Meredith comes to stand beside her.

"Is that so?" she counters with a snarl.

While Abby looks at Emma with unconcealed delight, my older sister glares maliciously.

"Is that a problem, Mer?"

"Not for me." She tilts her head to the side to take Emma's measurements. "But I'm sure Momma might be of a different opinion."

"I don't know if you've been paying attention or not, but our mother's opinion has never interested me in the slightest."

"Yes, I can see that. Come along, Abby. Let's leave Colt alone with his *girlfriend* and find Irene."

Her snarky parting comment makes me want to wring her little neck.

"You were right. Abby is lovely, Colt. Your older sister, on the other hand, is… what's the word I'm looking for?"

"A raging bitch? You can call her a bitch, Em. Lord knows she takes pride in being one. She takes after our mother."

"I'm sure she has her finer qualities."

I laugh.

"If you find any, let me know. Cause I sure as shit haven't found any worth mentioning. Come on. Let's find my friends. I want to introduce you to them." I place my hand on the small of her back, loving the fact that her black dress is backless and that I'll be able to touch her skin whenever I feel like it.

"Are you going to be introducing me to everyone tonight as your girlfriend?"

"Don't see why not?"

She pulls at my elbow and stops at the entrance of the ballroom to stare deeply into my eyes.

"How about we make this night as painless as possible and not do that."

"So, how do you want to play this?" I counter, crossing my arms over my chest, not ecstatic that she wants to keep us on the down-low.

"You can introduce me as your date, or your teacher even. I don't care. I just don't want to cause you any more grief with your family than there has to be."

Too late for that.

You shouldn't have told me they were members of the same society intent on ruining our lives.

"Whatever you need, Em. Just so you know, they'll figure out you're my woman, anyway, when they see me kissing the shit out of you at midnight."

"I forgot how incorrigible you are." She laughs.

"One of my best qualities, babe."

When she punches me in the gut for the nickname, I can't help but chuckle.

"Shall we, professor?" I wink at her, offering my arm.

She laughs under her breath as I lead her into the lively ballroom. As we begin walking through the crowd, my previous reservations come at me at full throttle. Every familiar face I encounter feels like an unseen threat that I should remain cautious of.

I watch Sheriff Lee stuffing his face with caviar and crème fraîche tartlets. At the same time, Betty Lee entertains herself by throwing fuck-me eyes over to Governor Peterson's young assistant across the room. Tommyboy's sleazebag of a father has a whole entourage surrounding him as he relays his presidential plans. Montgomery Ryland is trying to pretend he knows how to waltz on the dancefloor with who I would bet my left nut was my physics professor freshman year. I observe Walker's folks talking animatedly with Easton's parents, ignoring the passersby who give Naomi Price dirty looks.

I take stock of all of them, unable to tell the difference between friend and foe.

It's only when my gaze finally lands on the people that I trust with my life that my tense shoulders start to ease. I lock hands with Emma and slice through the busy crowd until I'm in the midst of my real family.

"Well, look who we have here. About time you showed up to your own party," Kennedy teases, her big blue eyes falling on our entwined hands. "Ms. Harper, I didn't realize you were going to be here tonight, too. What a happy surprise."

"Emma, these are my friends," I introduce proudly.

Kennedy, Stone, and Finn all greet Emma with warm, welcoming smiles, just as I knew they would.

"We missed you at the Price's over Christmas," Kennedy adds afterward, trying to hide the worry in her voice. "You and East still haven't made up, huh?"

"It's fine, Ken. Emma and I decided to stay home anyway."

"Did you, now?" she retorts playfully, her gaze sparkling with mischief.

"Has anyone seen my cousin?" I ask before Ken opens her mouth and puts Em or me on the spot.

I know it's futile trying to throw her off the scent that Emma and I are together. Especially since when Ken smells something in the works, the woman becomes a bloodhound and will chase you down until you confirm her suspicions. Can't get anything past this one. It's a fucking miracle we have been able to conceal The Society from her as long as we have, but then again, we had to for her protection.

"I saw him earlier tonight, but then I lost him," Finn explains, his gaze also promptly fixates on my date. Even Stone has a sly grin on her lips as she stares at both of us.

These fuckers act as if they have never seen me with a woman before.

Hmm. Come to think of it. They haven't.

But, fuck. Act cool, assholes!

"I um… I'm going to grab a drink. Be right back," Emma stammers, obviously unsettled by the way my three friends can't stop staring at her.

I kiss her cheek before she quickly goes about her business.

"Would you guys fucking cool it already? You're scaring my date."

"Oh, my God! You fucked Professor Harper, didn't you?!" Stone blurts out.

"Jesus, brat. My mom is right over there," Finn chastises, waving impishly at his mom, hoping Charlene didn't hear his girlfriend's outburst.

If Walker thinks his momma doesn't know his girl has a dirty mouth, he's living in la-la land. Stone rolls her eyes at him, pointing a knowing finger at me.

"Admit it! You banged our ethics professor?!"

"He did more than that, didn't you, Colt?" a familiar raspy voice utters from behind me.

I turn around to face Asheville's dark prince in his usual black attire, a timid Scarlett right beside him. Scarlett throws me a imperceptable nod and then goes over to greet the girls. Easton stays rooted to his spot, placing his hand on my shoulder and leaning into my ear so only I can hear the words that fall from his mouth.

"Not only did you fuck her, but you fell in love with her, too. Isn't that right?"

"That's none of your business." I grind my teeth, not liking the way he's talking about Emma.

He chuckles as his grip tightens on my shoulder.

"Tell me, asshole. What would you do if I went over to Emma right now and intimidated the fuck out of her? Put the fear of God into her—or in my case, the devil—and made her feel like she was as small as an ant that I could easily crush with my shoe. What would you do, Colt?"

I snatch his grip off me and stare him dead in the eye.

"I'd fucking break every bone in your goddamn body with a fucking smile on my face."

"I thought so. That's love, motherfucker. Welcome to the club."

My rapid heartbeat settles when his silver eyes turn from hellish retribution to the brotherly fondness I've been accustomed to since I was a kid. The need to apologize for my behavior with Scarlett burns in my throat since I finally understand his rage. However, when Kennedy squeals behind us, my apology gets cut short.

"Let me see it again."

I turn around and watch Stone and Ken fawn over the largest rock I have ever seen on a woman's finger.

"If you answered your phone once in a while, than I could have told you the news earlier. I asked Scarlett to marry me over Christmas. As you can see, she said yes."

"Congratulations," I mumble, sad that I wasn't there for such a monumental occasion in Easton's life.

His brows furrow in guilt.

"I didn't mean to do it when you weren't there, Colt. It wasn't intentional. I actually thought I'd only pop the question after graduation, but when Christmas came and I saw Scar so happy, I thought, why wait? When you know, you know. And I've known since I was thirteen years old. I think I've waited long enough."

With his proclamation of love still ringing in my ears, my gaze travels across the sea of people in the ballroom, only stopping when it finally locks on the woman who has my heart in a vise grip.

"Yeah, I get that."

His eyes follow mine, chuckling when he realizes where my mind went.

"I guess you do, don't you?" He squeezes my shoulder affectionately. "Who would have guessed there was a heart beating under that cold exterior after all?"

"If there is, then it's hers."

"Holy fuck," he snickers, but quickly hides it under a false cough. "You must have got it bad, son, if you're saying cheesy shit like that. Mazel Tov, brother."

"Finn! Finn! Come here, boy, and talk some sense into Price," Hank Walker calls out.

"How much do you want to bet it has to do with the new running back recruited by Chapel Hill?" Finn grumbles under his breath before walking over to his father.

"So Walker finally caved, huh? He's back to talking to his old man?" I ask Stone while observing a proud Hank Walker trying to wrap his arm around Finn's broad shoulders.

"Finn kind of felt he had to after all his dad has done for my family."

When the confused expression surfaces on my face, making it crystal clear that I have no clue what she's talking about, Stone elaborates.

"That's right. You've been MIA lately, so you don't know what's been going on. Charlene told Finn's dad that my father is getting out of prison. His hearing is in five days, and we all expect him to come home after the Richfield Foundation made the entire DA's office and sheriff's department look like incompetent jackasses. Since Charlene told him how worried she was that my mom and dad would still be living on the Southside, Hank immediately went into action and bought them a house close to theirs. He even has job offers lined up for my dad when he gets out. I think it was a play to tug at quarterback's heartstrings, but it worked.

It also helped that Hank gave Finn a heartfelt apology for his past behavior."

"I guess old man Walker knew he screwed the pooch and had to go to extremes to get on Finn's good side again."

"We all make mistakes. It's how you try to remedy them that matters."

"So does that mean Finn and you are moving out of Linc's place?"

"We already have. We found this cute little apartment close to school and moved in last week," she beams, a crimson blush dusting her cheeks.

"Well, look at you guys all grown up. New house. New job. Or did you not take Maxwell's job offer?"

"No, I did. I started a few weeks ago."

"And how has that been working out for you?"

I don't miss how Stone discreetly looks over at Kennedy before she replies.

"It's been educational."

Before I'm able to ask what she means by that, my phone vibrates in my pocket.

Linc: *Meet me in your room*

"Ladies, I've been summoned. Do you mind looking after Emma for a minute?"

I leave them to it, confident that Em will be in good hands while I go in search of my cousin. When I get to my bedroom, Lincoln's pissed off expression combined with the letter in his hands tells me all I need to know about this impromptu conversation.

"Got another one, I see?"

"You did," he snarls, his ocean stare so deep it threatens to swallow me under its tide. "Since The Society has always taken advantage of leaving a letter whenever there's been a big party, I thought it best to case your room to see if anyone came near it," he explains, dropping the letter on my mattress.

Guess I'm burning that shit now.

"And did you see anyone?" I ask, careful to keep a wide berth from my volatile cousin.

"No." He shakes his head. "When I got here, the letter was already on top of your bed. But *you* were the one that should have been here, Colt. Not me."

"Are you pissed at The Society or me, cuz?"

"Right now, at both. Why haven't you been answering my calls? No one has laid eyes on you in days."

"I've been busy over at Emma's." I shrug nonchalantly.

"Fuck, Colt!" He throws his arms in the air. "While you've been playing house, The Society has been getting restless. Read it."

He picks up the nefarious envelope and jams it into my hands. I take the letter out, trying to prepare myself for whatever fucked-up thing I'm about to read. But as each line blurs in my vision, all I can think about is the golden-eyed woman waiting for me downstairs and what their threat means to her.

Speak No Evil

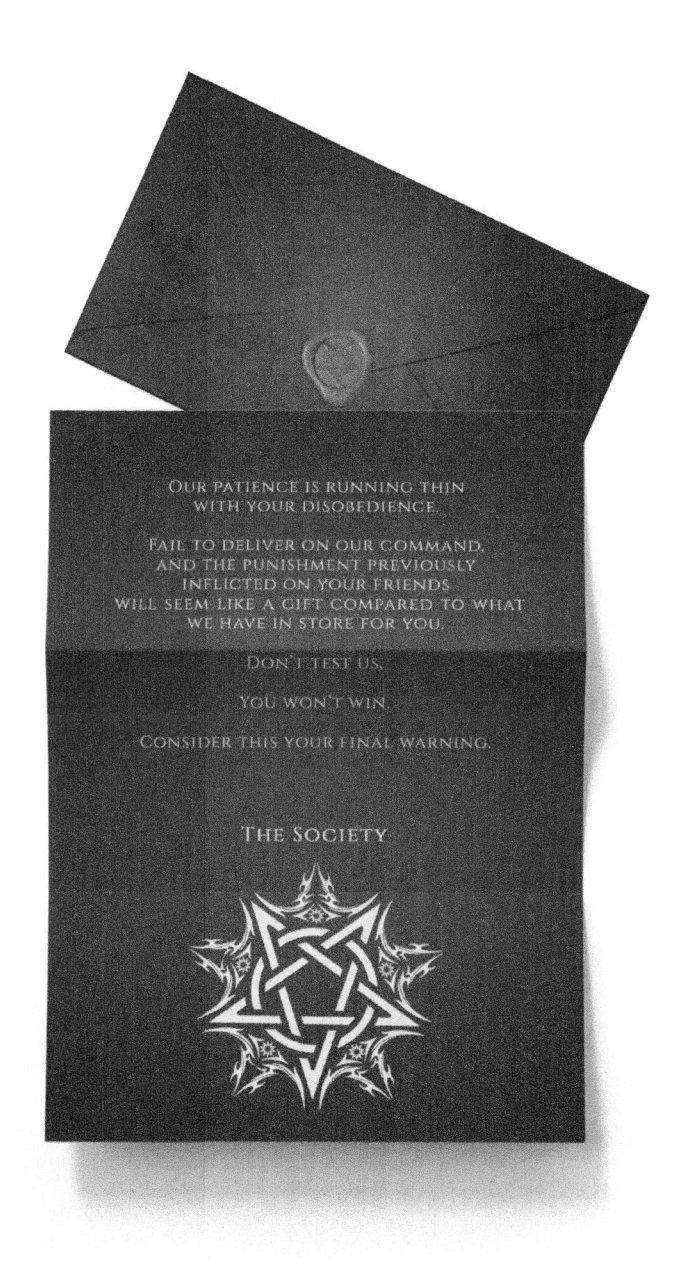

Our patience is running thin
with your disobedience.

Fail to deliver on our command,
and the punishment previously
inflicted on your friends
will seem like a gift compared to what
we have in store for you.

Don't test us.

You won't win.

Consider this your final warning.

The Society

"You better have some good leads, Colt, because I don't know what they'll pull next if they don't get their way. Were you able to get anything out of the professor?"

"Her name is Emma," I reply defensively, crumbling the letter in my hand and throwing it to the floor. I don't have to look at my cousin to feel his searing stare at me.

"And has *Emma* given you any idea of who The Society is yet?" he questions, his tone less heated.

I sit on the edge of the bed, loosening my bow tie.

"Yeah. She has her suspicions."

"And what might those be?"

"That we're fucked, cuz."

"More than we are now?" he goads lightly, sitting next to me.

"She thinks… fuck, just saying this shit out loud gets me nauseous. She thinks it's our family that founded The Society. Emma believes my dad is a member and, well, that you are one, too."

"Me?" He slaps his hand on his chest.

"That's what I said. And I've got to say, cuz, from all her in-depth research, I'm not sure I don't believe her."

I then enter into rant mode and tell him everything Emma discovered in her search to unmask our sworn enemy. From her parents' death and what sparked her interest, to the book she found in Charlotte, and finally, to the ledger entry she read right here in this very house. I spit it all out at rapid speed, hoping Linc can keep up with my manic explanation.

Lincoln doesn't even flinch at what I'm saying, preferring to keep silent throughout my diatribe until he's sure I've told him all I know.

"It does make sense, doesn't it?" he muses afterward, rubbing his chin in reflective thought. "Our family has always had its secrets. This being one of them doesn't surprise me."

"Do you think they would hurt us because we whacked Crawford? Cause I don't see it. My father never liked your piece of shit dad, so as far as I'm concerned, we did him a favor."

"Hmm. True. But that's if we're assuming your father is a member."

"As much as I hate my old man, I don't see him being this sadistic and cruel."

"Me neither. Uncle Owen wouldn't have the stomach for it, but then again, he's always been prone to secrets."

We both fall silent, staring at my carpet, wondering how things got so fucked up that we don't know left from right, up from down?

"What are we going to do, Linc? Do we tell the guys that the fuckers behind blackmailing us might be… well… us?"

I think about Naomi Price's sex tape and how East would never forgive me if he thought somehow I could have stopped it from being leaked.

"Let me think on it. I have to make sense of this because right now, I'm having difficulty seeing the whole picture."

"If you can't see it, then we are all screwed."

"Just give me time to piece this all together. I'll come up with something."

"What do I do about Emma in the meantime?"

"What do you want to do about Emma?" he retorts knowingly.

"I don't want to send her away, Linc. But if she has to leave Asheville, then I'm going with her."

"Yeah, I thought as much." He sighs. "Maybe that isn't a bad thing, Colt. Maybe you two can start fresh somewhere where they can't touch you."

"Her parents were killed in Boston. I think The Society's reach is pretty expansive. Besides, my family all lives here."

"But that's just it, Colt. Maybe it's our family you should be running away from. Think about Emma. Don't put her life at risk needlessly."

"Are you telling me to leave?" My chest tightens at the idea of leaving him behind to deal with these fuckers alone.

"I'm telling you to do what's right for you, brother. I don't think it's a question of us handing ourselves to the police anymore. If it was, then we wouldn't be having this conversation."

In other words, he would march downstairs right now and confess what happened when his parents died that fateful night if he thought it would spare me The Society's wrath.

I get up from the bed and walk to the door.

"Aren't you coming?"

"I think I'll stay here for a while longer just to get my head on straight."

"Okay." As I'm about to head for the door, he calls out my name.

"Colt."

"Yeah."

"I'm happy you found her at last. Finding your other half is rare, cousin. Treasure her and remind Emma that your heart isn't whole without her."

"How did you know?" I ask tentatively, gobsmacked at how well he can read me.

"Love has a way of branding us. It leaves a mark. Just be careful who you let see it."

I give him a curt nod and leave him to wrestle with his tormented thoughts, knowing he's speaking from experience.

As I'm about to walk over to the staircase, I see familiar silhouettes down the hall and away from the bustling party taking place in the ballroom on the floor below. Ever so discreetly, I watch Scarlett show my father her engagement ring. He pulls her into a bear hug, mumbling something in her ear that I can't decipher from where I'm standing. She then breaks away from him and heads back down to the party at rapid speed.

I keep myself hidden behind a grotesque statue my mother considers to be art and silently wait for my father to pass me by. From afar, he looked like the same carefree man I grew up with my entire life. It's only when he draws nearer that I see tears in his forest green eyes, filled with two contradictory sentiments that have afflicted my soul of late.

Utter joy.

And complete misery.

Chapter 26

Emma

"Emma, this is Lincoln," Colt introduces, his demeanor taut and apprehensive.

"I'm very pleased to meet you."

I offer to shake Lincoln's hand, but he surprises me by bowing down and planting a soft kiss on mine instead. I look over at Colt beside me, his impassive face giving me no insight as to what he's thinking.

"The pleasure is all mine, Emma. My cousin tells me you've been trying to meet me for quite some time now."

"Did he?" I slant my eyes at Colt, making a mental note to have a little conversation with him on boyfriend/girlfriend protocol.

Jesus, Emma!

Did you just refer to Colt Turner as your boyfriend?

You're as bad as he is now.

I shake the thought away and concentrate on the blond, blue-eyed man that is a total contrast from the one I've given my heart to. While Colt's eyes are clear, green meadows, his cousin holds a vast, lonesome sea in his. Lincoln's stare is so profound and blue that you feel you might drown in his deep watery abyss.

"How about we three go sit on the patio outside? The fireworks are bound to begin in an hour or so. I believe that gives us plenty of time to get to know each other better."

I offer him a tight nod, squeezing Colt's hand in mine with promises of retribution for his big mouth. Shoulder to shoulder, we walk through a large oval exit that leads to the mansion's backyard—if you can even call it that. This whole lavish affair feels like someone ripped a page out of *The Great Gatsby* and spun it to life. Their backyard is the gem of the evening—donned in beautiful décor, the lights twinkling on the vast horizon are sure to give the stars above a run for their money tonight. When the Richfields throw a party, they don't half-ass it, that's for goddamn sure.

Lincoln heads to a private corner of the large patio and takes a seat in one of the plush divans, indicating that we should join him. My mind is working double-time into summoning any topic that can be construed as harmless small talk when Lincoln surprises me yet again by getting to the heart of the matter.

"Colt tells me you're writing a book about secret societies. He also indicated that you believe I might be a member of one. Is that true?" he questions mirthfully as he waves for a passing waiter to bring us some champagne.

"You Richfield men," I smirk, shaking my head, "always so straightforward when the topic interests you."

"If you believe me to be part of such a secretive organization, then me speaking my mind so unreservedly should be a trait in complete contrast to your assumptions. Not in favor of them."

"The best liars are usually known for telling the truth. That's what makes them so good at it."

He smiles. His grin is not condescending at all, but it is telling.

"I'll keep that in mind. I have to say, it's a pity I've never been to any of your classes. I think I would have learned much from you."

"I thought you said this conversation was for us to learn more about each other. I don't need a classroom to teach a lesson."

Another broad smile.

"I can see why he fell for you."

"That must have been one hell of a talk you two had." I blush, unprepared to receive such a compliment. "Some things shouldn't be discussed so openly."

"Colt doesn't keep any secrets from me," Linc deadpans.

"Can he say the same of you?" I quip back with an arched brow.

I feel Colt's body go stiff next to me, but he never once interjects.

"He can. In fact, he's the only one who can."

My forehead wrinkles at his bleak remark.

"Sounds lonely."

"It can be."

This time the tug to his upper lip isn't as lighthearted. There is a flash of sorrow that holds him hostage, but just as quickly as it dominated his entire face, it disappears from view once the waiter arrives with our drinks.

"Somehow, we've managed to deviate from the real topic that piqued my interest about you. Although I personally believe it's nothing more than an urban legend, I am intrigued enough to want to understand why you think I could somehow be involved in The Society? Is it because of my bloodline? If that's your only justification, then wouldn't Colt be a member, too?"

"I thought so too once."

Colt's head swings in my direction with my admission.

"Don't worry, Colt." I squeeze his thigh reassuringly. "After having you as a student for one week in my class, I knew you could never be a member. The Society's whole foundation is based on selflessness. And you, my love, don't share in their values."

"I'm a selfish prick. I own it. And if that makes me less desirable to those fuckers then I call that a win," he replies, kissing the tip of my nose.

"So what Colt told me is true. You honestly believe that The Society is good at their core?" Lincoln adds inquisitively.

I don't miss how suddenly Lincoln is no longer putting up pretenses that The Society is just another glorified myth.

"I do."

"Hmm. That's disappointing. I can't in good faith put any belief that an organization, who punishes people for their worst mistakes in life, is morally good in any way."

"They only punish those who refuse to redeem themselves. Mercy is given to those who seek it."

Lincoln's scathing stare sends a fearful chill down my spine.

"Linc," Colt utters with a stern tone.

"Right." He clears his throat and takes a sip of champagne. "I'm getting sidetracked. Like I was saying, neither Colt nor I have ever had any contact with such an organization. So herein lies the issue. You told Colt that you believe it was a Richfield ancestor who founded The Society. If that indeed is the case, then why have neither one of us heard about it?"

"You're not the first sons," I explain with confidence.

"Colt is. He's the only male heir in his side of the family."

"He is, but we already established his many faults."

"Again, I'm not offended," Colt snickers.

"That means you think my brother Teddy could have been involved."

"I don't know much of your late brother's character to give an informed opinion, but it's the most likely conclusion, yes."

"And in your eyes, my uncle Owen is also a member, is that right?"

"I believe so, yes."

"You're wrong, Em. My dad is too busy being a two-timing asshole to also be involved in The Society. And anyway, you're the one who says they only want dogooders in their stupid boys' club. How does a cheating prick fit into that equation?"

"Even JFK had his extramarital affairs, and yet he is still remembered fondly as one of the all-time greatest presidents of this nation. His moral code was never brought into question."

"Linc?" Colt throws him an unreadable gaze.

Lincoln rubs his chin in contemplation, his long hair falling into his eyes while taking all my insights in.

There is one more piece of information that has been gnawing at me. If Linc really isn't a member of The Society as he claims, then it's only right I share it with him.

"There's something else," I begin, hoping not to open up old wounds with what I'm about to tell him. "It's about your parents."

Both Linc and Colt go pale at the mention of them. I expected as much since their passing wasn't so long ago.

"What about them?"

"I'm aware that the Asheville Sheriff's Department is having difficulty in finding clues to solve their murders. It pains me to say this to you, Lincoln, but I'm afraid they will never bring your parents' murderers to justice."

"Why do you say that, Em?" Colt asks beside me, dread tarnishing his beautiful emerald eyes.

I swallow dryly, facing his cousin instead, knowing this will hurt him more than Colt.

"If my research is correct, then just as Colt's father is a member of The Society, your father must have been one also, Lincoln. His death, combined with your mother's—an actual Richfield heir—would have gained The Society's scorn. To explain it plainly, whoever killed your parents has their days spoken for. The Society will make sure of it—if they haven't already."

The awkward, heavy silence that follows makes me regret that I had to be the bearer of such bad news. I know how devastating it is not to be able to bring the responsible culprits of the death of a loved one to justice. In my case, I forgave The Society for their part in my parents' demise a long time ago, blaming the wrongdoings of Judge O'Keefe instead. Unfortunately, Lincoln won't be so fortunate. Hopefully, with time, he'll heal knowing that someone else sought out justice for him.

"You know what? How about we talk about something else?" I state, anxiously wanting to move past this somber topic since both men look like someone just punched them in the gut. "I've heard marvelous things about the Richfield Foundation, Lincoln. I'm extremely curious as to what your contribution to it has been this year."

It takes him a bit to snap out of his stupor, but thankfully he grabs the lifeline of this new topic and rolls with it. For the following hour, he talks animatedly about his philanthropic work, successfully decimating the previous dreary atmosphere.

"Lincoln." We hear a soft voice call out.

We all turn around to find a pretty brunette shyly tugging a lock of hair behind her ear as she makes googly eyes towards our table.

"Who's that?" Colts asks as his cousin stands to his feet.

"That would be my date."

"Date?" Colt repeats in surprise. "Does Ken know you came with a date tonight?"

"Not yet. But I doubt it will bother her," Linc counters, taking the last sip of his champagne. "She's getting married, right?"

Colt's expression softens as he takes in his cousin's stoic countenance.

"It's the right move, cuz. It's time."

Linc nods sternly and then directs his attention back to me.

"It was lovely to meet you, Emma. I hope to see much more of you in the future."

"Oh, you will." Colt hugs my shoulder to him.

Lincoln walks off to his date, pressing a friendly kiss to her cheek when he reaches her.

"Ken is going to blow a gasket. Come on, Em. We don't want to be anywhere near this place when she sees that shit."

"Where are we going?" I laugh as he pulls me off the couch.

"We're going for a stroll, babe."

Colt takes me by the hand as we walk over to the large hedge maze at the very center of his yard. The green branches are all covered in twinkling lights giving it a fairy tale feel to it.

"Are you upset with me, Em?" he asks as we enter.

"If you keep calling me babe, I will be." I tease him.

"You secretly love it. Just admit it," he jokes, kissing my neck. "But seriously, are you pissed that I told Linc about what you've been up to?"

"I was at first. But then I saw you two together. There's a strong bond between the two of you, beyond cousin affection, isn't there?"

"I look up to him. I know we're almost the same age, but he's still the best man I know."

"Is that the only reason you admire him?"

"Linc hasn't had an easy life. Worse than mine, if you can imagine it. But he's never let it bring him down. He's always been a rock for all of us, even when his own life was a shitshow."

"Hmm."

"But enough talk about my cousin. Or do you want me to get jealous?"

"Could you even get jealous?" I laugh. "That doesn't sound like the cocky, self-confident man I know."

"You have no idea." He growls playfully, wrapping his arms around my waist. "When it comes to you, I can get real possessive."

"Is that so?"

"You bet your pretty ass it is." He nods, his eyes sparkling with desire.

"Hmm. You can't be possessive of what isn't yours," I tease, breaking free from his hold, sprinting into a run. "If you want that kiss at midnight, you better hurry up and catch me."

I run through the hedge maze, laughing while he runs after me. My heels are no match for his long legs, and before I know it, I'm being flung in the air, laughing so hard my stomach hurts. The slit in my dress lets me wrap my legs around him, his gentle grip already at my throat.

"Now, what was that you were saying about you not being mine?" His searing lustful stare so intense I'm left breathless and wanting.

My lashes flutter as I get lost in his loving gaze, unable to contain the feeling inside my heart any longer.

"I am yours, Colt. It's reckless and foolish to fall so quickly like this, but I am—completely and utterly yours."

His gaze softens even more, his hold on me tightening.

"I love you, Em. Don't let me fuck this up," he responds with genuine vulnerability in his tone.

"You won't."

"How can you be so sure?"

"Because I won't let you. I promise."

"I'm going to hold you to it, babe." He smirks before tipping my chin up so he can kiss me.

His lips press against mine, as sounds of fireworks spark up the night with light and color, yet none of it is as beautiful as this one moment where we bare our souls to one another. Our love might be rash, reckless, and too sudden for it to make sense to anyone else, but it's still real.

And it's still ours.

No one can take that away.

After we break apart from each other, Colt groans, placing my feet on solid ground.

"Let's go back to the party before I fuck you right here."

I laugh at his uncharacteristic restraint, knowing he's not giving in to his basic urges because he's not sure who might catch us if he does. Good thing, too, since before we make it out of the hedge maze, we bump into a very intoxicated Owen Turner, roaming aimlessly about with a bottle in his hand.

"Well isn't this a sight for sore eyes—my beloved son and his new conquest. I'm glad to see you finally found someone who grabbed your attention for longer than a weekend, Colt. I was starting to wonder if that would ever happen in my lifetime."

"You're drunk," Colt sneers, hugging me protectively to his side.

"Yes. Yes. I might have indulged in tonight's open bar more than I should. But I'm not too drunk to give out some fatherly advice."

He hiccups, slapping Colt's cheek repeatedly in a playful manner.

"Just spit it out, old man."

Colt slaps his father's hand away, taking a step back. Owen's inebriated gaze sloppily falls to me for a few seconds and then returns back to Colt.

"Never love a woman who can't love you back the same way. If you do decide to give your heart away, be sure the one you love reminds you that you still have a soul instead of making you sacrifice it. Trust me, son, your soul is too high a price to pay in the name of love."

"Are you done?"

"Ah. My dear sweet boy, my life was done for a long time ago."

CHAPTER 27

COLT

Another Saturday night wasted because of a fucking party I have to attend at the Richfield Country Club. Like clockwork, Asheville likes to do one of these kiss-ass parties once a month. Tonight's candidate to have the Northside elite pucker up and kiss his lily-white ass is the new district attorney who is rumored to be more corrupt than the scumbags he's vowed to put away. I'm so sick of having to put on a fake smile along with a stupid ass tuxedo just because my family's presence is always mandatory at these god-awful things. My skin crawls in disgust with every second that I have to put up with this charade, but unfortunately for me, my mother would have my ass if I dared to sneak home early.

I hate to say it, but sometimes I wish I could be more like Meredith. She always knows how to behave at these occasions. But then again, that's probably why she's Mom's favorite. If Lincoln were here, then at least he'd entertain me enough that I wouldn't want to bash my brains against the wall just because I'm bored half to death. But as my gaze lands on his parents' table, seeing Kennedy sitting so close to Teddy, I understand why he preferred not to come tonight.

Even the strongest stomach couldn't handle seeing that shit.

Once the four-course meal is finished with—a dinner I barely touched with the fucking view I had in front of me—everyone jumps out of their seats to mingle. I take that as my cue to get some fresh air. I sure the fuck need it since the air I have been breathing into my lungs is as stale as the conversations I had to endure listening to for the past two hours.

When I pass the country club's doors, I smirk when I see the dark prince already out here, sneaking in a cigarette.

"If Price catches you smoking, he's going to make you swallow the damn thing."

"Dick can blow me," he retorts, puffing smoke into the air.

"Those fucking things will kill you, you know?" I reprimand, unable to understand how anyone would willingly poison their body with such filth. But then again, this is Easton we're talking about. He's never had much appreciation for his life.

"Spare me the lecture. I get enough of them from Finn."

"Where is Walker anyway? I haven't seen him all night."

"Football practice."

Lucky bastard.

"Maybe I should take up football if it means I don't have to come to these things anymore."

"Like you'd ever risk hurting your face." Easton chuckles.

"True. It would be a goddamn shame to mess with perfection."

"Vain fuck," Easton goads, throwing his head back to blow perfect gray circles into the night sky.

The sound of heels coming our way makes us both turn around simultaneously to see who also decided they had enough of the partying crowd inside. Kennedy pulls at the elastic that has her blond hair trapped in a bun, cursing under her breath when she finally manages to get free.

"What's up, Ken? Not having a good time with your date?"

She throws me a scathing look as she tries to untangle her golden locks.

"Shut it, Colt. I'm in no mood to deal with you tonight."

"Ouch." *I press my palm to my chest.* "Is that any way to talk to your favorite future cousin? From what your father has been telling everyone with ears tonight, it seems like you and Teddy are fucking engaged already, rather than just hooking up."

"First of all, we are not hooking up. And secondly, my father likes to exaggerate. He always has."

"But you are dating him?" *Easton asks point-blank, never one to beat around the bush.*

"Yeah, I guess so." *She huffs out despondently, giving up on taming her hair.*

"You don't look so thrilled about it," *Easton continues to probe, trying to coax more details out of her.*

"Can we please talk about something else?! Please? Why didn't Lincoln show up tonight?"

"Ask your boyfriend. I'm sure he knows," *I sneer.*

It still boggles my mind how Ken, of all people, could ever date that creep. And worst of all, she knowingly did it, fully aware of the pain it would inflict on Lincoln. Not so long ago, I thought that my feelings for

Ken were just as strong as my cousin's. The day I realized all I had was a schoolboy crush on the girl who didn't give me the time of day was a godsend as well as one hell of a rude awakening. Because on that same day, I found out just what it meant to truly love someone.

Love, true love, is what Lincoln feels for Kennedy.

And because of it, his life will now be riddled with nothing but misery and suffering.

I vowed that day that love would never get its ugly claws into me. Not if I can help it.

When Kennedy's bottom lip begins to quiver, and her crystal blue eyes look away—so neither East nor I can see the shame and anguish in them—it's like a sucker punch to the gut.

Fuck.

I might not like the fact that she's dating the prick, but she's still my best friend. When one of us hurts, we all feel it. It's always been this way. It's not going to change now just because she got herself mixed up with Teddy.

"Come here, Ken," I whisper softly, opening my arms out for her.

She hesitates at first, but when I offer her a gentle smile, showing her I'm not pissed anymore, she instantly leans into my shoulder, letting me hug her.

"Life sucks," she mumbles.

"Preach, darling," Easton utters beside us, with his godawful attempt at a southern accent.

Her body continues to tremble against me, and it's only when I hear her sniffle that I realize she's crying.

"You crying, Ken?" East asks, his silver eyes growing wide at the sight.

Ken never cries.

Not even when her mom passed away did she shed a tear. She hates looking vulnerable in any capacity. Maybe it's because she grew up with us four guys as her best friends, or maybe it's just her way of trying to be the strong one of our little group. Whatever her reasoning, crying is a big no-no for Ken. But as she lifts her head, trying to clean away the mascara streaks running down her apple cheeks, there's no denying she's in a world of pain.

"Shit. Let's get you cleaned up before anyone sees you like this. Stay here, East. If anyone asks where we are, make up an excuse."

"Got it."

I keep her close to me as we both walk back inside. Instead of taking her to the communal bathrooms on the ground floor, I take her upstairs to a private one. When we get close to its door, she places her hands on my chest, stopping my next step.

"What's wrong?"

But before she can answer, I hear moans coming from inside the bathroom, indicating that someone must have ditched the party below for a quickie upstairs.

"Colt," Ken whispers, pulling my hand back. "We should leave."

"Are you kidding? And miss the show? Aren't you curious to see which uptight socialite is getting freaky in there?" I ask, thinking a little juicy gossip like this might lift Ken's spirits.

"God, you are such a horndog," she castigates, but there is a small smile on the corner of her lips that wasn't there before.

"Come on, Ken. Just a tiny look so we know who it is."

"Fine. We'll have a little peek, but I'm running if they realize we're watching."

"They won't." I wink.

Ever so slowly, I turn the knob, happy to see that in their haste to fuck, the couple forgot to lock the door behind them. Careful not to make a sound, I push the door open just enough to look inside. When I see a familiar reflection coming from the bathroom mirror, my whole body freezes in place.

Nothing could have prepared me for this.

With her dress up to her waist, the new district attorney's wife is being pounded from behind by none other than my fucking father. My whole body shakes with fury as I continue to hear her moan in delight, yelling that she's cumming while my father's eyes remain sealed shut, with an expression unlike anything I've ever seen on his face before. He doesn't look like he's in the middle of the throes of passion. He looks angry. So fucking angry that all he can do is punish the woman underneath him by impaling her with his cock.

Kennedy pulls my hand away from the door, closing it shut. I only realize that I'm the one crying now when she wipes the tears from my face. She grabs me by the hand, and in my catatonic state, I follow her lead downstairs.

Aside from Lincoln, I thought my father could do no wrong.

How could he fucking do this?

How could he fucking do this to our family? To my mother?

To me?!

I'm still trying to make sense of what I just saw when suddenly the ice queen herself appears in front of us as if she somehow heard me crying for her in my head.

"Kennedy. Colt." She greets coolly. "Have you seen your father anywhere? I can't seem to find him."

Kennedy's eyes instinctively go up the stairs in reply while I stand there in a daze.

I can't let her go up there.

My mother and I might have a difficult relationship, but she is still my mother. I can't let her see what I just saw.

I just can't.

When she begins to pass us by, her hand on the railing to go upstairs, I grab her wrist, stopping her next step.

"Mom, don't."

I'm not sure if it was the fact I called her mom—something I never do—or the devastation in my eyes, but it's enough to make her take a step back. Her blue gaze bounces off of me to Ken, and even though she looks like the same iceberg of a woman who gave birth to me, there is something behind her glacial stare—something that looks a lot like misery. It seems everyone I care for has been suffering from the same affliction lately. So much so that I've become an expert in identifying grief, and right now, I see it clear as day in my mother's eyes.

"No matter," she finally says, straightening her spine. "I'm sure he'll find me. Eventually."

Without another word, she turns on her heel and returns back to the party as if the awkward moment never happened. My mind is as numb to her reaction as it is to my father's behavior.

"Do you think she knows?" I ask an uncharacteristically silent Ken at my side.

Ken entwines her fingers with mine, giving my hand a gentle squeeze, placing her head on my shoulder.

"One thing I've learned about Aunt Colleen is that she knows everything. Even the secrets we try to hide from ourselves."

I hug Emma to me with one arm, brushing her thick raven hair off her face with the other hand. Instantly she melts into me, sighing in her sleep, confident that in my arms she is always safe. By the time we made it to my room last night, she was two sheets to the wind and dead tired. I would have preferred to take the two hours drive back to Charlotte, but she was too exhausted and needed to sleep.

I fall back on my pillow, staring at the ceiling wanting to purge memories of the past from my mind. Unfortunately for me, it's currently a minefield of troubled thought, keeping me wide awake, and all because my father decided to impart his fucked-up wisdom on me.

"Never love a woman who can't love you back the same way. If you do decide to give your heart away, be sure the one you love reminds you that you still have a soul instead of making you sacrifice it. Trust me, son, your soul is too high a price to pay in the name of love."

When another half-hour passes by without being able to get any shut-eye, I concede defeat. After leaving a kiss on Emma's temple, I gently pull away, careful not to wake her up. Thinking a swim will tire out my body and hopefully clear my head, I head to the pool for an early morning swim. But as I'm about to pass my father's study, I stop in my tracks when I hear his sobs.

"I can't do this anymore. I'm slowly dying inside, Colleen. Please, I beg you. Let me talk to them. Explain. I need this, Colleen. Please."

I stand silently at the doorway, a small crack enabling me to see my father on his knees, his head on my mother's lap. He looks like he's sobered up from when I last saw him in the hedge maze, but the anguish in his tone is just as present as it was earlier. Yet, it's not my father on his knees that baffles me. It's the tender way how my mother combs his hair away from his face so lovingly—much like I did to Emma not a few minutes ago—that confuses me. In my twenty-two years of life, I've never seen them share one caress, one kiss, nothing that would tell me that there was any affection of any kind between them. With my father fucking everything that walks and my mother being apathetic to his affairs, I always presumed their marriage was a sham.

But as I take in the sight before me, I know that couldn't be further from the truth.

"Please," he continues to beg, "please, sweetheart. I have given you everything you ever wanted. Give me this. Just this."

She raises his head from her lap, her blue eyes sparkling with unshed tears for her husband's suffering.

"If you do this, what will our children think of you? They won't understand. They'll hate you for it. Can you live with the girls' hate? Colt's? Because I can't."

"Colt hates me already." He huffs.

"We have that in common, my sweet husband. But we are also responsible for it, too. You know it would have been different if you just let me—"

He shakes his head.

"You promised me you wouldn't."

"I did." She sighs. "And you promised me that you were fine with Scarlett and Lincoln being kept at arm's length. I've kept all my promises, but now, here you are asking my permission to break yours." The deep melancholy in her voice is just as puzzling as the words she's uttering.

He rests his head back in her lap, my mother's fingers returning to fondle his hair adoringly.

"She's getting married. And Price will be the one walking her down the aisle instead of me. It should be me, Colleen. I'm her father. Not him."

"And when Lincoln also decides to marry? Will you demand to be at his side as well?"

"It's my right. He's my son, too."

My heart speeds up so loudly at their combined confession that I'm afraid I'll miss another word. Holding my breath, I lean in closer to the door, very aware that my entire body is shaking.

"You'll be able to perform your fatherly duties with our girls." My mother tries to console him. "And should Colt one day decide he wants to get married, I'm sure he will put past grudges aside and request that we share in his joy, too. From what I was able to observe tonight, it might be sooner than we both anticipated."

"I saw that, too." My father offers a lopsided smile to her. "She's good for him. We always knew whoever took our boy on needed to be a strong woman, someone with grit and passion. I think the professor will help him fulfill his potential instead of squandering it."

"I agree, although—"

"You don't need to say it. I know. I'll keep my ear to the ground."

"Thank you," she coos, bending down to kiss the top of his head. I watch as my mother caresses my father's scruffy beard, then lifts his chin gently up with the tip of her finger. They stare into each other's eyes, having a silent conversation that only they comprehend. "And what of Scarlett, my dear husband? Will you be content to play the role of the surrogate father figure that you've played so well all these years, or will you reveal the truth—a truth that will hurt more than it will heal?" He begins to shift his head away, but she brings it back to face her. "To the grave. Wasn't that what we vowed to one another? That our secrets would live and die with us? If we make an exception to reveal just one of them, what else might follow? Do you want to risk everything we've been able to accomplish over the years? Is your need to tell Scarlett or Lincoln the truth about who they really are to you so great that you would risk what we've bled for? Sacrificed for?"

I know he's conceded to her will the minute his shoulders square and his expression becomes one of deep resolve.

"To the grave."

"To the grave."

I give Emma's address to our chauffeur and then hurriedly put her inside the limo.

"Colt, what's wrong? Talk to me," she pleads for the tenth time since I woke her up. Her hair is in disarray, her golden eyes still foggy from sleep, her high heels in her hands, but right now, all I can think about is getting her as far away from my childhood home as possible.

"I will, Em. Just not right now. There are a few things I need to do first. But I promise I'll be home as fast as I can and explain everything to you."

"I like it that you call my little apartment home." She blushes sweetly, melting against the leather seat cushion while gazing lovingly at me.

"It's not the apartment, Em. We could live under a bridge, and I would still think of it as home. Wherever you are, that is home to me."

I lean in and press my lips to hers, deepening the kiss just enough to feel her goodness wash over my troubled soul. With much regret, I end our kiss sooner than I would have wanted, closing the passenger door next and slapping the roof of the car to order our chauffeur to take my heart safely home. I watch the limo pull away, wishing I was in it rather than being burdened with what I have to do next.

But like The Society, I've had enough of lies and hidden truths.

It's time they all see the light of day.

I get into my Bugatti and drive over to Lincoln's. It's barely dawn, and after last night's festivities, I'm sure he'll never see this early wake-up call coming, much less the bombshell I'm about to throw at him. I pound on his door, sighing out in relief when he opens it just a few seconds later. He's in sweat pants and nothing else. He must have been working out before he heard my knock. His chest and forearms show off the tats he got as an act of rebellion when he was younger, paired with a lonesome blooming rose in homage to his mom that he got over the summer.

Fuck. This is going to kill him.

"Put some clothes on. We're going for a walk."

His brows pull together tightly in confusion, but he does as I demand, picking up a nearby hoodie and pulling it over his head. As we walk silently step by step to the Oakley Woods, I'm reminded how these same trees have witnessed all the strife in our past. They, too, have been complacent in harboring our secrets. We keep walking until we arrive at the shed we used that fateful night to bury our most horrid secret, and the irony isn't lost on me that this will again be the place where I will have a hand in changing Lincoln's life forever.

"What's wrong, brother?"

My chest tightens at his word choice.

Brother.

That's always who he's been to me.

A brother I could look up to. A brother who defended me with every fiber of his being when everyone else just passed judgment. A brother who loved me for who I was and not what others wanted me to be.

"Colt?"

"Emma is wrong about it being our family behind The Society."

"Oh? Yesterday you seemed positive that we were."

"As cliché as it sounds, a lot can change overnight."

"Colt, where is this coming from? How can you be sure?"

Here we go.

"Because when The Society sent me the first letter, they also sent me a video recording with another set of instructions. They wanted me to discover a family secret and share it with the world."

His face remains stoic, but I see the disappointment in his eyes regardless of how hard he's trying to conceal it from me.

"And did you find it?"

"I did."

"And?"

"Let's just say that our family couldn't be involved since they don't want what I uncovered getting out. We're looking at the wrong people."

"You're deflecting, Colt. What did you find?" he questions sternly, losing patience with me.

"I found out that my father is Scarlett's dad, too."

"What?!" He takes a step back, the news taking him by surprise.

"Yeah. I didn't get the specifics, but I overheard my mom and dad talking about it this morning. She's his daughter."

"Hmm." He rubs his chin in thought. "Everyone knows Uncle Owen isn't the most faithful of husbands, but this would be quite the scandal for the Richfield name if it ever got out. Definitely something the family wouldn't want to make public. If The Society wants this publicized, then you're right, it can't be us. What's their game, then?"

I clench my fists to give me the fortitude I need to continue on while Linc is already trying to decipher The Society's Machiavellian reasoning behind their blackmail. Frankly, those assholes are the last thing on my mind. My only thoughts are of Lincoln and how I'm about to break him.

"She's not the only kid," I mumble, trying not to fidget in place.

"What?" he retorts absentmindedly, his head still in detective mode.

"I said that Scarlett isn't the only secret kid my dad has."

His forehead crinkles in confusion.

"Owen fathered someone else?"

I nod stiffly.

"Who?"

I look into his deep ocean eyes, unable to push the words out of my mouth.

"Colt, who?!" he shouts, his hands squeezing each of my shoulders, pain and anguish taking over his movements. "No, it can't be." He begins to shake his head profusely, taking a step away from me.

"You always knew you weren't Crawford's son, brother," I stammer, hating that he has suffered for so long when there was no reason to. "In these very woods, you told me how he confessed you were someone else's bastard and not his. We were thirteen, remember? We broke down. We cried. But it didn't matter because we knew we would always have each other to weather any storm. This is just another one we never saw coming."

His body is trembling so viciously that I can hear his teeth grinding.

"Linc." I hiccup, feeling his pain as if it were my own.

I try to inch closer to him, but he just steps away from me.

"That's not possible. It can't be possible," he mumbles under his breath.

"It is, brother. I heard my father confess to it himself. It's true. I swear on my very life. This is real."

"No!!!" He holds his palms to his ears, not wanting to hear anymore.

I seal my lips shut, knowing if I say anything else, it might push him past the brink of his sanity. Feeling powerless to stop his pain from consuming him whole is tearing me apart. Tears streak down his face as the truth takes its toll, his weak knees caving in, making him fall to the ground.

"They lied to me!" he wails, pounding the earth with his fists. "They both lied to me. They hated me so much they made me feel like I was an abnormal freak. That something must have been seriously inherently wrong with me. They let me believe that I was sick in the head. Twisted. Perverted."

"I know." I rush to his side, wrapping my arm over his shuddering shoulders.

"Why didn't my mother tell me?"

"My guess is she was too afraid of Crawford's retaliation if she ever told you the truth."

"Are you sure, Colt? Are you fucking sure?"

"I am."

His head falls to his hands, letting the cruel truth sink in. I hug him as years of self-loathing begin to lift from his shoulders.

"They told me she was my sister, Colt. My fucking sister! How could they do this to me? What fucking pleasure could they have ever had in making me feel like I was a depraved monstrosity for loving her?"

I don't say anything in return, praying instead that Teddy and Crawford are somewhere in hell paying for the pain they caused.

I hope you fuckers burn!

We must stay huddled together on the cold, dirty ground for hours, not that I care. I'd spend days rooted to this very spot if he needed me to. Luckily after a while, his anger simmers, as do his tears. It will take more than one day for him to wrap his head around this, but like me, he's come to terms with the fact that we have been lied to our whole lives by the very people that should have protected us.

"How do you want to play this, brother?" I ask him. "Are you going to confront him?" I don't need to say my father's name for him to know who I'm talking about.

"Yes," he replies sternly. "I need to know everything. No more lies."

"What about The Society? Now that we know this is what they were after all along, we've got to give it to them. All I need to do is make one call, and this shit will be broadcasted on every news channel and social platform within minutes."

"Your thirst for vengeance won't do us any favors, Colt. Even if it is what The Society wants."

"You of all people should understand why I don't give a fuck. My mom and *our* dad brought this all on themselves."

"Even so, let me talk to Owen first, then we can figure out what to do next."

I nod, conceding to his request. For now, at least.

"Let's go home," he retorts. "I have a lot of thinking to do."

I know he's right, but as we break from the woods and see a hunched figure sitting on his steps waiting for us, I don't think Linc will be thinking about what to do about my parents for a while.

Kennedy stands up, confused by the dirty state we are both in.

"Leave," he growls before walking with purpose in her direction.

I inwardly smile and head over to my car. As I sit in the driver's seat, I chance a quick glance in my rearview mirror and watch Lincoln grab a stunned Kennedy by the nape of her neck and imprison her with his lips.

About fucking time.

With Linc taken care of, I have one more place to go, and luckily for me, I don't have to drive very far to my next destination. Once I get there, I'm relieved to see Easton's truck parked outside the small cottage. She's sure going to need him beside her for this.

After my insistent knocking, a breathless Scarlett opens the door, Easton's arms encircling her waist from behind.

"I know we're back to being friends and all, asshole, but you've kind of come at a bad time."

"That's going to have to wait," I tell him, my pensive gaze taking in Scarlett in a whole different light.

"Everything okay?" she asks, reading my mood.

"You once told me you were tired of living a life filled with unspoken lies, that their only purpose was to cause pain, and you didn't want that anymore. Do you still think that way?"

"I do," she replies steadfastly.

"Well, then you best invite me in, sis. Cause I've got a whopper for you."

To the grave my ass.

Chapter 28

Emma

"How do you feel today?" I whisper in his ear, lightly running circles with the tip of my finger over his chest.

"Numb. Exhausted. Pissed. Anxious. Take your pick, Em, because I have no idea how I feel."

"It's perfectly normal to be overwhelmed. It's a lot to take in all at once."

He lets out a deep exhale before rolling me over on the bed, pinning my arms down above my head.

"Let's just leave. Go away someplace where we can forget that Asheville even exists."

"Is that really what you want, Colt? To leave Lincoln when he needs you the most?"

His head falls to my chest, releasing his grip on me.

"No." He huffs out.

"I didn't think so," I retort, playing with his hair. "Are you going to confront your parents?"

"I promised Lincoln I wouldn't. He wants to talk to Scarlett first so they can combine forces and do it together."

"Hmm. I have to say that even though this must be painful for all of you, it is nice that neither Lincoln nor Scarlett will feel so alone anymore. Now they have a family to fall back on."

"They always had a family, Em. Being blood doesn't change anything."

"You know what I mean. With Lincoln losing his parents so viciously this year and Scarlett being an orphan for most of her life, finding out you have siblings is comforting. They have each other now. They have you. It can be very lonely when you don't have a family to call your own."

He tilts his head up, his emerald jewels glistening with love.

"Is that how you felt? When you lost your parents, and then your grandfather? Alone?"

I nod. "But I don't feel that way anymore. I have you. You're my family now."

The words have barely left my mouth when I feel the swell of his cock hardening against me.

"Anytime you say romantic shit like that you get me hard, woman," he growls.

"I can tell," I snicker.

The wolfish grin that springs to life is the only warning I have that he's about to ravish me. His eyes go to the robe on the floor before leaning over the bed and grabbing its tie.

"What's that for?"

"You'll see." He licks his lips seductively.

He pins my arms once more above my head, lacing my wrists together with the satin tie. He then knots it on the bedpost, turning me sideways to ensure I'm comfortable.

"Mr. Turner, if you're going to fuck me, I suggest you get to it," I tease, squirming under him impatiently.

The spark of deviousness in his stare has me wet and wanting for his touch. Bound this way, I'm completely at his mercy, anxiously anticipating his ownership over every part of me—body, heart, and soul.

"Colt," I beg when his tongue begins to trail down my body.

"So impatient, professor." He tsks teasingly, his teeth scraping against my sensitive nipple. When he lightly bites my breast, my legs wrap themselves around his hips, desperate to have him possess me. He grabs my thighs, forcing them wide open, his head getting lost in between them. Colt fucks me with his mouth, making sure I cum on his tongue at least once before he has his way with me. I shout out his name when he succeeds in his mission, needing to touch him and frustrated that I can't.

"Colt," I beg pleadingly, tugging at my binding.

"Not yet. Only after I'm done with you."

In one fell swoop, he turns me over, grabbing my hips so that my ass is up in the air, and I'm left kneeling on the bed. When his tongue begins to play with my puckered hole while he gently rubs my clit, I feel like I'm going to pass out with the myriad of sensations he's inflicting on me. I bite my pillow to keep me from screaming, but Colt doesn't like that. He pulls at my hair, commanding my head back so that he can hear all my wails of ecstasy.

"I want to hear you scream out my name, professor. Let this whole damn apartment building hear you cry out who owns this pussy."

His dirty words, added with the forbidding kinkery of our foreplay, have me bending to his will, panting out unashamedly from how much I need him to fuck me. Hearing my call, one strong hand grips my waist and the other pulls my hair back. He thrusts deep inside me, giving me exactly what I want.

"Argh!" I cry out when all of him stretches me.

He ruthlessly pounds into my pussy as his thumb plays with my puckered hole, only heightening my arousal.

"One day, I'll own all of you. Your mind. Your mouth. Your entire body. I won't rest until all of you belongs to me."

I want to tell him he already does. That my heart and soul have his name branded on them, but words fail me. All I can do is call out his name as he continues to push me closer to the edge.

"That's it, Em. Fuck. That's it," he praises, my core clenching around his cock.

My eyes roll to the back of my head, finally succumbing to his forceful domination. My brain short circuits as the steamroller orgasm rips me apart, shattering reality and replacing it with nothing but white light.

"Fuck, I love you, Em!" he wails, cumming inside me.

I'm still in a post-orgasmic daze when he unties me, pressing butterfly kisses on my wrist before settling my body against his.

"I wish we could stay in bed all day," I whisper, hugging him to me.

"And why can't we?"

I sigh, saddened.

"I got an email from the dean asking me to meet him at Richfield this afternoon."

"What the hell does that fucker want? School doesn't start for a few more days."

"I'm sure it's nothing, but I still have to go."

"I don't like it." He tightens his hold on me possessively.

"It's my job, Colt. Besides, there are a few things I need to do back at the school anyway."

"Fine." He lets out a defeated exhale. "I'll drive you there and then go check on Lincoln to see how he's coping after yesterday's shitshow. Text me when you're through with the prick, and I'll pick you up."

"Sounds like a plan."

Colt lifts my chin from his chest to give me a kiss, the look of adoration in his eyes making my heart soar into the heavens.

"Go take a shower, Em."

"You're not coming?"

"I'll make some breakfast for when you get out. I was a little rough with you just now. If I have a shower with you, then I can't promise I won't fuck you against the wall just as hard."

"I don't mind." I flirt.

He laughs and plants another kiss on my lips.

"Go before you change my mind."

He slaps my ass before getting up from the bed. Still chuckling, he pulls on his boxers and heads to the kitchen. I lie in bed a little while longer, thinking of excuses to give the dean so that I don't have to show up today and just stay here in our bubble. I pick up my phone to look at my calendar to check what time he scheduled our meeting for when something else grabs my attention.

One.

Two.

Three.

Four.

Shit. Shit. Shit!

Five!

I'm five days late. My period is never this late. This must be a mistake. I count the days again, going back to last month to see if my calculations are wrong. But no, it's there in black and white. Wrapping a sheet over my body, I rush to the bathroom, opening up my medicine cabinet.

Shit!

I missed a few pills this month.

With everything happening with my research on The Society and Colt, it must have slipped my mind entirely. I close the cabinet and slowly walk out of my room, scolding myself for my reckless behavior and worrying how Colt will take the news. Rather than being in the kitchen as I expect him to be, Colt is standing in front of my living room window.

"Colt," I stutter. "I have to tell you something."

But he doesn't turn around.

"Colt, this is serious. I'm late. My period is five days late."

And though there is panic in my voice, he still doesn't face me. I walk over to him, entwining my fingers with his.

"Colt, did you hear me?" I ask worriedly, since he doesn't move an inch.

I squeeze his hand for a reaction, apprehension settling in my gut that something is very wrong here. Finally, he turns his attention from the window and onto me.

"Colt?"

"It's snowing."

"You're firing me?!" I blurt out.

"What did you expect me to do after you paraded yourself with your student at the Richfield party? You're a bright woman, Emma. You knew the stakes and the repercussions that would occur after making such a reckless decision. Don't tell me this comes as a surprise to you."

"Of course it does! There was no forewarning or any disciplinary action provided against me. You can't just fire me like this."

"I can and I will. Since it wouldn't be fair to your students that you leave midterm, you'll finish the school year as stipulated in your contract. That way you can save face and say that you left because there wasn't a vacancy for us to keep you any longer. We both know once rumors surface that you're screwing around with one of your students, it will be harder for you to gain employment elsewhere. Consider this a blessing that I'm being so benevolent with you and haven't had you removed from the premises today." Rage bubbles beneath my skin as his eyes lustfully skate over my body, even as his expression deems me to be nothing but trash. "As far as I see it, you should be thanking me."

"Thanking you? Is that what I should do? Tell me, Montgomery, how would you like me to thank you for this act of mercy? Would you like me to fall to my knees? Is that the thanks you had in mind?"

"If you opened your legs for that spoiled asshole, then opening your mouth for me shouldn't be too difficult for you."

I spit at his feet.

"You disgust me."

He rushes at me, his hand gripping my jaw.

"No! It's you who disgusts me. What did I ever see in a slut like you?"

"You saw what I wanted you to see. Now get your filthy hands off me before I sue you for harassment!"

"Like anyone would believe you." He smirks.

"I can think of one person who would. The same one that can snap his fingers and have you tossed on the street just as easily as you're trying to do with me."

His nails sink into my skin. I keep my eyes deadlocked on his so he knows I'm the last woman he should be fucking with.

"I won't say it again, Montgomery. Get your hands off me!"

But instead of doing what he's told, his grip only gets stronger as he pushes me against my desk, opening my legs with his knee.

"You'll pay for that." He grunts.

I don't think. I just react. I bite into his neck, my teeth piercing his flesh, and once his hold slightly loosens, I knee him as hard as I can in the crotch. Montgomery falls to his knees, wailing and groaning like the little bitch he is.

"You bitch! Get the hell out of my school! You'll never work as a teacher again! I'll make sure of it!"

I sneer, bending down to his ear and gripping his dirty blond hair so he can look me in the eye.

"You're wrong. I'm going to keep my job. You, on the other hand, have your days numbered. You messed with the wrong woman, Montgomery."

Before I stand up, I elbow him in his spine, leaving him on all fours in my office. I grab my handbag and rush out of there. I might be overselling my threat that he's out of a job, but when Colt finds out he put his hands on me, he'll pray that his prestigious career is all he loses.

I grab my phone from my purse to call Colt to pick me up, but by the way my hand can't stop trembling, I reconsider. I need to be calm when I tell him what happened just now. If he sees how rattled I am, he'll go off the deep end. No. I have to have my wits about me so I can protect Colt from his temper. I head to my classroom to buy some time to cool off when another Ryland surprises me.

"Kennedy? What are you doing here?"

"Professor Harper?" she says, surprised as if she weren't expecting my arrival.

"Is there something I can do for you?"

She wrinkles her nose, her eyes going through the room like she's looking for something.

"As a matter of fact, yes," she proclaims, straightening her spine and lifting her chin all business-like.

"Oh?" I ask, puzzled since I'm still trying to figure out how she knew I'd be here to begin with.

"Colt told me where to find you," she states, answering my unspoken question. "I thought we might have a little talk just us girls."

"Us girls?"

"Yes," she confirms, the unreadable expression on her face giving me pause.

"Colt tells me you might be pregnant."

"He did, did he?" I grind my teeth.

I really do need to have a talk with Colt about keeping our private business private.

"Yes. I didn't realize you two were so serious."

By the way she is taking my measurements from head to toe, I get the feeling she's not on board with our relationship. From the looks of it, my day is going to be filled with Ryland assholes. Good thing I'm fully prepared to put them in their place.

"We are. However, I don't see why that should concern you."

"Right. I guess you wouldn't, but it does. I grew up with Colt all my life. He's what you would call my annoying older brother in a sense."

"Colt has enough siblings."

More than you know.

"Doesn't change the fact he's still my family. And we protect our own."

"If I didn't know any better, that sounds vaguely like a threat, Miss Ryland. If that was your intention, I have to warn you I don't deal well with threats."

Just ask your father.

"Please, Emma. You can call me Kennedy. And no, I'm not threatening you. I just want to make sure your intentions with Colt are noble. However, if this baby is somehow the way you found to trap him, or if you don't care for him as he does you, then yes, it is a threat."

I place my bag on top of my desk and sit on its edge. Crossing my arms over my chest, I stare at the girl who thinks she can intimidate me.

"What some people consider to be actions based on wanting to protect their friends, others might call a toxic state of possessiveness. Immature jealousy or even envy of what they can never have."

She tilts her head back and laughs, sending a chill down my spine.

"You were always my favorite teacher, Emma. It'll be fun having you around," she singsongs and then waltzes out of the classroom with a spring to her step.

That family is one creepy nut job after another.

Thankfully Kennedy's little visit was enough to take my mind off what happened in the office with her father. Feeling calmer, I text Colt that I'm done for the day and that he can come to pick me up. Since I'm not sure if I'll have a job here anymore, I gather up my few belongings to take with me just in case.

With a few books and binders in my hands, I leave the classroom and head to the parking lot. The Hamilton Estate isn't far, so he shouldn't be long. Though it's chilly with the first batch of snow that fell overnight, the crisp air will do me some good and help keep my temper in check.

When I get to the steep steps that lead to the building's ground floor, I kick myself for my brilliant idea of bringing all this stuff with me. Forgoing holding onto the rail, I send out a silent prayer that I don't lose my balance and break my neck just because of a few school books.

I'm on the second step when suddenly I feel a shadow behind me. Before I have time to look around, two strong hands press on my back, pushing me into the air.

After that, everything happens quickly.

A loud cry leaves my lips as my body drops down the flight of stairs.

And as I'm about to hit the floor, knowing I'm seconds away from my head slamming into the stone ground, I think of Colt's emerald eyes and how I might never see them again.

Before everything around me fades to black, the last thing I see is a shadow of a silhouette and a wisp of blond hair blowing in the wind.

CHAPTER 29

COLT

"Looks like you two had fun," I smirk, walking into Linc's kitchen and finding Kennedy sitting on the kitchen island eating cereal out of the box in nothing but my cousin's T-shirt.

Shit, not cousin.

Brother.

It's going to take some time to get used to this.

"I... um... I'll leave you boys to talk. I'm going to grab a quick shower and get changed," Kennedy responds timidly, jumping off the countertop.

Before she can get very far, Lincoln pulls Ken by the waist, spinning her around in his arms and laying one dirty kiss on her. I avert my eyes to the ceiling because no one wants to see their brother make out with a girl who is like a kid sister to them.

When the two horny assholes don't break apart, I clear my throat to remind them I'm still here. Ken's hooded stare remains on Lincoln as he whispers something in her ear after their kiss. When her cheeks blush and his eyes fall to her lips again, I don't need to be a mind reader to know they still have sex on the brain. The smoldering look they give each other makes me wish I was still in bed with Emma and getting the same service, rather than having to watch them go at it.

"Ken, you said something about taking a shower, remember?"

"Right." She grins widely, pulling away from Lincoln's embrace and skipping out of the kitchen.

"And make it a cold one, Ryland!" I yell mockingly.

"Bite me, Turner!" she sings playfully from outside the kitchen.

"You sure didn't waste any time." I laugh, punching Linc on his bare shoulder.

"I wasted enough of it as it is. I don't want to waste another second."

His face is glowing with joy, warming up my cold heart.

"I like seeing you like this."

"Like what?"

"At peace. Happy."

His ocean eyes soften in my direction.

"Same goes for you, brother. I've never seen you this content."

"It's love. Who would've thunk it?" I laugh, gaining another radiant smile from him that shows just how happy he is for me. "Fuck, I feel like an asshole now, but we've got shit to deal with before we can all go on our honeymoons or whatever."

"Right. The Society." He huffs.

"The one and only. I don't know if you saw it, but my deadline is up. It snowed last night."

"Damn it, you're right. I guess my head didn't go there when I saw it fall."

"That's because your head was probably stuck in better places. Mine sure the fuck was." I walk up to the kitchen island where he's standing, placing my elbows on its edge, and lean against it. "They want me to tell the world about you and Scarlett, and I gotta tell you, Linc, that's exactly what I intend to do. All I need is your green light."

He grows quiet for a spell, deep in thought, but ultimately gives me a nod.

"I'll call Owen over today. I just need to talk to Scarlett beforehand. I didn't get to talk to her yesterday."

"Having the woman you love in your bed kind of took priority over talking to a sister you never knew you had," I joke.

The smile that crests his face squeezes my heart.

This was all he ever wanted. Since they were children, Lincoln and Kennedy gravitated towards one another—needing always to be close. Crawford made him feel like he was a perverted freak of nature for having such feelings for her, but now that we know it was nothing but a cruel lie meant to hurt him, Linc can finally have what his heart always desired.

"Once Scarlett and I speak to Owen and get some answers, then do whatever you need to. But Colt, I want you to think long and hard about what you are about to do. Once you tell the world about Scarlett and me, you can't take it back."

"Like I give two shits about my parents. They deserve this for lying to us all this time."

"I'm not talking about them. I'm talking about your sisters, *our sisters*. They are the ones I'm worried about. This will shock them to their very core. Owen is everything to them."

"What they did was wrong. Their lies messed with people's lives. They can't go unpunished for it."

"You sound like The Society."

"That's not fair," I retort, offended he would compare me to those fuckers.

"It wasn't meant to be. Yes, they lied, and those same lies affected how Scarlett and I grew up. But your truth—the one you want to shout out on the eight o'clock news—that truth will also hurt the people you love. And don't tell me that your parents suffering won't cause you any pain either. I know you, Colt. Like I know my own heart. If they suffer, so will you."

"You talk like I have a choice. I don't. You saw what The Society did to Finn, to East. We have no idea what they will do to me if I don't give them what they want."

"Do you even care if they go after you?" He arches a knowing brow.

"I'm not worried about myself. All I care about is Emma."

His eyes fall to the ground.

"I won't risk her just to avoid a scandal. And yes, my sisters might get their hearts broken when they realize that they have been lied to all these years, but I can't think of them right now. Not when Emma could get hurt."

"I get that. You love her."

"I do. I do love her, but it's more than that now," I croak, recalling her suspicions from this morning. "Emma might be pregnant."

"Pregnant?" he repeats, stunned.

"Pregnant?!" We hear Kennedy mimic from the kitchen entrance.

"That was a quick shower," I grumble, wondering how long she's been standing there. "We don't know for sure yet, but it's a definite possibility."

"And how do you feel about that?" Linc asks, trying to gauge what I'm feeling.

"Honestly, I'm not sure yet." I shrug. "Everything has happened so fast that I haven't had time to digest this news myself. Me, a dad? Why does that sound like a recipe for disaster? I'm going to fuck the kid up before he's even born. I just know it."

"Don't say that, Colt. You'll make a great father," Kennedy states comfortingly. "I know you will."

"I'm not so sure. It's not like anyone in this room has had the best role models when it comes to the dad department," I mumble, disheartened, but then shake the helpless feeling away to focus on something else. "Speaking of pricks, do you know why your dad asked Emma to come to the school today?"

"I have no idea. School stuff, I suppose. He is the dean, and she is a professor."

"Right."

I don't like Emma seeing Montgomery in any capacity, but I guess I'll have to swallow my hatred for the man since, technically, he is her boss.

"When do you guys find out about the baby?"

"I'm supposed to pick up some tests at the pharmacy later on before I pick up Emma from school."

"I have some errands to run in town, so how about I go with you and help out?" Ken asks while putting on her winter coat.

"That would be great."

"I wish I could tag along, but I have a few things to do here," Lincoln explains, his underlying meaning clear as day to me.

"Call me when you finish," I tell him and then direct my attention to Ken. "So, are you coming with me or what?"

"You know I am. Just need to do one thing first," she replies before flinging herself into Lincoln's embrace.

I roll my eyes and give them their privacy so they can properly say their goodbyes.

Half an hour later, Ken and I walk up to a pharmacy to buy some pregnancy tests. Thank God she offered to come with me because as I stare at the row filled with babies on the boxes, my heart starts to accelerate.

"Colt, you okay? You're looking kind of green there."

"I think I need some air. Can you sort this out?"

Her blond brows crease, but she nods, heading over to the cashier with five pregnancy tests in her hands.

I run out of there, gasping for air when I'm finally outside.

Shit!

How am I supposed to protect a helpless little baby when I can't even protect my friends?

FUCK!!!

"Colt?" Kennedy questions, concern evident in her voice, as she moves beside me. In her hands she's grasping the plastic bag that holds the answer to my future. "You're freaking out, aren't you?"

"Little bit, yeah."

She lets out an exhale, understanding swimming in her cornflower blue gaze.

"Come with me," she orders, pulling me across the street.

"Where are we going?"

"You'll see."

We walk a block until we reach a baby clothing store. My panic rises as Kennedy adamantly pushes me inside. Unwillingly I go in, overwhelmed with all the baby merchandise lying around. Ken goes right to the newborn section and begins to scour the various clothing racks until she finds what she's looking for. She unfolds a tiny little onesie with the words 'Daddy's Little Darling' embroidered on the front and places it in my hands.

I hold up the tiny piece of clothing, my heart doing laps around my ribcage.

"It's cute, right?"

"It's fucking terrifying."

She grabs my shoulders and gives me a thorough shake.

"Snap out of it, Colt. God! Will you stop thinking about yourself for one goddamn minute? You think Emma isn't as scared as you are right now?"

"She's stronger than me."

"No, Colt. She's not. Trust me. I know a thing or two about acting as you have it together when, in reality, you are just as terrified as the next person. Now stop being a little bitch and look at the onesie."

I do as I'm told and stare at the fabric.

"How can you be afraid of something that comes in such a small size, huh?"

Gently, I run my thumb over the wording.

"It is kind of cute, huh?" The corner of my lip twitches while imagining a mini Emma wearing it.

"It's freaking adorable."

"Hmm," I hum, looking over to a pale pink onesie on the counter that says 'Daddy's Little Princess.'

I pick that one up, chuckling under my breath at the small golden crown stamped on it.

"Tell me something, Colt. Do you love Emma?"

"With all my fucking heart," I deadpan.

"Then you will love this baby even more because it will symbolize what you two feel for each other. This baby will be the luckiest kid ever because it will be born with two parents who love each other just as fiercely as they will love it."

"You think so?" I croak, feeling emotional all of a sudden.

"I know so. Now, man the fuck up. And when Emma takes the test, you will be right at her side, supporting the result—baby or no. Have I made myself clear?"

"Yeah." I chuckle, my eyes sparkling when I see the tiniest little shoes.

"You kind of want her to be pregnant now, don't you?"

"Fuck yeah! Look at this!"

I pull up a little pajama that says 'Party at my crib. 2 a.m. Bring a bottle'.

We both start laughing as I continue to peruse more baby clothes. The sound of her phone vibrating interrupts our fun.

"Lincoln missing you already?" I tease, but when I look at her face, there is a dark shadow there. "Ken, everything alright?"

She places her phone back in her bag and throws me one of her fake-ass smiles.

"Yep, all good. You okay if I leave you? I've got something else that requires my attention."

"Sure. No problem."

She gives me a light peck on the cheek and goes about her business. I'm not sure her leaving me here alone was such a good idea since I end up going on a shopping spree for the next hour. I'm sure Em will laugh at me since we don't know if we're having a baby or not yet, but I can't help myself.

I'm still at the store when I receive a text from Emma telling me to pick her up. With a dozen bags in my hands, I walk the block back to my car. But as I get closer to the Bugatti, an eerie sensation runs down my spine. When I see a black envelope stuck to my car's windshield, I drop all the bags and run to it. My hands tremble as I rip open the Godforsaken thing to see what fresh hell they want to inflict on me now.

A LIFE FOR A LIFE.

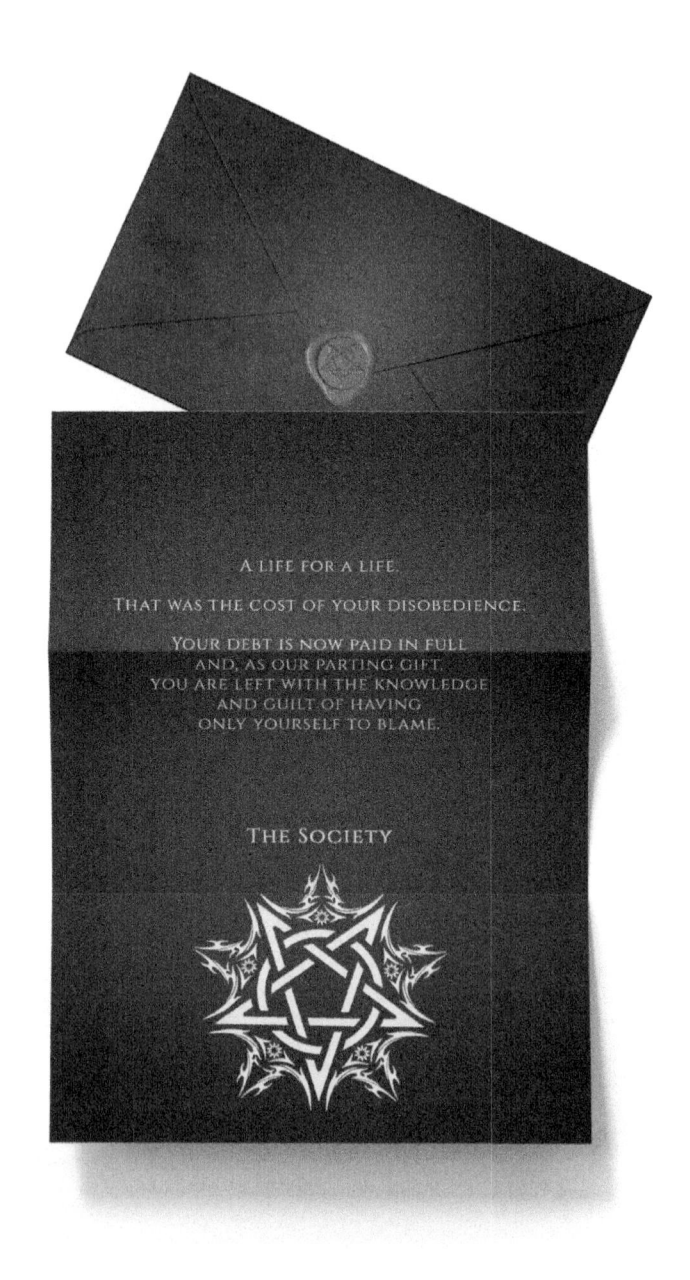

THAT WAS THE COST OF YOUR DISOBEDIENCE.

YOUR DEBT IS NOW PAID IN FULL
AND, AS OUR PARTING GIFT,
YOU ARE LEFT WITH THE KNOWLEDGE
AND GUILT OF HAVING
ONLY YOURSELF TO BLAME.

THE SOCIETY

Emma.

I jump into my car and drive like hell on wheels while yelling at my phone to call my woman.

"Pick up, Em. Pick up!" I yell, slamming my fist on the wheel.

A sense of dread clutches its ugly claws around my heart with each unanswered call. When I get to the school and see an ambulance there, my heart stops. I park the car in the middle of the road, leaving my door open to run to the ambulance as the paramedics close the doors. A crying Kennedy is shaking profusely as one of the paramedics tells her something before getting behind the wheel and taking off, all sirens blazing.

"Colt!" She cries when she sees me. "I'm so sorry! I'm so sorry!"

"Ken, who was in the ambulance?!" I shake her.

"There… there was so much blood. So much blood," she continues to stutter in her shock.

"KENNEDY! WHO WAS IN THE AMBULANCE?!"

Her watery gaze looks up at me with such despair, making me take a step back, my knees threatening to give in on themselves.

"Emma. It was Emma," she sobs.

I don't ask anything else and run to my car, pressing the pedal to the metal and racing to the hospital. I'm a total trainwreck when I arrive, earning apprehensive glances from passing strangers.

"Emma Harper! Where is she?"

"Sir, please calm down," the male nurse behind the reception desk orders.

I slam my fists on the counter before grabbing him by the lapel.

"I'll fucking calm down when you tell me where she is!"

He yells for security, two uniformed linebackers running toward us.

I throw each one a scathing look, my grip never wavering.

"Touch me and I'll make sure it will be the last thing you ever do," I warn, then turn my face to the trembling nurse. "Tell me where Emma is, or I swear to God I'll burn this whole place down to the ground looking for her."

I snap my hands off his collar, letting him sit back down in his seat and do what I ordered. He types on his computer, his nervous gaze shifting from the screen back to me.

"Yes, she's here. A doctor is currently with her."

"Tell him to get his ass in here when he's done. I need someone to explain to me what the fuck happened to my woman!"

"Yes, sir."

He picks up the phone while I pace the floor. Ten minutes later, a woman in a white coat comes through the double doors.

"Are you here for Ms. Harper?"

"Yes. How is she? What happened? How is Emma?!"

"She took quite a tumble. We're running some tests to make sure there isn't any internal bleeding, but so far, we are very optimistic that isn't the case here."

"So does that mean she will be okay? I was told there was a lot of blood."

"Right now, Ms. Harper has a concussion, which we would like to monitor overnight. In regards to the blood, when she fell, she cut herself very badly in the leg. A nurse is stitching her up as we speak. But apart from that, we don't see any real harm done. Nothing that a week or two in bed won't heal."

"And the baby?"

"The baby is fine. In the early stages of pregnancy, a fall like Ms. Harper experienced could have been lethal. She is fortunate that all she suffered were a few cuts and bruises."

I slam my back to the wall, pressing my thumbs into my eyes so the doctor doesn't see me crying. Relief like I've never felt before washes over me, mixed with pure joy from the doctor's confirmation.

Emma is pregnant.

I'm going to be a dad.

We're going to be a family.

I'm going to spoil this kid rotten because she's not even here yet, and already she owns me.

"Can I see her?" I finally ask once I've regained my composure.

"After we do some more X-rays and make sure nothing is truly wrong, I'll come back for you."

"Thank you, doctor."

"Of course." She smiles cordially before turning around and heading back to the woman I love.

Twenty minutes pass by and I'm still standing there, rooted to my spot, waiting for Emma's doctor to return, when I hear the last person I want to see frantically call out my name.

"Colt! Son!"

I turn around, my father rushing in my direction, Easton, and Scarlett right on his tail. My simmering rage bubbles through with the sound of his voice alone. Once he's close enough, I grab him by the shoulders and slam him up against the wall.

"Did you do this?!" I jam an accusing finger in his face.

"What?" he stammers, confused.

"Don't fuck with me, Dad. Did you fucking do this?! Did you hurt Emma?"

"No, of course not."

"Did The Society? Is this their handy work?"

His face pales at my remark.

"I don't know what you're talking about."

"Yes, you fucking do. I know you know who those fuckers are."

His expression morphs into one of utter sadness.

"Don't go looking for ghosts, son. All you'll find is death."

My nostrils flare with rage as I get into his face one more time.

"If I find out that you had a hand in hurting the woman I love, you're dead to me," I sneer through gritted teeth.

"I understand. I'd do anything for the woman I love, too. But you have to believe me. I'd never hurt her. I'd never hurt you."

"How can I believe a man who lies for a living?"

I pull away from him, not able to look at his somber face for another minute.

"Mr. Turner," the doctor calls out, eyeing my father and me cautiously. "You can see Emma now."

Thank-fucking-Christ.

I throw a nod over to East and Scarlett, telling them I'll be right out to give them the play-by-play of what happened after I've seen Emma.

"No need, Colt. Ken came over to Lincoln's and told us already. That's why we're here."

Scarlett looks concerned behind Easton's shoulder, thinking the same thing I am.

If Ken told them I was in trouble, then why isn't Lincoln here already? Why isn't she?

"Mr. Turner?" the doctor chimes in, reminding me that I have bigger things to worry about. I follow her lead until she ushers me to the room where Emma is lying in bed with a few scratches and bruises on her face. I immediately go to her side, gently kissing her lips, cheeks, arms, hands, and anything I can get ahold of.

"I was so fucking scared. So fucking scared, baby," I confess, emotion choking up my words.

"I know. I was, too."

"This was all my fault, Em. All my fucking fault." I hug her waist, kissing her belly.

"Shh," she hushes. "I'm fine. We're fine."

I lift my head to stare at her molten golden eyes.

"If anything ever happened to either one of you, I'd never forgive myself."

"Nothing is going to happen to us," she coos lovingly, running her fingers through my hair.

"I love you so much, Em. And our baby. I promise I will never let anyone hurt you again."

"I love you, too," she croaks, happy tears streaming down her face.

I slide beside her, needing to hold her in my arms. She places her head on my shoulder, running circles on my chest like she loves to do.

"So it's official. We're going to be parents, Colt. Are you okay with that?"

"Before this shitshow happened, I had spent over a thousand dollars on baby clothes. So yeah, I'm pretty okay with that."

The soft laugh that leaves her lips settles my anxious heart.

She's safe.

Our baby is safe.

That's all that matters.

"Em, do you remember anything at all of what happened? The doctor only told me that you fell back at the school."

"You know those stairs that lead up to my classroom? I fell from the first step all the way down."

"Jesus, Em. That was quite a fall." It's a fucking miracle she's here in my arms. A fall like that should have had a different outcome. Thank God it didn't. "Did you trip or something?"

She shakes her head, biting her bottom lip.

"Em?" I lean back to cup her face in my hands, her gaze falling to the blue hospital sheet instead of looking me in the eye. "Em? What is it? Talk to me."

"Honestly, I'm not sure what happened. One minute I was walking down the stairs, and the next I was falling."

"There's more to it, isn't there? What aren't you telling me?"

"I think I was pushed."

"Pushed? Pushed by who?" She continues to abuse her bottom lip with her teeth, trepidation keeping her silent. "Em, pushed by who?"

"I think… I think it was Kennedy."

My heart stops.

"What?" I gasp in horror.

"I can't be one hundred percent sure, but I think it was her, Colt."

My whole body shakes at this revelation, and suddenly another one slaps me across the face.

Lincoln!

I kiss Em's temple and run out into the hallway, calling Linc and then Kennedy, terrified that neither one of them answer.

"What's wrong? Is it Emma?" Easton calls out when he sees me.

"East, get Finn and find Lincoln!"

"What? Why?"

Just as I'm about to explain, Finn and Stone appear, both hyperventilating like they ran miles to get here. But my gaze doesn't stay on them for too long since it's fixated on the black envelope in Finn's hand.

I snatch it away and fall to my knees when I see that I'm too late.

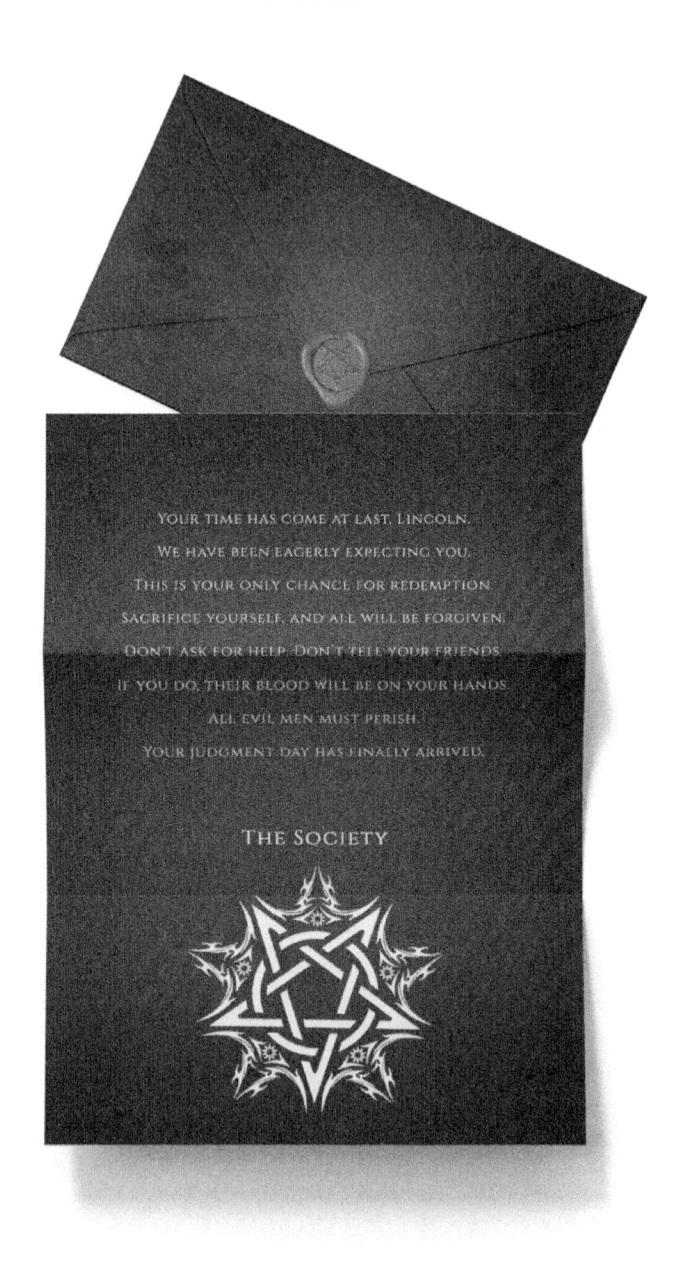

Your time has come at last, Lincoln.
We have been eagerly expecting you.
This is your only chance for redemption.
Sacrifice yourself, and all will be forgiven.
Don't ask for help. Don't tell your friends.
If you do, their blood will be on your hands.
All evil men must perish.
Your judgment day has finally arrived.

The Society

She has him now.

Epilogue

My teeth bite down on the pillow so hard I almost suffocate. When I feel my incisors rip through the silky Egyptian cotton, that one small act of defiance has me grinning into the pillow like a damn fool. I concentrate on the idea that somehow I ruined his perfect world—even in such an insignificant way—as he continues to grunt in my ear. He keeps to his ruthless thrusts as the sweat of his chest slicks down my back. I shut my eyes, wishing I could shut off the sound of his heavy breathing just as easily, but it's of little use.

Teddy wants me present to endure his vileness. Proof of that is when he grabs my hair, pulling my head up from the pillow so that he can hear my painful cries.

"Shut the fuck up. You know better than to make a sound," he sneers vehemently, as he slams himself into me.

I bite my tongue, drawing out blood as he keeps to his merciless tempo. No matter how many times he takes me, it never gets any easier. Teddy has no sense of giving pleasure—only pain. That's how he enjoys it.

Better it be me than…

"I like that you let your hair grow out." He snorts, forcefully pulling it in such a way my scalp is on fire. "But that's the point, right?"

I don't dare say a word in return because anything I do or say will piss him off. He might be delighted with the pain he's inflicting on my body now, but all it would take is one wrong word from me, and it could get so much worse. When his cock begins to swell inside me, I know he's close, and I mentally start counting down the seconds until he's finally done with me.

"Do you like my cock inside you, Ryland?"

No. I hate it.

"Yes," I lie.

"Tell me the truth. I want to hear you say how much you like me fucking your ass like this."

'I hate it. But not as much as I hate you,' I think to myself while lying beneath him, sucking in all his wrath as if it were my own.

"You fucking Rylands are all the same. Good little liars. But I'll tame you. I'll tame all of you," he belts, slamming his shaft into my tight hole until blistering light blinds me.

To my utter shame, I always cum.

Even when he takes what's not his, so brutishly, so violently.

Even when he humiliates and belittles me, intent on making me feel small.

In the end, no matter how grotesque the abuse, I always cum.

And that realization is worse than anything he could ever conjure up in his twisted mind to do to me.

When he sees that I've given him what he wanted, he buries himself to the hilt, muffling the sound of his cry by biting down on my shoulder.

That's another thing about Teddy. He's only truly satisfied once blood is shed.

After he cums, he falls to his side, perfectly content that he's ruined me physically, mentally, and emotionally with such ease. I lie still for a minute, not wanting to turn around and see his triumphant smirk on his face. He slaps my ass hard, with no care that it's sore from the way he's just brutalized it.

"You can go now. You've served your purpose for tonight."

I bite my inner cheek and get out of his bed as quickly as I can, hastily picking up my discarded clothes off the floor. I head to the bathroom to wash up, but before I've even made it inside, Teddy is already opening his nightstand drawer, preparing his second favorite vice of the evening.

It's definitely time to leave, alright.

Teddy is cruel sober.

But when he's high, he morphs into something completely inhuman.

I wash myself off and put on my clothes at a rapid speed, praying that I can get out of this fucking house before the drugs reach his bloodstream. Once it does, it will summon the living, breathing demon that resides inside him. I learned my lesson long ago to be out of arm's reach when that happens.

My fingers are on the light switch when a loud crash from inside the bedroom grabs my attention. Ever so cautiously, I open the bathroom door, stunned at what I discover. Teddy's lamp is shattered in small pieces on the floor, his whole body convulsing on top of his bed. I'm about to go to him when a knock on his bedroom door stops me in my tracks. Stepping into the darkness of the bathroom, I vigilantly watch Lincoln step into the room.

"Teddy?" he asks, slowly coming closer to his older brother.

By the way his expression pales to a ghostly color, there is no question he understands what's happening in this precise minute. Teddy is laid flat on the bed, drowning on his own puke, turning an ugly shade of purple. Lincoln doesn't move an inch and instead keeps staring at his brother's almost lifeless body. Each second that passes by is another taken away from Teddy's life.

He's going to watch him die.

Do it, Linc. Let him die! Do it!

But as I'm mentally ordering Asheville's golden boy to go against his basic instincts, the fucker shakes his head and hurriedly rushes to his brother's aid. He turns Teddy to his side so that the vomit spews all over the bedspread, instead of letting Teddy suffocate on it.

"I'm going to get help, Teddy! I'm going to get help!" he shouts frantically, leaving the room in a mad dash.

I slide the bathroom door open and bridge the gap between my tormentor and me.

"He was going to let you die, Teddy. Your own fucking flesh and blood was perfectly happy to watch the life drain from your body. Isn't that something?" Sitting by his bedside, I stare at the waste of human space I have been dealing with for longer than I care to remember.

"You're not worthy. I thought you were, but you're not," I continue to explain. "I'll find another way, Teddy. You're not it, unfortunately." I shrug before picking up the pillow beneath his head.

"I'll find another way."

Seeing as time is running out before the cavalry arrives, I place the pillow over his mouth and nose, ecstatic at how his dilated pupils go wide in terror. His entire body begins to shake again, struggling to gasp for air. He stirs so vehemently beneath me, his arms swaying left to right in panic, and yet somehow, I manage to keep my strong hold on the pillow. When his body stills, I let out the first relieved breath I've had in years.

It's done.

I place the pillow back beneath his head, giving the fallen god one last look. I fix the bangs away from his eyes but don't close them. The sick satisfaction of seeing his panicked eyes stare back at me, with unshed tears in them, feels like a warm, comforting blanket wrapped around my very soul.

When I hear loud footsteps running toward the room, I rush to his closet, opening the false door within it. I get inside just in time to watch Lincoln call on his fallen brother from the two-way mirror.

"You should have been the one to kill him, Lincoln. You wanted to. I saw that you did, which means you are just as unworthy. Teddy didn't hide who he was. Everyone knew he was a villainous bastard. You, on the other hand, play the part of the good brother. But you're not, are you? You're just as vile and wretched as he was. You just hide it better, which means you're not the way either."

But one day, I'll find it.

I have to.

I wake up in a daze, sweat pouring down my forehead, the memory of Teddy's bile invading my room. My body lifts from my bed, leaning against my headboard, trying to take shallow bursts of air into my lungs. I get up and walk over to my bathroom, splashing cold water on my face to clean the heavy sweat off my brow. Holding onto the sink, I stare at my reflection in the mirror.

I did find a way.

It was right there in my grasp, but Lincoln took it from me.

I don't care about the others.

It was never about them.

Only him.

Because of him, I lost everything I worked so hard to obtain.

Years of plotting, sacrifice, humiliations, I suffered them all in silence, knowing that victory would be mine sooner or later.

And Lincoln fucking stole it from me.

I can't let that go unchecked. He will suffer, and when he thinks he can't go on any longer, I'll erase the light from his eyes the same way I did his brother's.

The knot in my chest begins to loosen, my shoulders relax, and a true sense of calm settles inside me as my reflection smiles deviously back at me.

Judgment day has arrived for you, Lincoln.

No more games.

No more riddles.

No more.

It ends with you.

Just as it was meant to.

To be continued in

Do No Evil

THANK YOU SO MUCH FOR READING SPEAK NO EVIL.

If you enjoyed it, please consider leaving an honest review.

It may only take you a minute to write, but reviews is how books get noticed by other readers.

By writing a small review, you are opening the door for my love stories to be enjoyed by so many others.

I'd also love it if you would check out my author page: https://www.facebook.com/IvyFoxAuthor

And I invite you to join my Facebook group, Ivy's Sassy Foxes: https://www.facebook.com/groups/188438678547691

Much Love,

Ivy
XOXO

Ivy Fox Novels

The Society
See No Evil
Hear No Evil
Fear No Evil
Speak No Evil

The Privileged of Pembroke High
Heartless
Soulless
Faithless

Rotten Love Duet
Rotten Girl
Rotten Men
Rotten Love Boxset

Bad Influence Series
Her Secret
Archangels MC

After Hours Series
The King

Co-Write with C.R. Jane
Breathe Me
Breathe You

ACKNOWLEDGMENTS

There are certain people in my life that I'd be lost without.

My husband and my kiddo—my crazy life wouldn't make sense if you were not a part of it. I love you guys so much and I thank God every day to have been blessed with you both.

A huge hug goes out to my incredible PA, Courtney Dunham. These last few months have been super intense and I'm so glad I have you in my corner to deal with all my chaos.

To the wonderful women in my life, friends and author friends alike, who fix my crown when it sometimes tips over, thank you for always having my back and inspiring me to go after my dreams.

This book would have not been a reality without the assistance of my magnificent beta readers—Richelle Zirkle, Heather Lunt, Emma Brooks, Jesse Adler Wheeler, and Marjolein Van Laere. I adore you all, and will be forever in your debt.

To all the bloggers and instagrammers who have shared their love for The Society series and spread the word out about my new labor of love—thank you so much. You have no idea how thankful I am for having your support.

A huge thank you to my ride-or-die tribe—my Sassy Foxes. You know I love you, but I'll keep saying it until I'm blue in the face. You beautiful women make all my days shine and I'm so happy to have you all in my life.

And last, but never least, my last thank you is to you, my readers.

Words fail me in demonstrating just how much I appreciate all your support and love. As long as you pick up to read my book babies, I'll continue writing them.

With lots of love and gratitude,

Ivy
XOXO

About the Author

Lover of books, coffee, and chocolate ice cream!

Ivy lives a blessed life, surrounded by her two most important men—her husband, and son—and also the fictional characters in her head that can't seem to shut up.

Books and romance are her passion.

A strong believer in happy endings and that love will always prevail in the end.

Both in life and in fiction.

Printed in Great Britain
by Amazon